I0675838

= The Songline Series =

Book One: The Fall

Book Two: The Flight

Book Three: The River

Southwestern Songline

= The River of time =

*

Book Three:

= The River =

*

Written by:

Denver C. Davis

This is a work of fiction. Names, characters, places and incidents are either the products of the Authors imagination or are used fictitiously.

The Authors use of names of actual persons, places, and/ or characters are incidental to the plot, and are not intended to change the entirely fictional character of the work.

Published by Denver C. Davis
Copyright ©2015 by Denver C. Davis

All rights reserved. No part of this publication may be reproduced, distributed or transmitted in any form, or by any means, or stored in any database or retrieval system without the prior written permission of the Author.

www. DenverCDavis.com

Copyright © 2015 Denver C. Davis
All rights reserved

ISBN: 978-0-9961984-2-4

: This book is dedicated to a life of adventure:

To all of you who have been involved in the trip and are around to laugh about it still.
You know who you are.
   Thanks.
To those I've lost along the way,
   I miss you.
But most importantly, this book is dedicated to my friend, confidante, and partner in crime for lo these many years. She has remained by my side through sickness and in health, for richer and for poorer, and through a multitude of events that would have crushed a lesser woman.
Thanks J.J. My love is great, my sympathies legion.

*

As in all great adventures, there are people who enter one's life, and in some subtle way affect that person's storyline. For me, my old friend Eric Adams was one of those people. He unwittingly inspired me at a critical juncture, and that spark led to this novel.
   As for the rest: to list them all would be an impossible task. Therefore, and at the risk of slighting some, I will simply say thank you, and leave it you to sort it out amongst yourselves. But I will mention a few, whom without their help this book might still be in the works.
First, I cannot give sufficient kudos to my friend and neighbor Mark Shultise, whose computer savvy helped fill the massive void in my woefully inadequate skill set. And, to my friends Jackie Parkinson, Rick Pavek, and Sammie Biemborne, my love, and gratitude.

Denver.

Stories happen to those who tell them.

Thucydides

= Chapter 1 =

Carlton rolled his chair back and opened the bottom drawer of his desk. There were now *two* bottles of Pinch stashed behind the steel cashbox. The first was standard protocol: the second a recently added backup. Because if the past few days were *any* indication of what was to come, he was going to need them both.

The selling of Mr. Teller's stock had been easy enough: but timing it so it took place *precisely* at the last ring of the trading bell, while calibrating the transaction so it would not show on the Company books until the next quarterly report, well *that* was considerably more challenging.

But that had been Mr. Teller's request, and Carlton had pulled it off.

Removing bottle number one from the drawer, he peeled away the foil, twisted the cap, and poured until the amber liquid reached the top of the glass. Then, drink in hand, he stared at the cursor on the screen that blinked, no, *winked* at him. One press of a key, and his life would change forever.

1

With the weight of crushed dreams heavy on the finger that hovered over that key, he muttered, *"Fuck* James Carson" and let it drop.

Suddenly, Carlton felt lighter. . . as if he were pushing himself up. Up and away from his past and the burden it held. And now, nearly weightless, he leaned back in his chair to gaze at the ornate stamped copper tiles above.

"And *fuck* that ceiling too . . ."

The decision to defect had not been a difficult one; for while the money Teller offered was more than sufficient incentive, the larger issue was the stasis of his present life. And Kelly, looking as she had that morning, well, *that* made for a heady mixture. Sniffing the air where her perfume still lingered, he sighed, *'God . . . she's even more beautiful than Casey.'* but then immediately amended, *'No, not more beautiful. More achievable.'* Perhaps when this was all over he would ask her to dinner. But no sooner had the thought entered, the memory of the menacing tone in Teller's voice echoed in his head. Perhaps lunch was a better idea.

Bringing the glass of whiskey to his lips, he glanced again at the sequence of numbers on the screen.

That James would be murderously angry was a given; but in truth he didn't really care. Nothing he had done was illegal, or even unethical. The sale of one hundred thousand dollars worth of stock had been a legitimate transaction. The stock belonged to Mr. Teller, and he could sell any amount he wished, with, or without the approval of the stockholders. Or without consulting the board at all for that matter. And he could sign over the remaining percentage to whomever he wanted. Which in this case, was Miss Kelly.

Carlton closed his eyes, allowing the image of Kelly leaning over his desk to return: the auburn hair spilling over her shoulders ending where her breasts swayed against the soft material of sweater. Shaking that pleasing yet potentially dangerous image from his mind, he returned his attention to the paperwork spread out across the desk before him.

Once these documents were signed he would own not *only* ten percent of this transaction, but an additional ten percent of the LLC. But with that thought, his happiness flagged. *Everything* hinged on Mr. Teller keeping his word.

But then the worry vanished as quickly as it had arisen. James Carson *detested* Teller, and Miss Kelly believed in him absolutely. So, with that combination giving him a renewed faith in the outcome, he rolled the figures over in his head one more time and a glorious sense of rebellion mixed with relief filled him. For, while the money from Teller's generous offer was not sufficient to retire for life it was unquestionably more than he would *ever* see working here as James' whipping boy . . . and with *that* thought, Carlton leaned back in his chair and stared again at the ceiling.

When had things gone so wrong?

~

When the Corporate headhunters had first plucked him from University and offered him this job it had seemed a custom fit. What more could a young man have asked for? An all-expense paid relocation from the dreary east coast to a hip town in the Rockies, employment with a prestigious law firm, and a fine starting salary. It was everything an Ivy League kid could envision as a springboard for a successful career . . . with Casey as the golden ring.

Yes; everything had seemed perfect. But then James had entered the picture and dashed his dreams. The man was an arrogant, self-centered prick who showed little respect for her and none at all for him. No, Carlton had no moral misgivings with what he was doing, and the thought of helping Teller upset James' private kingdom brought him a great deal of personal satisfaction.

Pouring another splash into his glass he picked up the phone and chuckled, *'Karma, asshole . . .'* as he dialed.

~

Kelly heard the phone ring from the shower, shampoo dripping down her face. Under normal circumstances she would ignore it but these were anxious times.

With a curse, she rinsed, shut off the water and grabbed a towel, wrapping it around her dripping hair to reach across the sink.

Hello!?"

Shaken by the antagonistic tone in her voice, Carlton's sense of conviction faltered and he stammered out a weak, "Hello, Miss Rowan? This is Carlton. Is this a bad time?"

Scowling, Kelly punched the speaker button.

"No, no, Carl, it's okay, I'm sorry, I was in the shower. What's up?"

Relieved, Carlton started to speak; but with the image of her wet and naked overriding all else he struggled to remember why he had called in the first place. Squeezing his eyes tight, he pushed the visual from his head. "Oh, um . . . yes, yes, I just wanted to let you know I have the bank draft ready. Do you have the information?"

"Yeah I do. Hang on a sec."

Toweling her hair as she went to the closet, she took out one of Tellers old oversized T-shirts, talking as she pulled it over her head. "That was pretty quick Carl," she said, her voice muffled by the material. "Any problems?"

"No, not yet anyway. But then Mr. Carson doesn't know about it yet either."

"Good. Let's keep it that way for now. I'll be right over, just give me a few minutes."

"Alright, Miss Rowen. I'll be waiting."

Sensing anxiety in his voice, Kelly purred, "and Carl, please, call me Kelly." hearing no response, she cooed, "Carl, are you okay?"

Another second of silence followed, but he came back.

"Yes, just a little nervous."

"Don't be." she laughed. "You're not doing anything wrong are you?"

There was a short pause, but this time when Carl spoke his voice was much stronger.

"No. No, nothing I've done will create any legal disputes."

"Good. That's what Teller said. And don't worry Carl, he won't screw you out of anything he's promised. Whatever he offered, you'll get."

A tight-lipped smile creased Carlton's face.

"That's good to know, Miss Rowen, because once Mr. Carson becomes aware of what we are doing I will no longer work for this firm."

"And that's a problem?" she teased.

Surprising himself with a sense of freedom he hadn't felt since he realized Casey was an unobtainable goal he laughed,

"Hell no! Nothing has worked out for me since I took this position. *Fuck* James Carson *and* his jerk-off brother! I'm going on vacation."

"*That's* the spirit!" Kelly laughed. "Where will you go?"

There was a moment of silence, and Carlton's voice came back strong and bright. "I'm going to Disneyland!"

Hearing such strength in his voice made her happy, and knowing that it would please Teller as well, she chuckled, "Sounds perfect. I'll be right over."

Pulling the now damp t-shirt back over her head, Kelly tossed the phone on the bed and finished drying her hair. The day was starting well.

~

Standing in front of the full-length mirror, Kelly turned, and giving herself a quick review looked down at the clothing options she had laid out on the bed.

Hmmm,' she tapped her chin, *'sexy, or business?'*

Having set the hook, she saw no further need to tease poor Carl, so she settled for casual business with a sexy undertone. Hell, she *was* a woman after all.

Slipping into her chosen ensemble, she spritzed a cloud of perfume into the air, walked through the mist, and with a quick pirouette in front of the mirror, smiled at the reflection.

Perfect.

Ten minutes later there was a pause in the click of short heels on the halls terracotta tile as Kelly stopped in front of the oval mirror next to the front door.

Picking her purse up from the low table, she pushed a stray lock of hair back into place, tucked the bank information into the purses side pocket, and slipping a freshly painted finger through the ring of keys stepped out into the brilliant spring day dialing Teller as she walked.

— — ‑‑ ‑‑‑ ‑‑ — —
—— —— —— —
‑‑ ‑‑‑ ‑‑

= Chapter 2 =

Abbott was weary of waiting.

It had been more than a week since Teller's departure, and the only news that he had received so far was that he had met Billy's grandson in Tucson. Abbott frowned. That Billy had a grandson was surprising in, and of itself. And that he was meeting with Teller was more curious still. But when pressed for answers the old shaman had refused to go into any more detail than to assure him that Teller was fine and that things were progressing as they should.

'As they should . . .?' He grumbled, just what the hell was *that* supposed to mean?

Frustrated, Abbott had gone to the lake, where, sitting with his feet dangling over a sandstone ledge, attempted to compose himself by watching the wind ripple the surface below. But just as he was beginning to relax a sudden gust of cold air enveloped him, lifting the curly hair on his shoulders while sending a flurry of bright yellow Cottonwood leaves skittering across the slickrock; where they bounced against his legs before fluttering over the ledge and looping in lazy spirals towards the water. But as they twirled down, a second breeze struck: this one icy, and carrying with it the sensation of being watched.

Tensing, he laid a hand on the cliffs rough surface; and palming a small stone as he slowly turned, thought; *'a pebble for defense? Ludicrous!'* but as he completed his turn the stone fell from his grip.

There, not five feet away, was the very creature Teller had recently referred to as: 'The bane of his life.'

Abbott's first reaction was shock.

There had been no sound of the beast's approach; yet there it sat, resting on its haunches, scrutinizing him with piercing golden eyes as the cool breeze ruffled a luxurious coat of fur, that continually changed colors, rendering it nearly invisible against the sage background.

Never had Abbott seen a coyote so large, nor felt an aura of such immense power. But rather than wither under gaze of those ancient eyes he relaxed. For within their depths lie not danger, but wisdom: wisdom shrouded in boundless humor.

Bequeathing Abbott the canine equivalent of a smile, Coyote tilted its magnificent head, and from the deepest reaches of Abbott's subconscious rose a voice: a voice similar to Billys, echoing the same sentiment Billy himself had expressed earlier.

Take heart, my friend. Things are progressing as they should.'
Mesmerized by Coyote's shimmering presence, and oddly comforted by the sharp white teeth of that smile, Abbott's heart grew suddenly light.

With an infinitesimal nod, Coyote eased up on all fours. Then, with a shake of its magnificent coat, gave Abbott a golden-eyed wink, and vanished into the sage.

= Chapter 3 =

Teller lay in bed watching a morning re-run of 'The Daily Show' when the phone rang. Grumbling, he hit the mute button on the remote wishing it were a pause instead. He hated to miss anything Jon Stewart had to say regarding the absurdities of the previous day.

"Hi Tell!"

Kelly's voice was warm, satisfaction plain in her voice.

"I'm on my way to meet Carlton."

Tossing the remote onto the bed, he grinned, "Most excellent," both the news and her voice erasing his minor irritation immediately.

"Once that's done I can get the hell out of here. Jack and I are meeting with Billy's grandson again this evening"

Kelly interrupted. "Just a sec."

Against all odds she had found a parking spot on the street so, performing a neat three-point turn she squeezed into the slot, tucking the phone between her shoulder and ear as she stepped from the car, pulling her purse from the front seat while asking, "Billy's grandson?"

"Circles within circles, sweetheart."

"What?"

"Never mind. Just get that money transferred and assure old Carl that he has nothing to worry about."

Leaning back against the hood, she tipped her face to the warm sun. "He'll be glad to hear that. I think he's a little nervous."

"Tell him there is nothing to fear," Teller laughed. "He's doing nothing inappropriate and will be amply rewarded for his part in this endeavor."

Kelly closed her eyes; basking in the warmth of his voice as well as soaking up the sun. It was good to have him back. But then his voice intruded on her musings.

"Hey, you still there?"

"Yes, Teller." She smiled. "I'm still here."

"Good. Go take care of business and call me if there are any problems. I'll be right here."

"Okay." she smiled. "I'll call you either way."

Blowing a kiss into the phone as she hung up, and light of step crossed the street to James' office building.

With her reconnection with Teller leaving her exhilarated, she bounced up the stairs and into a short hallway, where the only door visible on the floor was a door with the word 'Accounts' hand-painted on its rippled glass.

Taking a brush from her purse she pulled it through her hair, straightened her blouse, and with a deep breath opened the door. But as she stepped across the threshold, Carlton's head jerked up, throwing a cautionary glance that stopped her in her tracks. Something was wrong . . . Carlton's expression was one of unadulterated misery: his blue eyes wretched behind his spectacles.

Kelly's survival instincts on alert, she took a quick step back; but too late. The door was pulled from her grasp, closing with a soft 'click' while from behind, a cold voice hissed,

"Well, well, well! If it *isn't* Miss Rowan . . . what a coincidence . . . *just* the woman I wanted to talk to."

Kelly stood immobilized as James stepped from the shadows, took her by the elbow, and led her to one of the chairs facing Carlton's desk. "Please," he said, his eyes as cold as his voice. "Have a seat."

She slipped Carl a questioning glace as she lowered herself into the chair but he just gave a tiny shake of his head as

James dropped heavily into the chair opposite hers, leaning forward with an artifice of great sadness in his eyes.

"Kelly, Kelly, Kelly. *What* are you trying to *do?*"

The question hung heavy in the room; but the oppressive silence was suddenly broken by the sound of glass clinking against glass. Both Kelly and James looked over at Carlton, who, with trembling hands, was pouring a healthy shot of liquid courage.

Kelly, however, showed no trepidation whatsoever.

Setting her purse on the floor she leaned back in her chair, and covertly slipping Carlton a subtle wink turned back to James, her face the picture of innocence.

"We've just been following one of Teller's requests prior to his relinquishing all holdings, James. There is absolutely nothing for you to worry about."

Her smile melted Carl's heart.

"It seems he needed to withdraw some funds for something he and Jack have going on. It's all on the up and up." Turning that smile to Carlton, she added, "Isn't that right Carl?"

Calmed by the whiskey and emboldened by Kelly's emotional control, Carlton spoke up.

"That's right Sir. It was a standard transaction involving a quick sale of stock and subsequent deposit of funds. All strictly legal, and all well within Mr. Teller's rights according to the company charter."

James was more than a little dismayed by the lack of fear he had instilled. Dropping his facade of false sorrow, he let his anger surface. "And *whose* idea was *this?*" But before either Kelly or Carl could answer he dug his elbows into his knees and ran his fingers through his hair. "Never mind." He growled, "That was a stupid question. It *had* to be Teller's."

Lowering his hands, he stood, thrusting the chair from beneath him and sending it spinning it across the floor where it crashed into a tall antique cabinet that held a mixture of law books, a tennis trophy from Carlton's college days, and glasses of various sizes and shapes. James followed the chair to the cabinet and stood with his back to them, clenching his fists while searching desperately for a position of strength.

Finally, with a slow exhale he opened his eyes, picked out the least dusty glass he could find, and with is jaw set in a grim line, marched back to the desk where Carlton sat, paralyzed, his blue eyes wide with fear.

Ignoring Kelly's smiling, arrogant face, James grabbed the nearly empty bottle of Pinch from the desktop and began pouring while glaring at the terrified man in front of him.

His glass filled as the bottle went dry; and choking the bottle by its neck, he shook the last few drops of the amber liquid onto Carl's desk where they pooled into perfect little drops on the highly polished surface. Never taking his eyes from Carlton, James carefully placed the now empty bottle directly in front of him, and growled, "How much?"

Carlton could only stammer, "Pardon?"

Glowering between furrowed brows, James leaned across the desk until they were nearly nose-to-nose.

"How much money did he take out of *my* company?"

Carltons eyes went to the empty bottle, but at the wasted drops that glistened on his desktop his dismay turned to irritation.

"Well, technically, he took no money at all from *your* company. He took the money from the sale of *his* property, which required no vote from the board. Each shareholder has certain rights −" Carlton wasn't given the chance to explain the legal aspects of the transaction any further. James exploded, "*I don't give a shit about the legal mumbo jumbo!!* I asked you a question Carl! How *much?*" The venom in James' voice set Carlton back in his chair, the ice in his glass rattling as he stuttered his answer.

"One hundred thousand dollars."

Impressed at the speed of which James' face turned red, Kelly tried to suppress a smile as his eyes bugged out and he swallowed the entire glass of whiskey in one massive gulp.

Then, making a concerted effort to retain control, he repeated, "a hundred grand?"

Carlton cringed. "Yes sir."

"One hundred thousand fucking dollars?"

"Yes sir."

"And you let this happen?"

Regaining some of his poise, Carl answered, "I did not let anything *happen*. I simply did my job at the request of a major shareholder. I *also* have the paperwork drawn up for the transfer of the balance of Mr. Teller's shares into your hands at fifty cents on the dollar, as well as give Miss Rowen her share of this year's projected profit if she chooses to leave before the season has ended . . ." with a deep breath he continued. "Mr. Teller is *still* fifty percent owner of this company until *these* papers," he tapped the ream stacked on his desk to make his point. "Are signed by all parties involved." It felt wonderful to exercise his authority, and Carlton actually smiled. "Which, I am happy to say, can be finalized as soon as I hear back from Mr. Teller. He has informed me that once the funds have been deposited in the account that Miss Rowen will provide, he will fax over a signed and notarized copy of the agreement, and I will send a copy to the bank receiving said funds. At *that* point, all business will be concluded between all parties involved."

"With one small caveat," Kelly chimed in.

James turned and glared at her, suspicion plain on his face. "And what is *that?*"

"Teller is giving ten percent of his shares to Carlton."

At this, James went apocalyptic. Strangling his glass, the veins in his forehead pulsed as his blood pressure skyrocketed.

"WHAT!!! No, no, no! There is *no fucking* way he is going to do *that!!*"

Watching James' hands, Carlton waited for the crystal glass to shatter while Kelly just smiled. "But there *is* James, and for two reasons. One, because he can. And two, because he *wants* to. But, to help ease the pain, he has asked me to do one last thing for you for old time's sake."

She paused, expecting another explosion. But James remained surprisingly silent, so she continued.

"*You* promise to stick to *all* the agreements you made at the lake, including this small element, and he will let you have the remaining forty percent at *forty* cents on the dollar instead of the original fifty cents. Teller felt that was a fair compromise for all concerned." She glanced over at Carlton, who was surprised by this new proposal but gave a diminutive nod.

James slowly lowered his glass and leaned back in his chair, shifting his gaze between them until his eyes came to rest on Carlton; and as they did, Carlton suddenly, and fully understood the phrase: "if looks could kill."

Another long minute ticked by while James' face went through a startling range of emotions. But finally giving the two of them a furious glare of resignation mixed with hate-filled fury, snarled, "I've no choice, have I?"

Kelly's response carried a note of obvious satisfaction.

"No, James, you do not."

The silence in the room grew oppressive; but Kelly casually leaned back in her chair and crossed her legs while Carlton, taking heart from her strength and attitude, tucked his fear aside and held out his hands, palms up. "No, Sir," he shrugged, "you really don't."

James' lips grew tight. "Very well then. I will accept his offer . . . but at the forty percent figure! Call me when you have everything in order." Lifting himself from his chair, he walked over to Kelly, who still harbored that infuriating smile. Resting a hand on her shoulder, he leaned into her ear and growled between clenched teeth, "I had hoped we could be partners, Kelly, but your allegiances are *clearly* elsewhere."

Her lips curling in distaste, she reached up, pinched his cuff with two fingers, and lifted his hand from her shoulder.

That was it . . . snatching back his hand, James stormed across the floor, coming to a halt in front of Carlton's desk, his face contorted with scarcely contained fury.

"And *you*! You *little* fucking *ingrate*, the *moment* this deal is closed you may consider your services no longer needed. Pack your shit, take your ten percent, and get the fuck out of this office, out of Telluride, *and out of my fucking valley!*" Trembling with rage, James hammered the polished desktop with both fists while bringing his face inches from Carlton's, clearly wishing he could rip out Carl's heart. But with a sharp intake of breath, he turned and stomped across the wooden floor, and throwing a dagger filled glance at Kelly as he gripped the doors glass knob, he turned, backed across the threshold, and slammed the door with such force that the window behind Carlton's desk rattled. Kelly stared at the shuddering door, fully expecting the rippled pane of glass to shatter and fall. But it held. Turning to Carlton, she giggled, "*That* went well, don't you think?"

That's when Carlton realized that he was still holding his breath. With a long, slow exhale, his trembling hand went to the desk's bottom drawer where his back-up bottle waited. Lifting the files that covered it, he pulled the whisky from its place of hiding, twisted the cork, raised it to his lips, and took a long slash. Then dragging his sleeve across his damp brow, he laid his forehead on the desk and muttered, "Much better than I expected."

Carl held that position as the whiskey warmed his blood and as his nerves steadied, he lifted his head to give a weak smile. "Well, I guess *that's* settled. I suppose I should start cleaning out my desk."

Pouring another finger into his glass, he corked the bottle, tucked it into his briefcase, and looked at Kelly. "Why don't you call Mr. Teller and let him know it's done. I'll take care of the change in percentages, finalize the wording on this document, and make a call to the Tucson bank."

Kelly smiled, nodded, and picked up the phone.

~

Teller was thoroughly engrossed in in 'The Word' segment of Steven Colbert's "The Colbert Report" when the phone disturbed him yet again

"Dagnab it!" he muttered. "Hello?"

"Well hello yourself!" It was Kelly, and she sounded pleased. "Everything here is a go, Tell. Carlton has the info you gave me and is talking to the bank manager as we speak."

"Wonderful!" he laughed, "Good job Girlie." then he glanced at the clock on the dresser. "Guess I better get down to the bank and sign the necessary paperwork. How's he sending it?"

Kelly looked over to Carlton, who was reciting some figures to the person on the other end of his desk phone.

"Just a minute."

All Teller could hear were muffled voices in the background, so he turned the volume on the television back up. But then Kelly came back on line.

"He's faxing everything you need to sign." There was a moment of silence, more muttering in the background, and she returned. "Just make sure you sign everywhere he has indicated with an asterisk."

Teller hit the TV mute. "No problem. That includes the transfer of his ten percent?"

There was another moment of silence as she confirmed with Carlton, then, "Yep!"

"Good. Then he's happy with the deal?"

Her warm laugh came over the phone. "Yes, Teller. Carlton's happy enough with it, but James was less than pleased when *he* found out."

"Fuck James." Teller said. "How much did you have to knock off?"

"What?"

"The final percentage darlin', how much did you have to take off of our fifty percent to keep him from having a heart attack?"

"Oh" she giggled, "I dropped it to forty, and he still turned red as a Baboon's ass"

Teller laughed. "If the color fits . . . my dear, we are well shed of that guy, but I think you may want to pack your things for an extended vacation."

"Why's that?"

"Because. I'm sure he fired Carlton, right?"

Now she was curious. "Yes, right then and there. How'd you know?"

"I know how James thinks, sweetheart. I told him to treat you with respect or I'd take away his precious Company, but by the end of today I will have *zero* leverage as far as that Company's concerned, and with no leverage I can do *very* little for you, *or* for Carl." Tucking the phone to his ear, he lay back with his hands behind his head and began to think, anticipating what James' next move might be.

Kelly waited through a few minutes of silence, then asked, "Do you really think he'll try something, Tell?"

Teller sighed. "With that guy, anything's possible babe. But the one thing I *am* sure of, is that as once I sign those papers, the only thing that will keep him in line is his fear of what I'm capable of doing to him if he tries anything stupid. And, as I said Kell, as sad as it may be, I know the guy and he *will* try something stupid. He won't be able to help himself." But then his tone lightened. "So, tell Carl to find a different place to enjoy his newfound wealth, and to forget about asking you out."

Her brow furrowed. "What are you *talking* about?"

"Kelly, Kelly, Kelly," Teller laughed. "What do you think made him agree to all this in the first place?

Thinking back on the clothes she had worn on their last meeting, and of Carltons reaction, she pursed her lips.

"You really think so?"

The warmth of his smile came over the phone. "Yes, Kelly, I really do. But that's now a moot issue. Tell him to watch *his* ass, not yours, and you go get packed. I'll be up to get you in a few days."

Carlton was on the other phone, saying goodbye to the bank manager in Tucson, but as he hung up his eyes drifted across the desk, roving over Kelly with thinly veiled desire; but Kelly, catching the track of his eyes drilled him with a bone-chilling stare. Carlton immediately began shuffling papers, and Kelly returned to her conversation with Teller.

"How shall I pack?"

"Pack for warm weather and bring a swimsuit."

"A swimsuit? Why? Where are we going?"

Teller turned the TV off. "Back to the lake. I need to talk to an Indian Chief and a Bear."

She grinned. "And just how long will we be gone?"

"As long as it takes. I'll see you in a few days. Now put Carl on the phone." Giving a cheerful, "okay," she made a kissing noise at the receiver, handed it over to Carlton and took a seat on the edge of Carl's desk so she could listen to at least one side of the conversation; and while Carltons answers consisted primarily of yes and no answers, she found the range of emotions that passed over his face astonishing.

Finally, after mumbling a quiet, "thank you." Carl hung up and sat staring at the phone while drumming his fingers on the desk. Kelly watched him until the drumming stopped. Appearing relieved, humbled, and elated all at the same time, Carlton looked up and gave her a bewildered smile.

"Your Mr. Teller is *certainly* an interesting man,"

Kelly's curiosity now overrode her annoyance with his previous display of lust.

"Why? What did he say?"

Slumping back in the plush executive chair while looking slightly embarrassed, Carlton mumbled, "He said not to push my luck."

"That's *it?*" she frowned.

Carl shook his head, "No, he also told me not to worry about James. That *he* would take care of any potential problems, but that I should leave Telluride." He paused, and his expression became one of puzzlement. "He also said he would be glad to help me out if I cared to invest in a project in Florida . . ." But then his bewilderment turned to delight.

"He also gave me Casey's personal number but said that he took no responsibility for anything that might happen if I chose to use it."

Kelly couldn't help but ask.

"Then why did he give it to you?"

"*That's* what's really odd." Carlton said, his blue eyes mystified behind his round spectacles. "He told me that a Coyote in a forty-eight Buick told him to do it.

= Chapter 4 =

Teller was in an extraordinary mood. Everything seemed to be falling into place, and with this, all seemed right with the world. But as he bounced down the stairs the old saw: *'don't count your chickens before they hatch'* suddenly crossed his mind. Stopping in mid-stride, the vision of Jack standing naked in the doorway with a room full of sputtering candles, empty bottles, and a smiling young woman tangled in sheets behind him returned; and with it, not *only* did Teller's good humor kick up a notch, a glowing sense of accomplishment accompanied it; and with that image planted firmly in his minds eye, Teller smiled and added a personalized addition to the old saying: *'But it only takes a couple scrambled eggs to make a meal.'*
Chuckling, he continued down the stairs.
He was still grinning as he rounded the corner to see a different girl behind the check-in desk.

Covertly inventorying the young woman's charms as he crossed the worn carpet, Jack's repetitive, *'college town'* remark came instantly to mind; and as if she had heard his thoughts, she looked up from her paperwork and smiled as he pushed the lounge door open with the flat of his hand; and just before he passed through he turned and slipped her a wink.

Teller let the door wheeze closed behind him, and as the last sliver of light blinked out he was transported into a different world; a world that was dark and cool . . . a most pleasant change from the bright hot reality of the Tucson morning. Pausing to allow his eyes to adjust to the dim light, he scanned the room.

Terry was behind the bar, buffing the inside of a glass with a rag that covered his hand like a puppet, while Joe was still sitting where they had left him the night before.

Sliding onto a stool, Teller smiled, "You ready to go?"

Terry glanced up at the clock, nodded and tossed the rag into the sink. "Hey Joe," he called out, "think you could watch the place again? We'll only be gone an hour or so."

Joe lifted bleary eyes from his half empty glass.

"Sure, Terry," he smiled, "no problem." But when he focused on Teller his smile brightened. "Hey Cowboy, what incredible adventures await you today?"

"Mornin' Joe." Teller waved, then held up a finger. "Just a sec."

Pointing to the half-full bottle of Johnny Walker Black on the top shelf, he opened his wallet and slapped a hundred on the bar. "Hand me down that bottle, Terry."

Terry was surprised, but he pulled it down and plunked it on the bar. "Anything else?"

"Two shot glasses and cold beer, any flavor," but then he corrected, "except Bud."

Terry chuckled as he dug through the ice, pulling out a Lone Star. "This do?" He asked as he dangled it from his fingertips.

"No." Teller said, shaking his head. "Dig a little deeper pal."

Terry stuck the bottle back in the cooler and plowed around, finally pulling out a longneck Coors. "How 'bout this?" Pinching the shot glasses between his fingers, Teller grabbed the Coors by the neck, wrapped his other hand around whisky bottle, and headed towards Joe's table.

"Guess that one's okay, huh?" Terry said to Teller's back.

"It'll do." Teller called over his shoulder as the whisky bottle hit the tabletop.

At the sound, Joe lifted his bowed head to see Teller swing a chair around, throw his leg over the seat, and plunk down two shot glasses.

"My adventures for today you ask? He grinned. "Why, Joe, today I am destined for classics and coyotes, subterfuge and Spanish gold, excitement and enlightenment."

Joe's bleary eyes cleared and he chuckled, "Sounds like a full day."

"Indeed it does, Joe," Teller laughed, splashing whiskey into the two empty glasses. "A full day and more . . ." Raising his glass, he smiled wistfully. "And then I shall be off to the red-haired Queen of the north." He tossed his drink back and turned the glass upside down on the napkin. "That's it for me, Joe. The rest is yours."

Joe gave a surprised smile. "Why, thank you sir, that is more than generous, but completely unnecessary. I can afford my own drinks. But, as I would not wish to seem unappreciative, I shall not refuse your kindness.

Pleasantly surprised, and agreeably impressed by the eloquence of Joe's response, Teller chuckled. It was not what he expected from a man dressed in the same wrinkled suit from the night before. With a smile, he asked, "And what does this bright new day hold for you, Joe?"

Joe picked up the glass and with a reconciled shrug, downed the whiskey. But when he looked up, the glimmer of a better man shone through. He smiled, and motioned Teller to pour again, to which Teller gladly obliged.

"Pretty much the same thing as you, sir." Joe smiled, "Except, of course, everything you said you were going to do between the time you sat down, and now." A sigh followed as the bright glimmer in his eyes faded. "No sir, I guess I'll just hold down the fort for Terry."

Teller gave a nod. "A worthy, if not lofty goal, and one no doubt filled with its own rewards." But as he pushed away from the table, he found himself suddenly curious.

"So, Joe. If you don't mind, just what *is* it that you do?"

Surprised that Teller would even bother to ask, the glimmer returned to Joe's eyes and a touch of pride entered his voice.

"I'm in sales."

The change in Joe's tone caught Teller's interest, and swinging the chair around, he sat back down.

"Sales you say? Well how's about just a *little* more detail, Joe?"

"Executive helicopter sales," he said. "Bell division."

Teller's eyebrows shot up. "Really!"

Joe nodded, picked up the bottle, and poured a little whiskey over the melting cubes in his glass.

"Yes, really. Why?"

Both surprise and humor shone in Teller's eyes.

"Two reasons Joe. First, the coincidences in my life are beginning to look less and less like coincidences . . ." His voice trailed off as a peculiar smile crossed his face. "And secondly, and no offense, but just *look* at you." Smiling, he waved a hand at their surroundings. "Cheap hotel, cheap bar, and worse yet, cheaper hookers." But pausing, he took the lapels of Joe's winkled coat between his thumb and forefingers and rubbed. "Altho' this is *not* a cheap suit."

His brow furrowing, he released the lapel and leaned back, eyeing Joe with an entirely new level of interest.

"Okay amigo. Now you've got my curiosity up. There's more to this story than meets the eye . . . spill it."

Joe opened his mouth to speak but Teller held up a finger.

"Wait, hold that thought." Turning, he called out. "Hey Terry, bring another beer and come sit down. I think you might want to hear this."

Following a few minutes of glasses clinking and ice rustling, Terry pulled up a chair and slapped Teller's beer onto the table.

"Hear what?"

Uncomfortable with this sudden scrutiny, Joe fidgeted while Teller refilled his glass. "Come on Joe," he smiled, "you're among friends."

In an odd combination of subdued defiance, Joe took a deep breath, raised his newly filled glass, and presenting a hung-over smile, said, "One word. Divorce."

Tipping the bottom of the glass to the ceiling, he drained it. Teller nodded, his voice reflecting sympathy. "That'll do it." He picked up the bottle, splashed a little more whiskey into Joe's glass, and leaned back in his chair. "Go on . . ."

"It's the same old story," Joe shrugged. "Successful young exec with a great career travels the globe selling high-end aircraft to high-end people," He let out an extended sigh, clouding his features.

"And *then* I met the girl of my dreams."

A grin spread across Teller's face. "I don't want to sound callous old son, but *that* contains the element of nearly every heartbreak song that has ever been written."

Joe's grin returned, and his mood lightened considerably.

"Oh, don't get me wrong gents." He laughed, "I'm not going to wring your hearts with tales of woe. I still have my stuff, I just have about fifty percent less of it. That woman was smart, beautiful, great in bed and ruthless in court. Turns out she's the perfect ex-wife."

Throwing his head back, Teller let go an enthusiastic laugh. "Now *that* is a great line! I once wrote a song titled, 'I'm not broke, but I'm badly bent.' and I'll tell you what, Joe. It sounds as if it could have been written just for you. Hey, if you don't mind, I may try to work that brilliant phrase into the song in your honor." As his laughter faded, he looked at Joe with newfound respect. "So then, you still in the helicopter game?"

Joe rattled the ice in his glass and smiled. "I'm not broke, but I'm badly bent huh? I like it! yes sir, that describes me to a 'T." Picking up the bottle, he poured a splash and gave Teller a disheveled grin. "however, in answer to your question, yes, I am. Why?"

Teller glanced over at Terry, picked up his now empty beer bottle, and gave it a little shake. Taking the hint, Terry went to the bar, and once Teller was holding a fresh Coors he continued. "Because Joe, if you're still in the game, I may have *just* the client for you."

Terry flashed a suspicious glance but Teller just smiled.

"Don't be concerned lad, there is nothing inappropriate, or illegal going on. It is simply that the same set of circumstances that has allowed me to purchase that fine old automobile of yours will also provide the financial wherewithal for my partner Jack to replace his ragged old chopper with something more befitting his desires."

With a mighty grin, Teller raised his beer in a toast.

"To fast rafts, cold water, and sun-drenched titties!"

Neither man had a clue what Teller was talking about, but able to appreciate the concept nonetheless, both men lifted their glasses to Teller's bottle, and smiles lit the table.

Teller drained his beer and looked at Joe. "So, are you still in any position to provide sales representation?"

Joe's demeanor transformed instantly. Suddenly he became less the unkempt door-to-door encyclopedia salesman and more a polished professional lying dormant under an expensive, but rumpled suit.

"Of course, but what exactly is your friend in the market for?"

Teller clapped his hands merrily and laughed, "*That* I couldn't tell you Joe, for it is not my area of expertise. But I can tell you this. It must fly fast, silent, *and* be appealing to pretty girls."

Here he leaned back, his smile growing warmer.

"Ahh, but the man himself can give you all the dirty details. In the meantime, Terry and I have a little business to take care of. But I'll call Jack and get him down here so you two can discuss the particulars."

At the mention of Jack's name, Joe perked up. "*Jack* is the guy who needs a new chopper?"

Lifting his bottle, Teller smiled, "One and the same."

Putting it to his lips, he drained it, plunked the empty onto the table between them, and turned to Terry.

"You ready to go?"

Terry nodded, stood, and pushed his chair back under the table. Teller followed Terry's example, then reached across the table to shake Joe's hand.

"Stick around amigo, this sale might make your month."

= Chapter 5 =

Stepping through the same exit door as yesterday, Teller followed Terry into the warm morning. It was still early, and the sun had not yet turned the car into a mobile oven.
Grateful for that small boon, Teller slid into the passenger's seat, rolled down his window, and slipped on his shades.

"Well son," he grinned, "by now my confederates up in Telluride should have succeeded in transferring the necessary funds into a branch of the Wells Fargo bank down here in Tucson at . . . wait a sec." Teller pulled a folded piece of paper from his pocket and checked the address. "Ahh. It appears to be the Wells Fargo bank on north Campbell Ave."

"That's just a few miles from here." Terry smiled. "Buckle up!"

As they drove, Terry brought up Jack.

"So, your friend is a Helicopter pilot?"

"Yes, he is." Teller grinned, "he is that and much more, and had I known old Joe was in the chopper game, Jacko would be that much closer to his dreams." He turned to look at Terry. "Did *you* know that Joe was a sales rep?"

Terry shook his head. "Well, I knew he was a salesman, but I *didn't* know he was involved in Helicopters."

Teller grinned. "Just goes to show that you can't judge a book by the cover." Nodding in agreement as the Bank came into view, Terry whipped the steering wheel, pulled under a tree, and turned off the ignition.

Teller swung the car door open. "You just wait right here son." But just as the toe of his boot touched pavement, he stopped, sat back down, pulled the door closed and resting his elbow on the seatback, looked at Terry.

"How would you like your money lad? Cash, money order, or deposited into your account?"

Terry's brow wrinkled, and he drummed the steering wheel with his fingers. "I'm not getting involved in anything that can cause me any trouble, am I?"

Teller grinned and shook his head.

"No, Terry, the money's legit. I simply cashed out of a business up in the Rockies. Everything's on the up and up, so there's nothing to concern yourself with."

At the news Terry slumped back into the seat with a sigh of relief. But Tellers reassurances notwithstanding, he was still out of his element in regards to banking procedures.

"Heck, Teller. I have no idea. What do *you* think?

"Terry," Teller sighed, shaking his head. "I'm not your financial advisor." But then a small smile touched his lips and with a slap on the dash he swung the door open, stepped out, and leaned back into the open window. "I'll take care of it kid." He winked, and spinning on one heel, walked away.

Watching him disappear into the bank, Terry smiled, shook his head and turned on the radio, nervously glancing at his watch every few minutes until finally he closed his eyes and dozed off . . .

In his dream he was six years old, playing in the lake with his sister. They always had such fun splashing in the cool water chasing minnows and jumping from the rocks, especially when the big dog with the yellow eyes would come down and . . . Suddenly, in a rush of hot air his childhood evaporated and his eyes popped open to see Teller toss his deerskin pack between them as he slid in.

Slapping Terry's shoulder, he grinned, "Okay young son, let's go get that car."

Terry, still foggy from the dream, wanted to speak, to tell Teller of the dog, but Teller silenced him with a wave of his hand. "Later Terry, whatever it is, it'll wait." Laying his head back against the seat, he closed his eyes and didn't utter another word for the rest of the trip.

Terry didn't mind at all, for while they maneuvered the same quiet deserted streets they had traveled the last time, the silence gave him the opportunity to recall the dream; it had been so real he could *still* feel the cool water on his skin, and *something* about that huge yellow-eyed dog seemed critical: as if it, his memory, and Teller were all wound up together somehow . . . But the harder he tried, the quicker both the dreams imagery, and its importance faded, and by the time the two big boulders that stood sentry came into sight it was all but gone. Frustrated, Terry put the car in park and tapped Teller gently on the shoulder. "We're here," he smiled, and got out to unlock the big wrought iron gate

"Fantastic." Teller yawned, opening one eye and leaning his head out of the window to hear the sound of the car's tires rumbling over the bricks of the driveway for the second time that week.

As they rolled beneath the canopy of broad-leafed Catalpa trees, Teller looked up and saw that the buds had blossomed since their last visit: the rich, velvet colors of the orchid-like flowers were now in full display, adding a stately elegance to the Victorian home. But the coincidence of their sudden bloom also enhanced the sense of providence that lent itself to this unlikely tableau; but saying nothing, Teller laid his head back and watched the flowers disappear as Terry steered the car from beneath the trees and down the winding drive to the Porte Cochere where Terry put the car in park, looked up at the house, and turned to Teller.

"So, what did you decide at the bank?"

Teller waggled his eyebrows. "*You* are about to be a rich young man," he grinned. "Don't sweat the details."

Grabbing his pack, he swung the car door open, slung it over his shoulder, hopped out of the car and headed up the steps; but on not hearing the slap of a second set of feet behind him, he stopped to glance over his shoulder.

Terry had not moved.

Spinning on his heel, Teller went back to the car and leaned in the window.

"Is there a problem?"

Terry sat with his hands resting lightly on the wheel, chewing on the inside of his lip. He remained quiet for a moment, then said, "No, no, there's no *problem*. It's just that this is all so weird. Two days ago I was wondering what I was going to do about the mortgage, the kids . . ." He paused and turned a curious eye to Teller. "Moneys been pretty tight lately." he sighed, relief and perplexity equally evident in his eyes. "And then *you* walk into my shitty bar and *everything* changes."

Teller slapped the roof of the car. "I understand completely lad, but don't blame *me*." Stepping back, he began waving his hands at right angles above his head, laughing as he waddled around, "I'm just another puppet."

Completing his spasmodic circle, he lowered his arms, dropping the marionette act. "Let's go, I want to take my new old car for a cruise."

Chuckling as he slid from behind the wheel, Terry stepped onto the familiar driveway. Looking first at the gabled roofline of his Grandfathers home, he then turned his eyes to his new acquaintance turned benefactor who was bouncing up the entry steps two at a time: and as he did, he wondered again why *he* was left the old car. With that question heavy on his mind, Terry went up the steps to find Teller leaning against the doorjamb.

"You feel that?" Teller asked.

Terry paused. A sense of expectation charged the air, and he could feel the energy; the very molecules surrounding them seemed to pulse.

"Yes . . . yes I do . . ." he nodded.

Both curious, and slightly nervous, he went to the two lion statues that sat at the top of the stairs guarding the entry; and reaching into the left ones mouth he removed a key.

Looking at Teller, he slid it into the ornate lock with trembling fingers, and pushed . . .

The two heavily carved wooden doors swung open; and as the warm light of the day brightened the foyer, a rush of cool, musty air blew past them, ruffling their hair as it collided with the early afternoon heat.

It felt as if the house had just breathed a sigh of release.

With goose pimples raising the hair on the back of his neck, Terry slowly turned to Teller who had a big smile spread across his face. "*Someone*'s glad we're here," he whispered, and stepped into the path of light.

Terry reluctantly followed, surprised to find that a sense of peace infused the air. And while the cool, quiet atmosphere calmed *his* frazzled nerves, that same strange sense of welcome intrigued Teller; and as he stood in the shadowed room, he was struck by the feeling that some cosmic gear was about to slip into place.

Scarcely breathing, he cocked his head, fully expecting to hear an audible 'click'.

Nothing.

Hoping for *something* more tangible than just a nebulous sense of impending arrival, Teller held his breath . . .

Still nothing.

But just as he decided it was all in his head he looked down at the beam of sunlight that fanned in from the door, lighting a path on the floor before him. His first thought was of the yellow brick road in the, "Wizard of Oz" but as his eyes followed that trail of light into the gloom, he saw that not *only* were the tracks that he and Terry had left on their previous visit still visible in the dust, there were a new set of prints . . . those of a *very* large canine.

Shaking his head, he chuckled, "Well, well, well."

Hearing Teller's suppressed laugh, Terry turned, and seeing the tracks gasped, "Where the hell did *those* come from?"

Teller's eyes sparkled.

"You remember a few minutes ago when you mentioned that I walked into your bar and everything changed?
Terry gave a nod. "Yeah . . ."

"Well, welcome to *my* world." he hooted, and raising his hands over his head once again, began his marionette dance, walking in jerky syncopation towards the kitchen.

"Walk this way," he called over his shoulder, the jubilant tone of his voice echoing throughout the empty room; and Terry, recalling Marty Feldman's 'Igor' in the old Mel Brooks movie, shrugged and stepped behind Teller, walking through the living room while waving his hands above his head in a comical imitation while being careful not to step on the ghostly tracks as they followed the canine trail through the dining room.

By the time they reached the kitchen, Teller had ceased his puppet walk and now, standing in the filtered light that came through a dusty window waved Terry forward while pointing at the door to the garage.

"Sir, the honors are yours."

Terry nodded, stepped around, laid a hand on the glass knob, and swung the door open.

Another blast of cool air hit them, duplicating the air in the entry; charged with a mysterious, and extraordinary pulsing energy: and while the room was dark, the sense of emptiness that had previously permeated the gloom was gone.

Puzzled, but also comforted by the odd feeling of un-emptiness in this empty house, Terry reached into the darkness, sliding his hand along the wall until his fingers touched a switch; and with a flip, the bare bulb hanging from the wooden rafters exploded in light, chasing the shadows into their corners and illuminating the stunning old motorcar. Teller's eyes went wide.

The creamy yellow paint so fashionable at the time gleamed elegantly: glowing with opalescent radiance while the abundance of highly polished chrome reflected the single bulb's light from every point.

Teller stepped into that light, slowly approaching the car to stroke the hood with loving reverence.

"She's beautiful," he purred, walking down the old autos side while letting his finger trace the curve of the front fender, his hand sliding down the side of the car, along the raised bodyline, and coming to rest on the large silver door handle. "Just beautiful . . ."

A smile crept across Terry's face. There could be no argument that *this* was the man who should possess this car. He could feel the approval of his grandfather.

Teller paused to look through the window, and seeing the keys dangling in the ignition, pressed the large silver knob on the handle with his thumb; his smile growing wider as the mechanism clicked softly. With an intake of breath, he slid behind the massive wheel, closed his eyes, and turned the key.

Nothing.

"He took the battery out."

Terry's voice fetched Teller back to the present.

"What?"

Terry pointed over to a six-cell battery on the wooden bench in the back of the garage.

"He always took the battery out when he parked it for any length of time. Like I said, he didn't drive it all that often."

Tellers disappointment vanished. "Of course. . ." he smiled and tapped the horn.

Silence.

As he slid back out he drug his fingers along the seat, the touch bringing a subtle tactile pleasure.

"Pop the hood young son," he grinned, "and I'll put the battery in. I want to hear this baby run."

Terry nodded and went to the front of the car, fumbling between the spaces of the huge chrome grill as his fingers searched unsuccessfully for the latch.

Teller watched for a moment, then stepped in and bumped him out of the way. "Move aside junior. I'll do it."

As Teller jostled him aside, Terry snapped, "I told you, I don't know *anything* about old cars."

But Teller just laughed as his fingers slipped between the gleaming chrome bars. "No insult intended lad, it's simply that when it comes to beast's such as this, you are hamstrung by your youth." Fingering the latch, he looked up with a grin as it clicked. "But don't worry, you'll outgrow it."

Terry's feelings soothed, he laughed at Teller who, waggling his brows, rubbed his hands together and lifted the massive hood.

"Well then, let's just see what we've got under here."

The motor was immaculate.

A light coat of dust covered the engine, but that was it. No oil, no grease. Nothing but fine dust.

Teller shook his head in amazement.

"Your Grandfather really loved this car, didn't he?"

Terry nodded as his fingertips grazed the curve of the fender. "Yeah, he did. I think this old car and my grandmother were the two things he loved most."

Teller smiled. "She must have been one hell of a woman."

"Yeah," Terry chuckled. "Granddad sure thought so."

Seeing the car with new eyes, random childhood memories sprung forward. "Don't get me wrong, he loved us all. But it was when he hit the road in this cruiser and did whatever he did up on the Reservation that I saw him the happiest."

With a smile and a nod of understanding, Teller went over to the old six-volt lead cube. It was also covered with fine coat of dust. So, wrapping it in an old towel that was folded neatly on the shelf above, he slid it from the countertop and nearly dropped it on his foot. He was *not* ready for that kind of weight in such a small package. Bringing it up to his waist, he straightened his back and bounced it a few times.

'Damn, this thing must weigh 50 pounds!'

Putting a little more muscle into it, he lugged it across the garage and lowering it into its holder, jiggled the terminal cables onto the posts.

"So, Terry, where might one find a wrench?"

Terry just smiled and pointed to the rolling tool chest against the far wall. "I don't know *anything* about cars, Teller, but I *think* those are tools over there."

"Smartass." Teller chuckled.

It didn't take long to find what he needed. The tools in every drawer were laid out neatly: either in type, in order of size, or both.

Finding the wrench he was looking for in the second drawer among a row of its clean but dusty cousins, he smiled. He was impressed, and just a little put out by the level of neatness and organization that Terry's Grandfather exhibited. It was a trait that he wished he had developed to a greater degree. Vowing to begin a new regimen in the near future, he picked up a half-inch open-end wrench from the row; and slapping it against his palm as he crossed the garage, he waggled it at Terry like an old school Marm with a ruler as he stuck his head under the hood, his voice echoing inside the steel shell.

"Well Terry, I may not know much, but I *can* tell you this with the full confidence of personal experience. A cool car, a fine guitar, and a good woman will unquestionably increase a man's sense of joy, and thus, make his life just a little more worth living."

Cranking down the last nut, he pulled his head from beneath the hood, wiped his hands on the rag, and looked at Terry, his eyes bright and sincere.

"Now, I'm not saying that there's nothing more to happiness son, but without those three items, I can assure you *I* would be a far less jovial fellow." With that, he slowly brought the massive hood down, pressing gently until it locked into place with a solid, 'snick.'

With that, Teller rubbed his hands together, smiling as he imagined the look on Jack's face when he rolled up in this classic: but now, thinking of Jack, Teller dropped a hand on Terry's shoulder and squeezed.

"Let me add one more *very* important item to that list of happiness son. Make sure you've got a few good friends."

With that, he slid behind the wheel and turned the key.

The starter whirred and the motor caught on the second revolution. There was a slight hesitation but giving it a little gas, the big engine sputtered a few times and came to life.

Teller feathered the pedal, frowning when he heard a barely audible valve clatter; but as oil reached the upper cylinders the noise quieted and he smiled in satisfaction.

Once the motor smoothed out, Teller pressed the pedal, and the engine roared. Its deep rumble set Teller to laughing; and raising his face to the roof, he gave a long howl and pointed to the swing-out garage doors.

"Prepare for lift off!" he shouted.

Laughing along with Teller, Terry flung the doors wide, and the choking blue smoke billowed out, coloring the air until the breeze caught it, and whisked it away.

Teller took his foot off the gas and the old Buick coughed a few times but quickly settled into a smooth idle: hitting solidly on all eight cylinders and purring like a lion at rest.

Tellers grin was enormous as he jumped out, and with a quick search, found a floor jack to lower his dream to concrete. He frowned as the car settled on deflated tires; but not about to have his fun spoiled by such trivial matters as lack of air, a second look around turned up a compressor, and ten minutes later the wide white walls were standing proud.

Stepping back one final time to admire the car, Teller whispered, "Perfect" and reached through the window to grab his deerskin. His smile had not diminishing one iota as he looked Terry squarely in the eyes and added one last item to his previous statement.

"And, of course, my young friend; last, but not remotely least, there is *one* final equation to ones' happiness in this world . . . *money.*" Throwing open the flap on the deerskin, Teller removed a fat Manila envelope and placed it in Terry's hands. "As agreed," he grinned. "Sixty thousand dollars."

Holding the envelope, Terry's heart and mind were a mix of disbelief and trepidation. He had a sudden, and unfounded feeling of regret at the selling his Grandfathers car, but his apprehension was slightly alleviated by the envelope's weight.

"Go ahead lad," Teller beamed. "Open it up!"

Terrys smile was one of disbelief as he folded the flap back and fanned through the stack of bills; but faltered when he saw that among the neatly banded bundles were five certificates. Pulling them out, he asked, "What're these?"

With a sigh, Teller tossed his pack through the driver's window and leaned up against the fender.

"That, son, is sixty thousand dollars that the I.R.S. doesn't need to know about. You wouldn't give me an answer at the bank, so I was forced to make an executive decision."

Terry's face remained blank. "Meaning what?"

"Give me that!" Teller snapped, snatching the envelope from Terry's hand; opening the envelope to remove the packs of banded hundred-dollar bills. Then, handing them back to Terry one at a time, he counted: "Fifteen thousand in bills, and five nine thousand dollar cashier's checks. You see, junior, under ten thou at a time, no need to report it." He winked. "It'll just be our little secret. Now, sign over the title."

Terry nodded, laid the manila envelope onto the hood, and signed the title and its accompanying paperwork in all the required spaces, feeling like he was in a dream as he passed it back to Teller.

Giving it a quick once over, Teller smiled a satisfied smile and put the title and registration into the massive glove box. Then, going to the driver's side, he took a deep breath, opened the door, and slid in, pulling the heavy door closed, relishing the solid sound as it shut. Grinning through the open window he turned the key with a flourish.

As the powerful engine roared to life, Teller reached up to unlatch the clips at the windshields frame; and once released, he pushed the large chrome button on the dash.

Motors whirred and the canvas top lifted, rising and folding back into its compartment.

Rolling down the windows, Teller reached out and took Terry's hand.

"Thanks for making a dream come true my friend." He said, his grin growing larger as he pulled out of the garage and circling the roundabout twice, he hung his arm out the window and hollered, "See ya back at the bar!"

The old Buick rumbled down the drive, the sound of tires slapping the bricks echoing as the Sun's filtered rays flashed through the leaves of the Catalpa trees, dappling the cars painted surface; flashing along the chrome as it disappeared through the wrought iron gates; and hearing Teller's laughter rising above the wall beyond, Terry joined in.

~

Racing down the winding road of the upscale neighborhood, Teller checked himself in the rearview mirror.

With the wind whipping through his hair, he smiled at his reflection. He felt like a King.

Adjusting his sunglasses, he turned the big ivory knob on the radio; the dial lit up, and classical music poured from the big dash speaker.

"No! No! No! *Not* what I want." he growled, pushing the big chrome buttons beneath the glass-covered tuner.

Rewarded with nothing but pop music and advertising, he yanked off his shades and glared at the radio as he pressed the very last button in the row. Suddenly Carl Perkins blasted from the speaker:

'You can do anything that you want'a do, but buddy lay offa my blue suede shoes!

"Yes!" Teller laughed, pressing his shades back into place with one finger while he cranked the volume up and shouted, "Take *that* Elvis!" into the desert sky.

Laying his weight onto the gas pedal the engine roared, leaving a trail of exhaust, and Tellers joyous singing mixed in the wind.

= Chapter 6 =

Putting knuckles to eyes, Abbott rubbed, dropped his fists, and stared again at the spot in the sage where the air still shimmered in a vague outline of the canine. But it was only as a bird gave a few tentative chirps did he realize how utterly silent the desert had become: and with even the breeze having quit, the previously swirling leaves seemed to wait for permission to move on. . . but then, with those first sweet notes of birdsong the winds caress returned, lifting the colorful leaves up and sending them dancing away while filling the desert with a symphony that he had not noticed until it was gone. With a sigh, he lay back on the warm sandstone and stared up at the clouds that floated by.

'My, my, my, that was certainly enlightening.'

As he lay there, Abbott began to contemplate what had just occurred, and in doing so realized that not only was he adrift in uncharted waters, he was without compass or sails.

He needed to talk to Billy.

Locking his calves against the rock face for leverage, he hauled his considerable frame up into a sitting position, then, rolling onto one knee he pushed himself up to stand with his face into the light breeze that now blew from the direction the Coyote had trotted off.

"Thanks." He called out, muttering as he walked away, "I guess . . ."

Abbott's trek across the sunbaked land started out normally enough, but he found that his senses intensified as he walked. Suddenly, every step he took felt as if the earth softened slightly, giving way to his weight. Hard stones turned their sharp edges away, sagebrush twigs bent rather than snap, and the soles of his feet seemed to sense the movement of each grain of sand as it shifted . . . it was as if he were walking on a living surface rather than the stone floor of an ancient seabed.

Slowing, he looked about, noticing lizards that were no more than scurrying flashes of movement earlier, now stopped to watch him pass giving sly reptilian smiles beneath hooded lids that held glittering eyes. Uncomfortably aware of their scrutiny, Abbott continued, and when his feet finally touched the wooden steps of the store he found himself unexpectedly relieved to feel the solid reality of the building beneath him. Taking a deep breath, he stepped into the shade, wrapped his fingers around the handrail, and looked back across the now unremarkable desert landscape.

He needed to find Billy.

Turning away, he pushed through the front door, causing the little bell to tinkle out its sweet note. He glanced around, hoping that Billy might be close but the store was empty. Frowning, he marched through the double doors at the rear of the store and peeked into Billy's office. The ceiling fan spun in lazy circles, but there was no sign of the man. Turning back around, he flipped the fan switch off, walked back to the wall cooler, took out a cold six-pack, and passing through front door a second time, sent the little bell singing once again; and with that sound the only constant, Abbott went to edge of the porch, brought his hand up to shade his eyes and gazed across the desert. No sign of Billy.

With a sigh, Abbott flopped into the rocker and opened a beer. He knew that if he waited long enough Billy would return, And, if there is one thing an Archaeologist learns, it is patience.

Abbott thought about Coyote as he rocked. This adventure was becoming more complex with every passing day; and, with this last appearance an entirely new twist had been written into the script . . . sipping his beer as he puzzled just how this sighting might affect him, he heard the porch steps

41

creak, and looking up, saw Billy, wiping his hands on a rag greasy from working on the old Scout. Seeing Abbott, a magnificent smile lit the shadow of Billy's face from his beat-up cowboy hat.

"Mr. Bear, you were looking for me?"

By now Abbott had become somewhat accustomed to Billy's prescience, and while he tried to match the old mans smile, he was easily a thousand watts shy.

"Yes, Billy, I was. I just had a visit from our friend."

Billy's expression did not change as he continued to wipe his hands.

"And?"

"And he indicated Teller is fine."

Raising his eyebrows, he nodded, and took a seat on the bench next to Abbott.

"Did he come in the guise of Coyote, or human?"

"A Coyote, and a very healthy one at that."

Billy pushed his hat back and pulled his sleeve across his forehead. "Interesting," he murmured. Then, gazing intensely into Abbott's eyes, he asked, "has he ever appeared to you as human?"

Abbott gave a shake of his woolly head. "Until now he's never appeared to me at all. And I've never heard Teller say anything other than coyote."

"Hmmm." Billy nodded. Then, putting both hands on his knees, he stood and walked into the store. A few minutes later he returned with a glass of water and sat back down, but didn't drink, he just stared off at the buttes in the distance.

The silence stretched, and Abbott closed his eyes.

It didn't take long before the glass in Billy's hand began to sweat and with the sensation of cool water trickling down his fingers he was brought back to the shade of the porch. Taking off his hat, he set it on his knee and turned to see Abbott's eyes were closed. He gave a quiet cough and smiled as Abbott's eyes popped open.

"Let me ask you a question, Sir Bear. What do *you* think Coyote has in mind for your friend Teller?"

Abbott blinked, taking a moment to think. He had no misgivings of his role in this adventure so far, and he certainly held no suspicions regarding the man sitting across from him now. But the question seemed beyond his ability to answer with any relevance. Taking a deep breath, he spoke slowly, putting great consideration into each word.

"Sir, you are asking me to invoke my interpretation onto something beyond my grasp. How could I possibly assume to guess the intentions of a deity I did not think even existed until a short while ago?"

Billy's eyes twinkled. "It is as I thought. You are wise, Sir Bear, and the perfect choice of companion. *No* one can know Coyote's intentions." He paused, then spoke softly. "I often wonder if he knows them himself." But quickly turning his attentions back to Abbott he smiled, "But that is not my point. Coyote's game is his own to play, and quite often he picks a unique individual that either suits his needs, or whose personality is in sync with his own. In *this* case, I believe it is the latter." Taking a sip of water, Billy's eyes returned to the horizon, locking on some point in the distance. He fell quiet, and several moments passed before he spoke again.

"I think our friend Teller is a man whose heart is very close to Coyotes, and for that reason Coyote has chosen him to be the recipient of his attentions." Again, he paused and smiled. "There are many stories in my people's long history of Coyote; telling of the tricks he has played on both the heroes and the fools of the past. But rarely does he grant the boon of guidance as well as fortune, to a man without exacting some form of payment."

At this, Abbott's brow creased. "And just *what* constitutes payment?"

Billy steepled his fingers and leaned back.

"Ahh. That *is* the question, isn't it?"

= Chapter 7 =

At the sound of hammering on the door, Jack stepped out of the shower, wrapped a towel around his waist, and leaving a trail of wet footprints on the carpet went to the door and peeked through the peephole. With a sigh, he flung the door open, sweeping his low arm in welcome.

"Come on in, Tell . . ."

Teller stuck his head through the door; casting a wary eye around the room. "Where's your date?"

Chuckling, Jack pulled the towel from his waist and started rubbing his scalp; turning to follow his wet footprints back to the bathroom. "I sent her home." he said, his voice muffled beneath the cloth. "You said we had a meeting tonight."

"We do." Teller answered, averting his eyes from Jacks naked ass as he went to the window and pulled back the curtain. "And please, cover yourself."

Jack's laugh was cut off by the closing of the bathroom door, only to be followed by the sound of running water.
After a bit of banging around, the door swung open and Jack emerged through a cloud of steam, rubbing his face briskly with aftershave. The smell wafted across the room, assaulting Teller's nostrils and whipping around, saw that Jack had wrapped a towel around his waist.

He thanked the powers that be for small favors.

"So," Jack smiled. "What time is the meeting?"

"Old Spice? Teller groaned, wrinkled his nose. "Jeezus Jack, couldn't you get more original?"

Jack ignored the comment. "What time?"

Coughing melodramatically, Teller turned, and went to the mini-fridge for a beer. "We're supposed to meet Junior at six." He said as he pulled the door open. No beer, just a half-melted Popsicle and a frozen rose. He looked up at Jack and grinned. He understood the rose; but was reasonably sure he didn't *want* to know the details of the Popsicle.

With a shake of his head, he closed the refrigerator door, went to a chair near the window, flopped down and flipped on the T.V.

"So, how did everything go with what's her name?"

Jack pulled a comb through his hair. "Patty?"

"Yeah, Patty."

"She's a nice girl Tell." Jack grinned, "Thanks for the intro."

Teller turned off the television, stood, and threw an arm over Jacks shoulder. "I missed you Jack. This is like old times. Hey! I got rid of the rental. Wait 'til you see our new ride."

~

The evenings light reflected off of the hood of the Buick as they cruised the Tucson streets. Jack had his cap pulled down tight, his right elbow resting out of the window, while Teller, the wind tousling his hair turned and grinned.

"Hey Jack, you remember rumpled Joe?

"The guy at the bar? Sure I do Tell, Why?"

Teller hung his wrist hung over the mammoth steering wheel and leaned back into the seat. "Because, Amigo, the guy is a hotshot for the Bell helicopter Corp, and just *may* be the man who can sell you that new chopper you've been dreaming about."

Jack sat up straight, pulled off his cap, and rubbed his scalp. "*That* guy? What makes you think that?"

"Cause that's what he told me."

"People tell you a lot of things, Tell." Jack chuckled. "That don't make 'em true."

"Point taken." Teller nodded, "But some things aren't hard to prove. Once we're done with this thing tonight we'll know where we stand financially. *Then* we'll pin Joe down and talk about fancy helicopters."

Jack nodded. "Sure, Tell. But Joe . . .? I just don't see it."

"Yeah, I know." Teller smiled, "But stranger things have happened." Poking at one of the big chrome buttons on the radio, the music of Wynton Marsalis spilled from the big speaker in the dash, and with the dulcet sounds of Wynton's trumpet blending beautifully with the wind whistling through the car, the two men lapsed into silence, each caught up in his own personal fantasy . . .

Jack buzzed low over a river filled with pretty girls on rafts, all wet and waving, while Teller was on a houseboat in the shade of a massive wall on Lake Powell, stretched out on a reclining chair with a cold beer in one hand and a fishing pole in the other. Kelly came down the ladder from the sun deck: topless, and slippery from sweat and oil. Reaching out and taking off his sunglasses, she pressed her warm lips to his, and slid onto his lap . . .

"You think Junior's for real, Tell?"

Jacks voice reeled Teller from his daydream back into the Tucson night. Ignoring him, he squeezed the steering wheel and tucked that pleasant vision into his long list of things still to do.

"Teller?" Jack repeated, raising his shades and leaning forward.

"Sorry man." Teller smiled, "my mind was elsewhere. Yeah, I believe he is. I have a good feeling about him, and that gives me faith. And being Billy's nephew certainly adds a positive to his credentials."

"True." Jack nodded, falling silent as his eyes went back to the road. Teller glanced at Jack, mentally shrugged, and turned his attentions back to his present surroundings. It may not be a houseboat with a beautiful woman, but it *was* a lovely warm evening. And with the last light of day bouncing from the clouds onto the rounded hood of the car, he forgave his friend for disturbing his illusion. With a grin, he cranked the wheel, heading down 22nd street to cruise past Santa Rita Park where a group of old men sitting at a bus stop saw the Buick glide by . . . years suddenly scattered and as one, the old fellas sprung from the bench, whistling and hollering shouts of approval as the steel dream of their youth rolled by.

Teller waved and hooted back, his smile nearly as large as the Buicks grill until the bus stop disappeared in the rearview mirror. But then turning to Jack, his smile turned petulant.

"You haven't said a word about my car, Jacko. What? You no like?"

"Course I do, Tell." Jack smiled, patting the steel dash. "What's not to like?"

"I'm just hurt that you haven't shown more enthusiasm."

Jack took off his hat and threw it onto the dash.

"Christ, Tell, come on . . . .. I'm tired, I'm hungry, and my dicks sore . . . none of which are your fault. Hey, wait. Now that I think about it, you *are* peripherally responsible for the latter."

Teller shook his head and smiled. "Jack, Jack, Jack. *I* only made the introduction. Whatever that lovely young woman did with your dick is none of my concern. As a matter of fact, I would greatly appreciate it if you kept the dirty details to yourself. However, I *can* do something about your hunger." With that, he whipped the wheel to the right, and into the parking lot of the restaurant.

"We're here." He grinned, powering up all the windows, and, with a flourish, pushed a big chrome button above the radio. Motors began to hum, gears engaged, and with a symphony of whirring and clicking, the folded top rose from behind the back seat; the canvas popping like a tent as it stretched on the framework to reach its full extension, and in a glorious demonstration of 1950's automotive technology, slowly lowered itself into place.

Locking down the chrome leavers attached to the windshields frame, Teller slid from the front seat, walked to the front of the car, and standing in front of the gleaming grill gave a slight bow and extended his arm towards the entry.

"After you, stud."

~

Teller followed Jack into the bustle of the restaurant and looked around. The place was packed, barmaids weaving through the crowd with their trays held high, and as the girls shuffled by, he spied Junior in the booth where they had first met, semi-hidden behind a girl writing in her pad.

It was Susan, and scribbling as she turned to see Teller, she tucked her pen behind her ear, smiled, and took a step towards him; but as she did she happened to glance up just in time to deftly avoid a collision with a college kid nesting at least a dozen open beers in his arms. Stepping aside while shaking her head with exasperation, she stopped long enough to give his cheek a light kiss.

"Hi handsome. We missed you last night."

With a wink she turned and walked away, her hips swaying gracefully as she moved through the crowd.

Jack sighed and threw his arm over Tellers shoulder.

"I don't know how you do it buddy," he smiled as he squeezed the back of Teller's neck. "You're *not* that handsome. But if you could bottle whatever it is, you could make a fortune."

Tellers eyes followed Susan's rear until she was lost in the crowd; then turning, he waggled his eyebrows. "You're just jealous . . . come on, Junior's waiting."

Seeing them coming his way, Junior's face lit up and he threw his napkin onto the table as he stood and held out his arms. "Teller! Jack! Good to see you both! Have a seat!" Gesturing towards the table, he grinned, "Susan's bringing the drinks. Negra Modello's alright?"

Teller's smile nearly equaled Junior's as he slid into the bench seat. "Just what I would have ordered myself, young Bill. Thank you. And how are you this evening?"

"Outstanding!" Junior smiled, his teeth flashing white against his dark skin. "Outstanding! I can't thank you enough for convincing me to go out last night."

Teller gave a nod and looked towards the bar.

"So, where is she?"

William gave a conspiratorial wink. "It's her night off."

"So?" Teller shrugged.

"So she's at my house napping until I return."

"Ahhhh," Teller smiled, giving a sage nod. "Well played young Bill, well played . . ." but leaning back into the seat, his smile turned to an exaggerated frown of self-pity. "So, it seems everyone but me had a very good time last night."

Susan stepped behind Teller with a tray of drinks just as he finished the sentence. Dropping a napkin on the table, she centered his beer on it and looked into his eyes.

"You had your chance." she smiled, and with an air of dismissal placed the two remaining drinks in front of the other two men. "Anything else I can do for the two of you?"

Junior fidgeted uncomfortably while Jack ordered a second Scotch, neat. Susan nodded, but as she turned to go, a bright smile lit Teller's face and he reached out to lay a finger on her wrist. "Darlin,' it's only through sheer willpower that I refrain from inviting your delicious self to join me in the back seat of my big, beautiful car to ravage you nose to toes, whilst my companions here remain to enjoy their meal."

Taking a leisurely drink, he looked into her face as he placed his bottle on the table and smiled sadly. "But alas, my young beauty, my heart belongs to another."

His eyes held hers, judging her response.

A small smile played across her lips. And while both Jack and Junior held their breath waiting for all hell to break loose, Susan simply nodded, and tapped her pen on the top of Teller's beer bottle.

"Alright. I'll give you one more chance."

With that, she took his hand, scribbled her number onto his palm, and folded his fingers over the ink. *"One* more chance." she smiled sweetly, adding, *"Don't* blow it." Picking up the empties, she walked away.

Teller smiled as he watched her leave, then turned to his friends. "Alrighty gents. Where were we?"

Junior, who was most anxious to tell them not only of his decision to help them, but also of his finding a reliable buyer for the stones decided to ignore the scene that had just taken place. So, clearing the table directly in front of him he brought his briefcase up, snapped the latches and opened his mouth. But before he could speak, Jack held up a hand. An inquisitive expression crossed Junior's face; but he said nothing.

Jack looked at Junior, nodded, and turned to Teller.

"Teller . . ."

"Yes Jack?"

"She seems like a nice girl."

Teller looked to the bar where Susan stood at the drink station, her toes resting on the foot rail.

"A beautiful girl." he agreed.

"Then why are you teasing her?"

Teller leaned back in the booth. "I'm not teasing her, Jack."

Jack picked up his drink. "Okay then," he smiled, taking a slow sip. "what *are* you doing?"

Teller's eyes narrowed. "You need to be a little more specific amigo. I'm not quite sure what you're getting at."

"Come on, Tell." Jack sighed. "You've got a gorgeous woman waiting up in Telluride. What are you doing chasing tail in Tucson?"

Sitting up straight, Teller wrapped both hands around the bottle and looked into Jack's eyes. "First, let me say that 'Chasing tail in Tucson' sounds like a *great* song title. But more to the point, Jack, is that enjoying the attentions of a pretty girl does not challenge my ethics, nor dirty my soul. It simply means I'm not dead yet. And did I, or did I *not*, tell her that I am spoken for?" A smile of amusement crossed his lips. "Besides, it don't hurt to flirt." He gave Jack a dismissive nod and turned back to Young Bill.

"Now, you were saying?"

Jack threw up his hands. "Forgive me trying to be the voice of your conscience. Carry on."

Junior's assessment of these two men raised another notch; silently appreciating the level of this friendship as he placed a manila folder on the table.

"What I was *saying*, is that I've contacted some business associates regarding the articles in question."

"And?"

"And," he said, picking up the folder and pinching open the clasp, "I have some *very* good news."

He handed the envelope to Teller, who, removing the contents, scanned each page. His smile grew larger with each page he flipped over, and by the time he had reached the last his smile was one of complete satisfaction.

Susan bounced up with a fresh round of drinks just as he laid down the report.

Seeing the enormously pleased expression on Teller's face she looked at him suspiciously. "As my Grandmother used to say, you look like the cat that just ate the canary."

Teller's grin growing larger, he tucked the papers back into the envelope.

"Better than that," he winked, "I'm the Coyote that just ate the canary-fattened cat."

— — -- ---- -- — —
—— —— — —— —
-- --- --

= Chapter 8 =

Adjusting the small Tiffany lamps rectangle of light onto the page he was reading, James ran his fingers through his hair and looked at the pile of paperwork that lay spread across the eight-foot slab of highly polished Brazilian Cherrywood that served as his desk.

There, within those pages, Teller had laid out the details of his severing their partnership in the Telluride Corporation; and on reading the details, James found himself besieged with mixed emotions. On one hand, his wish had been granted, Teller would be gone and the business would be his and his alone. But at the same time another small voice whispered through his greed. It was the voice of his higher self, lamenting the loss of the friendship they once shared.

Squeezing his eyes tight, James put the heels of his hands to his eyes and rubbed vigorously. Not only was his conscience bringing up emotions he did *not* want to deal with, he was discouraged. Having spent the past few hours pouring over the contracts fine print, he could find absolutely *nothing* wrong with the wording. It was written in straight, uncomplicated language, leaving him no legal advantage. Leaning back in his chair, he scowled at the ceiling.

~

Earlier that evening, Carlton had delivered the package that now lay before him; and from the moment the man had stepped through the door, James had sensed a change.

Gone was the cowed, hesitant shuffle he had come to expect. Instead, a new, and mysteriously self-assured Carlton had walked boldly up to the desk and unceremoniously dumped the severance agreement onto its gleaming surface; offering an uncharacteristic smile of satisfaction as he slid his own letter of resignation into that rectangle of light.

James had sneered as he picked up the document, framing a cutting remark calculated to destroy Carl's newfound confidence as well any idea he may have of leaving this room a winner. But when he looked into Carlton's eyes he saw a different man: and the reason for that perception was that Carlton *was* a different man. His meetings with Kelly had reinvigorated his repressed sex drive, and Teller's pep talk, combined with his generous gifting of stock, had re-instilled the bravado and confidence that was his before James had crushed his dreams.

Carlton felt reborn.

"Well, Mr. Carson," he smiled, "I wish I could say that it has been nice working with you, but that would be a lie. And, while I am quite aware that you no longer require, nor wish my services, I am going to give you one final bit of advice. Be cautious in your future dealings with Mr. Teller. He is a *very* clever man." With that, Carlton had turned on his heel and walked out of the office.

Struck dumb, James' wicked remark was left twitching on his tongue like a dying rodent; and staring at Carlton's retreating back while Teller's letter of resignation shook in his trembling hand, his paranoia of suspected conspiracy between the two men returned; cemented by Carltons smug, confident smirk.

~

Dismissing Carlton from his thoughts, James turned again to the paperwork on the desk; forced to allow a modicum of grudging respect to Teller's ingenuity. The man missed nothing. The contract was simple and direct, with none of the loopholes or grey areas that *he* would have included.

'Well. At least now the company is mine to do with what I please. No more of Teller's endless bitching of it no longer being any fun. Fuck him! Making money is fun!'
But then a pang of regret stabbed at his conscience as he once again realized that Teller was now truly lost as a friend.

Dabbing at the water forming in the corner of his eye, he mumbled, 'Light in here's bad.'
With a sweep of his arm, the paperwork flew from the desk; and as the pages fluttered to the floor, James reached down and removed his Scotch from the bottom drawer.

— — ▬▬ ▬▬▬ ▬▬ — —
▬▬ ▬▬ ▬▬ ▬▬ ▬▬
▬▬ ▬▬▬ ▬▬

= Chapter 9 =

"Again, you bring up Coyote?"

"Pardon?"

Junior's black eyes were serious. "What did you mean about Coyote?"

Teller leaned back. "What I meant," he sighed, tapping the packet with his finger, "was that after reading through all that information, is that while I've *no* idea *why* I am *where* I am" Jack chuckled, and Teller, giving him an evil squint, growled, "Shut up, Jack." then turned back to Junior. "As I was saying, although I've no idea *what* this golden-eyed jester has in mind, it seems that this merry chase is about to reap *considerably* more than spiritual benefits alone."

He picked up the envelope and handed it to Jack, who took it, looked at Teller questioningly, and began to silently read.

Now it was Tellers turn to ask the questions.

"So, young Bill, what made you decide to trust *us*? Other than the goodwill of last night's romp with . . .?"

"Sheila."

"Right," Teller smiled. "Sheila."

Junior shook his head as if to say, 'she has nothing to do with it' and raised his eyebrows. "I called my grandfather."

At this Teller was genuinely surprised.

"Really!"

"Yes," Little Raven nodded, smiling with the memory of the warmth and wisdom that had laced his grandfather's voice. "My grandfather thinks you are a *very* interesting man."

Hearing the comment, Jack look up from the papers and squinted at the two of them.

Junior smiled, "He thinks quite highly of you as well, Jack."

"And I, he." Jack nodded, his eyes returning to the contents of the envelope.

Grinning, Teller turned back to Junior. "Well, Young Bill, I have been called many things in my life, and although interesting has no doubt been used, I'm quite sure the context at the time was less than flattering. But, considering the fact that it came from Billy, I will take it as a complement."

Junior nodded. "Yes, Teller, you *should* be flattered. My grandfather is a good man, and a gracious man, but he takes few into his heart. Particularly you Billagaana." He sipped at his drink, quietly waiting to see Teller's reaction.

There was none.

"The truth of the matter," Junior continued, "is that he is intrigued by the fact that Coyote has taken such interest in you. And more so still, in that he has chosen to reveal to *you* the remainder of the gold that has helped our people for so long." He paused, his black eyes searching Teller's as if the answer lay hidden behind them. But then, with a small cough, he went on.

"The stories passed on by our family's elders have always claimed that the gold was only a portion of what the dark shaman carried. So that Coyote has led *you* to the remainder of the missing treasure, well, that, Teller, *that* is a thing that puzzles my grandfather greatly."

Teller turned up his palms. "*That,* Little Raven, puzzles me as well."

Jack chuckled, tucked the papers back in the envelope, and dropped the packet on the table. "Junior," he drawled, "Your grandfather has always been an excellent judge of character, and I can, and will, personally vouch for Teller here being more than merely *interesting* . . ." He tapped the envelope with his finger. "But let's concentrate less on the 'why' this fortune has fallen into our hands and get down to what we're going to do with it."

A smile lit Tellers face as he pushed the envelope to the side. "Always the pragmatist eh, Jack?"

Jack pushed his cap back. "Tell, as intriguing as this mystery may be, the *fact* is this. *You* now are in the possession of a shitload of stones and coins that, according to the information in that packet, stand to make you *quite* the fat rat." It was at that moment Susan came out of the crowd with fresh drinks, and on hearing Jack's comment she looked down on the men.

"Now we're talking rats?"

Teller grinned. "River rats. The worst kind."

She nodded and set the drinks on the table; and again, she didn't pour Tellers glass.

"Don't mind him," Jack said. "Just bring some menus on your next pass."

"And another round." Junior interjected.

"Will do . . ." Susan nodded. But her gaze settled on Teller. "So, which car is yours?"

Caught off guard, Teller lacked a snappy comeback. "Pardon?"

"I checked the parking lot," Susan smiled. "Which 'big, beautiful,' car is *yours*?"

"Oh." Teller frowned, picking up the bottle and pouring it into his glass, obviously disappointed at her oversight. "It's the old Buick."

"I thought so." she said, and with a sweet laugh walked away.

Teller's expression was one of consternation mixed with disappointment, and seeing this, Jack grinned.

"What's the matter Tell?"

Teller sat silent as Susan melted into the crowd. Then, turning, grumbled, *"That."* frowning in the direction she had gone. "Every woman I've ever met can do it."

"Do what?"

"That laugh." Teller said, his scowl slowly giving way to humor. "Over the course of my life I have heard it in every conceivable context. From the reaction to a comment over dinner, to the accompaniment of pleasure between the sheets, to the morning after's goodbye. And I've *never* been able to figure out just what it means. Whether it was delight, satisfaction, or something that exists in the soul of a woman that those of us with testicles are not privileged to understand."

"Teller," Jack laughed. "They're *women*. Those of us with testicles aren't meant to understand them. Hell boy, you're old enough to know that. As a matter of fact *you* that have pointed that detail out to me on numerous occasions."

"Yeah, well," Teller started, but Jack held up a hand to silence him, tugging the brim of his cap low on his forehead and sliding the envelope back to the center of the table and tapping it with his finger. "But putting *that* mystery aside for the moment, let's get down to more pressing, and personal business. Junior, how would *you* suggest we approach this thing?"

Junior studied the faces of the two men sitting across from him for a moment, and white teeth flashing, reached into his briefcase.

"Really, gentlemen," he said, placing a legal tablet on the table between them. "There's nothing to it. It is simply a measure of trust. Teller, you supply me with the amount of coins and stones you feel comfortable with, and I will convert them to cash. I would suggest no more than a quarter million at a time. After our first transaction, if everyone involved is happy, we will continue." He looked again at both men. "Is that acceptable to you both?"

Jack looked to Teller, and Teller nodded. "*More* than acceptable Young Bill."

With a return nod, Junior went on. "Fine. Now, what I intend do with whatever amount of goods you choose to provide, is-" But before another word could be uttered, Teller held up his hand, stopping him in mid-sentence.

"No need to go any further Bill. Unless it is absolutely necessary for me to know the dirty details, I don't *want* to know." Teller leaned his elbows on the table and looked deep into the eyes of Billy's nephew.

"*Do* we need to know?"

Junior's black eyes held Teller's gaze. "No, not if you don't want to. Although nothing I do is illegal. Just slightly under the radar."

Teller nodded and leaned back into the booth.

"Good. *That* is an area I'm quite familiar with and would much prefer to remain. I will happily supply you with whatever you feel is best and you do whatever it is you do, sparing us the details unless you feel it is absolutely necessary." Turning from Junior, he looked over to Jack. "That okay with you, partner?" But Jack's attentions were focused on a pair of young women sitting at the bar. He had made eye contact and was mildly flirting.

"Jack!"

Offering the girls his most winning smile, Jack grudgingly turned his attentions back to Teller.

"Yes?"

Teller shook his head. "As the voice of my conscience you set one piss poor example . . . So, if I can have your attention for a moment, do you think I could I talk you into flying us back to the lake tomorrow? I'd like to get this show on the road"

Jack smiled, but his voice took on a note of reluctance.

"I don't know Tell, those two are awfully cute. Besides that, I thought you said you were going to drive."

Teller looked across the room and winked, prompting smiles. "Yes, Jack, they are. But we have bigger fish to fry."

Jack opened his mouth but Teller cut him off.

"No jokes concerning Tuna, sushi, or any other slippery marine delicacies Jack. I'm serious. Can we leave tomorrow? I've changed my mind about driving."

Jack shrugged. "Hell, Teller, I'm just in this for the ride. A little over a week ago I wasn't sure how I was going to make my payments. If it hadn't been for fate dragging me to Lake Powell, I wouldn't be here now. So, my friend, taking a lesson from the pages of your life's book, I will go in whatever direction the winds may blow . . . in other words I'm with you. We'll do whatever you think is right."

Teller spread his hands. "Good. Then its settled."

Turning back to Junior, he asked, "How would *you* like to handle this?"

"Actually," Junior said, "As Jack just said. It's up to you."

"Well, in *that* case," Teller smiled, rubbing his chin, "I *do* happen to have a rabbit hide pouch with some of the stones out in the car. I'll be glad to give you those tonight, but Jack and I will need to go up north to gather the rest of the loot. Besides, I need to tell the third Musketeer what's going on." Turning to Jack he was pleased to see that his attention was with them; not on the girls.

"So, Jack, can we fly out tomorrow?"

"Sure Tell. I don't see a problem with that."

"Fan*tastic*." Teller grinned, rubbing his hands together.

Teller was in high spirits. With a new game afoot, he was just about to begin discussing the details with Junior when Susan stepped up, with a tray of fresh drinks.

Laying a menu in front of each man she gave Teller a sly smile while pouring his beer as provocatively as she had that very first night.

"There you are, Gentlemen, I'll be right back to take your order." But as she turned to go, she gave Teller a teasing wink. "By the way, I like your car." And with the same sweet laugh, walked away.

Teller threw up his hands. "That's *exactly* what I mean!" he cried, prompting Jack to break into laughter.

Junior followed, and within moments Teller was laughing along.

~

Teller and Junior worked out the final details of their arrangement during their meal while Jack, marveling at his good fortune mentally shopped for helicopters. But eventually both the meal, and the discussion came to an end; and on Susan's next pass, Junior requested the tab.

Susan returned with the bill, which Junior paid for in cash, including a *very* substantial tip; and after presenting Junior a sincere smile as well as heartfelt thanks, she turned to Teller; arms crossed as she seemed to weigh him with her eyes. A few uncomfortable seconds ticked by, and finally, flashing a smile, she blew a kiss and walked away. All three men watched her melt into the crowd. Once gone, Teller continued to stare while the other two men stood silent and waiting. Finally, Teller turned to Junior.

"Well then. I guess I'll call you in the morning."

William, out of his element as far as flirting waitresses were concerned, was at a bit of a loss, but smiled when Teller turned to Jack and saw that *his* concentration was now on a new group of women at the bar. Giving him a sharp kick under the table, Teller hissed, "Cut it out, Jack! It's time to go. You gotta pilot us outta here in morning."

Jack puckered up for the girls, then turned, laughing at Tellers expression as he reached out to William, shaking hands to seal the deal. Junior obliged. Then, turning to Teller, wrapped both of his hands around Tellers and smiled, "I have a feeling that this is going to be a *most* interesting partnership."

Giving one of his easy laughs, Teller laid his free hand on Junior's shoulder. "There you go again, using that word."

Junior smile dropped, and he went silent, looking slightly confused until Jack interjected, "Interesting. The word was interesting."

"Oh . . .? Oh!" Junior chuckled. "Well. I'm sorry Teller, but it *is* fitting."

"No worries my friend. I wholeheartedly agree. Although through these eyes, interesting does not nearly *begin* to describe it . . . and, oddly enough, you, and this business arrangement have proven to be the sanest part of this entire month."

Jack laughed, adding, "*And* the most lucrative."

"*Oh* yes . . ." Teller smiled. "Without doubt, the most lucrative." Freeing his hand from Junior's firm handshake, Teller turned to walk away. "Come with me Young Bill and I'll get the stones out of the car." But stopping in mid-stride, he turned at Junior. "Oh, by the way, as my plans have changed do you think I could leave the Buick with you until I return?"

"I don't see any problem with that." William shrugged. "Just drop it off at my place before you leave."

Teller grinned while patting William on the shoulder.

"Thank you, Young Bill. It seems our partnership is off to a good start."

= Chapter 10 =

His wrist hanging loosely over the wheel, Teller steered the big Buick through the warm Tucson night; his thumb tapping to the beat of the passing lamp posts. This went on for several miles until, finally, he turned to Jack.

"So, amigo. What do *you* think?"

Jack was slouched low, his head resting against the back of the bench seat. Without moving a muscle, he muttered.

"Bout what?"

"Well hell, Jack." Teller grinned. "About anything . . ."

Jack closed his eye and grumbled, "I think I'm tired."

Teller tsk'd and shook his head.

"Mr. Hawkins. Fornication is exhausting business. At least if you do it right. But your fatigue elicits no sympathy from the likes of me."

Rolling his head, Jack turned a tired eye to Teller. "Fuck you Tell. I don't want your sympathy, I want some sleep."

Teller nodded. "And fuck you right back, Jacko, *I* wasn't the one who kept you up all night."

"No," Jack glared, "but you were the one who started the whole thing."

"I started nothing, Jack!" Teller said, slapping the steering wheel as his grin grew larger. "I simply introduced you, and thus planted the seed of lust in that young woman's heart."

Jack closed his eye. "That's what I said. You started it."

Teller's silence lasted less than a minute.

"Alright then. I grudgingly accept responsibility. But considering things in *that* light, I must admit I am rather hurt by your lack of gratitude."

Jack's eyes remained closed as they pulled into the hotel parking lot. But then a smile touched the corners of his lips, and his voice held a note of artificial sincerity.

"Fuck you, Teller. Very much."

Teller laughed brightly. "You're very welcome, Jack."

~

The rays of the rising Sun illuminating the slopes of Mt. Lemmon; they also lit the side of the chopper as it flew north, stretching the shadow it threw over the desert below and winking from the lenses of Jacks shades as he hummed happily along to the music in his headset while Teller calculated the potential value of the treasure still in the cave on the spiral notebook in his lap. Without looking up from the numbers he shouted to be heard over the engine.

"Hey Jack, what kind of helicopter were you going to get?"

Receiving no response, Teller looked up, but with Jack's eyes hidden behind his aviator shades Teller couldn't decide if he was being ignored, or if he couldn't be heard.

"Jack!"

"What!"

Just as he thought. Ignored.

"Answer my question."

Jack exhaled, pushed his headset back on his neck, and turned to look at Teller over the top his shades.

"What difference would that make to you?"

"A hell of a lot." Teller smiled. "I want to know what level of comfort I'll be traveling in."

Jack pushed his sunglasses back in place and turned off the stereo. "Bullshit, Tell. What's on your mind?"

"I'm just curious. Six mill is a *lot* of spending money."

Jack nodded and adjusted course another eight degrees northwest. "Yeah. But like you said, we won't get it all at once, and I sure can't run out and buy a new chopper with an I.O.U. from a coyote." Then he laughed. "Not with *my* credit anyway."

"No," Teller agreed. "But the Corporation we are going to form can buy one."

Now Jack's curiosity was up.

"*What* Corporation?"

Teller grinned. "While *you* were busy fantasizing over those girls last night, Young Bill and I were discussing the best way to deal with our sudden influx of fortune."

Jack turned a wary eye to his friend. "And?"

"And," Teller said, waggling his eyebrows, "the only way we are *ever* going to realize the full benefits of this turn of luck is to play the game by the rules the big boys have established: A non-profit for profit Corporation."

Jack's brow furrowed. "Teller, that doesn't make sense, even coming from you."

Teller laughed. "I know, it *is* a bit of an oxymoron, but Little Raven says it's our best way to go, and I trust the guy." Tapping his bottom lip with his pencil, he eyed Jack seriously. "What about you, Jack? you trust Young Bill?"

Jack weighed the question, then nodded. "Yeah, I do. I've known his grandfather for a lot of years and I've never heard him say anything he didn't mean." He paused, and a slow smile spread across his face. "Altho' it *is* often rather ambiguous . . . but, Billy has never lied to me, and he *did* send us down here. So yeah, I trust Junior."

Teller conceded Jack's assessment, adding only, "It's a *lot* of money, Jack."

Glancing at the instrument panel, Jack could feel Teller study him while he considered the full scope of the issue: but then he smiled, "Yeah, but I'm good with it."

Teller nodded. "Good. Me too."

"Alright then Boss," Jack laughed, "Just what are you going to call this ragtag company?"

Teller frowned, turning away to gaze through the window; and watching him, Jack fancied he could hear the gears turning in his partners head . . . a few seconds passed and Teller looked up with a mighty grin.

"How about, 'Hole in the Wall Investments'?"

"Perfect!" Jack laughed, pushing his shades back in place while grabbing the joystick.

"Let's ride, Sundance!"

The Sun flashed in the twin mirrors that were Jack's shades, and the chopper jumped forward; the sudden increase in the rotors R.P.M's drowning out the angst in Teller's voice.

"Wait! What if *I* want to be Butch?"

= Chapter 11 =

The first knock on the door was so faint Kelly nearly missed it. But with each following knock seeming incrementally louder, she put down her much-anticipated bottle of wine. She wasn't expecting anyone; certainly not at this hour and especially not after the scene in the office earlier. So, puzzled as well as slightly apprehensive, she made a fist around the corkscrew she held, leaving the sharp tip poking between her knuckles as she made her way down the tiled hall. She wrapped her free hand around the doorknob just as the forth, and most aggressive knock yet hammered the thick wooden door. Tightening her grip on the corkscrew she muttered; "this had better not be *James*," and slowly opened the door to the limit of the security chain.

Peeking through the crack she saw Carlton shuffling nervously on the entry's little landing, his eyes on the sidewalk and a bottle of wine cradled in his arm. But on hearing the rattle of the chain, he looked up to see a blue eye peering at him through the gap.

Adjusting his eyeglasses, he gave a meek smile.

"Hi Miss Row- excuse me, Kelly." Extending his arms to present the proffered gift, he began apologizing. "I'm sorry to bother you this late, but I'm leaving town first thing tomorrow and I wanted you to have this."

Relieved that it wasn't James, Kelly relaxed her grip on the corkscrew, unhooked the chain, swung the door open and stepped back. "It's fine Carl, you just surprised me . . . Please, come on in." Accepting the bottle as he stepped across the threshold she closed the door behind him. "follow me." She smiled.

Carlton trailed her into the living room where she closed the lid on the suitcase open on the couch and put it on the floor.

"Have a seat . . . I was just opening a bottle of wine myself. Would you like a glass?"

His anxiety plainly evident he stammered out a, "No, no thank you." as he took a seat on the edge of the couch, then, in a near whisper, asked, "You wouldn't happen to have any Scotch, would you?"

Kelly found his shy nervousness rather charming.

"I doubt it." she smiled, "but I'll check."

Carl nodded; and as she disappeared into the kitchen the memory of her breasts swaying beneath her sweater as she leaned over his desk earlier that day returned, stirring his feelings of unrequited lust: but directly on the heels of that memory Tellers not-so-subtle "advice" echoed in his mind, crushing his hunger. But still struggling to dispel the softness of the sweater, Carl looked down at the tips of his shoes and attempted to conjuring up unpleasant thoughts; with James heading the list just as Kelly stuck her head back through the door. "Sorry Carlton," she said, smiling apologetically. "No Scotch. You sure you don't want some wine?"

With a deep sigh, Carlton pushed his lust, and his thoughts of James aside. "I've never been able to say no to a pretty girl. Sure, I'll have a glass. Thanks."

"Great," she laughed. "I hate to drink alone."

She disappeared back into the kitchen.

Drumming his fingers on his knee as he waited, Carl reflected on how quickly, and how thoroughly, his life had changed. But his moment of self-examination was interrupted as Kelly returned, a bottle of Merlot, and two long-stemmed wine glasses in hand.

Pouring each half full, she placed his on the coffee table and stepped back; attempting to appear casual. But Carlton could see that she plainly wished to avoid sitting beside him on the couch. Instead, she rested her hip on the edge of a well-used antique table that held a vase filled with flowers and a half-dozen framed photographs, and lifting her glass to her lips, she raised her eyebrows.

"So, Carl, why are you here?"

Caught off guard by Kelly's bluntness, Carlton swirled the ruby liquid, watching it run down the vessels curved sides while thinking how best to answer; while Kelly, clearly aware of his discomfort, sipped her wine, the silence stretching as the clock on the mantle ticked the minutes away. Finally, with a submissive sigh, Carlton's eyes left the glass. Looking up, he started to speak, but the moment he made eye contact a second sigh deflated him and he lowered his glass, staring at his lap in silence: the only sound in the room being the ticking of the clock.

Kelly watched the second hand swept the clock face two more times . . . That was enough.

"Okay, Carl," she said, leaning in. "Speak up. What's on your mind?"

Carl coughed. Both eager and reluctant, he had been rehearsing what he was about to say all day. But looking into her eyes was much different than looking into a mirror; and now, under her scrutiny all his earlier self-assurance fled.

"Miss Collins," he blurted out, but in his nervousness his voice squeaked like a anxious teenagers, its tone leaving him mortified now as well as apprehensive. In an effort to compose himself he took a slow, deep breath, and tried again.

"May I call you Kelly?"

"Of course, Carl," she smiled. "I thought that was already settled."

Carl's brow furrowed as a small smile crossed his lips.

"Ohhh . . . oh, yes . . ." nodding as he set his wine glass down he smiled shyly, "Yes, we *have* discussed that haven't we?" And while Carl's tension dissipated slightly, when he removed his eyeglasses his blue eyes were filled with apprehension.

"Okay. First, I want to thank you for your help today with James."

At that, Kelly giggled. "Oh, no need to thank me for that! The pleasure was *all* mine."

Carlton gave her a thankful, but shy smile.

"Yeah," he chuckled, "did you see him almost explode?"

"Yes!" Kelly sputtered, "beautiful, wasn't it!" Attempting to contain her delight by squeezing her lips tight, her cheeks puffed out like a chipmunks, and moments later she burst into laughter.

For a split-second, Carl hesitated. But her laughter was so infectious he couldn't help but join in, and in doing so the chill that surrounded them was replaced with warmth; melting the ice of his unannounced drop-in and allowing Carlton to forget his anxiety.

"Well then Miss- oops, sorry- *Kelly* . . . the reason I am here is this. As Mister Carson has made it abundantly clear that I am no longer welcome in Telluride, I was wondering what, after all the financial dust settles, *you* were going to do?"

Kelly's smile not only vanished, it seemed to Carlton as if the room temperature dropped ten degrees instantly. Her voice cold steel, she asked, "Why?"

Carltons blue eyes went wide behind his glasses. "No, no, no!!" he stammered out, "It's nothing like that! no!"

Seeing his reaction, Kelly visibly relaxed while Carlton shifted uncomfortably; his anxiety returning full force.

"I was just curious, that is *all!* You see, I find myself displaced, alone, and nowhere to go, and, as I will soon have more money than I would have *ever* made working with Mr. Carson, I was just wondering what you and Mr. Teller might have planned."

Kelly searched Carlton's face for signs of duplicity. But his innocence was real: and seeing he harbored no nefarious schemes, she laughed delightedly. "Carl, you obviously have had *no* experience with *Mr.* Teller."

Seeing Carltons expression shift from hopeful to baffled, Kelly realized that further clarification was necessary.

"What I meant, Carl, is that wherever it is that Teller might be headed, the odds are greatly against that being the place he'll end up." She looked at Carlton hopefully, but if anything, his expression was even more perplexed.

Chuckling, Kelly set her glass down, placed her palms flat on the table and straightened her legs, crossing them at the ankles. This was going to be more difficult than she had hoped. So, looking to the ceiling, she searched for a more cohesive explanation.

"Teller is like a force of nature, Carlton. The best I've ever been able to do is guess what direction he'll be coming from, and how much damage he'll do as he passes through."

Carltons brow furrowed.

"That certainly doesn't sound encouraging."

Kelly laughed a sweet and loving laugh.

"It sounds worse than it really is. My point is that I would never make any plans with that guy with the expectation of having them turn out the way they were planned." Carlton gave a befuddled nod as he pushed his glasses back onto the bridge of his nose, but he appeared no less perplexed.

Kelly was at a loss as just how to clarify when an epiphany struck. She had come to accept Teller's ways so completely that the thought of others finding them crazy had long ceased to be a consideration. Pondering this minor enlightenment for the briefest of moments, she smiled. Then, picking up the bottle, poured the last of the red wine into her goblet and gave Carl a contrite shrug.

"Well. I can see that didn't clarify a great deal, but it's as good as I can do . . . Teller is just Teller. But now it's my turn. Why do you ask?"

"Well," he started, but hesitated. He was obviously uncomfortable with what he was about to say, but was determined to say it anyway. Gathering his courage, he spoke.

"The reason I asked is because now that I am no longer under any oath of fealty to the Tyrant of Telluride I was hoping I might be allowed to travel with you both. At least for a little while."

Now it was Kelly who was baffled.

"Why in the *world* would you want to do that?"

Carlton's eyes were hopeful behind his spectacles. "Well, mostly because I owe my present economic boon to Mr. Teller's generosity. But I also think that I might be of some use."

"I'm sorry Carl," Kelly smiled, "and I mean no offense, but how?"

A conspiratorial grin transformed his features.

"Because I know *every* financial secret Mr. Carson is hiding. After all, I'm the one who keeps-" a flicker of resignation crossed his face. "Excuse me, *kept* the books for the company."

Kelly slowly smiled as his point became clear.

"So," she nodded. "*You* could prove a valuable ally in the event of James' trying to pull some sort of double cross."

Carl's response was enthusiastic. "Yes! Exactly! Not that there is much chance of that, of course. Mr. Teller's agreement was brilliantly simple, leaving very little room for misinterpretation. But, nevertheless . . ."

Kelly grinned. "Yep, that's Tell. Simple, but wily. Oh, but Carl, when you *do* talk to him, just call him Teller. Drop the Mister."

"You don't think he would mind?"

Kelly rolled her eyes. "God no! On the contrary, he will be *far* more likely to talk to you."

"So I should ask him then?"

Kelly shrugged. "Sure, no harm in asking. But as far as I know we're just heading to Lake Powell, and I seriously doubt he will want any company. . .no offense."

Carl's expression went from questioning to disappointment as Kelly motioned to the wall clock.

"It's getting late, Carl. Time to go."

Carlton's eyes followed hers. "Oh! You're right! I'm sorry Miss Rowen, I didn't realize the time." he stood, quickly finishing his wine and slipping on his jacket.

Kelly took his empty glass and walked him to the front door. "Don't worry Carlton, and remember, its Kelly, not Miss Rowan. As for Teller, I'll call you just as soon I hear from him. By the way, how will I find you?"

Carlton took out his wallet and handed her a card along with a hopeful smile. "I'll be at home. My number is on this. Just call." He took the four steps down to the sidewalk and turned. "Thank you again Miss Rowen."

Wiggling the card between two fingers, Kelly stepped back into the house. "It's Kelly, remember?" And as the door closed, Carlton's face lit up.

"Right! Kelly!"

— — -- --- -- — —
— — — -- --- --

= Chapter 12 =

James' eyes went the rented hospital bed, then turned away. While he felt pity for the boy, with tubes running from multiple bags suspended from poles and pumping god knows what into his arms, he felt no guilt. And regardless of Casey's accusations, he refused to accept any culpability for Benny's being there. With a final glance at Ben's sallow, drawn face, he pulled the bedroom door closed. *'No,'* he told himself. *'I didn't cause this.'*

But self-reproach still niggled at his conscience as he plodded down the hallway. He was tired. Tired of arguing with Casey, tired of the battle to keep his company *his*, and tired of trying to outmaneuver Teller.

With a weary sigh, he latched onto the handrails of the wide staircase and pulled himself up and into the huge open-beamed living room of his mountain retreat: and, as always, its grandeur lifted his spirits. A mans home was his castle, he thought, and this house, built with Casey's grandfathers money, was as palatial as one could hope for.

Crossing the gleaming hardwood floor, he glanced through a plate glass window that spanned half of the west-facing wall. Ordinarily he swelled with power at the sight of Telluride spread out below him. But not today: today the magnificent view seemed meaningless.

With a second, and much deeper sigh, James shuffled to the liquor cabinet, grabbed a bottle of Glenlivet by the neck, and dragging two crystal glasses through the ice, continued until his bare feet were warmed by the exquisite Navajo rug on which the carved legs of an expansive leather couch rested.

Casey closed her book and looked up.

"How is he?"

"Crazy," James said, and with a third sigh, plopped down and leaned back into the leather cushion.

Giving a furious scowl, Casey lowered her book onto her lap. "And whose fault is *that?*"

James was too tired to argue. Instead, he poured Scotch over the ice in both glasses, shook it down, and held one out to her. "Goddammit Casey, I'm *not* the one who put him in the hospital."

Accepting the glass, Casey held it in both hands, her expression accusing. "No, but he wouldn't be there if you hadn't sent him to spy on your-" she paused, correcting her near slip with a malicious smile. "*Teller's* girlfriend."

His anger spiked, but just as quickly dissolved.

"I'm tired of this argument, Casey. You win."

Tucking her feet beneath her rear, a cruel smile twisted her lips. "I don't care if I 'win' James," she said, giving a slow shake of her head. "that's not the point. *I* know you will never possess Kelly. She loves Teller and nothing you can do will ever change that. Your delusions regarding it no longer bother me. What *does* bother me is the fact that you refuse to accept that fact and get on with *our* lives."

She stared at him, waiting for a response. But steadfastly refusing to acknowledge the truth in her statement he simply closed his eyes and laid back into the deep cushions.

"You know what that bastard did today?"

Casey cupped her glass, unfolded her legs, and stretched out. "No, James." she sighed. "What?"

— — -- ---- -- — —
—— —— — —— —
-- ---- --

= Chapter 13 =

The Sun glinted from the snow-capped San Francisco Peaks in the hazy distance; and with their appearance Jack adjusted course. But the moment the rotor speed changed, Teller, slouched in the co-pilots seat asleep, opened his eyes.

"We here already?"

"If that's the way you want to look at it."

Stretching as best he could in the small cabin, Teller frowned, "What's *that* supposed to mean?"

"It means that 'already' only applies to those of us who have slept for the past two hours."

Teller gave an exaggerated yawn. "Do I detect a note of hostility, Jack?"

"No," Jack said, "but if we continue to do this, *you* are going to get a pilot's license."

"No problem." Teller grinned. "Happy to oblige, but those are long term goals . . . what about our immediate future? hmm? What's the plan for Flagstaff? We gonna gas up and go, or am I just gonna watch that pretty woman chase you around the airport?"

Jack chuckled, but there was a hint of underlying resentment in his voice. Drop it, Tell. Max is a subject that is off limits as far as *you* are concerned."

Teller raised his eyebrows. "Whattaya mean off limits? I'm not -" but Jack cut him off. "It means just that. Off limits. End-of-discussion. But now that you're awake, let's talk about our options. First, what are we going to do?"

Teller decided to let the comment regarding Maxine go. He stretched and yawned again. "Options?"

"Tell, don't play stupid. I mean, are we going to go directly to the cave? Are we going to stop and get Abbott? Are we going to bring everything here, or stash it at Billy's? Christ, Teller, there are a *lot* of things to consider here."

Teller bowed his head, rubbed his scalp roughly with both hands, and sliding his palms slowly down his face, looked at Jack as if he were a slow child.

"Yes, Jack, I am aware of the *many* considerations. But relax . . . it's not nearly as difficult as you're making it out to be. These are all fairly simple logistics. First, I need some new clothes, or at least a washing machine."

Jack wrinkled his nose. "Right. We go to my place."

"See how easy that was?" Teller smiled. "You got any duffle bags at your place?"

Jack answered with a nod.

"Good again!" Tell smiled and patted Jack on the shoulder. "See? Nothing to this. You got Billy's number handy?"

Again, Jack nodded in the affirmative.

Following his nap, Teller was refreshed and rolling. He held out his hands. "So there we are brother. Problem solved. Set this bird down, get some gas into her, and let's go clean up and get something to eat. *Then* we call Abbott and Billy and figure out all the minor details of this thang . . . you'll see. It'll all work out."

Jack frowned. "But what if-"

Teller cut him off with a swipe of his hand. "Cut the negative vibes Moriarity! If I say they'll be a bridge, then they'll be a bridge!"

Jack's brows came together. "What in the fuck are you talking about *now*?"

Teller reached back over his seat, grabbed his pack and pulled it onto his lap. "Just a line from an old movie."

Jack's expression of complete befuddlement made Teller laugh.

"Donald Sutherland . . .? Kelly's Hero's . . .?"

Jack's expression conveyed no enlightenment whatsoever, prompting Teller to give him a sneer of mock disgust.

"Philistine! Never mind, just land this thing and let's get to your place."

"Tell," Jack sighed, "you've got a mind like a corkscrew."

Pulling his headset back on, he double clicked the handset and made contact with the Flagstaff tower for permission to land; but as he made the call he silently prayed that Maxine would be off duty. He had *no* desire to go through another introduction with Teller. And while his prayer was inconsequential, it was answered. But as with most answered prayers, not in the manner hoped.

Old Sam had been the comptroller at the Flagstaff airport for as long a Jack could remember, but he was retiring, and the new controller-in-training was Sam's nephew out of Phoenix. He was a nice enough kid, but being fresh out of the military he was just a little *too* anxious to impress everyone with his Government supplied skills. And after years of Sam's relaxed, jovial intercom banter, this kid's impersonal, clipped patter brought back unpleasant military memories.

Following a long list of landing instructions interspersed with smatterings of static, Jack finally glared at the microphone and growled through clenched teeth, "Just give me a goddamned spot to land!" Teller grinned and gave an exaggerated salute, to which Jack gave him the finger.

Ten minutes later they were on the ground, and before the rotors stopped spinning, Teller jumped out, but turned, setting one foot on the rail while leaning back into the cab.

"Just like old times but better, right, Jack?"

Jack hopped out and tugged at his cap. "Why better?"

Teller just shrugged, "why not?" and walked away.

Jack slammed the choppers door, shoved his hands into the pockets of his leather flight jacket and followed Teller across the tarmac shaking his head.

"Sometimes I wonder just what the hell is *wrong* with you."

Having been friends for far to long to take anything phrased like that seriously, Teller turned, and put a hand onto Jack's chest stopping him in mid-stride.

"No reason to be grumpy, amigo. It's nothing a shower and some food won't fix." But taking note of Jack's expression, Teller paused, then grinned. "Ahhh, *you're* upset about Max, huh?"

Teller was both right and wrong, but Jack would never admit it, especially not to him, and especially not now.

"I told you, Tell. Off limits."

Teller also knew Jack well enough to know when to stop. "Fine, Jack, fine . . . then give me your phone, I need to call Billy."

Jack tossed the phone over the roof of the truck.

"Number's in the phone."

Teller caught the phone as it sailed by; sliding onto the seat and giving Jack a disgusted look as he cranked down his window. "Jeeze Jack, what crawled up *your* ass? Things are going great, and you are very close to an early retirement. Wait. Let me re-phrase that. *We* are very close to a not-so-early, very unexpected, but most assuredly well deserved, retirement. Yet you insist on retaining your shitty attitude."

Unable to keep from smiling, Jack loosened his stranglehold on the steering wheel. "Sorry, Tell. I guess I'm just a little edgy. So much has happened so fast. A simple, random phone call from Billy a week ago and my life completely changed." But then a note of annoyance crept into his voice. "And I had forgotten just how *hard* you are to keep up with."

Teller looked at his old friend and grinned. "Jack, Jack, Jack. Again, it's all perspective. It's not that *I'm* so hard to keep *up* with, it is *you* who have slowed *down*."

"There's a reason for that, Tell," Jack sighed, taking off his cap and running his hands across his scalp. "It's called getting older and wiser, and it's something *you* are going to have to face at some point."

Teller looked at Jack, insult plain on his face.

"I've heard the rumors regarding *that* particular, Jack, but I refuse to comply. I simply don't see the advantages. But that aside, I've been thinking that the phone call Billy made to you originally was neither simple, nor random." Reaching over, he pulled out the ignition key and the engine died, leaving the truck's cab silent.

Now he had Jack's attention, but it was beginning to turn into anger.

"Dammit Tell, what are you *talking* about?"

Closing his fist around the keys, Teller laid his head back against the seat and closed his eyes.

"Look man, haven't you ever felt as if you're just a player in some elaborate script?"

Jack muttered under his breath, reached over, and prying the keys from Tellers grip, restarted the truck and threw it into reverse. "You need something to eat," he growled as he backed out of the parking space.

"Damn it Jack!' Teller shouted, "I'm serious!"

"I know you are Tell, but we've had these discussions before. And brother, I *never* feel any better after one of them."

Teller leaned his head back onto the seat and gave a long and weary sigh.

"A wink is as good as a nod to a blind horse . . ."

Jack looked over and squinted, *"What . . . ?"*

Teller's eyes remained closed, but the slightest of smiles touched his lips.

"Nothing, Jack. Nothing at all."

— — -- --- --   — —

—— ——   —— ——

-- --- --

= Chapter 14 =

James looked at Casey in disbelief. He had just finished the story of how Teller had screwed him out of forty percent of the company, and she was smiling?

"What are you smiling about?" he said, anger coloring his voice. "How is *any* of this *funny* to you?"

Casey set her glass on the table looked at him and shaking her head. "Teller did not *screw* you out of *anything*, James. And I admire him for what he did for poor Carlton. I've told you more than once that it would be a mistake to push him, but *you* wouldn't listen. I think you should count yourself lucky."

James eyes widened in incredulity. "Lucky? *Lucky!?* How in the *hell* do you figure losing over a hundred thousand dollars in cash and forty percent of the company is *lucky?*"

Picking up her glass by the stem, Casey put her eye to its curved surface, and looked at James' distorted image through the wine. Thinking that it fit him well, she smiled and lowered the glass to gaze at him over the rim; her expression one of cold amusement.

"Because, James, he *left* you with sixty percent."

She stood and smoothed her dress. "And, as there is nothing to be done about it now, I think you should concern yourself with the much more pressing problem of what *you* are going to do about *Ben*."

Tipping her glass to him, she turned towards the kitchen.

— — -- ---- -- — —

— — -- ---- -- — —

-- --- --

= Chapter 15 =

Billy tucked the map of the lake into the bag next to a few other goodies the young father had bought for his daughter. They were down from Salt Lake and the little girl was waving goodbye with a child's delighted joy as her daddy pulled her through the screen door. Billy wiggled his fingers to her as he picked up the phone.

"Hello?"

"Hi Billy. Teller here."

Billy's thousand-watt smile ignited.

"Teller! How are you?"

"Doin' good Billy, doin good. I want to thank you for the introduction to your grandson."

"So," Billy's dark eyes twinkled. "Little Raven will be of some help?"

Although Billy couldn't see, Teller's smile nearly equaled his own. "Yes Billy, I believe he will be of *considerable* help."

Teller sat at Jack's kitchen table, pushing a Robin egg-sized green stone around on the surface with a pair of chopsticks he had found on the floor.

Pinching the stone with the chopsticks, he held it up to the beam of light that streamed through a clean spot in the dirty window. The deep green hue nearly glowed.

"But you already knew that."

Billy's eyes drifted to Abbott, who was sleeping peacefully in the rocker. Turning on his heel, he went back to his office, pulled the door shut, and took a seat in his high-backed chair.

"Yes, Teller, I suspected that he could. But please understand that had I told you more than I did, not only would I have put myself and my family at some risk of exposure, *you* would have had a different set of expectations, and *that* may have affected the outcome."

Teller rotated the stone in the light. "How so?"

"That's just it," Billy smiled. "One never knows how, but one's expectations will *always* affect the outcome of *any* endeavor. Certainly by now you have realized that Coyote's game is more than just a game."

Teller's lips curled into a grin, and he dropped the stone back on the table. "Billy, I am not a fool, but a riddle is still a riddle."

"No!" Billy laughed, "of course you are not! But then the fool is always the man who thinks he *is* no fool but refuses to recognize it when proven to be so . . . *that* is the riddle the fool never solves."

Teller spun the stone on the tabletop, and his smile grew introspective. "So, Billy. Is that Zen, or wisdom?"

Following a brief moment of silence, Billy smiled.

"What's the difference?"

Teller's reply was immediate. "Only a fool would attempt a guess."

Bursting into laughter, Billy spun his chair and put his boots on the desk. "Yes, in circumstances other than this, that *would* be the case. However, in you, Coyote has not chosen a fool, so that leaves guessing our only option."

Billy's laughter slowly subsided and his voice turned serious.

"In my dreams I was told only of your impending arrival, and with it, the implication that, if I wished, I was to help the man who was about to enter my life." There was a long pause, then he continued. "In you, Coyote chose wisely, and I am delighted that he sent you my way."

Billy dropped his boot heels to the floor. "So, what have you decided to do?"

Teller pushed the dull green stone off the table's edge, catching it as it fell and returning it to his pocket. "At the moment, the plan is for Jack and I to be back there tomorrow to pick up Abbott, and then go retrieve the rest of the goods."

"Of course. And then?"

"Billy, I am always reluctant to make plans, even in the most normal of circumstance. So in *this* case, I believe I will just wait and see what our friend Coyote has in store for me before I make any further efforts to plot my future."

Again, Billy chuckled. "And there, my friend, is your proof."

At that moment Jack walked through the door. He had just hooked up the propane tank for the grill and shot Teller a questioning glance as he went by.
Teller simply smiled and returned his attention to Billy.

"Proof of what?"

"That you are no fool."

Teller's response was measured. "Forgive me if I find that less than reassuring." But then, with a quiet laugh, added, "Although in truth, I've rarely been sure of anything."

There was a moment of silence, and Billy replied, "And that, Teller, is proof that you are wise."

Teller's smile grew. "And the difference between the wise man and the fool?"

The silence on the other end was so complete that Teller thought the connection had been lost. But then Billy's laughter rang through and he chuckled, "I've never been real clear on that."

Teller laughed.

"Thanks for the vote of confidence Billy. We'll see you tomorrow, and please, tell Abbott to be ready."

Just then the bell hanging over the front door rang, and Billy stood. "I will do that, Teller. Say hello to Jack for me and tell him to give my regards to that pretty girl at the airport."

"I will, Billy, and thanks again."

He hung up just as Jack was walking by with two seasoned steaks on a plate. He paused and asked, "What did Billy have to say?"

"He said that you should quit running."

Standing with the plate in one hand, and a beer in the other, he gave Teller a wary look.

"Running from what?"

Teller stood, walked over, and pinched Jack's cheek. "Love, Jack. Love . . ."

Growling, "*You* are an asshole, Teller." Jack turned and stomped through the door. But Teller was on his heels, catching it before it slammed.

"That may be true, Jack," he called out, "but rumor has it I'm no fool."

___ ___   __ ___ __   ___ __

___ ___   ___ ___

__ ___ __

= Chapter 16 =

Pleased by the news of Teller's impending return, Abbott pressed Billy. "Tomorrow, he said?"

"Yes, Abbott."

Billy stood over a pile of mesquite coals basting the Antelope steaks that a relative up on the Wind River Range in Wyoming had sent. He received wild game every hunting season; and this gourmet meal was the result of that generosity. So, with both the evening and the conversation warm, Billy placed a plate of sizzling steaks onto the picnic table, pulled out the bottle of Bordeaux he had taken from his hidden supply and dusting it off with a dishtowel, offered Abbott the honor of relieving the neck of its cork. Abbott happily complied, and pouring two glasses, slid one across the table to Billy.

"So," he asked, "was Teller's trip to Tucson successful?"

Billy did not immediately reply. He had spent the morning sequestered in his ancient cave above the greenhouse in deep meditation; puzzling the ramifications to that very question. Because regardless of the results of that meeting, the mere fact that Coyote was involved meant the future now had multiple outcomes.

Saying nothing, he turned his weathered face towards the first bright stars of the evening and closed his eyes; and Abbott, seeing this, set his glass down on the rough table. He had come to accept the inevitable silence that preceded any answer of a question involving Teller, or any explanation regarding the nature of Coyotes interest in him. Swinging his leg over the bench seat, he smiled. "The wine is excellent Billy, but I think I'll get a beer."

Billy's eyes opened.

"Yes Abbott. I believe he was."

Abbott nodded but continued towards the trailer.

"Good. You can tell me all about it when I get back."

"No," Billy smiled, shaking his head. "There is nothing for me to tell."

Abbott turned, walked back to the table, and dropped onto the bench. "What does *that* mean?"

"It simply means that there is nothing for me to tell you of Teller's trip. Any questions that you might have you will need to ask yourself. After all, he is coming to get *you.*"

Abbott nodded, set his elbows on the table, and looked into Billy's bright eyes. "Alright then, what about Coyote?"

"You needn't worry, Abbott," Billy smiled. "Coyote will be accompanying you."

Abbott scratched his chin through his beard. "That is *not* what I meant."

"I realize that, Sir Bear." Billy replied, but pausing in mid-sentence cocked his ear as if he heard something in the distance . . . then, with a hint of amusement flashing across his dark features he smiled, "have another piece of Antelope."

Abbott acquiesced. He knew there would be no more information regarding the matter, and the meat *was* delicious. So, with beer now forgotten, he limped to the grill and dropped another steak onto his plate, but by the time he made it back to the table, he saw that there would be no further conversation.

Billy sat, eyes closed, his finger making slow revolutions around the rim of his partially filled wine glass. The result was a beautifully pitched harmonic: one that was a haunting accompaniment to the deserts evening song. And as he listened Abbott felt the cool air from the higher mesas drift down, lightly caressing his skin while the evening shadows stretched across the valley, deepening in the dusk and adding yet another dimension to an already extraordinary landscape.

Lifting his eyes to the twinkling points of light above, he sighed, *'this is truly lovely . . .'*

That thought foremost in his mind, Abbott looked across the table. Billy had not moved. His eyes remained closed, his finger still gliding around the top of his glass and creating that one, beautifully sustained note; his expression matching its ephemeral quality . . . Abbott smiled, poured a little more wine into his glass and stood, flexing his ankle. Still tender, it was a great improvement, and with Billy's assurance that it was mending, he felt a small degree of comfort.

It was then he noticed a tattered, but still inviting old lawn chair beckoning from its place beside the massive red rock that shaded the trailer. Accepting the chairs invitation, he limped over, turned it to face east, and settled gingerly into it.

"Ahhh," he sighed. "*Much* better . . ."

With his glass resting on his belly, Abbott watched as the Moons pale edge slowly peeked over the Eastern horizon: and as it rose in glorious fullness he was reminded that it had now been over a month since his first encounter with Teller.

'Amazing,' he thought. *'A lifetime's worth of adventure in only thirty days. And while seems as I've known him for years, it seems as if I met him only yesterday.'*

Shaking his wooly head, he glanced over at Billy once again and smiled beneath his beard.

'And who'd of ever thought I'd be sitting here now, with a man who could offer such an all-encompassing, yet simple concept of Prophecy rock. . .' then he blinked and smiled to himself. *'Hell, who'd of thought I'd be sitting here at all?'*

It was with the enormity of *that* thought he attempted to put in order the kaleidoscopic sequence of events that had taken place between Moons.

It had all started with Teller . . . no, it had all started with his decision to go on the river trip . . . no, he thought, it had really begun with his decision to take a hiatus from the museum and explore Prophecy Rock on his own. Well, but then, of course, he had stopped in Telluride and met Kelly, who had suggested the river trip . . . Which then led to Teller, which brought him back to here . . . his head swimming with the multitude of small, and seemingly inconsequential choices that had led him to this spot; this here, and this now; he closed his eyes and let his thoughts drift . . . *'what are the limits of free will?* Suddenly, a coyote yipped in the distance, it's haunting laugh bringing him back to the moment.

Looking up, he saw that the Moon now seemed to be balanced on the very tip of the tallest of the rock spires that lined the horizon . . . so close Abbott was sure he could touch it: and, as he reached out to dip a finger into its powdery surface it disappeared, eclipsed by the outline of Billy's head as he stepped between them.

Then, he smiled . . . for a magical moment, it appeared as if the Moon's pale light shone through Billy's mouth: but then he spoke, and at his words, Abbott wondered if he had been thinking out loud.

"It began," Billy said, his voice velvet. "the moment Coyote recognized you as a necessary part of the story and no decision you could have made would have altered your participation."

Abbott blinked, finding himself only mildly surprised by Billy's apparent knowledge of his thoughts.

"So," Abbott countered, "you're saying there *is* no free will?"

Billy's clear laughter rang through the night air.

"No! No, of course not! But keep in mind that free will and destiny are not mutually exclusive, and that Coyote often blurs the edges of both."

"So I've noticed . . ." Abbott murmured.

Billy squatted at the foot of Abbott's chair. "What I am saying, Abbott, is that you were destined to be involved. But it was your *choices,* along with Coyotes nudging, that determined where, and how deeply that involvement would be; and so, it has been the resulting mix of both free will *and* destiny that have brought you, here, now, with me."

He paused, and with the light of the moon surrounding his head like a halo, he placed one hand on Abbotts injured foot.

"And I am *very* glad of it, Sir Bear. Very glad indeed."

Billy gave the foot a tender squeeze, and a peculiar tingling passed through Abbotts toes. A vibration that felt akin to a molecular interpretation of the harmonics Billy had produced on the rim of his wine glass.

With Abbott a Cheshire Cats smile, Billy stood.

"Teller will be here tomorrow morning and he will be anxious to go. You should rest. He is going to need you."

His smile winked out, and he turned, and vanished into the night.

Abbott squinted into the darkness at the place where Billy had been and wiggled his toes.

They felt *much* better.

= Chapter 17 =

Leaving the airport, Jack flew the chopper over the same course he had taken to rescue Ben. It was the same red, parched, and desolate ground that passed beneath them, yet *nothing* was the same.

Teller was in great humor, while Jack, still amazed that his friend had not sabotaged his chances with Maxine on their first meeting, was doubly thankful that the second had held none of the horrors he had envisioned.

~

Upon landing for refueling, it seemed his fears would be realized. Teller had demanded a coffee for the road; and, as was inevitable when dealing with Teller, whatever it was that Jack wished to avoid would be precisely what was bound to occur. So, naturally, as Jack followed Teller through the airport they ran into Max. But to Jack's astonishment, Teller had been a true gentleman.

Following a short reintroduction, he had politely excused himself to go for coffee: and as they had watched him walk away, Max had said that he seemed very nice, throwing in a comment about his being quite handsome as well.

Jack was well aware that her remark was meant to be teasing, but still, he bristled, and seeing his reaction she had added, "but not *nearly* as handsome as you, Jack." She followed her comment with a warm kiss on the lips, and that, of course, had been the moment Teller chose to return; grinning as he held three double latte's.

Slipping a covert wink at Jack, Teller presented one of the cups to Max with the same playful smile he seemed to give every woman, which irritated Jack to no end. Then, touching his cup to Maxine's, he had handed Jack the third cup, knowing full well that Jack drank his coffee black.

Jack had managed to extricate them from the situation by stressing that they were in a rush. But as he towed Teller away by the elbow, Teller had the audacity to promise that he would *personally* make sure Jack called her just as soon as they landed.

~

Shaking his head at the memory, Jack suppressed a frustrated, but warm grin as his eyes shifted from the console to Teller: who's forehead was pressed against the window watching the landscape wiz by below; and seeing the happy expression on Tellers face, the last of Jack's residual anger vanished. In retrospect, the damage had been minimal, and he was still feeling *enormously* pleased with the kiss she had given him.

As if reading his mind, Teller turned from the window.

"I think Max likes you old boy. I'm glad I could help."

Jack's previous irritation immediately returned; but before he could react, Teller's sly grin turned to authentic enthusiasm. "I'm really looking forward to learning to fly one of these, Jacko."

Jack gritted his teeth, and glared suspiciously, but Teller was so sincere that his grimace became a grudging smile.

"Good. I'm looking forward to being chauffeured."

But as they broke through a ceiling of low clouds and Glen Canyon Dam materialized, Teller's smile vanished.

Green and shining in the desert sun, the miles of water that filled the myriad of small canyons radiated out like the roots of a massive tree.

"Damn." he muttered. "As much as I hate that thing, it sure as hell is impressive."

Jack nodded and pressed the joystick with his knee, altering their course slightly.

"Yeah, it is . . . Okay Tell, we're going to make a quick stop at Bullfrog to top off our fuel. I want to be sure we have plenty for the extra mileage, *and* the extra weight."

Teller's angst evaporated as suddenly as it had appeared.

"Exciting, isn't it?" he beamed.

Turning the mirrored lenses of his shades to his smiling passenger, Jack pushed his headphones back onto his neck.

"Have I ever told you what an unbelievable pain in the ass you are?"

Teller stared at Jack, but as all he could see was his own smiling reflection he smiled, "More than once, Jack."

Jack nodded. "And have I ever mentioned how *every* time you get involved in my life, you somehow manage to fuck up whatever plans I was trying to make?"

"Yes, Jack . . ." Teller's expression took on a sense of droll forbearance. "I believe you have made *numerous* comments along those lines."

"And you *do* realize," Jack continued, "that this is due to your habit of leading the innocent astray?"

Teller, tremendously amused, tried to appear properly chastised. "But as you pointed out earlier, Jack, no one is innocent."

Jack smiled. "That being true, have I ever really thanked you for it?"

Teller scratched his chin.

"No, Jack, I don't believe you've ever done that . . . at least not to my satisfaction." He paused. "Or, if you have, you've never done so with any real sincerity."

Tilting his head, Jack regarded Teller over the top of his shades. "Well. Once this is over, remind me to thank you properly."

Teller's green eyes sparkled. "I shall be sure to do that Jack."

For a moment, the only sound was the 'thwop' of the rotors echoing within the cab. But then Jack began to laugh, and a second later Teller joined in.

Suddenly the clouds broke and the marina came into sight. Five minutes later and still chuckling, Jack set the bird down near the pumps.

It was a quick stop, and within minutes they were back in the air, northbound, the next part of their adventure already underway.

= Chapter 18 =

Swirling Scotch in his cut crystal glass, James stared at the doorway through which Casey had just disappeared. "She's a Bitch," he growled, pushing himself up from the couch. "But she's right." Grumbling, he shuffled over to the massive window that overlooked the valley.

The heart of Telluride was lit; the residential lights in bright clusters in the center, diminishing as they crawled up the mountains steep slopes with the few near the peak twinkling in competition with the stars.

Rocking on his heels, he brought his drink to his lips. It seemed this was a case of the old, 'good news, bad news' scenario. The good news was that Teller was out of the picture. The bad news was that Kelly would follow.

But as he contemplated how to make the situation work to his advantage, he caught sight of his reflection in the massive pane of glass. Startled, he lurched backwards, nearly spilling his drink. He scarcely recognized the man.

His hands shaking, he poured the Scotch down his throat and stepped close to the window to squint at the ghostly reflection.

'Christ!' he murmured, scrutinizing the forlorn figure that stared back. 'Do I *really* look that bad . . .?

Forced to accept the unpleasant truth, James frowned. *Well, I guess it's no surprise with what Teller and that fucking kid have put me through.'* Shaking the ice in his now empty glass, he sighed, "guess I'll freshen this up and go see how the little bastard's doin'." While at the same time

thinking, *'It may not be a solution, but at least it's a step in the right direction.'*
But as he took that first step, he cocked an ear to the sounds coming from the kitchen.

For the briefest of moments, James thought Casey might be fixing something to eat and his stomach growled in subconscious reflex. But just as quickly the hope vanished. The woman might be beautiful, he thought, but she couldn't cook to save her soul. So, dismissing the thought with a second sigh he turned to cast another glance at the valley on the other side of the window; but finding himself facing that miserable man's reflection where *his* should be, he threw out his chest in defiance. "Goddamnit!" He hissed, "This is *still my* Kingdom!' and forcing a bravado he couldn't truly muster, went to the liquor cabinet.

Dropping three fresh cubes into his glass, he poured a double, tossed it back, and refilled the glass to the very top in order to steel himself for the unpleasant task ahead: then, turning to the stairs that he had trudged up earlier that day, he mumbled, "It might be step in the right direction, but its sure as hell not a walk I look forward to taking . . ."
Suddenly his reluctance was replaced with anger.

"That goddamn kid has always been a problem,' James snarled his lip curling as he lifted his glass. *'Just like his worthless fucking father.* But as the liquid touched his tongue a different sound caught his attention.
Over the rattle of ice, he heard a vehicle rev its motor in the garage. *What in the hell?* but tilting his ear towards the kitchen he could still hear Casey banging around. So, he wondered. If *she* was still here, who was in the garage? Suddenly, the engine revved up, the sound shaking the ice in his glass, followed immediately by the squeal of tires on concrete. For a moment, James stood baffled, his mind scrambling to process the information. Then it dawned on him. There was only *one* other person that it could possibly be, and that realization hit him like a baseball bat.

Sprinting to the window, he saw the brake lights of his Hummer flash once and disappear down the long driveway.

"Goddamn it!!!!" he shouted.

With glass still in hand, he spun on his heel and took off across the room, bounding down the grand staircase three stairs at a time, gaining velocity with every step, hitting the door of Ben's makeshift hospital room with such force that the doorjamb splintered; leaving the door hanging from its hinges as James stood, staring in stunned silence.

The boy was gone,

The mattress was ripped open, laying half out of the frame with the bed sheets shredded and knotted around the metal I.V. stand that, once holding bags of life-sustaining fluids now lay broken on top of a dresser: its chrome frame reflected in its shattered mirror with every drawer pulled out and the contents flung across the room.

Stunned, James took a tentative step into the chaos.

There was a snapping crunch of glass beneath his feet and startled, he ducked, fearing gunshots; but realizing his mistake and chastising himself for his cowardly paranoia, he raised an expensive loafer. He was standing on the splintered picture frame that had once contained that glass . . . letting his eyes follow the trail of broken shards, they led to the remains of the bed, where the photograph that had been ripped from that frame lay. It was a photo taken of he and Teller, taken in the earlier, happier days of a budding partnership.

In it, two proud young men smiled into the camera, their arms thrown over one another's shoulders as they stood in front of the New Sheridan Hotel in downtown Telluride: The Aspens in the background splashed in the colors of fall.

Memories came flooding back and James nearly smiled as he reached for the crumpled photo. But that too-brief moment of pleasure dissolved when he saw Ben had shoved the bloody I.V. needle through Tellers eye, pinning it to a plastic bag that now lay deflated, the last of its contents leaking onto a soaking pillow. The gruesome image was too much, and James' hand involuntarily opened, allowing his glass to drop to the carpet where it splashed Scotch and ice onto his shoes as the glass bounced once, then came to rest between his feet. But as he gazed down at the photo a second time his paralysis broke. Kicking the glass away, he sprinted to the bathroom; hoping to find Benny lying on the hard tile unconscious or dead. . . preferably dead. That would save him a *great* deal of trouble. Torn between hope and fear, James stuck his head into the darkened room, flipping the light on to yet one more unanswered prayer.

Benny was *not* there.

With his hopes of an easy solution dashed, James trudged dejectedly back to the room where he leaned on the doorjamb shaking his head in amazement. It looked as if there had been a small explosion within these four walls and the level of hatred reflected in its magnitude was alarming. But as the reality of it all sunk in, James' selfish frustrations increased. This was yet *another* example that the world had suddenly turned against him.

Balling his fists, he lifted his face to the ceiling and screamed; *"What the fuck is happening to my life?!!*

His angry shock morphing into self-pity, he kicked his way through the wadded sheets and scattered medical gear, where, righting the mattress, he dropped to his knees, dug his elbows into the stuffing's, and lowered his head into his hands.

Had anyone looked in, they might have thought he was praying in a battle zone.

Holding that position, he stared at the ravaged photograph.

"This *can't* be good," he mumbled while delicately plucking the IV needle from Tellers eye.

Smoothing the photo, he slowly stood, folding it into his back pocket as he went to the door, picked up his glass and headed upstairs to the bar. He needed a drink.

Once back in the living room, James leaned wearily on the polished bar to stare again at his reflection superimposed over the lights of Telluride; and seeing that the man in the reflection looked even worse than before, he nearly cried.

His entire world was coming apart.

James stood like that for a few minutes more, then shaking his head he straightened his spine and wiped the moisture from the corner of his eye.

He had no time to waste on self-recrimination.

Giving the refection a final glance, James reached into the liquor cabinet, wrapped his fingers around the neck of a bottle of red wine, and clutching his bottle of Scotch close to his heart strode to the couch, taking the crumpled photograph from his pocket and smoothing it on the coffee table.

Flopping back into the feathered cushions, he poured a tall glass of wine for Casey. Then filling his to the very brim with Scotch he shouted. "Hey Casey. Get in here, we have a problem."

~

Ben, confused, had driven well over a mile before he even bothered to turn on the headlights. His morphine-dilated pupils absorbed sufficient light to negotiate the deserted road and memory alone would have allowed him to drive it blindfolded if necessary; but struggling to remember what had happened, he slowed the vehicle slightly.

He had awoken in a panic, still shaking from the residual memories of the brutal nightmare.

In the dream he was drowning, struggling desperately to rise from the frigid depths of the river. But every time he broke the surface; frantically gasping for breath while clawing for the shore, a man would appear, standing between he, and the safety of land; laughing while he poured shiny coins over him: loading his pockets as their weight pulling him back beneath the fast moving current . . . where once again he bounced helplessly along the boulder-strewn bottom, his bones splintering; their snapping filling in his ears.

Ben's eyes opened in terror, still in the bed of his uncle's house; feeling more prisoner than patient.

'Teller caused this!' His fevered mind screamed! *'Teller wanted to kill me for trying to save Kelly from him!'*

Feverishly flailing at the knotted sheets wrapped around his sweat-soaked body, he knocked over the I.V. stand and it fell on him. Twisting in agony, he picked it up and threw it with all his strength at the dresser, where it shattered the mirror, dropping onto the photograph of his smiling nemesis; breaking both glass and frame while sending Tellers mocking grin fluttering to the floor.

Ben, tangled tightly in bedsheets, stared at that photograph, his mind twisting in rage as Tellers smile drove him further into madness; until, weak, sobbing, and quaking from delirium, he tore the needle from his arm, falling from the bed to crawl across the carpet, cutting himself deeply on sharp shards of broken glass to reach the photograph.

Tears pouring down his cheeks he finally reached his goal, and grabbing the picture, viciously jabbed the needle through the eye of the smiling man.

"Die!" He sobbed, then collapsed.

~

Something in Ben's fevered mind had splintered that night in the tent next to the river; for while the injuries he had sustained from his aborted boat heist had been treated, his sanity had continued its decay.

It was not Teller's fist that had done the damage. but the blow, compounded by his unrequited love of Kelly, magnified further by his uncle's perverse attraction to the object of his affection, had been the cleaver that had finally separated Ben from his tenuous grip on reality. And now, with the unerring instincts of a mad dog he knew *exactly* where he must go. The location was imbedded in his mind as clearly as the photograph he had just destroyed.

It was a small dock on the lake, just downriver from his first sighting of the strange and wonderful Coyote.

That is where Teller would be. And it was there that he would kill him.

Tearing off what was left of his gown, Ben had gone to the closet, dressing in whatever he pulled off of a hanger: then, allowing his madness to guide him ghost-like through the house, he found himself in the huge, six-car garage, standing in front of a locked steel door.

Completely unconscious of his actions, the silky voice in his head whispered to him, speaking of the treasures that lie behind the door; and when he rattled the knob to find it securely locked, it led him to a large toolbox.

Lifting its lid, he discovered a steel bar, and lifting it from its confines he checked its heft, and finding it sufficient, jammed it behind the padlock, twisting until the lock first bent, then easily snapped.

At the success, the voices in his head were giddy with excitement, praising him as he reached for the light switch: and with a 'flick' the room was illuminated.

Cheers filled Ben's head as his eyes adjusted.

Five halogen lamps hung from a bar on the rooms ceiling, each throwing a bright, white beam on the wall opposite: each beam highlighting a different, very expensive, and *very* lethal hunting rifle.

Shivers of joy tingled Ben's skin, as revenge pumped hot in his blood. For placed strategically on a brilliant white wall, and supported by highly polished Gabon Ebony racks, were the weapons of a madman's dreams:

Mid-wall a Nosler M-48 shone; while gleaming next to it the Sauer 202 vied for attention.

To its left a Weatherby Mark XXII whispered seductively, while the stunning Savage MKII caught his eye, as did the Cooper M52 . . .

But it was the Sako Finnlight that *called* to him . . .

It's deadly black stock, coupled beautifully with chrome throw-bolt and barrel was the perfect weapon to rid the earth of his adversary.

~

Driving through the starless night, the orange dash lights intensifying the psychosis in Ben's eyes.

But as he navigated the winding mountain road he cursed the faint, but insistent, voice in his head that cautioned him that the laughing man in his dream more closely resembled his uncle than it did Teller.

= Chapter 19 =

Flying low, Jack skimmed over the convoluted sea of red rock until he saw the Sun flash off of Billy's old Airstream trailer in the distance. Banking, he aimed for the shimmering lake that had settled over dusty parking lot in front of the store.

Abbott was also staring out over the parking lot from the rocking chair, contemplating the irony that in the hottest, driest places on earth, God chose to tease the dying with imaginary water. The thought titillated his thirst, and he raised a cold Coors to his lips and flexed his ankle.

The pain he had suffered since he had jumped into that damned hole with Teller over a week ago was nearly gone now; better than he could have ever hoped since Billy had done whatever it was he had done when he touched it the other evening. And while he was immensely pleased, he was equally curious. He was just about to ask Billy how he had accomplished so much with no more than a simple touch when the 'thwop' of rotors sounded in the distance. Smiling, he slipped on his boot and pushed himself out of the chair. The question would have to wait.

As he stood, Abbott looked over to Billy and saw that although his hat was pulled down over his eyes his smile was expanding. He chuckled. He doubted he would get a satisfactory answer anyhow.

Still limping out of habit, Abbott took his first few steps towards the porch railing; but by the fourth step he realized that he felt no pain. Pausing, he wiggled his toes. Then, rotating his ankle, a joyous grin lit his face and he looked over at Billy a second time and decided that no answer was necessary. But deciding that a malt beverage was in order to celebrate this minor miracle he detoured to the cooler and rustled through the ice.

Clutching a cold beer, wearing a warm smile, and feeling much better about life in general, he completed his journey to the porch railing light of step as the black insect-like craft circled to the front of the store; hovering as the blades kicked up a cloud of dust while blowing tumbleweeds in a wide arc. Suddenly the side door slid open and Teller appeared, his deerskin pack slung over his shoulder and a grin that could be seen even through the dust. Setting one foot on the landing rail he leapt, disappearing into the billowing dust as the swaying machine settled to earth and through a cacophony of of noise and flying debris, burst through the dirty cloud like a movie hero.

Abbott laughed with joy as Teller spied him in the shadows, shouting over the noise of the props, "Abbott! Old shoe!" while bounding up the steps to throw his arms around the big man and squeeze him in a powerful hug.

Unfortunately, Abbott's beer can was between them at the time; and at the sudden dampness, Teller stepped back and looked down. Both of their shirts were soaked.

"Is that beer or are you just glad to see me?" Teller laughed, pulling a hastily folded t-shirt from his pack to wipe at the suds. But as he was patting Abbott's belly, Billy walked up. Teller immediately quit dabbing and shoved the wadded shirt into Abbott's chest. "You're on your own, pal." he grinned, turning to take Billy's calloused hand in his own.

"So, Chief, what's word from the Gods?"

Billy's smile was brilliant.

"Rumor is that we are still on our own."

"I don't believe that for one second Billy. Teller chuckled, tossing his pack onto the bench.

"Wheels within wheels, gears within gears, atoms in orbits, a certain Coyote has his paws in a lot of pies . . ." he paused and snapped his fingers. "Wait a sec, I'll be right back."

He disappeared into the store just as Jack came up the stairs slapping the dust from his cap as he acknowledged the two men. "Billy, Abbott." he drawled.

"Good morning Jack," Billy smiled, "How was Tucson?"

The bell on the screen door tinkled again as Teller returned holding a six-pack. "Don't ask *him*," he laughed, pulling the tab on one of the cans. "He had his fingers in a few pies as well."

Jack chuckled and tipped his head in Teller's direction.

"Always the wit."

Teller's grin doubled in size as he went to Abbott, taking the crushed can he still held and replacing it with a full one while giving a pat to Abbott's damp shirt and the ample belly beneath. "There ya go, pal, a freshie with my apologies."

Taking a seat in the rocker, he leaned back, directing his attentions to Jack, his smile bright and happy.

"It's the truth, Jackie boy, and you know it."

Jack began a half-hearted denial but Teller held up a wagging finger. "Save your stories for the ladies, Jacko, you can't bullshit a bullshitter." But then his grin faded as he motioned for them all to sit. The men all looked to one another as Teller waited for everyone got comfortable. But when he spoke, his tone was serious.

"Billy, you never mentioned a second carving."

Abbott blurted, "A *second* carving?" and as Teller silenced him with a wave, a small smile crossed Billy's dark face.

"You never asked."

Bringing his hand up, Teller squeezed the bridge of his nose. "Of *course* I never asked!" he sighed in exasperation, "Why *would* I?"

"Why would you not?" Billy countered.

Sliding his hand down his face, Teller's green eyes flashed with annoyance, but calming quickly, he smiled. "Zen?"

"No." Billy said, "wisdom. How will you understand the answer if you do not ask the right question?"

Teller leaned forward and put his elbows on his knees, his humor gone. "Alright then, Chief, here is my question, and answer me true. What is the other carving doing in the dash of an old Buick?"

At this, Billy's eyebrows shot up in surprise; but then, closing his eyes he leaned back in his chair and the smile on his dark face changed, reflecting a warm and pleasant reminiscence. "Ahh, Sebastian *did* love that car . . ." then, very slowly, his dark eyes fluttered open, and he turned them to Teller.

"May I ask what led you to his car?"

"You know very well that it was not *what,*" Teller growled, "but *who.*" but his tone softened and he smiled, "And I am thankful."

Abbott's curiosity could no longer be kept in check. "*What* are you talking about?? What *car*, and what *carving?*"

Teller turned and gave him a look of exasperated humor. "It's a long story, Griz, and you'll hear it soon enough."

Turning from Abbott's hurt and bewildered expression, Teller turned back to Billy.

"Well . . .?"

Billy studied Teller for a moment, then turned away, focusing on the horizon. Teller stared at the side of Billy's head as minutes ticked by; and just as he reached the end of his patience, Billy murmured, "This is *quite* fitting,"

Then, turning his luminous eyes back to Teller, smiled, "so *you* now hold both carvings? Yes . . . yes . . . quite fitting . . . yes indeed . . ." Billy suddenly rocked forward and stood.

"I am going to make coffee, would anyone like some?"

"Yeah, I'll take a cup," Jack said.

Billy nodded, and looked down at the other two men. "Anyone else?"

Abbott declined but Teller looked up at Billy. "Sumatran?"

"I'll check," Billy replied. "But if not, would you find any substitute acceptable?"

Tapping his chin as if this were a major decision, Teller's brow furrowed. Then, pursing his lips, shrugged, "Whatever you have will be fine."

"Good." Billy replied. "Then I shall see what I have."

The little bell chimed as the screen door opened and closed, and everyone listened to Billy's boot heels click across the old wooden floor.

Once gone, Abbott turned to Teller.

"You bought a *car*?"

Teller's green eyes twinkled, and a smile of unfettered joy lit his face. "No, my dear Abbott, I did not buy a *car*, I bought a dream. A beautiful steel dream." Glancing over to Jack, he smiled, "am I right Jack? Is that not a piece of sculpted art with wheels?"

"Yes Teller." Jack nodded. "A veritable feast for the eyes."

Teller gave a derisive snort. "Screw you, Jacko. You've no appreciation for anything that doesn't have tits or propellers." Jack smiled, inserting one correction. "Or rotors."

"Semantics, Jack," Teller said. "A rotor is just a horizontal propeller."

Jack laughed. "Point taken."

Through the laughter the sound of the bell on the screen door announced Billy's return; holding a tray with three cups. He handed one to Jack, who dipped his head in thanks, to Teller he said, "I'm sorry Teller, no Sumatran. Is Guatemalan satisfactory?" Teller took the cup, bowing his head ever so slightly. "It would be rude of me not to accept. After all, you've gone to the trouble."

Billy took his seat in his rocker.

"How *very* kind of you."

"And you're very welcome." Teller replied. "But Chief, you've yet to answer my question."

Billy's dark eyes peered over the cups rim. Then, blowing a cloud of steam as he brought the cup to his lips he smiled,

"Which one?"

"The one concerning Sebastian," Teller said, lifting his own cup and tipping it at Billy. "*Including* the Buick, and more importantly, Coyote."

Billy's smile shone within the cloud of steam.

"Yes, yes, of course . . . questions require answers do they not? But first, while it is quite obvious Coyote accompanied you to Tucson, I would very much like to hear *your* account of the story. Once I've heard that, I will be in a much better position to provide those answers. So. *If* you would be so kind, the details please."

Teller glanced over at at Jack, then leaned forward, cradling his cup in both hands . . . In order to streamline the story he decided to omit the girls and the hotel, concentrating primarily on the more relevant aspects of the trip. And, surprisingly, and against all inclination and habit, he did not bother to exaggerate. There was no need to do so. There was absolutely nothing he could add to make the truth more entertaining.

~

The Sun was closer to the horizon and another pot of coffee had been drank by the time Teller wrapped up his much-abbreviated story. Jack had said nothing at all during the retelling, and Abbott had remained unexpectedly quiet as well. So, with Teller leaning back in his chair scrutinizing Billy's face tor reaction, the other two Musketeers waited in silence.

Finally, Billy spoke. Slowly at first; as if he were excavating precious memories; methodically sorting them into their proper places. This took time, for much had transpired over those many years . . . but once started, the tale grew stronger in the telling.

"I met Sebastian soon after I returned from the war." Billy began, placing his palms on his knees and sitting straighter. "He was a young archaeologist," here a paternal grin lit his face as he looked at Abbott. "And, like our friend here, was also fascinated with Prophecy Rock."

Billy paused again, organizing his thoughts. Then, shaking his head ever so slightly with pleasant recollections, smiled.

"As a matter of fact, he was *very* much like you Abbott. Independent, smart, and driven to find answers. Perhaps that is why I feel such kinship to you. It is much like having my old friend with me once again."

Humbled, Abbott smiled and Teller thought he saw a blush of color under his beard. Billy saw this as well and it brought yet more warmth to his eyes. "But back to the story."

"Many years ago I was deer hunting in the canyons north of here when a violent summer thunderstorm hit the mountains not far from where I was. I could see that it was raining hard on their peaks, and soon I heard the rumbling of water in the distance. Being familiar with how quickly flash floods strike in this country, I was wise enough to realize that I needed to get out of the canyon I was in and to higher ground. It was this foresight that saved my, for by the time I had scrambled onto the rim, a monstrous wall of dirty water came rushing through the canyon."

Billy stopped, his expression one of awe at the memory.

"The power of a flood like that is truly remarkable." he said. "The skies above may be clear, but the rain in those far away hills can still be deadly."

"Yeah," Teller said, raising his eyebrows. "I got caught in one in the Big Thompson canyon in Colorado once. It wiped out the whole place . . . scary shit."

"Scary shit indeed."Billy chuckled. "Anyway, from my place on the canyons ledge I watched the rushing water carry away everything in its path while the deep, hollow rumblings of large boulders tumbling down the watercourse echoed within the canyon walls. But most wretched were the few desperate animals that had survived by clinging to logs or tree branches as their dead cousins floated by in the flotsam and froth. The sight was both impressive and terribly sad.

But the water drained away nearly as quickly as it had come, and with my hunt ended I began my journey home, staying high on the rim in case there was more rain in the mountains. But then, in one of the side-canyons I came across a wounded young buck. The poor fellow had escaped the floods wrath but had broken a leg in doing so. Seeing this gift, I thanked the Sprits for their providence and relieved the creature of its pain. However, once done, as in all things, both the good and the bad came into play. For while I now had food, carrying the heavy deer over my shoulders slowed my progress and after a few miles of difficult hiking I paused to rest. But as I laid the deer onto the ground, I happened to look into the canyon below. There I saw a very strange sight. Pools of water from the flood had gathered at the base of several large boulders, and from between those rocks a pair of legs stuck up like some strange plant, waving about in the air."

Glancing up at his audience, Billy gave a little smile.

"To say I was surprised would be an understatement. But thinking some poor soul had been caught in the flood and was now somehow stuck, I made my way down to help. But when I reached the canyon floor I saw that while it *was* a man, he was in no trouble at all. He was squeezing between the boulders trying to reach something that had been exposed by the rains washing clear the sand."

Here Billy paused, and with his companions riveted to their chairs he smiled, knowing the value of timing.

Taking a sip of coffee, he continued.

"This fellow had not yet seen, nor heard me. So, staying the shadows, I waited for him to retrieve whatever it was he was straining so very hard to reach, and finally, when he pulled himself up I was startled to see that he was a young Billagaana. Then as a flash of gold glittered from a small hole in the leather pouch that he now held I was shocked a second time, for I recognized the pouch immediately. It was the same as the ones my Grandfather had in *his* possession. Therefore I knew that the coins this stranger held was the same as my family kept hidden."

Billy paused yet again, the three men still spellbound.

Suddenly the silence was broken by the carbonated hiss of a can being opened. Turning as one, they all looked at Abbott, who gave a sheepish smile and tipped the can to his lips.

"Very much like Sebastian." Billy chuckled, then turned back to his tale.

"This was a terrible situation and I was unsure just what I should do. This stranger's good fortune had the potential to create problems for my family *and* my people. But I am no thief, so taking the pouch from him was not a consideration. So, you see my dilemma. I could not simply take the pouch, but neither could I let him keep the coins of my family. And please, keep in mind that in those days things were *much* different between the white man and the Navajo. So to say that I was conflicted would be a tremendous understatement. So I watched from the shadows as this young man opened the pouch and spilled a few of the coins into his hand. To my great surprise, he simply looked at them. That he was pleased I could tell, but in his face I saw no greed: only curiosity. Seeing this, I studied the man before me with new eyes."

Here Billy turned his obsidian eyes on Teller.

"Sebastian was also very much like you, Teller. A man with no avarice in his heart . . . I find having met two such white men in my life quite extraordinary."

"Thanks," Teller smiled. "I guess."

Billy's teeth flashed against dark skin. "You are very welcome." But his smile slowly slipped away as he said, "Have I mentioned that Coyote has been an integral part of my life from the time of my birth?"

Teller looked at the other two men, and then back to Billy.

"We know only what little you've hinted at."

Billy nodded thoughtfully. "Well, then we shall talk more of that later. For now, it is enough for you to know that I have always been able to feel Coyotes presence. Because of this I could feel ancient power emanating from the pouch, drawing me from the shadows of my place of hiding. It was then that I *knew* Coyote was involved in my life once again.

So I called out, stepping from the shadows and into the light." Suddenly Jack's phone shattered the suspense, and growling he thrust his hand into his pocket to turn it off, but Billy smiled, tipping his head. "Answer it Jack. It may be important." With a reluctant a nod he yanked the phone from his pocket and snarled, "*Hello?*"

"Jack?"

"You called. Who were you expecting?"

"Well. I see you've become no more pleasant than before. This is James, James Carson."

Jack's eyebrows shot up in surprise. "Jim . . ." he said, his tone sarcastic. "It's a *pleasure* to hear from you. How may I be of service?"

The voice on the other end was equally scornful.

"Look, Jack, I'll waste no time on pleasantries. This is simply a courtesy call."

Hearing James' name, Teller held out his hand. "Give me the phone," he insisted, but Jack waved him away.

"Well," he said, "I must admit I'm surprised."

Teller waved his hand at Jack and growled, "Gimmie the phone!" Jack pulled away, delighting in Tellers frustration while putting a playful tone to his voice. "But I *will* accept the courtesy." He smiled, giving Teller the finger and returning his attention to James

"So, just what is this 'courtesy" pertain to?"

It was difficult, but James managed to hold his temper.

"I called to talk to Teller. Is he there?"

"Just a moment," Jack said solemnly, "I'll check." Looking over at Teller he laid the phone against his thigh and grinned, "Its Jim, would you like to speak with him?"

Glaring, Teller held out his hand. "Just give me the goddamn phone!" Pulling away, Jack brought the phone to his cheek and sang, "Just a min-ute . . ."

Teller snatched the phone from his grasp, and giving him the finger, walked down the stairs and away from the crew.

Abbott threw a puzzled glance at Jack, but Jack just held out his hands in a: "I dunno" gesture.

From the shade of the porch the three men watched Teller as he walked in loops; one hand stabbing the air as he talked, becoming more agitated with every loop: and after circling the helicopter several times he flipped the phone shut and stood, staring off towards the lake. Minutes passed, with no other sound than the wind whistling across the desert: but then, turning his face to the sky, Teller shouted.

"SON-OF-A-BITCH!"

His voice was picked up by the wind, blown against the sandstone walls, and sent bouncing back across the sage; and as the echo faded he turned, and walked slowly back to the store. But as he came closer, Billy noticed that with Teller's every approaching step the ever-present wind grew quieter; the unusual silence amplifying the sound of his boots as he took the wooden stairs to his coffee cup.

Empty.

Frowning, he turned it upside down and looked at Jack.

"How soon can we leave?"

Teller's expression bothered Jack, but he had known him far too long to ask unnecessary questions.

"We're ready now."

"Good." Teller nodded, "we're leaving in about thirty minutes. But first, we're going to hear the rest of Billy's story." Taking his seat, he put his elbows on his knees, shifted to make himself comfortable, and looked at Billy; his expression serious, and expectant.

Billy returned his gaze but remained silent.

Finally, Abbott's curiosity got the better of him.

"Captain, I know I speak for us all. . ." and pointing to the phone that Teller still held, said, "But *what* was *that* all about?"

A murmur of agreement sounded from the other men.

"Oh." Teller said, looking down at the phone as if he had forgotten all about it and handing it back to Jack with a preoccupied smile.

"*That* was James."

"And?"

"Well," Teller said. "Apparently that crazy little fucker Ben is on his way down here to kill me."

— — ˉˉ — —
— — — —

= Chapter 20 =

Kelly sat on the edge of the couch with wine glass in hand.

Having spent the past three hours packing she was now frustrated. She had no problem with what to do with *her* things, but Teller's eclectic collection was something else entirely; and looking around the room she allowed herself a smile. It was not so much a home as a museum of his life.

He had acquired the two-story, 1890's Victorian house years ago from a vibrant ninety-year-old widow. This was long before she and Teller had met, but with Teller serving as common ground, over the years she and Grace had become friends. And now, sitting there among his possessions, Kelly smiled as she recalled the story Grace had told her of her first meeting with Teller.

~

It had been late fall, Grace had said, and the first big snow of the season had been a brutal one. But that night she and the bartender were safe in the warmth of the 'Last Dollar Saloon,' making small talk when the front door suddenly burst open, filling the entry with swirling snow. She had paused then and laughed, saying that it had come in with such force that it seemed its own small, but wicked storm. But as the door was kicked shut and the fat flakes settled, she saw that a stranger had blown in with the squall. Stomping his boots, he stepped in, unwrapping a thick woolen scarf from his broad shoulders as he crossed the room; and leaning against the bar he gave Grace a warm smile and ordered a double Courvoisier in a heated snifter from the surprised bartender.

Grace's eyes sparkling, she told Kelly that there was *some*thing in his smile that had charmed her from the very beginning.

~

Once the bartender recovered from his shock of a customer appearing in this weather he acknowledged the strangers order and snuck a glance at Grace, who just smiled and nodded. The bartender remained wary: but accepting her judgment, reached for the Brandy.

Seeing the exchange, Teller winked at this elegant woman in fur and as his drink was prepared, moved towards the crackling warmth of the fireplace, blowing into his cupped hands as he settled back into one of the soft armchairs that faced the flames; and seeing the firelight play across Tellers rugged features, feelings thought long gone returned with a warm, tingling flush.

'There's a man who's no stranger to living.' Grace smiled and turned to check the bartender's progress.

Having always been bold, Grace had been considered quite salacious in her prime; and now in her mid-eighties, had slowed only slightly.

Looking again at Teller, she decided she was bored.

She waited patiently as the Bartender warmed a large snifter, gently pouring the amber liquid into the heated vessel. But the moment he turned his back in order to return the bottle to the shelf, Grace picked up the now warm brandy along her drink, and went to the fireplace where Teller, thawing in the comfort of the armchair heard a voice purr over his shoulder.

"Here's your drink, handsome."

Teller's forehead creased; he didn't recall a waitress when he had ordered. But when Grace stepped around the chair he smiled. Although time had left its mark, the soft firelight was kind, and the glamor of her youth still shone in her eyes.

Pushing out of the chair, Teller stood, giving a slight bow as he took the goblet. "Why, thank you Miss."

Presenting a daring smile, Grace brought the glass to her lips, her eyes dancing over the rim.

"You are *quite* welcome."

Smiling at her flirtatiousness, Teller swept an arm in the direction of the chair opposite his. "It's cold, and the fire is warm. Would you be so kind as to join me?"

She accepted, and while the storm raged outside, they spent the next few hours in the light of the fire, trading stories while playing backgammon for drinks: but eventually the logs burned down.

Teller glanced reluctantly at the window.

It looked as if the brunt of the storm had passed, for instead of blowing sideways the snow was now drifting gently, burying the cars on the street in a blanket of white.

With a sigh, Teller smiled, "It's past my bedtime Grace," moving his last piece to close out. "And you are a formidable opponent."

"And you, Sir, are a gallant man who loses well." She countered.

Teller's eyes glittered as he looked into hers. "Five out of ten Grace. That means I won fifty percent of the time."

The orange glow of the dying fire lighting her face, Grace rested a hand on his knee. "But, my good man," she laughed, "It also means you've lost as much as you've won."

Tilting his head, Teller thought how well the fire's warm light echoed her past beauty; and Grace, looking back into his eyes, smiled as if she could read his mind. Graciously accepting the truth, she removed her hand, but did so with no shame.

Teller winked, and called to the bartender for the tab.

The big man had been watching from behind the bar the entire evening, and having known Grace since he was a child, felt a familial protectiveness. But having witnessed Grace's delight he found himself pleased, as well as impressed with the stranger's style.

Throwing the bar towel over his shoulder he went to the fireplace, stepped between the two chairs and held out the bill. Grace reached up but Teller laid his hand on her wrist, gently pressing down. "No, Grace. Not tonight."

His eyes never leaving hers, he handed the barman a hundred, increasing the bartender's positive impression exponentially. Taking a step back he smiled, "I'll be right back with your change, sir." but Teller held up a resolute hand. "No, mate. Keep it. It's a small price to pay for shelter from the storm, *and* the company of a beautiful woman."

Here he paused, and asked, "But would you happen to know of a place for rent?" A fresh gust of wind rattled the door and he smiled, "It looks like winter's just kickin' in and this seems like a good town to spend it in."

The Bartender looked genuinely sorry. "No, buddy, I don't. Things get pretty tight around here in the season."

"Yeah," Teller sighed, unenthusiastically pushing himself up, and out of the comfortable chair. "They always do . . ."

Lifting his scarf from the hook on the mantle, he wrapped it around his neck. "Well," he shrugged, "I've got a room over at the New Sheridan if you hear of anything."

Holding out his hand, he smiled. "Name's Teller."

The big bearded fellow hesitated. Like all locals in hip mountain towns he held a proprietary attitude regarding outsiders. But for some reason he liked this man.

Taking Teller's hand, he smiled, "Nice ta meet ya Teller. I'm Mike." Two strong hands clasped, and as Mike released his powerful grip, Teller turned to Grace.

"And, Madame, it has been a pleasure meeting you as well. Perhaps we can do this again sometime soon." With a bow, Teller took her hand, bringing it up, brushing her fingers lightly with his lips. And while it was hard to tell in the bar's dim light, Mike was sure he detected a blush on the old gal's cheeks.

"I believe I would enjoy that very much, Mr. Teller." Grace said, reluctantly taking back her hand. "But if I may be so bold, are you interested in a house, or are you simply looking for a room?"

Teller was surprised but answered quickly.

"A house would be preferable. Why?"

"Because, my good sir," Grace smiled, "back in the forties my husband and I acquired several homes here, thinking they might come in handy in our retirement. But, as he is no longer able to enjoy that retirement, with his being dead these past twenty years, that is no longer a concern. And *I* now find myself forced to leave for Washington State next week to stay with my younger sister."

A shadow of annoyance crossed her face.

"Poor old thing, she's just not getting around as well as she used to, and has asked if I would come up and help her for a while. So, as it stands, I've recently sold all but two of the houses. One I still live in, but I believe that the one that now sits empty may suit you just fine. Would you care to see it tomorrow?"

Mike shot a look of disbelief, as a slow smile lit Teller's face.

"Grace, I would *love* to see your house."

~

And now, sitting in that very house, Kelly refilled her wine glass and looked around again at the many odd, but interesting things Teller had collected.

'Eclectic is putting it lightly,' she smiled, *'But every piece is him.'* But having no idea of what he might want to keep, or what he might throw away, she frowned, and lifted her glass to her lips.

'What would he do?'

It came to her in a flash. She knew *exactly* what he would do. He would say: "*fuck it. Pay the rent for a year and use the house as storage. Why move this shit just to store it somewhere else?"*

Smiling at the simplicity of the solution, as well as pleased in knowing he would approve, she picked up the phone and dialed Grace.

Following a pleasant greeting, Kelly explained the situation, and in the hope of placating any possible problems, offered to pay the year's lease in full.

Grace had made noises of refusal at first, but with Kelly's playful insistence, she had eventually capitulated. But at the end of the conversation, Grace asked if the two of them were parting company.

Surprised, Kelly blurted, "No! Why would you ask that?" But Grace had only laughed and said that Teller's shoes would be welcome under her bed anytime.

"It's not his shoes that take up the room." Kelly had countered.

"Well," Grace had giggled. "You know what they say about big feet."

Laughing, Kelly said goodbye, went to her desk, wrote a check for the year's rent, and tucked it into an envelope for mailing. Satisfied, she looked around the room, and went back to packing her suitcase.

= Chapter 21 =

Abbott's reaction to Tellers statement was one of disbelief while Jack just lifted his coffee cup and chuckled,

"One more on a long list."

Teller looked at him in surprise. "You're awfully cavalier about my impending death, Jack."

"Come on, Tell." Jack shrugged. "A lot of men have threatened to kill you."

"True." Teller nodded. "But this is a *little* more personal."

"I would think that *anyone* wanting to kill you would be considered personal." Jack countered.

Tellers lips tightened. "You're funny . . ."

Jack just smiled and turned his pale blue eyes to Billy. "What do *you* think, Chief?"

Billy sat quietly, his weathered face in peaceful repose. So much so, Jack thought he might be asleep. But then his bright black eyes popped open, striking in their vibrancy.

"I think the boy is poisoned by hate. And hatred is a dangerous thing."

"You're stating the obvious." Teller said as he spun in his seat, "And that wasn't the right question Jack. The question *should* have been, what do you think will *happen?*"

"Ahhh," Billy smiled. "As always, straight to the heart of the matter." Standing, he shook his cup and looked at them one by one. "But that is another issue altogether . . . Let me warm this and I will finish telling you of Sebastian when I return. *Then* we will talk of this new problem." He walked through the door, the bell rung, and as the screen door squeaked closed, Abbott looked at it, then turned to Teller.

"Do you *really* think Ben is coming to kill you?"

"Oh yes, Abbott." Teller nodded, "I do, and for two reasons. One, the kid is a fucking loony. And two, as I am *quite* sure James is none too happy with me right now, I am equally sure he would be more than pleased to have me out of the picture altogether, and the fact that he bothered to call and warn me at all indicates I should take this *very* seriously." But before Abbott could respond, Billy returned, holding the dented stainless-steel coffeepot. Holding it out, Teller declined while Jack held his up for a refill.

Billy poured, and set the carafe on the floor.

"Now," he said, settling into his chair, "Where were we?"

Anxious to talk about Ben, Abbott started to speak, but Teller looked at him and held a finger to his lips; then he turned to Billy. "So then, you were telling us of Sebastian and the Coyote."

"Ahhh yes . . ." Billy nodded, closing his eyes and returning to that moment so many years ago.

"I could see, even from a distance that this man displayed no greed for the coins of my family, and more importantly, the spirit of Coyote emanated strongly from the confines of the bag he held. So, I watched for a few minutes more, then, calling out to make my presence known, I stepped out of the shadows. He was surprised of course but made no attempt to hide the bag he held. This impressed me, greatly, so I made my way across the riverbed to a man who would become my friend for the next seventy years."

Teller glanced over at his companions, thinking of his chance meeting with Jack nearly three decades ago, and his more dramatic run-in with Kelly and Abbott more recently.

"Funny how fate throws people together." he smiled.

Billy gave a meaningful nod. "Some say that fate, destiny, providence, or whatever you wish to call it are all merely results of our own subconscious desires." His eyes pivoted to Teller, and he smiled. "Others say that in certain cases, Coyote is instrumental in all the above . . . but back to the story. As I said, although this young Billagaana was startled when I suddenly appeared, he made no attempt to hide the pouch or the coins he held. So, introducing myself, I asked him what he was doing here in the middle of everything, yet so far from his home."

Abbott laughed. "I bet I know what he said."

Billy waited, his smile brilliant in the shade of the porch. "Yes?"

"He said, I have no home."

Billy smiled. "Very close, Abbott, but no. He said: "In the middle of everything, how can I *not* be home?"

Teller chuckled. "That is a *much* better answer."

"Yes," Billy said. "And it was that response that was the basis for the very long friendship that followed." With warm memories in his eyes, he went on.

"I held out my hand, palm up, and with no reluctance whatsoever this young Billagaana placed the pouch in it. The boldness compelling me to such action startled me even as I held out my hand, and his lack of hesitation of placing it there surprised us both. He then laid the coin on top of the pouch but said nothing more. Now, the coin was familiar, of course, but it was the power radiating from the bag that intrigued me, for I had never felt it's like. So, excited, I shook the bags remaining contents into my hand, and along with more gold coins tumbled out the Coyote carving that you found set in the dash of Sebastian's car. I had never seen it's like before, nor had I heard of any like it until you arrived with the one from the cave." Pausing to take a drink, he looked at Teller. "May I see the one *you* carry?"

Taking the carving from his pocket, Teller placed it in Billy's hand; but as Billy's calloused fingers closed over the carving he released a soft exhale. . . suddenly, there was a gust of wind and a tumbleweed bounced up the stairs; rolling across the deck to bump against Tellers feet. Billy's eyes opened and his glittering gaze went from the coyote statue, to Teller's face, and finally, down to the western icon that nudged Teller's boots.

His eyes turning back to Teller face, his smile was enigmatic. "It is time for you to go, and to take Abbott with you as well. We will continue this story upon your return"

Reaching out, he took Tellers hand and laid the coyote gently onto Teller's palm; but maintaining a light grip he folded Tellers fingers over the mysteriously warm carving.

"You must take care, Teller, for you now possess not only the Coyote of the ancient ones, but the one that was given Sebastian so very long ago." But his somber mood abruptly vanished, and a smile burst forth. "And his car as well! *That* is *truly* a revelation . . . one that I did not expect, but one, as I said, that is quite fitting."

Jack stood and swallowed the last of his coffee. "Well if Billy says it's time to go, it's time to go." Taking the steps towards the helicopter he called over his shoulder, "grab what you need, boys. I'll do the flight check."

Shoving the coyote to his pocket, Teller looked at Abbott.

"What are you waiting for Griz? Grab some grub and some beer. We'll be gone a day or so at least."

Abbott's face split into a broad grin. "Aye, aye, Captain." he saluted. Teller laughed and waved him away, but the moment he passed through the screen door, Teller turned to Billy, all traces of humor gone and his expression deadly serious. "Look Chief, if that crazy kid *does* come down here, you be careful."

Billy smiled, and while his smile was comforting, his words were not.

"It is not me the boy wants Teller. It is you."

"Good point . . ." he nodded, "but still, be careful."

Picking up the coffee pot, he shook it. It was still half full. "Mind if I take this?"

"Just bring it back."

"Haven't I always?" he grinned, taking a step towards the stairs, but then stopped.

"Hey Billy,"

"Yes Teller?"

Before he could say more, Abbott came through the screen door, carrying a cooler in his hands and a big bag of chips between his teeth. Bumping into Teller, he mumbled, "Thxushe me," and headed towards the chopper.

Teller watched him trundle down the steps, then turned back to Billy. "Damned bears are hard to train." he grinned.

Billy chuckled as they watched Jack load the cooler and help Abbott into the rear seat. Ready to go, Jack motioned to Teller to come, and jumped up into the pilot's seat.

"Hang on!" Teller shouted and turned to Billy.

"You wouldn't happen to know anyone with a nice houseboat for sale, would you?"

Billy's smile became one of mild surprise. "Why?"

"Cause I'm thinking of spending a little more time down here and your trailer is to damn small. Besides, it doesn't float."

Billy nodded, and a brilliant smile crossed his face.

"You are a *very* fortunate man, Teller, and it seems Coyote favors you greatly."

Teller was already at the bottom of the stairs, but he stopped and turned. "And why is *that*?"

"Because a man I know down at Wahweap Marina happens to have a very large, and very luxurious boat that he would like to sell very quickly."

The corners of his mouth lifting into a suspicious smile, Teller went back up the steps and stepped into the shade of the porch. "Chief, in *my* experience, very large, and very luxurious, is almost always followed by *very* expensive."

Billy's smile was untroubled. "That, I do not know. But I will call and ask."

"You do that Billy." Teller nodded. "And if the price is right, call your grandson and see if he has secured any funds from the stones I gave him. If he has, and they are sufficient, buy it." Bounding back down the steps, he called over his shoulder. "Do it Billy!"

Billy smiled as the helicopter lifted off in a cloud of dust.

"I will do that, Teller."

His statement was seconded by a howl in the distance, and within moments the helicopter was no more than a speck in the blue sky.

"Treat them well." Billy whispered, and turned away.

= Chapter 22 =

The Cave's coordinates were logged from the last flight, so Jack didn't need to rely on Teller's tour-style directions as they flew. Consequently, before the Sun had made its march halfway across the sky the same lush, green meadow they had landed in on their first trip came into view: impressing Jack for a second time with the way the cliff wall rose majestically from the carpet of wildflowers.

Swinging low, Jack hovered over the meadow, looking for the best spot to land. But Teller couldn't wait. Flinging his door open he stepped out onto the landing rail and jumped, hitting the ground at a run and loping towards the cave that had sheltered he and Abbott on that first snowy night.

~

The blades were made their final slow 'swoops,' when Teller came walking back across the meadow: a smile on his face and a small chest under his arm. Stepping close, he handed Abbott the chest. "Griz, would you be so kind as to tuck this away somewhere safe?"

Abbott nodded, and put the chest in a cubby behind his seat.

"Thanks, old bear." Teller smiled and walked away. But as he strode through the flowering meadow he hollered impatiently over his shoulder. "Well, come on lads, our fortune awaits!" and moving quickly, he blended into the shadows of the pines. Grabbing his small pack, Abbott turned to Jack who was still flipping toggles and switches.

"Come on, Jack." he cried as he took off.

Jack watched Abbott lumber across the field, grinning as he took off his shades, pulled out his shirttail and cleaned the

127

lenses. Then slipping them back on followed the trail of bent grass and broken flowers to the caves small entrance.

Taking off his shades again, he stepped into the darkness to find Teller kneeling, examining the ground for signs of unwanted visitors. But finding nothing more than the tracks of their last visit immortalized in the dried mud, he stood, brushing away the dirt from his knees.

"Well boys," he grinned, "it's time to make history." he then turned to Abbott. "Right Griz?"

Abbott's brows rose, and he scratched his chin.

"Are you *sure* you want to be famous, Cap'n?"

"Only for my sense of style my friend," Teller laughed. "*You* are welcome the glory, but as I told you before, keep *me* out of it."

"And as I told *you*," Abbott said, dropping to his knees and sticking his head through the little entry. "If this gets out, *you* will have no choice."

"Then in *that* case, Porto's," Teller frowned, placing the heel of his boot on Abbott's behind and giving a hard shove,

"Silence must be this band of brothers' bond."

Abbott was propelled forward with a grunt; only to be brought to an abrupt halt as his waist hit the constricted opening . . . now wedged half in and half out, he struggled as he listened to Teller's muffled laughter.

Jack shook his head. "Jesus, Tell, sometimes you can be such a dick . . . now how are *we* supposed to get in?"

Grinning, Teller stepped back.

"Don't worry, Jack. Bears have an amazing ability to squeeze through small passages . . . Watch . . ."

His humor increased as he watched Abbott's legs kick, digging in the dirt for purchase while his upper torso squirmed and twisted, working himself further into the cave while the muted resonances of his extensive, and creative, cursing echoed within; but Teller was proven right. Abbott finally managed to squeeze through.

Breathing hard in the darkness, Abbott rolled onto his back, forcing his breathing to slow as his irritation increased. But with his aversion to confined spaces quickly overriding his anger, he was soon looking longingly at the circle of light that was the caves opening. Suddenly the entry's light was extinguished as a deerskin pack was pushed through, followed by a lantern, followed immediately by Teller's face. His voice serious,he said, "Porto's, if you're gonna take up spelunking, you're gonna need to trim down a bit."

Abbott grabbed the lantern, fighting the urge to crack Teller on the head with it while Teller, seeing Abbott's anger, smiled soothingly. "Griz old chum. I was just trying to expedite our entry, *and* make my point. As far as the treasure goes, you may do whatever you want with your share of fortune, and the fame that may come. But I've told you twice. Keep *me* out of it." Picking up the lantern, he smiled sweetly, and turned to see Jack, upon clearing the entrance, roll onto his back and look up at the stalactite-covered dome.

"Wow . . ." he whispered,

Both men's eyes followed.

The lanterns yellow light created dancing shadows among the stalactites; the flecks of mica and fool's gold laced within glittering like stars to create a sparkling canopy

Teller smiled. "I fully agree Jack. *Wow.*"

Going to his knees, he stood and slung his pack over his shoulder. "Come gentlemen, let us gather our long-lost fortune and be gone from this Paleolithic deposit box."

Abbott's anger had been slowly eroded by the beauty of the glistening stalactites and what remained of his annoyance evaporated altogether at Teller's comment.

Chuckling,"Well phrased Sir, well phrased." he took a step to follow as Jack laughed from behind, "The man has a way with words, of that there is no doubt."

This being Abbott and Teller's second visit, they wasted no time exploring the main gallery but went straight to the second room.

Estebanico's skeletal remains lay as they were first discovered although now slightly rearranged due to Abbott's previous exam. However, the gourd displaying the painted image of the Aztec coyote still sat near his right hand.

"Looks like he doesn't want to let it go," Teller teased Abbott. "You should have taken it the first time when he wasn't paying attention."

Abbott picked up the gourd and spun it in his hands.

"I wanted to give us reason to return at least once more Captain. I needed the time to decide the direction of my future." Jack snuck a glance at Teller, who, acknowledging it, held the lamp up to Abbott's face.

"Would you mind elaborating on that?"

Abbott lowered himself onto the dirt, set the gourd aside, and resting his elbows on his knees, put his whiskered chin in his hands. "Captain, you would probably not understand, and it is very difficult to explain . . ." Turning his brown eyes to Teller he sighed, looking forlorn. "You see, my entire *life* has been dedicated to studying the past. I have spent *years* wandering the southwest looking for clues, insights to our history through the variances of cultures. Then, through a simple twist of fate, *you* come down a river and change my entire *life*."

Teller looked at Abbott; not sure whether he should be insulted, indignant, or proud. After all, what*ever* he had done had been unintentional. He had put no planning into the meeting, or its outcome.

"Okay," he said. "I'm either sorry or I'm not. What's your point?"

At first, Abbott looked perplexed, but then he laughed.

"No. No! The remark was not meant to be disparaging Captain! My dilemma is my own, and it is this. I need to decide whether I am going to divulge the location of our long-lost friend," he glanced over to the bones of the dead man. "Or not . . ." turning back to Teller, his expression became wistful.

"To do so would invite me into the rarified circle of men of discovery, such as Howard Carter and Harry Bingham. Garnering fame and leaving me to spend the rest of my life in academia, writing dissertations and giving lectures."

He went silent; but as his reflective mood passed, he lifted his eyes from the bones, and turned them to Teller.

"Or do I leave him to rest here, as he has for the past five centuries while I, with the help of this newfound fortune, pursue my own interests. At my leisure, with the likes of you, and Jack."

Teller looked at Jack.

"Well, one certainly *sounds* like more fun than the other."

Jack nodded, adding, "But of course that depends on your definition of fun."

"A *very* valid point, Jack." Abbott chuckled, holding out his hand to Teller. Teller laughed, reaching down to clasp Abbott's outstretched hand and pull him to his feet.

"Well, I can only say that I hope you make the right choice, Porto's, for it would be a shame to break up the Musketeers." Letting go of Abbott's hand, Teller bent to pick up the painted gourd; spinning it so the Aztec image faced Abbott. "Mischief," he grinned, "and merriment!"

Abbott's melancholy lifting, he took the gourd from Teller's hands and laughed, "All for one!" But as the words left his lips his joy faded, and his eyes dropped to where the literal bones of his dilemma lie.

With a sigh he kneeled next to the somehow still elegant remains and laid his finger on Estebanico's skeletal hand.

Bowing his head, he whispered reverently. "Rest in peace, my brave black friend, for you accomplished far more than most in your time. In my heart I always doubted that you had been slaughtered at the hands of savages, and now that I know that you were not, it makes me *very* happy."

Holding the gourd toward the grinning skull he finished.

"Your secret is safe with me and I thank you for this. It will be well used."

Teller, impressed with Abbott's heartfelt entreaty, laid his hand on his friend's shoulder.

"As I have said before, my dear Abbott, you can be quite eloquent on occasion. But what say we head back to the lake and wrap up a few minor details there?"

Abbott gave a slow nod, picking up the silver spear tip that still lay in the dirt and dropping into the gourd where it clinked among the coins. "Yes, Teller. It is time to go." But he suddenly gave Teller a worried look. "Do you think we'll have a problem with Ben when we get back?"

That very question had been weighing heavily on Teller's mind as well; he snuck a covert glace at Jack, but all he got was a grim shrug. Nodding, he patted Abbott's shoulder.

"We shall see what we shall see my friend . . . Jack, you ready to fly?" Jack nodded, but as he turned, the beam of his flashlight bounced from something beneath one of the shelves. Curious, he went over and knelt.

Something *was* back there.

Lying on his belly, he reached back and pulled out the object that had reflected the light; it was a hammered copper bracelet, encircling an ancient parchment scroll.

Teller stepped over, his curiosity piqued as well.

"Whadja find, Jacko?"

"I don't have a clue Tell," he said, handing Teller the flashlight. "but let's see . . ."

As he slipped the scroll from the bracelet, it began to tear and seeing this Abbott lunged forward. But Teller's arm shot out, and with his hand pressed against Abbott's chest, brought him to a halt. With a moan, Abbott's eyes searched Teller's beseechingly. Teller let his hand drop and Abbott took one more step, holding his breath as Jack carefully slid the scroll from its copper ring and unrolled the parchment.

A few long seconds ticked by and he shrugged. "I can't read it Tell, it's in some strange language."

Abbott, quivering with excitement, reached out and took the scroll, his eyes widening as he read.

"It's Arabic." he said softly, "And appears to be some sort of diary." But as he unrolled it further, the ancient parchment began to crumble. Abbott lightened his grip but the paper continued to disintegrate. With a gasp, Abbott put one hand underneath the curling document, desperately attempting to catch the falling pieces. But the parchment fragmented further as it touched his palm. Frozen in place, Abbott's expression was one of agonized despair as the ancient work crumbled through his fingers. Teller watched the pieces of the tattered scroll flutter to earth; and while he could not help but feel great empathy for the Archaeologist, he knew nothing could be done.

Stepping forward to tenderly remove the bracelet from Abbott's trembling hand, he squeezed the big man's shoulder. "Let the mystery rest my friend. That was just Estebanico saying goodbye."

Nodding miserably, Abbott looked down at the small pile of yellowed dust at his feet; and putting a finger to the corner of his eye brushed away a tiny teardrop as he spoke, his voice quiet, but strong. "You're right, Captain. Let's go."

But as they took their first step, a vicious crack of thunder boomed; its force rattling the earth as a gust of wind shrieked across the dome above their heads.

Another burst of thunder shook the cave, and Teller looked up to see the massive stones that were blocking the hole in the roof collapse. Jumping sideways, he reached out and yanked both Abbott and Jack to the ground, pulling them away as the rocks tumbled inwards, snapping the rungs of the ancient ladder and landing with heavy thuds, raising a cloud of dust where the three men had stood yet leaving the bones of Estebanico untouched. Again, lightening flashed, and the hidden corners of the cave were illuminated through the now gaping hole in the rock ceiling. . . Teller glanced up, instantly mesmerized by the black clouds materializing in the once blue sky: building at an incredible rate to tower into the heavens, churning as they spun; the sight both terrifying and beautiful; and shaking his head to quiet the strange electric buzz that filled in his ears and lifted the hair on his arms, Teller pushed himself up from the dirt.

Suddenly, the heavens split to form a hole: a hole that swallowed all light; and from that tear in the sky, a diffused ball of color appeared where it floated for a moment. Then, rushing through the hole in the ceiling, this strange, pulsating sphere of plasma hovered directly in front of them.

Suddenly it began to whirl and twist, spinning across the floor of the cave: changing shape until finally becoming a black waist-high tornado; its whirling eye an endless black hole filled with spinning stars.

Dancing madly across the floor, the vortex whipped and churned, first harvesting the remnants of Estebanicos diary; then, making its way to the ancient bones, the small cyclone's tail whipped back and forth across the surface of the skeleton, sucking up tatters of skin like a vacuum, pausing here and there to collect heavier material, dipping into the eye sockets of the skull to clear the tiny debris that remained. The cyclone paused as if making sure it had gathered every last bit of Estebanico's earthly remains: and with flakes of parchment and dust gathered within the funnel spinning in crazy patterns, the cyclone ran the length of Estebanico's skeleton one last time.

Done, the tail whipped once, giving a final lick; twirling back to join the cloud of dust that swirled from the caves floor. Together they pulsed, and with a final sucking sound vanished up and into a thunderous sky; leaving the three men in speechless awe.

Teller's eyes lingered on the bank of dark clouds that had birthed the phenomenon but were now rapidly dissipating; then with a sudden and brilliant flash of light illuminating its interior the last black cloud raced away, leaving only clear blue skies in its wake.

Teller smiled and thought of Coyote.

In the eerie calm that followed the three men threw puzzled glances to one another as if to verify what they had clearly seen. But as words were meaningless, they simply turned; skirting the pile of boulders that now lay bathed in the bright rays of sunlight pouring in from the hole in the ceiling: departing the cave in silence, their bond of friendship made tighter still by the supernatural experience.

And Estebanico, now free, spun into the cosmos.

Having lain undisturbed for half a millennium among the wealth he had coveted, he was now no longer bound by guardianship of these worldly baubles. For, with Coyote's intervention the men who had been led to his tomb had removed the anchor of his possessions; and in doing so, they had unchained his soul. And the cave, now empty of its treasures held only the cleansed bones of an extraordinary man who had crossed Coyote's path so many years ago.

~

The three men trudged in holy silence towards the chopper, for what was there to say? The incredible event might possibly be explained away as some sort of natural phenomenon; but each knew better. Teller most especially, as there was now no doubt who had been manipulating his life since he had walked out of Jake's office back in Moab in what seemed a lifetime ago.

Reaching the helicopter, Teller opened the dusty Bell's door, removed the small cooler, and raising an eyebrow in Abbott's direction walked over to a thick Ponderosa pine where he plopped down in its shade to rest his head against the trunks fragrant bark. Abbott, still smiling in wonder, set the illustrated gourd on the helicopters seat. Then following him into the shade, lay down in the pine-needle strewn grass; crossing his fingers over his belly to stare into the sky.

For the first few minutes no one spoke; then Teller broke the silence. "So, professor. What do you think?"

"I think I would like a beer, please." Abbott sighed.

With the comment bringing an element of normalcy back into the afternoon, Teller chuckled. "How did I know you would say that?"

"Because," Jack smiled, stepping into the shade of the tree while lighting a cigarette. "That seems to be his mantra." Flipping his lighter shut, he took three beers from the cooler, tossing one to each of them. Catching his one-handed, he gave Jack a look of reproach at the cigarette.

"I thought you quit."

Jack smiled and released a stream of smoke from the corner of his mouth. "Oh, I have. Several times. And I will again. This just seemed like an appropriate time for a smoke."

Teller shrugged and turned back to Abbott. "Well old chum," he smiled, "considering what we have just witnessed, *surely* you've something to say . . ."

Abbott simply gave a slight shake of his head, taking time to mentally phrase his thoughts. In the ensuing silence, Teller looked to Jack, who shrugged and blew a smoke ring.

But then Abbott finally spoke.

"Well, Captain," he frowned. "I see no need to divulge any of this to anyone within historical circles. It would serve no positive purpose, and there would be little, if any, proof. Particularly as there is now nothing but the bones of a large man and some empty gourds . . . without the stones, or the gold present any attempted determination would be nothing but educated conjecture."

A smile tugged at the corners of Teller's lips.

"And, there is no diary, nor written records of any sort."

Abbott's brown eyes were solemn. "No, there is nothing like that . . . if asked, I would be unable to produce verification of any kind. No," he continued, "if I were to try to submit this to any archeological society I would be put into the category of liars and charlatans seeking to expand their academic careers through wishful thinking.

And, more importantly, it would drag *you* into the picture, and you have made it *abundantly* clear that you have no interest whatsoever in any type of fame."

Teller's smile grew. "Good! You *have* been paying attention."

"Therefore . . ." Abbott smiled, and straightening his arm from his prone position to hold his can above his chest, shouted, "All for one!"

Teller's smile turned to laughter and motioning to Jack, the two men clinked their cans to Abbott's.

"And one for all!"

Jack wiped his mouth with the back of his hand, looked at the horizon and stubbed his cigarette out on the heel of his boot. Shoving the butt into his shirt pocket, he said,

"Time to go, gents."

Teller looked at Jack, nodding as he stood, and reaching down, pulled Abbott to his feet. "You've made a wise choice Griz," he said, giving Abbott's shoulder a brotherly squeeze. With that he turned and walked towards the sound of the helicopters cranking motor.

Abbott nodded, turned, and cast one last forlorn look in the cave's direction. "The only choice, really." he sighed.

~

Jack sat in the pilot's seat, shades on, while Teller stood on the rail, waiting for Abbott. The rotors whipped fiercely, creating a downdraft that pushed the grass onto its side, sending spinning petals from the spring flowers into the air where they danced across the meadow like brightly colored confetti.

Teller helped Abbott into his seat as the chopper began to lift, remaining on the rail; a smile lighting his face as he silently thanked Estebanico for the colorful send off.

"Get your ass in here Tell!" Jack shouted.

"Sure, Jack." Teller grinned, and with a final glance at the scattering petals, he slid in, pulled the door shut, and took his place as co-pilot.

Jack looked over his shades. "You ready?"

Teller reached back over his seat, slapped the Aztec coyote-faced gourd that sat in Abbott's lap, gave Abbott a thumbs up, and turned back to Jack.

"Born ready, Jack."

Jack smiled and shook his head. "Yeah," he said, pulling the joystick back. "I think you were."

The chopper lifted, banked, and sped southwest towards Billy, and the Lake.

— — ‾‾ ‾‾‾ ‾‾ — —
— — — — —
‾‾ ‾‾‾ ‾‾

= Chapter 23 =

Hanging up the phone for the second time, Billy leaned back in his office chair. It had been a busy morning.

Following Teller's request, he had first called his grandson in Tucson in order to ascertain the status of Teller's funds. Following a few pleasantries, Little Raven assured his grandfather that a sizeable portion of both the stones and coins had been sold with the monies funneled into the shell company. Therefore, if Teller so desired, he could withdraw a substantial amount of cash.

"But tell him," Junior had cautioned, "that it would be wise to invest the money into something physical. Something that may be used as a company write-off."

Billy's Hollywood smile revealed itself.

"A boat, perhaps?"

There was a pause with Junior's voice sounding intrigued.

"Yes . . .that would work, but the company would need to utilize it."

With a nod, Billy suggested, "What if it were a secondary residence?"

Sitting in his office chair, a duplicate of his grandfather's smile spread across Little Raven's face as he picked up the gold coin Teller had given him the night they had met: the very same night Teller had convinced him to meet the girls at the nightclub, which, had culminated in an amazing night with Sheila. Consequently, he now considered this coin his lucky piece. Flipping it, he caught it in the air, slapped it on the desk, and lifting his hand, his smile grew wider.

Heads.

"Yes Grandfather." he chuckled, pocketing the coin. "I do believe that would qualify. Oh, and please have Teller call me at his earliest convenience, would you?"

On the other end, Billy's smile matched Little Ravens, but for much different reasons.

"Yes, of course. He is north of here at the moment, but I believe he will want to speak with you as soon as he returns."

"I see. So he is following Coyote?"

"I am not sure who is following who, but yes."

"Is that all then?"

"Yes, Little Raven, that is all for now. I am looking forward to seeing you again. When do you think you will be up this way next?" Junior could almost feel his grandfather's smile over the phone. "Well, there *is* a beautiful old Buick in my garage that is overdue for a spin, and I would very much like to see both you and Mr. Teller again. Do you think he would mind?"

If possible, Billy's smile grew larger.

"No, I think our new partner would appreciate your delivering Sebastian's pride and joy to him."

Junior's feet dropped from the desktop, and lightly touched the floor. *Partner. . . ?*

Junior had learned not to question his grandfather: and while this was *certainly* an unexpected development, he had also learned that not *only* were his grandfather's decisions seldom up for discussion, they were rarely wrong. Regardless, the prospect of a road trip was pleasing, and getting away from Tucson for a few days would be a welcome change of pace.

"Well then. Give me a day to get ready and I'll drive up."

"Wonderful! Oh, and Little Raven,"

"Yes?"

"Don't forget to bring some of that Mesquite honey along with the company checkbook."

Junior gave a chuckle. "Yes Grandfather."

~

140

Finishing his conversation with Little Raven, Billy picked up the phone and dialed Neil, a boat broker he knew down in Phoenix, and one who handled nearly every watercraft transaction that took place on Lake Powell.

As the owner of a marina, however small it may be, Billy was privy to the gossip and rumors that spread throughout the tightly knit community, and just last week he had heard rumor of a houseboat that was for up for a quick, and discreet sale down at the Hanging Rope Marina.

The story shared by the wagging tongues, was that a high-rolling CEO from Silicone valley had tucked a luxurious houseboat away in the remote dock as a floating love nest for his clandestine romps with his mistress. Regrettably for said mogul, it was not remote enough to remain hidden from a suspicious wife nor the lens of her investigator's camera. Consequently, he was unloading it for pennies on the dollar in order to satisfy the increasing demands of his soon to be ex, and to pay off the only people who ever win in these situations: Attorneys.

~

Following the normal banter of two friends catching up on events an intense but friendly bargaining session ensued, eventually bringing the two men to a verbal agreement on the price: with the only caveat being that the boat would be motored up to Billy's dock with full payment upon arrival. With that, the deal was sealed.

The broker joked that for the price he was paying, Billy should swim down and pick it up himself. But Billy countered that Neil should be happy that neither the wife, *nor* the mistress had stuffed the body of the philandering husband in the walk-in closet and sunk the boat in revenge. So, with *that* in mind, Neil should consider himself fortunate to have the boat in his inventory at all, and therefore content with whatever profit there was to be made.

Chuckling, Neil promised to have the boat delivered by the end of the week; and, as it was already Wednesday, Billy found the bargain satisfactory. Telling Neil to give his wife a kiss, he hung up and leaned back in his chair, smiling as he lifted his coffee to his lips.

= Chapter 24 =

Glass in hand, Casey gazed through the massive window at the folds and valleys of the San Juan Mountains admiring the way the Sun backlit the higher peaks were backlit above the subtle depths of shadow that filled the valley's below.

Swallowing what remained of her wine, she turned to look at James, her expression a mixture of worry and anger. Only moments ago, she had insisted they notify the San Miguel County police of the theft, but he had refused. He just stood, hands clasped behind his back, a furious statue with eyes focused on those same snow-covered peaks.

Frustrated, she went to the liquor cabinet, grabbing a second bottle of expensive wine and flopping onto the couch, but as she remover the cork and poured, her shaking hands splashed blood-red droplets across the wrinkled photograph.

Turning from the window, James looked down at the photo: a frozen piece of time where two old friends stood in a happier past. But now the photo, like the memory it captured, was damaged beyond repair. The enormity of the loss was beginning to finally sink in; but her whining, petulant voice cut through his sorrow.

"*Why* won't you call them?" she sneered. "Are you afraid your precious standing in this bourgeois little town will be harmed?"

The cords in James' neck tightened.

Covering the distance between them in three quick strides, he snatched the glass from her hand.

"The *reason,* you stupid bitch," he snarled, leaning within inches of her face, "is that if I were to call the redneck cops

143

in any *one* of these counties, you wouldn't be visiting him in the hospital, it would be the morgue."

Casey's eyes widened in fear and she stammered, "but you could *tell* them he's not dangerous . . ." With that, her voice broke, and she collapsed into the couch's soft cushions, her shoulders shaking as she pushed her face into a pillow and began to cry.

Her tears diluting his fury, James reached down to lift her chin with his finger.

"Except that's not quite true now is it, Casey? He's taken a high caliber weapon, stolen my truck, and is on his way to kill someone. *I'd* say that's pretty *fucking* dangerous, wouldn't you?" Rattling the ice in his glass he took a step back to allow that small bit of reality to sink in.

Casey's breathing became less ragged as the shaking of her shoulders diminished; soon her weeping ceased altogether.

"You're right, James." she nodded.

Her voice still trembled, but her tone was stronger as she brushed back a stray lock of hair and looked at him through tear-reddened eyes. "But what do we do *now?*"

Infused with the relief of her recovered control, James handed her back her glass, and smiling weakly she accepted, clutching it with both hands.

Pleased with the passing of *that* small crisis, James went to the bar, scooping his tumbler through the ice while speaking over his shoulder.

"I don't know, Casey, I just don't know. I called Teller and warned him so at least Ben no longer has the element of surprise." James' lips tightened as he poured Scotch to the very rim of his glass. Re-corking the bottle he returned to the massive window. "I know Teller can take care of himself," he said to his reflection. "But he is at a *serious* disadvantage"

Gazing at the peaks, James thought back to last fall's hunting trip, and the ease with which he had taken down 1200-pound elk from a quarter mile away with the very same rifle Ben now carried.

Lifting his glass, he took an enormous drink

A shudder ran through his body that was brought on by more than just the alcohol: and as he stared at his reflection in the window, he whispered, "but I'm betting someone's going to die."

Mercifully, his voice was too low for Casey to hear.

— — ‌‍ — ‌‍ — — — — — — — —
— — — — — — — — —
‌‍ — ‌‍ — —

= Chapter 25 =

Tap, tap, tap . . . tap, tap, tap . . ..

Sleeping with the side of his head pressed against the driver's door window, Ben didn't so much hear the sound as feel the vibration against his skull.

Tap . . . tap, tap . . .

Groggily cracking open one eye, the bright morning Sun flooded Ben's retina like molten glass sending tendrils of fiery pain burning through his nervous system.

Stifling an involuntary scream at the sudden agony, his eyes slammed shut and he jerked away from the window.

Startled by the driver's reaction, the Montrose County trooper stepped back; unbuckling his holster and laying his right hand on the pistols grip while making a twirling motion with the fingers of his left.

"Roll down your window, Sir."

The troopers voice seemed to come from far away, muffled in a fog of pain and confusion: but Ben's animal sense of survival awakened, and clawing its way through his fear, a silky voice hissed, *'Open your eyes. . .'*

Doing as he was told, Ben's lids lifted, squinting at the Troopers wary expression through the glass as the madness subsided. . . and where before hatred burned, a cold, calculating rage now pulsed beneath his skin: thumping with each beat of his heart.

Holding his hand up to block the brutal light, he pressed the window switch and the glass slid away.

"Yes Sir?"

Surprised by the driver's unexpectedly calm response the trooper paused, thinking that he may have overreacted. But caution had kept him alive for many years, and in his line of work there was no room for mistakes.

Remaining wary, he took a step forward while keeping a ready hand on his pistol. Setting his boot heels in the dirt, he leaned towards the open window.

"Sir, are you alright?"

~

Walter was a grizzled veteran of the Denver Police Department; and having spent twenty-five years serving on the mean streets of the inner city had recently transferred to the Western slope; and, up to now, his life had been routine.

Not so many few months earlier he and his wife had talked of retirement and how, when the time came, they would gladly leave the city to live out their lives in a more peaceful environment. But retirement had been five long years away so the conversation had taken on the quality of just another pipe dream. But then, out of the blue, the opportunity to transfer to Montrose presented itself.

It had been an excited Walter who discussed it with his wife over dinner that night; and with her blessings he filed with his commanding officer the very next morning.

His request was accepted, and they had never looked back.

Pam was thrilled with the move.

Having grown up in the small town of Delta, she had reluctantly moved away from family and friends due only to her love for her husband, and that love demanded she follow him when his career took him to the city. And now, overjoyed with the chance to return to the less hectic, and considerably less dangerous atmosphere of a small town, she had slipped effortlessly into the role of the rural policeman's wife. While Walter, after nearly three decades of well-founded inner-city paranoia was still having difficulty adjusting to the 'Mayberry' atmosphere of rural Colorado. And now, standing on the gravel roadside next to a hundred thousand dollar vehicle with this peculiar young man at the wheel, the odd conversation with his wife that morning came back . . . Pam had been unusually quiet during breakfast, and fretful as they cleaned up. But when asked if she was okay, she had simply smiled, saying that she knew she was being silly, but would he please be extra careful today?

Her look of worry flashed through his mind as the kid set his glasses on the bridge of his nose.

~

"Yes Sir, I'm fine." Ben smiled. "I just got tired of driving last night and thought it best to pull over and get some sleep."

The boy's response was exactly right: but there was *something* slightly off in his eyes. Walter had noticed it from the beginning, but it had been ambiguous. But now, behind the eyeglasses magnification he could see it clearly.

Something was wrong.

Sensing danger on a primitive level, Walter's heartbeat increased: and while his instincts may have been dulled by the peaceful routine of the past few months, his years of training kicked in subconsciously.

Un-holstering his weapon, he took another a step back, waving the guns barrel to encompass the vehicle.

"This yours?"

"No Sir, it's my uncles."

Officer Peterson took in the custom metal-flake paint and extensive chrome that covered this obscene toy.

"Pretty good lookin' rig you got here son. Does your uncle know your cruising around in it?"

With the powerful element of survival fully engaged, Ben made an effort to look properly abashed. "No, Sir, he does not. But-"

At Ben's feigned humiliation, Walter relaxed slightly.

"No but's now, son. Why don't you just hand me the registration to your uncle's vehicle, along with your driver's license. You *do* have those with you, don't you?"

Squeezing his eyes shut against the worms that squirmed in his mind, Ben reached into his back pocket.

"Yes, Officer . . . just a minute." Tugging his wallet free, he flipped it open and held it through the window, but Walter never took his eyes off of Ben's face. Instead, he nudged the wallet with the barrel of his 45.

"Remove the license please."

Tears began to seep from the corners of Ben's eyes as he complied, and seeing this, Officer Peterson began to soften. His gentler nature assumed that they were the tears of a spoiled kid caught doing something that might affect his allowance. Against all intuition he lowered his guard and holstered his weapon.

'This kid isn't crazy, just scared. And what a way to start a morning' he thought shaking his head as he scanned the picture on the license *'to step into some rich family's problems . . .'*

"Registration please."

Ben nodded, fighting back increasing tears.

Unbeknownst to Sheriff Peterson, the tears Ben struggled to squeeze back had nothing to do with fear. They were the result of his losing battle with his grip on sanity.

Leaning across the seat, Ben reached down and popped the glove compartment, knowing that the registration lie neatly folded within a booklet containing all the legal documents and receipts that went with the vehicle. If nothing else, his uncle was an organized man. But as he reached into the glove compartment his eyes caught sight of the handgun on the floorboards that must have slid from beneath the passenger seat. It was then that he remembered that his uncle always kept a fully loaded Smith and Wesson 500 50 Caliber Magnum in the car for what he referred to as: "unforeseen eventualities."

James *loved* the movie: 'Dirty Harry.' and ever since he had seen Clint Eastwood terrorize the "punks" of the bay area, he had wanted that gun. And now, with the bigger, and if possible, even more dangerous version of that handgun within his reach, the only thing now standing between him and his rescue of Kelly was this hick fucking Sheriff. . .

Feeling as if his skull were being shredded, the demon within began viciously peeling away the thin veneer of sanity that still remained, screaming at him to just kill this smug bastard and *go- find -Teller!*

Ben pushed his tear-streaked face into the passenger seat, struggling to wrest control of his trembling hand and the desire to wrap his fingers around the pistols grip. All he need do is pull the trigger and his problems would be solved.

Somehow, he held the madness at bay, slowly withdrawing his hand from the recesses of the floorboards to reach into the glove compartment and present the booklet with shaking hands.

Walter took the paperwork from Ben's trembling hands, and while the last names matched he gave Ben and the picture on the license a long once-over for comparison. Feeling slightly better, but still obliged to follow protocol, he began to turn to his cruiser to call in for any outstanding warrants: but at the anxiety on Ben's face, compassion overcame his remaining suspicions. Lifting his hand from the now holstered weapon, he leaned into the window.

"You okay, kid?"

Walter's concern was real, but his training was second nature. So, as he laid his elbow on the window's opening he snuck a glance over Ben's left shoulder. The gleam of chrome against black on the rear seat flashed, and his professional instincts immediately kicked in.

His hand went to his holster and he took a quick step back.

"Son, I need you to-" But before he could finish the sentence, something dashed from behind the huge tank-like vehicle. Lightning quick it was across the road by the time Walter dropped to one knee and gone by the time he had drawn his gun, leveling it at the now quivering branches of sagebrush.

Slowly rising, he re-holstered his weapon and bent to pick up the driver's license and leather registration folder that he had dropped in his haste. "Just a damned coyote." he mumbled with a nervous laugh and brushing the dust from his knee. But as he handed the documents back to Ben, he noticed that all fear and confusion had vanished from the young man's eyes.

"Yes Officer." Ben said, his voice distant. "I believe it was. Those filthy things are *every*where."

The comment struck Walter as peculiar, and the feeling of dread that pricked the hair on the back of his neck intensified when he noticed that the tears that had reddened the boy's eyes earlier were gone.

They were now dry, and chillingly clear.

With his cop instincts humming, Walter slapped the legal documents in his palm as he took a step back.

"So, *where* was it you said you were headed?"

Ben's empty, intense gaze gave Walter the creeps.

"I didn't, Sir, I borrowed my uncles truck because mine is in the shop. I need to go get my girlfriend. She's in trouble."

Walters's suspicions increased. "What *kind* of trouble?"

The ease of the lie came with the lack of conscience that all psychotics display. "She's having trouble with an old boyfriend. I need to go pick her up and bring her back to Telluride to stay with my family for a while . . . at least until we get married."

'*Dysfunctional family*' Walter thought. *I knew it.*'

The voice of the city cop in him said that something was fishy here. And while the voice of the rural sheriff, close to retirement, suggested that he let it go, his suspicions argued that he not. But just as he decided go to his cruiser and call it in, his wife's worried smile over blueberry pancakes flashed through his mind: and it was with that image that Walter decided that the boy's explanation was sufficient. His suspicions seemed unfounded, with this no more than a domestic affair he wanted no part of. . . By all appearances the kid had legitimate possession of the family vehicle and had wisely pulled over to get some rest rather than drive.

Holstering his Smith and Wesson M&P.40, Walter snapped the keeper strap, handed Ben back his license and registration, and touching the brim of his Trooper hat with two fingers, took a step back.

"Have a nice day Mr. Carson. And good luck with your girlfriend." Turning on a polished boot heel, Walter walked back to the cruiser.

Ben's facade crumbled.

His mind twisting violently, he strangled the steering wheel as the taillights of the cop car flashed red and the right rear wheel spun in the dirt of the roadside; throwing up dust and sending a shower of gravel that rattled against the Humvee's chrome grill. The cacophony ringing in his ears like the chimes of hell.

— — ·· ··· ·· — —
— — — —
·· ··· ··

= Chapter 26 =

At the sound of the helicopter in the distance, a smile began to shine in the shade of Billy's cowboy hat; and as the chop of the blades bouncing through the canyon walls grew louder he squeaked open one eye.

Abbott leaned on the porch rail, excitement lighting his face

Billy's smile grew larger still, and that smile was one of immense satisfaction. He had lived a very long, and very interesting life, and it seemed as if the events of these past few weeks were the culmination of a story long in the telling: for his was the bloodline of a family whose lineage could be traced to the beginning of the world, and the emergence of the mud people. And now, he was the last of the shaman. For the world had moved on, and it seemed his kind was no longer needed. He was simply a dream of the past: floating away on the river of time . . .

Ahhh, but then a familiar thought surfaced. It was one he had considered many times over these many years; and was yet to be answered to his satisfaction. Was it *he* that floated upon times waters; or was he left to stand upon the banks shifting sands as time flowed past . . .

He chuckled. Perhaps *that* was a question *with* no answer.

Whatever the resolution, both his son and his grandson had been able to change with times extraordinary turnings; and for that, he was glad. For in order to survive one must adapt. *This* was a lesson that had been forced upon his people, and it was one his people had learned. Time was long, or short, depending on which end of the experience you were on: and history was full of those who had failed to see the difference.

~

From the moment of the Billagaana's arrival, the world of the People had plummeted into a state of unbalance. For the white man's greed provided no equilibrium. Their appetite for the treasures of the earth was endless: and they gave *nothing* in return. But all things have purpose, even the inexplicable. And as these bewildering men were beyond comprehension, because Coyote's ways were also ways of chaos he found these new and ignorant men to be a source of endless amusement. And by leading the black Spaniard to Hawikuh, Coyote had placed these strangers' wealth into the hands of Billy's long-dead ancestors. And in doing so provided the circumstance that had helped to right the imbalance. *'Yes.'* Billy smiled. History was littered with those who had failed.

It was with this thought the helicopter appeared; blowing his musings away in a cloud of dust.

Waving that dust from his face with his battered hat, Billy stood and made his way to the edge of the porch in order to greet the arrival. And watching the strange, insect-like craft settle, he smiled yet again. *Yes,* he thought. Once out of balance, harmony was difficult to re-establish, and the Gods seemed slow to act. But Coyote bringing Teller into his life had been proof that the scale of time was much different for the Gods. And man, despite his impetuous nature, was forced to learn patience.

Suddenly, the door flew open, revealing a dust-shrouded Teller. He stood for a moment, then leapt to the ground, the deerskin pack slung over his shoulder and the smile of a reprobate shining in his eyes.

Chuckling, Billy understood why Coyote had chosen him. They were *very* much alike.

~

Immediately on Teller's heels came Abbott, his grace belying his large size, clutching what appeared to be a gourd.

Billy laughed aloud at the sight. They made an unlikely, but perfect pair. Again, Coyote had chosen well.

"Hey Chief!" Teller shouted as he stomped up the stairs, pulling the dusty, and slightly dented coffee pot from the pack on his shoulder, handing it to Billy as if presenting a rare gift. "Here you go. Don't let anyone say that I am not a man of my word."

Billy accepted with aplomb. But Teller, his grin at Billy's expression turning serious set his pack in the chair and asked, "Any sign of the kid?

Billy had no opportunity to either thank Teller for the coffee pots return or answer his question as Abbott marched past them both without a word, bumping Teller aside and dropping the gourd into Billy's rocker as he marched through the screen door, cold beer on his mind.

Frowning at being jostled, Teller watched the screen swing shut. But then his grin returned. "Well, the man *does* have his priorities, I'll give him that . . ."

Turning back to Billy, he asked again, "So, what's the word?"

Billy didn't answer as his eyes went to the gourd in the chair. *'Ahh . . . another piece of the puzzle.'* But gradually bringing his attention back to Teller, shook his head.

"I've heard nothing during your absence. But do you really think the young man is capable of such action?"

Before Teller could speak, Abbott banged back through the screen with a glorious smile and handed him a beer.

Gratefully accepting, Teller popped the can and took a dust-clearing swallow. "Absolutely, Chief." he smiled. "That kid is crazy as a shithouse rat, and he sure has a bug up his ass regarding me." His eyes lit as a half-smile crossed his face. "But it seems that bug has migrated north and is now nibbling on his brain stem."

Taking another drink, he turned his grin to Abbott.

"What's *your* educated opinion on Ben's mental stability Griz?"

Abbott crushed his empty can and opened another.

"I sadly concur, Captain. Shithouse rat crazy."

Teller gave a nod. "And there you are, Billy. A second expert diagnosis." Abbott was chuckling as Jack walked up the stairs and into the tail end of the conversation.
Nodding to Billy, he looked to Abbott and held out his hand. Abbott grinned, and filled it with a cold can. Nodding his thanks, Jack turned to Billy.

"As I recall, Billy," Jack said popping his beer, "You mentioned something being wrong with the kid when I picked him up."
Billy's black eyes glittered. "Yes, Jack, I did. I felt something dark in his soul. At first, I thought it might have been Coyote's influence. But I now realize that something far much more dangerous is in play here. Coyote may have touched the boy, but the moment the window in between worlds opened something black crawled through and linked with an existing weakness within." Suddenly a chill breeze blew across the porch and the three men looked at him.
He shrugged, not helplessly, but with a sense of inevitability.

"But I fear there is little I can do if he has let the darkness win."

Swallowing the last of his beer, Teller crushed the empty can and turned to his companions "Well then." He said. "I suggest we keep a sharp eye out. Jack, hand me your phone please."

— — -- ---- -- — —

— — — — —

-- ---- --

= Chapter 27 =

Out of habit, William Gaagii Knowles came to a full stop, looked left, and then right: but there was nothing to see. The empty highway was nothing more than a ribbon of faded asphalt stretching across a desolate landscape.

Pulling away from the gas station and back onto the two-lane road, he adjusted his rearview mirror and watched the little reservation town of Kayenta slip into the distance.

Once gone, he turned his eyes back to the horizon.

The vast panorama of the Navajo Nation always stirred something deep within the recesses of Williams' ancestral memory: and as the wind blew through the open windows he could hear the faint strains of a wooden flute concealed in its song. It was a song that matched the pulse of his heart as it beat out the rhythm of two hundred years of suffering.

'This land was not always a cage,' he thought. *'At one time, this was our home.'*

Blinking back the moisture forming in the corner of his eye, William aimed the hood of the massive car towards the spires of Monument Valley and laid his weight into the gas pedal. The wind picked up as the beast began to roar: and the music of the flute was lost.

Pushing the in-line, eight-cylinder, 320 cubic inch motor to its full potential the speedometer needle quickly passed eighty, and the towering red monoliths that had been the backdrop of so many old movie westerns rushed towards him. Hanging his arm out of the window, he imagined John Wayne galloping along beside him, leading the 54th Calvary as they chased a whooping band of heathen redskins towards their inevitable doom.

Extending his arm, Little Raven leveled an imaginary Colt 45. And taking careful aim, a bittersweet smile touched his lips as he uttered one simple word. "Pow!"

In his fantasy, smoke puffed, and the King of the cowboys clutched his chest, tumbling from his horse to be trampled into the dirt beneath the flurry of hooves that charged from behind.

Shouting, "Take that Pilgrim!" William watched the ghosts of the past ride off into the wind: and in that wind the sound of the flute returned, his pain softening as the spiritual sorrows of the past drifted away in the imaginary smoke.

With this small, personal exorcism complete, William took his foot from the gas pedal and coasted to a stop.

It was a beautiful day he decided, *far* too nice not to be one with the sky. So, pushing the big chrome button in the middle of the dash, William smiled as the top folded back into its platform behind the rear seat to reveal the great expanse of blue above. With the sun on his face, he put the car in gear, rolled back onto the empty highway, and reached down to press the volume button on the new stereo that he had taken the liberty to have installed in the trunk of the old Buick.

It was a multi-disc CD player, and the sound coming through the Bose speakers that were cleverly hidden in six different locations was simply amazing. And as the intro to Pink Floyd's classic song, "Money" came through the speakers, he thought back to the clunky eight-track car stereo that had been the latest thing in automotive sound in the first car he had owned.

"We've come a long way baby" He grinned as the car vibrated to: "Boom, boom ba boom boom ching! Boom boom ba boom boom ching!"

'How fitting,' he laughed, and with the thumb of one hand tapping against the steering wheel he reached over to pat the briefcase that held the cash from the sale of the coins and stones Teller had left with him.

Junior was sure that Teller would appreciate the enhanced sounds, as well as the ability to access satellite radio stations since he had also paid for a year's subscription to Sirius radio. His only concern was that he had been forced to remove the original radio to make room for the new equipment. But as it fit nicely into the original space, *and* he had gone to great effort to locate a somewhat retro looking unit, he figured the trade-off was worth it, and trusted that Teller would feel the same. But just to cover all contingencies, he had made sure the installer put the original radio in a box and placed it in the trunk next to the spare.

So now, with the top down, and the wind blowing through his hair, he sang along.

"Money! It's a crime. Share it fair-ly but don't take a slice of myyy pie!" As he sang, Junior noticed a large shadow crossing the gleaming hood. Looking up, he smiled.

Against the incredible blue of the southwestern sky, a Golden Eagle soared, its flight matching exactly the speed of the classic automobile.

Taking both hands from the wheel, William Gaagii Knowles turned his face to the Sun and held out his arms as if to embrace the magnificent bird.

"Lead on Brother! There is still hope!"

The Eagle screamed and wheeled North.

Laughing, Little Raven stepped on the gas, chasing the bird down the shimmering black ribbon.

— — -- ---- -- — —
—— —— — —— ——
-- ---- --

= Chapter 28 =

Kelly had finally finished unpacking all of the same things she had packed up before her conversation with Grace.

Looking at the now empty boxes stacked next to the door she glanced up at Teller's wall clock. Checking her phone for the second time in twenty minutes she grumbled,

Why hasn't he called?

Frowning, she flopped back onto the couch, her frustration slowly building into anger. Just then the phone rang.

Snatching it up, she growled, "Where *are* you?"

"Hey, Kell. Are things alright up there . . .?"

"Yes. . ." she answered, the tone of his voice put her feminine suspicion on immediate alert.

"Why? What's wrong?"

"Nothing serious. Have you heard from James?"

Now her anger was replaced with apprehension.

"No. Should I have? Tell, what's wrong?"

Teller had somehow hoped that he might avoid telling her about Ben but could see now that there was very little chance of that happening.

"No Kell. Truthfully, I would have been surprised if you had."

She allowed only a moment of silence, and asked, "what's up, Tell?"

Teller smiled and sighed at the same time. Women. Somehow, they always know . . .

Standing, he walked down the steps and away from the crew, slipping into the shade of the chopper while trying to sound nonchalant. "Small glitch in plans babe, I've got a few things I need to do before I can come up and get you.

Abbott, Jack, and I just got back from Estebanico's cave." A chill ran up his spine as he recalled the numinous event, but he shook it off.

"So, short story is all financial elements are now in play, but I was hoping you wouldn't mind holding off a day or so before joining me." He paused, knowing full well that what he was about to say would not go over well.

"But I want you out of Telluride."

Now her anxiety was tinged with suspicion.

"Why's *that*?"

Realizing there was no way that he could dance around this ugly turn of events, he leaned against the helicopter and slid down the smooth body.

"It's that little shit, Ben." He said, running his fingers through his hair. "James called me with a bit of disturbing information."

Kelly relaxed, but only because he was confiding in her.

"Disturbing in what way?" she asked.

Teller squeezed his eyes tight and rubbed his forehead.

"Disturbing in a pyscho killer stole a car and is on his way to murder you kind of way."

Kelly digested the statement in utter silence, which disturbed Teller more than anything else she could have done: and just as he was about to speak she shouted, *"What!"* However, Teller, being who he was, couldn't help but find humor in the situation.

"It seems your wannabe boyfriend has finally slipped a gear and decided to win your heart by eliminating the competition."

"That's *not* funny, Teller!"

"Everything's funny sweetheart." He replied, pushing himself back up the slick aluminum body of the chopper to head back towards the store. "Look Kell, the kid's a loon, granted, but he's nothing I can't handle. I just don't want you anywhere near here."

Kelly was not *worried*. She was *angry*.

"That is *bullshit* Teller! I am *not* going to sit *here* while you're down *there!*"

Teller went up the steps and into the shade of the porch holding the phone to his ear. "You are absolutely right Kell. You're *not* going to sit up there. You're going to go down to Durango and wait till this thing blows over."

"Durango? Why Durango?"

"Because it's safe, Willie's there, and it's a straight quick shot with the chopper." Turning to Jack, he asked, "how long to get to Durango from here?"

Kelly could hear muffled voices in the background and a few seconds later Teller came back on the line.

"Jack says he can get there in a couple of hours, so I'm going to call Willie and tell him you're coming. I'm also going to call the Strater Hotel and book you a suite for the week. So, what I want you to do is get down there and hang out until you hear from me." He laughed, "Hell Kell, enjoy yourself. Willie can be a real hoot if you overlook his proclivities."

That garnered a chuckle from Jack.

Kelly had already decided a stay in a nice room at the Strater would be a welcome relief from this lonely house; but the comment regarding 'proclivities' raised her antenna.

"What's *that* supposed to mean?"

"Nothing babe, it means nothing. Willie's a great guy, and he'll show you a good time."

She heard talking in the background and Teller laughed.

"Jack says to go The Lost Dog, ask for Kip and tell him his dad wants him to prepare for a homecoming party and to invite the girls. Oh, and to tell Willie to re-load his cannon."

Now she was *completely* baffled.

"And just what in the hell is *that* supposed to mean?"

"I don't have a clue, Kell, but Jack says do it, so do it."

"Okay, Tell . . ." she said, massaging her forehead with her fingertips. "Just be careful."

"I will Kiddo," he chuckled, "just like always."

"That's *not* very reassuring."

"No, but it's gotten me this far. Get moving. I'll call you tomorrow night at the Strater. Be there!"

He hung up.

Kelly hit the 'off' button and closed her eyes.

She was angry, and worried as well. But he was right; he *had* always managed to survive. But as she thought about Durango, and a suite at the Strater, a loving smile touched her lips.

"That son of a bitch . . .."

= Chapter 29 =

Teller hung up and turned to Jack.

Eyes closed, he sat in the rocker with a half-smile on his face, his daydream in full force: only *this* time, his new helicopter was ruby red.

"Hey Jack' Teller said, giving the rocker a kick. "Didn't James put you up at the Strater when you first came down here with Ben?"

A lengthy pause ensued, and a self-satisfied smile crossed Jacks face before he opened his pale blue eyes.

"Yeah, Tell, he did. A very *expensive* suite. Why?"

Teller gave a sly smile. "You think you could re-book it?"

He slowly quit rocking and his eyebrows rose; his smile shifting from daydream to the weighing of favors that might be accrued for later collection.

"Under James' name and using his credit card no doubt."

"Well," Teller shrugged, "with his credit card anyway."

Jack leaned forward, and took his wallet from his pocket, thumbing through multiple scraps of paper; each bearing a women's phone number until he finally found a piece of hotel stationary with a short sentence followed by a longer sequence of numbers. Written in a flowing, feminine hand it was tucked in amongst a few dollar bills.

"Ahh," Jack nodded. "*Here* it is . . ."

Seeing the pile of scraps scattered in Jack's lap, Teller laughed. "I knew you were good for more than just borderline criminal acts, Jackie boy. But I must ask, how did you get *those* particular numbers?'"

Jack the slip of paper between his thumb and forefinger and waved it back and forth. "Insult me if you will, but sparing you the dirty details, I convinced the desk girl I needed them the night I checked in. However, I *was* forced to promise her things I've yet to deliver . . . So," he said, bequeathing a devilish smile, "it's going to cost you."

Teller's eyebrows rose.

"Cost me? *Cost* me? Jack, I've made you a rich man and *now* you're trying to squeeze me for small change?"

Jack added a hint of sleaze to his lowlife smile.

"Well, *yesterday* you may have been generous, but what have you done for me *lately?*"

Turning a disappointed eye to Billy and Abbott, Teller sighed and shook his head sadly. "And *I* have the poor judgment to call this ungrateful ne'er-do-well a friend."

Abbott nodded in commiseration. "It is indeed a sad situation Mon Capitán, and you have my condolences. Perhaps you should seek a better class of friends."

"Thank you Grizzly," Teller nodded. "I shall take that under advisement. But in the meantime, *Mr.* Hawkins, would you be so kind as to give the hotel a call and reserve a suite for the next two weeks?"

Jack held up his phone with one hand while wiggling the slip of paper with the credit card numbers in the other.

"Say *please* . . ."

Teller's eyes went cold.

"Do you *really* wish to be pauperized so soon?"

Jack's grin turned to a frown, and as he dialed he muttered, "You're a hard man, Teller."

— — ··-- ---- -- — —

— — — —

··- ---- --

= Chapter 30 =

Kelly fell back onto the couch still clutching the phone.

What could have *possibly* happened to make Ben want to kill Teller? She considered calling James but immediately thought better of it. Really, what would she ask?

Drumming her fingers nervously on the tabletop, an idea came to her and she began rummaging through the pile of paper on the coffee table, searching for the card Carlton had given her the previous night. For a brief moment she worried she might have thrown it away, but finding it, she punched in the numbers.

"Hello?"

"Hi, Carl? This is Kelly."

"Miss Rowen!" Carl stammered, "this *is* a surprise . . . What can I do for you?"

Pushing a lock of hair from her eye Kelly leaned further back into the plush pillows. "Well," she cooed. "For starters you can quit calling me Miss Rowen. It's Kelly."

"Okay . . ." Carl said. "How may I help you, *Kelly?"*

"Have you talked to James lately?"

Kelly could almost feel the cold silence.

"No, I have not. Mr. Carson and I are no longer on speaking terms. He made that *quite* clear when he fired me." But then a laugh came over the phone, muffled as if it were coming from a small, enclosed space. Puzzled at first, she suddenly recognized the audio imagery.

He was talking into a glass.

"Carlton." she teased, "Are you drinking?"

"Yes, Miss Rowen," he replied, his voice regaining its clarity. "I am. But no more than the situation requires. I am in my office, excuse me, my *former* office, packing up the last of my personal belongings and preparing to leave this soul-sucking town." The clink of ice dropping into a glass punctuated the statement.

"I see . . ." Kelly giggled, "and may I ask *when* you intend on leaving?"

Taking another sip of the expensive Scotch he had lifted from the liquor cabinet in James' private office, Carl held it up as if in toast. "I shall be leaving forthwith and posthaste!" Kelly laughed, and it was music to Carl's ears.

"And just where would one find that on a calendar?"

"One moment," he said, the words working around the ice in his mouth. "Let me check." a moment of silence followed, and his voice returned. "It appears that would be tomorrow." Kelly had never seen this side of Carl's personality, and she rather liked it. "Well, Carl, would it be too bold of me to ask where you might go?"

Puzzled by her interest, Carl was also intrigued.

"No, not too bold, but I'm afraid I am unable to tell you."

Now Kelly was intrigued as well. "Really? And why not?"

Carl set down his glass, placing it exactly twelve inches diagonally from the corner of his desk, and while he was putting up a bold front, the melancholy in his voice was plain. "Because, Miss Collins, it now seems I have nowhere inparticular to go."

Carlton couldn't see, but Kelly was smiling.

"Well, Carlton, I may be able to help you with that little problem. How'd you like to drive me to Durango?"

Carlton's melancholy was suddenly supplanted with hope.

"Drive you to Durango? Me? Why?"

"Because, Carl, I need a ride. And if you've no better plans, then why not?"

It took him all of one second to consider her offer. She was right. He had nothing better to do, so why not?

With his future suddenly, and unexpectedly, much brighter, a smile of optimism lit his face, and he stuffed the cork back into the bottle. "Well then, what time would you like me to pick you up?"

Kelly smiled, and shook her head. Men were *so* easy.

"Pick me up at nine and we'll have breakfast. And Carl, could you do me a favor?"

"Of course, Miss Rowen. What would that be?"

"Have you heard anything about Ben?"

Carlton's brow creased. "No, nothing in particular, but then I'm not privy to family affairs. May I ask why?"

She hesitated, unsure how much to reveal: but curious as to what he might *not* know she asked, "Well, did you know he was in the hospital?"

"Yes, I heard. Didn't Mr. Teller have something to do with that?" Kelly frowned at the implication. "Yes, he did, but his reasons were well founded."

"Oh, I'm sure they were." Carl said. "The kid's a prick."

Kelly blinked in surprise. Ben had always seemed so quiet and kind.

"Really?"

"Yes. Really." Carl said. "He hid it well when it served him, but there was always something off about him. Very much like his father. *And* his fucking uncle for that matter. Excuse my language Miss Rowe- Kelly."

Kelly said nothing. She had never really thought about it. But now that Carl mentioned it . . .

"Are you still there, Miss Rowen?"

Snapping back to the present, Kelly nodded. "Yeah, Carlton, I'm still here . . . so, do you think you can find any information regarding where he is?"

Carlton chuckled, smiling a wicked smile.

"Miss Rowen, as I mentioned, my access is primarily to financial interests, not personal affairs. But I'll see what I can do." Tucking the bottle into the top desk drawer, he pushed it closed, shut his briefcase, and rolled the carved oak chair away from the desk.

"So, I'll see you at your place tomorrow about nine?"

Kelly was still distracted by Carl's comment concerning Ben. Maybe Teller was right all along. God. That would typical, but she'd *never* admit it to him.

"Yeah . . . nine's perfect Carl, I'll see you then." Hanging up, she relaxed a little. Teller *could* take care of himself, and some time in a nice hotel would be the perfect balm for the insanity of these past few weeks. Yes, she smiled. Getting away might be *just* what she needed.

~

The coffee grinder went off at exactly seven.

Kelly preferred to use the grinder as her alarm since it served two purposes: first, the sound was more agreeable, and second, it created that moment of overused phrases, 'Wake up and smell the coffee." For some reason that saying never failed to amuse Teller; and the thought of his delight made her smile. She lay thinking of him for a few seconds more, then, with a jaw-cracking yawn threw back the covers; swinging her legs over the edge of the bed, scrunched her toes into the rugs soft pile, and padded into the kitchen.

The first rays of dawn streamed through the big bay window; lighting the worn Oak planks of the floor in a pool of warmth. Stepping into it, she looked out at the sun on the mountain peaks. It was going to be a beautiful day. Her smile harmonizing with the brightness of the new morning, she took a clean cup from the dish drainer, poured coffee, added honey and little milk, and headed to the bathroom.

Twenty minutes later the wooden door swung open and Kelly emerged through a billowing cloud of steam: clean, refreshed, and naked but for the towel that wrapped her hair.

Leaving wet footprints down the hall and across the kitchen floor, she poured a fresh cup of coffee; cradling it in both hands as she went back into the sunlight that streamed through the window. It *was* a beautiful day but there were things to do. Turning reluctantly from the warm sun, she went down the hall light of step.

Her step was light, and for several reasons. The first was that she was leaving Telluride . . . the town seemed oppressive since her confrontation with James, and the house seemed exceptionally lonely in Teller's absence. Bringing the cup to her lips, she took a sip as she looked around.

'I don't think the guy realizes just how much space he takes up . . .' Releasing a loving sigh, she fluffed her hair and dropped the towel, kicking it through the bathroom door as she headed to the bedroom.

Slipping on a pair of cotton panties, she pulled on her jeans, took a shirt from the closet, and giving a quick turn in front of the full-length mirror, allowed herself a quick smile of approval. "Not bad." she chuckled, taking her suitcase and tossing it on the bed.

Ten minutes later, packed and nearly ready to go, she brushed her hair back, twisted it a few times and it into a high crowned ponytail as she went to the dresser. A slight frown touched her lips as she hesitated, then opened the bottom drawer. There, hidden beneath her winter sweaters was the pistol that Teller had given her some time back.

A small caliber derringer.

~

At the time, Kelly felt it only natural to ask him where he had gotten such a cute little gun. But he had danced around the question trying his best to change the subject.; but his avoidance only increased her curiosity, and badgering him until he relinquished, he finally told her that he had procured it from a hitchhiker that he had picked up outside of some little town in Utah long before they had met. Pressing him for details, he had just smiled, and told her to put on her jacket and come with him. She had done as he asked, but they both knew that the matter was far from settled.

She smiled at the memory.

It had been a perfect fall day. The sky was a flawless blue, Teller silent as they drove through mountains awash in color; winding up the old highway and over the pass to an abandoned Marble quarry on the other side where a half-century of excavation had left a hideous gash in the mountain; its only use now was as a practice range for the locals.

Parking the truck, Teller had pulled a few empty cans from the bed, set them up on bullet-riddled log ten feet away, then loading the pistol had put it in her hand, pressed himself against her rear and resting his chin on her left shoulder.

Lifting her arm at the elbow, he pointed her towards the target. "Just squeeze." he had whispered.

Giving him a peck on the cheek, she smiled, "I bet you say that to all the girls."

His breath warm on her neck, she could feel his smile as he wrapped his hand loosely around hers to put a gentle pressure on her finger. "True," he chuckled gently in her ear, "But I pack a *much* more impressive weapon."

The trigger clicked, and the can went spinning.

Her grin growing, she turned her cheek to his. "But why are the cans so close?"

Teller had placed his palm under her elbow, gradually raising her arm and aiming the little pistol a second time.

"Because, my dear, this is a short-range firearm. This little popgun is only good for close encounters with the dangerous kind." Squeezing her finger delicately, the can went flying.

Lowering her arm, but still holding her hand, he turned her face to his. "I want you to have this just in case you ever need it. But remember, this thing is *only* good close in. You've got two shots, and within ten feet, if you're quick, you can get both off and probably hit whatever you're trying to hit. Aim for the chest. That's your biggest target and one hit'll slow 'em down. But never, ever, fire this unless you have no other option, and then aim to kill."

"Except for practice." she said, frightened by his intensity.

He re-loaded. "Except for practice."

After shredding the last of the empty cans, Teller emptied the spent shells and went to the cooler in the truck for another six-pack. "We still have a half- box of shells," he said. "Let's try a few more before we lose the light."

Taking a seat in the scattered shade of a stout Aspen that had managed to find purchase in the loose rubble of the pit, he popped two beers, leaned back, and patted the ground next to him. "Have a seat and empty a target."

Taking him up on his offer she sat and leaned her head against his shoulder. "So, where *did* you get this?" She remembered explicitly the smile that had crossed his face as he lifted his beer.

He was returning from visiting an old friend in Idaho, he had told her. A trip made in order to road-test the 1950 Chevrolet he had just restored; and, as it needed some break-in highway miles he figured Idaho was as good a destination as any. Here he had leaned his head back against the tree, his expression dreamy. It was late summer, he said, and the creeks were running clear, the trout were hungry, and the Chevy ran like a dream. But, after three weeks on the road he was ready to sleep in his own bed again. So, pleased with his car, and tired of fish, he was on his way home. But then he had laughed, saying that even alone fate can often be a funny companion. And in the shade of that lone Aspen, he told her the tale.

~

He had been driving the old frontage road east of Grand Junction: winding along with the bends of the Colorado River when he came across a fellow walking along the shoulder of the road: dressed in an expensive, but worn suit, and carrying nothing but an old valise.

Curious, Teller had pulled over to offer a ride.

At first, the man declined. But seeing Teller's conspiratorial smile of kinship, the once well-dressed tramp accepted; the only stipulation being that they stop at the nearest liquor store. A request that Teller was more than happy to fulfill.

Soon they were tooling along the old highway laughing and telling lies. Spirits grew high as the miles passed, and eventually Teller's curiosity got the better of him.

Gently questioning his rider for the reason he was on this lonely stretch of road, the man confessed he was on his way to Vail, where he had once been a member of the police force. At that Teller chuckled. Now he *had* to hear the rest of the story. And, as if living proof of the old adage: 'You can't judge a book by the cover,' the fellow proved to be both articulate and thoughtful, despite his dusty jacket. And so, as they cruised the old two-lane blacktop, his passengers story unfolded with as many turns as the bends of the river they followed. He had moved to Aspen in the late sixties: living the crazy blur of those heady rock and roll days of the 70's: that short, sweet period before the Roaring Fork Valley became a developer's wet dream, and the town had been turned into semi-private club for the filthy rich. He even told of how, during these wild times that he had voted for Hunter S. Thompson when he had run for the Sherriff of Aspen under the "Freak Ticket" in a glorious, yet doomed bid to save the soul of the town. Losing the election by a hair.

Yes, the times they were a-changing, to quote Dylan, and fun was being re-defined by the wealthy. And, as if more proof were needed, along with this influx of rich assholes, the price of real estate was rising as quickly as the tides of change; the resulting high water washing the working classes, as well as some long-time residents, down-valley to the more affordable towns of El Jebel and Carbondale, all the way to Glenwood Springs. Here the dusty tramp had paused, saying *he* had been at a crossroads as well.

For years he had served as the dogcatcher for the town of Aspen. But with the skyrocketing prices of rising real estate, a dogcatcher's salary could no longer pay the rent. And, to add to his woes he was suffering from an existential dilemma as well. . . He had come to *despise* these new out-of-state residents for their absurd desire to remake *his* town into some elitist hip fantasy, for it reflected their complete disconnect from reality. But the final straw, he had told Teller, occurred one morning upon his arrival to work.

He felt it the moment he had stepped from his truck. Something was amiss, but he couldn't quite put his finger on it. Then it struck him. It was the silence. Normally on hearing his truck arrive, the dogs would go mad with joyful barking. But *this* morning it was different. *This* morning, the only sound was the chirping of a few birds. Worried, he made his way cautiously to the back of the building where the bizarre sight that greeted him explained the silence.

The chain-link fence that had once held the impounded animals had been pulled down and now lay stretched across the compound with a severed piece of climbing rope still attached to one of the upper bars.

Staring in shocked puzzlement at the scene before him, he noticed a piece of paper fluttering in the morning breeze, taped to the only post still standing.

Going to it, he peeled it from the post and unfolded it.

It read, "Free the gods! They cannot be caged! Sorry, dyslexia. I meant dogs. Signed, Heyduke."

Folding the note and shoving it into his pocket he took a final look at the twisted fence, kicking the six feet of frayed rope that lay at his feet as he shuffled across the pavement.

Pulling the office door closed, he flopped into his desk chair, took the note from his pocket.

As he re-read it, he began thinking about what had happened. And the more he thought about it, the more he decided it was a sign, a boot in the ass from the powers that be that it was time for a change! time to quit straddling the metaphorical fence. . . and now, he smiled, that fence had been quite literally torn down. So, deciding to go with the: "God moves in mysterious ways," concept, he had taken off his uniform, placing it on his desk along with his badge, his ring of keys and a neatly typed letter of resignation.

That done, he had dressed in his civilian clothes and walked away, his heart as free as the no-longer caged dogs.

Whistling cheerfully all the way home, he had packed a suitcase and grabbed his fly-fishing gear, his destination Wyoming for an extended vacation.

Here Teller had smiled, saying that after the story's retelling, the fellow, proud beneath his soiled suit, had said that the breakout had come at the perfect time. That it had been both symbolic and cathartic; for he had found himself on the horns of an existential dilemma. While he *hated* locking the dogs up, he truly enjoyed caring for them, developing an odd kinship for each sorry pooch incarcerated. And, having come to love each and every one of the hounds, had been finding employment as their jailer less rewarding every day. So that some unknown assailant had set them free on that glorious morning was a sign that he too, should run as fast, and as far as he could before his own personal fence grew too tall to climb. But then, pausing in his story the fellow's eyes had narrowed.

"I remember picking up a young hitchhiker as I drove past the new Snowmass turn-off that day." he had said, scrutinizing Teller's profile while trying to clear decades of dust. But then he had shaken his head and frowned,

"Naah, couldn't be."

~

Teller emptied his beer and threw the undamaged can out among its hole-filled cousins.

"What that poor bastard didn't realize," he smiled, "is that it *was* me he had picked up all those years ago."

Kelly remembered saying, "small world," and Teller kissing her forehead while laughing, "yes, it is. But what makes it smaller still is that it was also *me* who freed the hounds."

That had surprised her, and she pulled away sputtering,
"What . . . ?"

But Tellers grin only got bigger. "Yep. I was only eighteen at the time, and friend of mine and I were working up on Snowmass creek doing the surveying for what would become the inevitable rape of yet another beautiful valley."

His smile faded, then slowly returned.

"Anyway. Every Saturday night my partner and I would leave our camp to go into Aspen for some fun. And every time we did his damn dog would follow us into town and get locked up. So, every Monday morning we would have to go back to town and bail him out. Well, as usual, one hung-over Sunday morning the damn dog was gone from camp; and, as usual, we were broke. And as I was *very* tired of throwing what little money we had at Pitkin County for the stupid offense of 'dog at large.' that night I went to town, tied a rope from the bumper of the truck to the fence, yanked it over and loaded Dave's dog into the truck, leaving the others to follow their noses in whatever direction interested them. The note was added as a humorous afterthought in deference to Edward Abby. Anyway, on the drive back I decided I'd had enough of the whole thing. So I took the dog back to camp, packed my stuff, and headed out."

Leaning back against the tree trunk he chuckled at the memory while Kelly, laughing along, joked, "I never realized the extent of your criminal past! Doggie jailbreaks. Wow."

Bow –wow . . ." Teller had grinned.

~

Smiling at the recollection, she wrapped the little derringer in a sock, tossed it into her suitcase, and glanced up at the clock. It was nearly nine.

Carlton would be here any minute.

Again, her mind drifted back to that day at the quarry. She hadn't thought about it at the time, but in retrospect she remembered the peculiar look that had crossed Teller's face as he quietly added, "I had forgotten about the entire thing until that day . . . what are the odds I'd end up giving that same guy a ride all these years later?"

176

~

What Teller could not have known, as he retold his story to Kelly that afternoon beneath a lone aspen in a small corner of the world, was that it had been that one small act of chaos that had captured Coyote's attention.

~

Teller went silent after telling his tale; leaning back against the Aspens trunk while watching the clouds gather over the higher peaks, changing color as the sun moved west.

"So. How'd you end up with the gun?" she asked.

"Huh?"

"The gun, Teller. Where'd you get it?"

Tellers attentions were already elsewhere, the past packed away in favor of the beauty of the afternoons dancing light.

"Oh, yeah." At her question, he continued the tale.

"Well, the guy had gone to Wyoming after his epiphany with the dogs, but as Fall arrived he knew that winter wasn't far behind. So, using some of his connections in Aspen he got a job in Vail as a town cop." Here Teller reloaded the little pistol and stood; but when he tried to pull her up she had refused, insisting that he finish the story.

With a long sigh, he sat back down.

"Well. I guess he was an avid golfer, and one day out on the back nine he heard someone yell, "fore! Unfortunately, he didn't react quickly enough and got beaned by a Titleist three."

She flinched. "Ouch."

"Yeah, ouch!" Teller had laughed, tossing a newly empty can out into the rocks and popping off a shot. She still remembered the high-pitched whine of the ricochet.

"And?"

"And," he had said, "It turned out the errant golf ball was a slice by none other than the illustrious Gerald Ford."

"No way! The President?"

She remembered his expression clearly. It had been a mix of disgust and depressed humor.

"None other . . ."

She pressed on. "What happened?"

His sparkle returned. "Why, he was offered a job in compensation for his injuries of course! Following the laws of The Peter Principal, and with his extensive experience in the dangerous field of canine law enforcement, he was given a job as chauffer for the Presidential limo!" Teller had been absolutely beaming as he made the statement, and while Kelly was thrilled with his good humor, he still had not answered her question.

"The gun, Teller. What about the *gun?*" then, as an afterthought, added, "and what was he doing walking along the road anyway?"

"Ahhhh. *That* my dear," Teller smiled, "is the best part of the story! The reason he was walking down the road is that he had quit his job." Here he went silent yet again, forcing her to ask the obvious question.

"Why?"

"Because he had a soul." Teller grinned. "When Ford pardoned that vile piece of shit Nixon for his crimes against this nation, our friend found that he could no longer bear to be part of any system so mindlessly corrupt, regardless of the perks. So, he told Ford to take this job and shove it, he ain't workin there no more."

And?"

Teller stood, picked up the two fresh empties, and placed them on the log. He was tired of the story now. Walking back towards Kelly, he spun on his heel and fired two quick shots. Both cans spun away into the dusk.

Nodding in self-satisfaction, he turned. "And I traded him a couple lines of coke for the pistol and one of the cufflinks Jerry wore."

"A cufflink?"

The smile returned. "Yeah, a very cool cufflink, one with the presidential seal, the kind you seal wax on envelopes with. It had his name engraved on the back too. He said he found it on the floor of the Limo."

"You traded him *cocaine* for a pistol and a cufflink?"

Teller's face was one of innocence combined with pride.

"Hey," he had said, pulling her to her feet. "He *was* from Aspen."

"No! That's *not* what I mean. . . I *mean*, you had *coke* to trade for guns and Presidential cuff links?

Teller had feigned indignation, but the sadness in his voice was very real. "You may be too young to remember my dear, but once upon a time, not so very long ago, before everyone's asshole clamped shut, the world was a *lot* more fun. People didn't take themselves so goddamned seriously, and recreational drugs weren't nearly as frowned upon as they are today." His smile slowly returned, and his eyes twinkled. "Hell, for some of us they were a way of life." With that, he had taken her by the hand, given her a kiss, and pulled her towards the truck.

"Come on, it's gettin' dark."

~

She smiled again at the recollection. Why did a story like that *not* seem crazy?

The answer was simple. Because it was Teller.

Throwing a jacket over the sock that held the cold blue steel of the little pistol. And as she closed the case a horn honked outside.

Time to go.

— — -- --- -- — —

—— ——   —— ——

-- --- --

= Chapter 31 =

"Okay Tell," Jack said as he hung up. "Kelly's set. And not only will her suite will be ready, I told 'em to have a bottle of bubbly chilled and waiting."

"Nice touch Jack. Thanks."

Smiling, Jack held up his hand, dangling the piece of paper with the numbers between two fingers.

"Nothing to it pal, she's a good woman and deserves a little pampering."

Teller, with a smile of his own placed a firm hand on Jack's shoulder. "I fully agree pard, and shall consider charging James for these small luxuries partial compensation for the inconvenience of his nephew's desire to kill me."

Abbott, who had been sitting silently in the shade, chimed in. "*Speaking* of that, just what are we going to do to prevent him from succeeding?"

Teller shrugged, dismissing Abbott inquiry completely. Then turning to Billy, stroked his mustache and asked, "Well, Chief, any success on the boat?"

Everyone looked to the old Indian.

Billy's eyes were closed. But Teller, having become used to his prolonged pauses between questions and answers, reached into the cooler, pulled out a beer, and waited.

~

Billy was *much* older than any of the men present suspected: thus, he possessed the wisdom of the ancients. So, while to his companions he appeared to be resting, in truth he had entered the spirit world to search for signs of either Coyote, or the shadowy madness of Tellers foe.

Feeling the presence of neither however, he shuffled the countless planes of overlapping realities like a deck of Tarot cards: and flipping over the card of the now, he slowly opened his eyes. "The boat. Yes, yes, the boat! So many things to remember! So many things to consider! Yes Teller, the boat. It should arrive tomorrow."

Teller, pleasantly surprised, leaned forward, his elbows on his knees. "Tomorrow huh? Well, may I be so bold as to ask what *type* of boat?"

Billy's face grew brighter. "I may be old, Teller, but my memory is still strong. Did you not request a boat on which you might live?"

Teller countered with a sincere smile.

"I have great faith in both your recall, *and* your capability Chief, but we seem to have a small problem here."

Billy appeared not at all concerned. "And that would be?"

Teller's smile disappeared and he held out his hands, palms up. "Money for one. I've not yet reaped any of the rewards of our discovery."

Billy's resulting grin was magnificent.

"Faith, Teller! One must have faith! *You* of all people must certainly understand that!" He reached down and picked up his coffee cup. "Little Raven is on his way as we speak, bringing you what was once Sebastian's car, and with him is the first dividend on your investment in the R.R. Salvage Company." The smile beneath his battered cowboy hat radiated unfettered joy.

Teller's first thought was that he no longer needed to go back to Tucson. His second was surprise.

"Young Bill is on his way with the Buick?"

"Yes Teller. And with funds sufficient to purchase your boat as well."

Turning to his companions with a look of supreme satisfaction, Teller grinned, "See Jack, ya just gotta have faith!" But Jack shook his head. "You have *got* to be the luckiest sonofabitch I have *ever* met."

181

Teller's response was tempered. "It's not luck, Jack."

Jack, rocking forward to snag the bottle at his feet, pulled the cork. "What would *you* call it then?" he asked.

Teller glanced at Billy, but saw he could expect no help from that quarter. The expression on his weathered face was non-committal. Accepting his silence with a nod, Teller stood: and giving a slight bow, smiled, "It's just my part in the play, Jack. I don't write the script." but as a melancholy shadow passed behind his eyes he quietly added, "and it's not all *good* luck . . . after all, someone *is* trying to kill me."

At the shift in Tellers humor, Abbott pressed a freshly opened beer into his hand. "Thanks, Griz," he said, tipping it to his lips. With the swallow his sorrow dissipated, and he smiled. "And I am more than happy to play the role in which I have been cast." but looking at Jack his expression turned serious once again. "And let us not forget, my friend, that *you* have a starring role in this passion play as well."

Allowing Jack no time to respond, Teller returned his attention to Billy. "So, Chief. You say Young Bill is on his way with my car, *and* my new digs are motoring up the lake?"

"Yes, Teller, and both should be here tomorrow."

"And what kind of houseboat did you find?"

Both Abbott and Jack cried out in unison, "*House*boat!?" Ignoring both them and their outburst, Billy smile was enigmatic. "Oh, I think you'll find it acceptable."

Teller laughed and tipped his can in the direction his two friends. "Will there be enough room for characters such as these?"

Billy's smile did not dim. If anything, it grew brighter as he turned his dark eyes on them. "Yes, there should be more than adequate room for this pair."

"Good!" Teller grinned, his smile only marginally less luminescent. Then, turning his smile to Jack, he raised his eyebrows. "You ready for a little vacation?"

"Sure," Jack nodded. "As soon as the kid's no longer a problem." Teller nodded back and turned to Abbott.

"And you, old bear?"

Abbott's teeth shone through his beard. "As Jack said. As soon as Ben no longer represents a danger."

"Well then." Teller shrugged. "I guess we wait."

~

The four men sat in silence as the Sun rolled across the sky; the breeze from the river cooling the air as each nursed their private thoughts. Teller's breathing smoothed, and settling into a slow, steady rhythm his eyes fluttered closed. Suddenly a loud burp shattered the peace. Glaring through one eye he growled, "can't take you *anywhere*."

Abbott simply shrugged and gave an embarrassed grin, while Teller, his reverie disturbed glanced over at Billy, whose eyes remained closed.

"Hey Billy."

"Yes, Teller . . ."

"Did you say the name of your Company was R and R salvage?"

Billy shook his head.

"No, I said, R period, R period, Salvage. No '*and*'"

"Okay. . ." Teller nodded. "So then, what does the 'R. R.' stand for?"

Billy never opened an eye but his dazzling Hollywood smile nearly lit the porch. "On paper it stands for: 'Reclaim, Re-sell. But that is only a legal formality."

Teller knew when he was being baited but he smiled.

"Okay, I'll bite. So what does R. R. *really* stand for?

Opening his eyes, Billy slowly sat straighter in his chair. And while the pause was unintentional, the comic timing was impeccable. His smile gleaming from beneath the shadow of his hat, said, "Redman's Revenge."

There was a moment of absolute silence, then everyone burst into laughter; everyone but Teller, because, for the briefest of moments it felt as if all of his troubles had dissolved and blown away on the desert wind . . . but then, throwing his head back, his laughter became the richest of all.

Amid the laughter, a coyote yipped in the distance as if joining in; and as the joy faded, Teller pulled the back of his hand across his eyes, wiping away the happy tears.

"*That* is brilliant Chief. I believe I'm going to enjoy working with you."

Billy's return smile was one of increasing affection and respect.

"And I believe I shall enjoy your proximity as well, Teller, as I wish to be present for what Coyote has in store for you next . . . never have I been this close to his influence."

Teller shrugged. "Neither have I, Chief. Neither have I, but I guess I'll adapt." Recalling a line from one of his songs titled, '*I ain't that kinda guy,*' Teller sung out loud.

"As influences go, I confess to a few, but under and bad were my favo-rite two . . ." He finished the beat with his fingers on the low table, adding, "but they pale in comparison to this Coyote." Grinning, he turned to Jack., "Hey, Jacko, you got Willie's number in that phone?"

Jack tossed the phone at Teller who snatched it as it sailed by. "Nice catch." Jack smiled, waggling his empty glass. "Go ahead and take a look. I'm going to go get some ice." Teller gave him the finger, but Jack just walked away.

Chuckling at Jack's retreating back, Teller dialed.

Waiting through six long rings, Teller was expecting voice mail, but on the seventh it stopped to what sounded like a great deal of commotion in the background.

~

Willie was in his truck, driving into Durango for the night's show when the phone in the ashtray buzzed. He had just set a fat, burning roach on its lip but the phones vibration jiggled it out and it tumbled to the floor where it started smoldering among the diverse collection of trash on the floorboards. "Damn!" Willie hollered, grabbing the phone before it followed the joint onto the floor.

Catching it with one hand he brought it to his ear; steering with his knee while retrieving the remains of his joint from a burning burger wrapper.

"Willie?"

"Ouch, shit! Yeah, yeah, yeah . . . who's this?"

"It's the guy you steal all your good songs from."

Willie's brow furrowed. "Who the fu. . .?"

Shoving his thumb into his mouth, he thought for a second, then pulled it out with a 'pop'. "Teller, you *dog!* Where *are* you?" he laughed, then, "and I hate to burst your bubble, but they aren't all that good."

"Says the guy who can't write a song." Teller chuckled.

"True, true," Willie said, "but I'm a better musician. Hey, I met one of your old friends a couple weeks ago."

"Jack? Yeah, he mentioned it. Matter of fact he's down here with me now."

"No shit! Funny guy that one. So, what are *you* doin' Tell?"

Teller leaned back, a more serious tone in his voice.

"That, Amigo, is a *long* story, and will be told in full when the time is right. But for now, I need a favor."

Cramming the roach back in the ashtray with his blistered thumb, Willie relaxed, and spun the steering wheel right, following the old highway into town. After all these years he still hated that new four-laner that ran through Bodo industrial; and as he drove past the site of the long-gone sawmill where he and Teller had once worked the night shift so many years ago, he thought: '*Cosmic that he's on the phone right now.*'

"Sure, Tell. You know I'm always here for you."

"Yeah, I know, Willie, and have always appreciated that fact." Teller's smile came across in his voice. "And this small favor should be a relatively pleasant task.

Willie drove on, one hand on the wheel while squeezing the phone to one ear with his shoulder and searching for his lighter in the fold of the seat with his free hand.

Digging deep he finally found it, taking the roach from the ashtray and spinning the striker with his burnt thumb.

"I'm always up for pleasant." he said, taking a deep drag and releasing the smoke through the wing vent. "There is *sooo* little of it these days."

"All too true." Teller agreed.

"So, what's the favor?"

Jack returned with his glass of ice, and looking over to Billy and Abbott, Teller silently thanked the stars for his friends.

"I'm dealing with a small problem Willie, so I need you to keep Kelly company for a few days."

Following a massive inhale, Willie started coughing; squeezing his eyes shut as he came to a full stop at the corner of third and Eighth Street. With the doobie in one hand, he wiped away the tears and looked both ways twice.
He was always exceptionally cautious when he was stoned.

"Hell, Teller, that sounds like more of a wish come true than a favor."

Teller laughed. "Glad you feel that way old chum. She'll be at the Strater by tonight. Give her a call and let her know you're around. You two can figure it out from that point."

Turning right on E. Fifth Avenue, Willie slowed to a near crawl. He didn't remember the paint on these Victorian homes being so colorful . . . and the trim detail . . . that was different wasn't it??? and the trees lining the street, they seemed to have an exceptionally mellow vibe today . . . Shaking his head he grinned. "Sure, Tell. What room's she gonna be in?"

"I don't know, Willie. Call the hotel and ask for her."

"Okay, what's her last name again?

Teller rolled his eyes in exasperation. "Rowen. Kelly Rowen. And Willie,"

"Yeah Tell?"

"Do this and you can forget the royalties you owe me."

"Teller," Willie laughed as he pulled into the parking lot of the 'Lost Dog.' "What royalties?"

The phone went dead.

Abbott looked to him and asked, "Everything alright?"

Teller grinned and tossed the phone at Jack.

"Couldn't be better Griz, couldn't be *better*. Hand me a beer."

= Chapter 32 =

Breakfast at the Bakery had been no more than a quick stop. Kelly wanted a poppyseed muffin and a latté to go, while Carl had been hoping for a leisurely breakfast with a beautiful woman.

Predictably, it was he who was disappointed.

As they waited in line, they discussed their best route to Durango; and, as they were in no hurry they decided that rather than backtrack over Dallas pass through Ouray, they would take highway 145, down the west side of the San Juan's and through the old mining towns of Ophir and Rico, where they would hit Delores and head southeast to Mancos. So, with coffee and muffin in hand, they left Telluride.

As always, the drive was spectacular, Kelly sharing Teller's opinion that there was not a prettier stretch of road anywhere in the state. But as they passed the newly graded turnoff to Dunton Hot Springs, her mind wandered back to that first crazy weekend spent with Teller.

~

She had never met a man quite like him. He was funny, with a quick-wit and an odd charm. And while he was undeniably good-looking in a rough sort of way, he didn't seem to be overly aware of it. She found the combination to be a curious, *and* attractive package, and one that only got more interesting once opened.

The days following were spent in a tangle of tequila, damp sheets, hot water and laughter; and on the fifth night she felt something open deep inside: a vulnerability that had frightened her in its intensity. But the dream-like week came to its inevitable end, and as it did she feared that once they returned to Telluride the magic would vanish as quickly as he likely would.

Surprisingly, that proved not to be the case.

Instead, he introduced her to his partner, James, along with the Telluride crew.

Soon they were working side by side. But as thrilling as all this was, she kept her job at the bar. She had been hurt before, and just in case things went south she wanted to have a backup position. But against all odds, nothing really changed. Teller simply incorporated her into his life, and the intensity of their lust was polished into something slightly more manageable.

By summer's end she shared his house, finding her life to be not only surprisingly satisfying, she secretly hoped things would never change. But now, she realized, her wish had come true. He *hadn't* changed. He remained as impetuous as ever. Impossible to pin down, and as just as likely to take off on some crazy personal tangent as when they had first met. And, to make it even *more* frustrating, the recklessness she had found so attractive in the beginning, was the very same impulsiveness that had taken him away from Telluride: forcing her present state of personal re-evaluation. But then, remarkably, fate had delivered him back to her on the banks of the river.

Closing her eyes, she squeezed them tight and smiled, *'Teller, Teller, Teller.'* Then, as if she needed yet further evidence of life's propensity for irony, she opened her eyes to Carlton's profile behind the wheel . . . Here she was, riding next to James' excommunicated bookkeeper; an innocent man who was yet another victim of James' insatiable egomania, as well as one whom she had, at Teller's request, blatantly, and successfully, manipulated in order to bring into their camp; thus making him a reluctant co-conspirator in a game of wills.

A game that Teller had won.

Closing her eyes a second time, she leaned her head back against the seat. She could almost hear him laugh.

Carlton's voice cut into her sleep. "Would you like something to drink?"

Her eyes popping open, she glanced around. They were in Delores, parked in front of a little market, Carlton looking at her quizzically. "Would you like something?" he repeated.
In deference to the man she was missing, she smiled, "How about a Moosehead? And if they don't have that, Coors."
Carlton frowned as he restarted the car.

"For that we'll need to go to the liquor store."

Driving south to 3rd Street, he parked for a second time, stepped out and leaned in through open window. "Be right back!" he said, his smile bright.

It seemed as if she had barely closed her eyes when Carlton returned, sliding behind the wheel and rattling the paper bag he set between them as he pulled out two green bottles. In the act of the gentleman, he took one, wrapped his fingers around the cap, and gave a twist; resulting in little more than the near peeling of skin from his soft accountant fingers. *Oww!"* he cried in surprise, "It's not a twist off!"

Clenching his hand while looking both pained and apologetic, he mumbled, "I'll go back and get an opener."
But with a smile that made his heart flutter, Kelly took the bottle from his wounded hand "I've got it Carl."

Taking the seatbelt clip, she pulled it across her lap, placing the flat of metal against her thumb and forefinger to leverage the edge under the lid. The cap popped off, and she handed him the foaming beer bottle, repeating the process with the second, stuffing the caps into the ashtray
Carlton nodded at the seatbelt. "Clever trick."

"One of Teller's," she grinned, taking a drink. And licking a spot of foam from her upper lip, nearly broke Carl's heart.

With a sigh, he started the car. "The guy's full of tricks, isn't he?"

"He's full of something Carl," Kelly giggled, "and I suppose 'tricks' is as a polite way as any to phrase it."

Carlton smiled in return, but only in the hopes of buoying his sagging spirits.

Pulling out of the parking lot, they headed down Main Street towards the highway; but Kelly touched his elbow and smiled, "turn left here Carl. If you go down Riverside to Fourth, we can cross the river and take the old county road that hooks up to 184 about seven miles south of here. It's a lot nicer drive." Carl nodded, but as the tires rattled across the wooden slats of the bridge she noticed him giving her a questioning glance.

"He knows a lot of back roads too." she shrugged.

Dust roiled behind the car as they cruised down the empty dirt road, and as promised the short cut was far more pleasant than the highway.

As he drove, Carlton snuck casual glances at Kelly, who, slouched in the seat with one foot propped up on the dash, stared straight ahead; the Juniper trees outside the window providing a scented backdrop for her profile.

"A penny for your thoughts?"

At his voice, she rolled her head on the seatback to look at him, her gaze uncomfortably intense.

"Did you find anything concerning Ben?"

He hadn't anticipated *that* response. As a matter of fact, he had forgotten about Ben completely.

Refocusing, he shook his head. "No. Well, not really. Casey took him out of Denver General a few days ago. According to them he was scheduled for home care."

She said nothing, but her scrutiny was making him nervous. Focusing on the road ahead, he asked, "Why?"

Kelly relaxed slightly. Her suspicions of Carl were minimal but at this point *everyone* was suspect. She was reasonably certain that he hadn't heard about Ben's vow to kill Teller, but her curiosity as to how he might respond prompted her to tell him now. So, as they rolled up to the stop sign that terminated County road 30 onto Highway 184, she dropped the bomb.

"Because he stole a rifle from James, took the Hummer, and is on his way to Lake Powell to kill Teller."

Carl's mouth fell open in disbelief and he managed to stammer out a, *"What?!"* as a semi roared by, its steel trailer packed with cattle and splattered with dung. Rolling up his window against the unpleasant wind that rocked the car, he turned. "Say that again?"

"Ben is going to try and kill Teller." she repeated.

Carl's grip on the wheel tightened, and the expression of incredulity on his face erased any thoughts she might have had of his involvement.

"So *that's* why you asked me to find out about Ben?"

She nodded.

Carl nodded back. "But why would Ben want to kill *Teller?*"

The question hanging in the air, Kelly shrugged, "I don't know, Carl."

Suddenly there was a short honk from behind.

Carl glanced up into his rearview mirror to see an old green Ford truck full of hay waiting. Giving an apologetic wave, he hit his blinker and pulled onto the highway. The old fellow driving the truck responded with a 'no problem' gesture and turned the opposite way, heading towards Cortez.

"So, do you have any ideas why?" Carl pressed.

"Well," Kelly said. "You know it was Teller who put Ben in the hospital, right?"

Carl nodded, "Yeah. Well, no, not really, but I suspected as much. As I may have mentioned yesterday I am hardly the confidante of the Carson family. All that I *knew* was that he was seriously injured and had been medevac'd to Denver."

Kelly looked at him suspiciously. "You knew *nothing* of Teller's involvement?"

Carl's forehead wrinkled. "No, no more than I could discern from conversations within the office. When James

192

first flew to Durango there was nothing said about Teller particularly, but his name came up later on."

Kelly nodded, her lips tight. "That was because no one knew at the time that he was on the river with us."

Carl's expression of puzzlement increased.

"Wait, I thought Teller disappeared after their falling out at the bar." As he finished the statement he smiled. "I heard *that* was quite the interesting discussion."

Kelly nodded, but she did *not* smile. "Oh, yeah. But from where I stood it was not so much of a discussion, as two bears deciding on who was going the carcass they had stumbled across."

"So the carcass was the business?" Carlton asked.

"No," Kelly frowned. "The carcass was Telluride." Turning, she looked at Carl, her eyes harboring residual anger. "But the business *was* part of it, and for a while I thought that *I* was included." but then, her anger in her eyes was replaced with a reluctant smile. "At least until Teller showed up on the river."

Carl was hoping for more, but Kelly had fallen silent, giving no indication she had any more to say on the subject.

Cresting the rise into Mancos in silence, they began their descent into Durango; the La Sal Mountains rising in snowy majesty on their left.

As Carl drove, he mulled the story over until his curiosity could no longer be ignored. "So then, *how* did *he* end up meeting you on the river?"

Her eyes closed and her head back against the seat, Kelly gave Carl a sad smile. Then, with a deep sigh, said, "You're not going to believe this, but . . ."

―――― ― -- --- -- ― ――――
―――― ―――― ―――― ――――
-- --- --

= Chapter 33 =

Ben's head jerked from the padded headrest, pulled from his catatonic sleep by dark, probing fingers.

'Where am I?' he slurred, his swollen lips trying to form the words as he squinted through a windshield laced with spiderweb cracks. He blinked, trying to focus on the large tree that leaned over the hood; looking as if it were growing there. Confused, he pushed the door open and crawled out. He was deep in a canyon . . . one that he had no memory of driving into the night before.

Baffled, he turned and looked at the vehicle.

The passenger's side fender was crumpled around a tall, thick, cedar tree; the bumper buried deep into its splintered flesh. Sap oozed from the deep gash, pooling in the concave remains of the broken headlight, and having filled the glass bowl, now stretched to the ground like an amber stalactite.

Turning in a slow circle, Ben struggled to put together the pieces of the past few days . . .

He remembered nothing.

Suddenly, a blast of wind rattled the trees, but as he whipped his head towards the sound the movement drove spikes of pain through his skull, dropping him to his knees.

The damage to his jaw was far from healed, and the rough four-wheeling that had gotten him into this lost canyon had done the weak mend no good. And now, with a thousand hot knives slashing at every nerve, Ben collapsed onto the grass, clutching his head between his palms and writhing in agony.

Slowly, the pain subsided, leaving Ben peeking through his fingers, his eyes bleary with tears of pain. He had no clue as to where he was, and equally confused as to why.

Then, as suddenly as it had come the wind stopped, and in that silence, voices came as the chaotic fog clogging his mind cleared; leaving a raw, searing hatred in its place.

'It was Teller!' the voices screamed.

Now Ben remembered. *Teller* was responsible for this misery! *He* was the man who had taken his love from him against her wishes!!

Ben's jumbled memories were like a jigsaw puzzle that had been kicked apart then put back together by a demented child. He clearly recalled having devised a brilliant method for their escape: but during his daring rescue of Kelly, the brute Teller had caught them. And after beating him cruelly, had tried to kill him by drowning. These twisted memories brought the pain rushing back and Ben's hands went to his temples to squeeze away the torment. . . but then, through the stabbing pain a strange laughing cackle drowned out the mad chatter in his skull.

Lifting his eyes from trembling hands, he looked up.

There, perched on the tree that leaned against the hood of the Hummer, a large raven sat, its head cocked and looking terribly amused.

Ben's hatred exploded. Pushing himself to his knees, he stumbled to the rear of the Hummer, throwing open the door to pull the gleaming black rifle from its case and draw back the bolt. Smiling wickedly as the shell clicked into place, Ben jammed the bolt forward, stepping around the vehicle to sight on the black demon. With a vicious laugh, he squeezed the trigger. "Goodbye, Teller."

Bens eyes shut in reflex as the gunshot shattered the silence and the bird's otherworldly scream echoed against the canyon walls. As the echo died away, Ben opened his eyes.

The branch the creature had been sitting on was splintered: the bird gone . . . but as the gunshot's echo faded, he heard a rustle of feathers and looked up to see the Raven flapping high into the sky above him.

At the apex of its rise, the bird spread its shadowy wings to their full span, and with glittering black eyes focused directly on Bens frightened face, folded those wings, and dove.

Ducking, Ben swung the rifle as the black form swooped by but his efforts were futile. Razor sharp talons carved flesh from bone; gouging deep furrows into his skull. . . but Ben felt no pain, only rage; a rage that burned hotter than the viscous fluid that poured down his face.

Releasing the madness that rent his very soul he pulled a trembling hand across his face, smearing the blood in horizontal streaks. Then, turning the grotesque visage to the sound of retreating wings he screamed, "TELLER!!!"

The words were lost to the wind that carried a laughing caw back to him; one that burned his ears as he watched the Ravens glistening black wings carry it south: a bloody scalp dangling from one claw.

= Chapter 34 =

James struggled to keep his eyes open as a huge yawn stretched his jaw; and with a shake of his head, refocused on the dark highway in front of his big Chevy trucks headlights.

It had been an extremely difficult night and he was glad it was over. His discussion with Casey regarding Ben had begun deteriorated as the two Valium she had taken earlier mixed with the red wine, with each successive glass making her less and less coherent. Finally, exhausted and emotionally drained, she had allowed James to put her to bed. And while she had put up a nominal argument, at *least* he had gotten her to understand that bringing the cops in would solve absolutely *nothing*.

Tucking her in, James stood at her bedside waiting until her breathing became a soft steady snore. Then, going to his dresser took out the Magnum that was the twin to the one under the seat of the Hummer.

Hefting its deadly weight, he pointed it at the mirror.

"Yes, he muttered with a twisted smile. '*This* will take care of any problems I might encounter."

Sighting down the weapon once more, he reached behind his socks for the box of shells he kept hidden there.

Rattling them, Casey snort he shoved them into his pocket.

he froze, glancing over at the lump beneath the blankets. Absolutely still, he waited for her to fall back to sleep. Soon she was snoring peacefully and he tucked the Magnum into his satchel, pulled on a sweater, and walked out into the chill mountain morning.

But as he drove, he considered his dilemma.

When he had wished Teller dead, he hadn't meant it *literally*
. . . what was that old saying. . .? 'careful what you wish for?
'What a fucking *mess,*' he mumbled, shaking his head in
frustration

Steering with his knee, he reached over and grabbed the
satchel he had tossed onto the seat. Unzipping it he yanked a
half-empty bottle of Scotch out, bit the cork and pulled;
filling the cab with its pungent odor. Wrinkling his nose, he
pushed he cork back into the neck.

'Maybe coffee is a better idea.'

~

Idling at a red light, James realized that it had been a *very*
long time since he had last been in Cortez: and while its
outskirts were just as dirty and run down as he remembered,
Main Street had been upscaled. Where he recalled only
defunct business and liquor stores there were now new-age
candle-slash bookstores and coffee shops: complete with
brand-new, and, up until recently, non-existent parking
meters.

Spying a parking space in front of a newly refurbished
building with the name, 'Spruce Tree Coffee House,' etched
into the glass of the front window, he maneuvered his truck
into the slot. He despise the entire concept of "new-age," but
it was a coffee shop and he needed coffee.

James mood darkened the moment he pushed the front
door open. The room was filled with cheerful chatter; and
with recent events having left him feeling persecuted the
jovial banter only increased his sense of isolation.

Frowning, he took his place in line.

Ten long minutes later a smiling barista called out his
name; handing him his coffee while glancing meaningfully at
the tip jar. Making a show of pocketing his change, James
pushed his way through the crowd to the condiments. But
just as he stepped up to the counter a young woman with a
child slung on her back bumped him aside; and, with no

apology whatsoever, began fine-tuning her latté as the child waved and giggled.

James was stunned. Not *only* was the mother's rudeness an affront, the joyful innocence on the baby's face compounded his fury. Looking over his shoulder to make sure there were no witnesses, he leaned within inches of that cherubic smile, and made a hideous face. For the first few seconds the child was absolutely silent. Then, eyes going wide, air was sucked in as tears welled, the rosy glow of healthy cheeks blossoming red, and with the shaking of tiny fists, the baby released a howl so astonishing in volume that all conversation ceased, and the room went silent.

Panicked by the incredible power of her baby's wail, the young mother swung around, attempting to comfort the screaming child while at the same time searching for the source of its distress. Following the child's teary gaze, she noticed the smile of supreme satisfaction on James' face.

Pulling the child close, she cooed soothingly, snapping the lid on her coffee while offering him her nastiest scowl.

Returning a 'fuck you' sneer, James bumped her purposely as she walked away; stepping up to commandeer the entire table. He was feeling better already.

Pushing the crumpled napkin she had left onto the floor, he grabbed a handful of sugar packets; tearing them open one at a time; slowly stirring each in, and taking a test sip after each packet.

As he performed his ritual, the grumbling of those in line increased with each person added, and by the fourth packet, the mood had turned sour. But just as the crowd's patience reached its limits, James' sweet tooth's demands were satisfied and he turned, glaring at the annoyed patrons as he pushed his way through their ranks and out the door.

Picturing the baby's expression, he bounced down the steps, laughing out loud; gloating in his disdain for the lower classes. But as he approached his truck the ticket beneath his windshield wiper cut his pleasure short. Setting his coffee on the hood he took the ticket and tore it into little pieces; scattering them into the breeze.

"So, give me a fucking ticket for littering too, *Barney*," he grumbled, grabbing his cup and climbing into the cab.

But his boldness wavered as he turned the ignition and checking his side mirror just in case; he pulled out into the empty street.

By the time James cleared the town limits the caffeine had begun to clear the fog of last night's Scotch; but now with his head slightly clearer, he realized that not *only* was he without a game plan, he had no idea at all where Ben's might be. All he *knew* was that the little fucker had snapped and was on his way to kill Teller. Yet here he was, pointlessly driving south, with no clue as to where to go. Cursing himself for a fool, he turned around, only to have the Old Ute coffee shop and diner come into view and with it, ghosts of the past returned.

Back in the old days when money was tight, he and Teller had eaten there more often than he cared to remember.

'Tight? He muttered grimly. How about non-*fucking-*existent . . . '

James nearly smiled. For some reason Teller had always loved places like that, and he could never figure out why. He *hated* the greasy feel of the diners and their worn-down waitresses. But then his mind jerked back to the present and the memories vanished.

What the hell did he think he was doing? He and Teller were *done!* He owed him nothing! And now that he thought about it, not only had Teller taken half of his money, he had ruined any possibility of his cajoling his way back into Kelly's good graces. But as his anger returned and his resentment increased, Casey's words during the drive to the hospital in Denver came back to him.

"*It means that you're just like my father,*" she had said. "*He's also an egotistical asshole who thinks he should have everything. Whether he deserves it or not.*"

Recalling the sarcastic smile on her face, James' blood pressure began to rise. She was right, damn her! Kelly was never going to leave Teller. As much as he hated to admit it, Teller simply had class. He had bet the farm with that coin toss and won it all.

The bastard was *born* lucky.

Crumpling his now empty coffee cup, he tossed it onto the floorboards. 'Screw it!' he said aloud, and in a hollow attempt to assuage his guilt told himself, *there's nothing more I can do. I called and warned him and that's more than he deserves. He's on his own.'* But a tinge of repentance tickled at his soul as the Montezuma County Airport sign came into view; and as the memory of Janey and Leroy leapt forth, so did the sense of loneliness he had felt that afternoon they lifted from the tarmac: his face pressed against the cool glass as the gruff old woman waved goodbye.

Suddenly, it was all too much. Spinning the wheel, he headed towards the Airport. He could use some breakfast and wouldn't hurt to tell Leroy what Jack was up against. After all, they *were* his friends. And who knows? That big son of a bitch might have an idea.

~

James removed his sunglasses and pushed through the terminal doors. The concourse was empty but for a few sunburned tourists flying home from Mesa Verde; and over the rows of empty seats James saw that the Coors sign was lit, only now the 'r' was flickering.

'How about that.' he thought as he laid his palm on the diner's door. *'Its real neon.'*

Janey stood with her back to the door, her head wreathed in smoke as she fiddled with the coffee maker. but hearing the squeak of the stool, she mumbled around the cigarette that dangled between her lips. "Be right with ya."

Replacing the filter and adding fresh coffee, she pressed the start button as she turned; blowing a thin stream of smoke from the side of her mouth while she reached into her apron for her pen and pad.

"What kin I getcha?"

"I didn't know there was anywhere left that you could still smoke in public," James answered. "How do you get away with it?"

Jane's eyes narrowed as she raised her head, ready to challenge whoever the hell was sitting there regardless of their official status. But it took only a second to recognize him and giving a double take at his disheveled appearance her cantankerous attitude vanished.

"Slick!" she said, "ya look a mite rougher than the last time I seen you. What the hell are you doin' *here*?" But then her eyes brightened as they danced towards the door. "And where's Jack?"

James sighed as he ran his hand through his hair and looking at Janey through bloodshot eyes, shook his head.

"I don't know, Jane, but do you think I could get some coffee?"

Jane gave a nod and extinguished her cigarette, frowning at his unshaven face as she pulled a cup from beneath the counter and walked towards the urn.

"Hey Jane?"

She glanced over her shoulder. "Yeah?"

James gave her a tired smile. "None of that, please. Do you think you could you brew up some of that stuff we had last time?"

Jane set the empty cup back down. "Sure Slick. I forgot what a connoisseur you are." Wiping her hands on her apron, she smiled, "I'll be right back."

The bat-wing doors to the kitchen had barely swung to a stop when she stepped back through, setting them in motion once again.

"Give it a few minutes Slick," she said, picking up a lipsticked butt from the overflowing ashtray. "I put on some of the 'spensive stuff my daughter sends."

Putting her cigarette between her lips she re-lit it, shook out the match, and resting her bony backside against the counter, crossed her arms.

"I may be an old woman, Slick," she said, giving him a penetrating gaze. "But I know what trouble looks like, and it looks like it's got it teeth sunk gum-deep in your ass. So, tell me, why is it that *your* here, and Jack aint?"

For all his arrogance, James felt intimidated by this skinny old woman. He frowned, but his expression held none of its previous superiority.

"I know you think I'm an asshole, but while we wait for that coffee do you think I could get a drink?"

Janey shrugged. "Bein' an asshole ain't a prerequisite for drinkin' Slick." Turning to stand on her tiptoes, she pulled the bottle off the shelf, took a glass from beneath the counter, plunked in a few ice cubes, and poured.

"Stoli, right?" she said, sliding the glass in front of him. He gave a nod and lifted the drink, saying nothing.

Janey took a long drag on her cigarette while she studied his face. Then, exhaling over her left shoulder, said,

"Altho' for some, they go hand in hand."

Smiling in spite of himself, James plunked his freshly emptied glass. "Yeah, well, you're not the first who's thought as much . . . think that coffees ready yet?"

```
____ __ -- --- --  __  ____
____ ____  __  ____  ____
      -- --- --
```

= Chapter 35 =

Over the years that he had worked in the Telluride office Carlton had heard a multitude of stories regarding Frank Teller. Some sounded merely unlikely, while others plain crazy. But, while each person's take on the man was different the one thing they had in common was a degree of admiration. And, while none of the wild rumors came as close to revealing Tellers true nature as what he had just heard, together they made him realize that what may have seemed preposterous, they were based in fact. So now he was left with no option but to accept that the minor legend that was Teller, was, for all intents and purposes, true. These newly revealed details also provided two reasons why James' attitude over the course of these past few years had become increasingly hostile.

One: he was jealous.

And two: his clear, and overriding, desire for Kelly.

However, in mulling those two factors over, Carlton was forced to admit that while his own attraction to Kelly had not diminished in the slightest, his admiration for Teller had grown by leaps and bounds. Sneaking a glance at Kelly's profile, hurt his heart. Her love for Teller was clear, which in itself left him out of the running. But more to the point: if even only a *small* portion of what he had heard was true, Teller was a force to be reckoned with and he seriously doubted that *he* was the one to do the reckoning.

Kelly wrapped up her improbable story: a tale that was at the very least, riveting, and at times, unbelievable; and now, with tires thumping across the Animas River Bridge, directed him left on 550, then north to West 7th Street.

Carl made the turns while she rolled down her window and pointed to a five-story red brick building with the faded lettering: The Strater Hotel.

"There it is." She smiled.

With a nod, Carl spun the wheel, pulled into one of the diagonal parking spaces on the Hotel's north side and turned off the ignition as his eyes drifted to the large gold Gothic font lettering on the plate glass window that read: '*The Diamond Belle Saloon*' But as he looked at the smiling happy people on the other side of the glass, Carlton suddenly felt disconnected. As if he were no more than a figment of his own reality. The story he had just heard made his life seem painfully ordinary; and he didn't like it; but like it or not he had been sucked into this Teller vortex, and it had made a shambles of his once orderly life. Laying his forearms wearily over the steering wheel, Carlton turned and gave Kelly a tired smile. "Does your Teller change the life of *everyone* he meets?"

Kelly was quiet for a moment, then smiled. "Yeah Carl, to some degree, he does."

Carltons eyebrows rose, resulting in an expression that generated a modicum of pity from Kelly. But as tired as he might be, *her* exhaustion was multiplied many times over; and that, combined with her heavily edited re-telling of the river journey, had left her emotionally drained.

Consequently, her sympathy was at an all time low.

She had told Carlton nearly everything: including their unlikely reunion on the river, leading to the events that resulted in Ben's broken jaw. She had also included her initial introduction to Billy as well as Teller's second miraculous appearance on the mesa. She had, however, purposely left out the treasure, *and* the Coyote.

But her mood had darkened when she described James's unexpected arrival, and the business agreement that he and Teller had struck. She apologized again for that deal having cost Carlton his position in the company.

But at least the re-telling of *that* meeting had garnered a chuckle.

Emboldened by the shared closeness of the story, Carl motioned through the windshield. "So, Miss Rowen. Would you care for a drink?"

For a moment, it seemed as if she was going to accept. But the moment passed. "I don't think so Carl," she smiled apologetically. "Not tonight. I'm beat."

That was the answer he had expected. But she surprised him by adding, "But what are *you* going to do?"

Carlton, startled by the question, also found himself inordinately pleased. For while he was quite sure it was no more than friendly conversation, he was in desperate need of a friend.

"I have absolutely no idea." he shrugged. "I've nowhere to go, and I'm in no hurry to get there." Kelly gave a sweet laugh. "Sounds like one of Teller's songs."

Her instant referral to him sent a blade of jealousy through his heart but he buried the resentment just as quickly. He had no right to *any* proprietary feelings: and, having seen where that attitude had gotten James he had *no* desire to find himself on Tellers bad side. Or hers for that matter. . .

In truth, he had considered booking a room at the Strater, but in fear of appearing as some type of stalker, thought better of it. "I'll probably go somewhere to grab a bite and get a cheap room. As I said. I've nothing at all to do so I'll probably just hang out for a few days while I figure out what to do with my new life." He grinned, "I am, after all, without obligations at this point."

"As are we all, Carl." Kelly smiled, opening the car door. "As are we all . . ." but as her heel touched pavement, Carl suddenly felt the thin thread that had been holding him together since leaving Telluride unravelling; and just as it was about to be severed and he set adrift, she leaned back in.

"I'm glad you're staying, Carl. "she said, her smile warm. "Teller should be here in a few days, and I think he would very much like to meet you."

Carl's thread rewound. He had fervently hoped she would invite him to stay.

"Thank you, Miss Rowen."

Kelly gave him a playful look of reprimand. "Carl . . ."

"Sorry." he blushed, "I meant, *Kelly* . . . and I would very much like to meet Mr. Teller as well."

"Just don't call him Mister." She laughed, "and you'll be fine. Give me a call tomorrow morning and we'll have coffee. You can get my number from the front desk." With that, she picked up her bag and walked away.

Carl let his eyes follow the curve of her silhouette as she placed her right hand on the brass rail, took the four steps up to the entry door, and disappeared into the lobby.

Carlton's eyes lingered for a heartbeat longer.

'You might be a world class prick, James.' he thought, *'but I can certainly sympathize with you.'*

Putting the car in gear, he backed out of the parking space, pulled forward to the stop sign on Main and turned left.

He was in Durango, and on his own.

— — -- --- -- — —
— — -- --- -- —

= Chapter 36 =

Kelly entered the room and turned full circle.

It was lovely . . .

Smiling, she crossed the thick rug that softened the oak planks of the floor and going to a tall, west-facing window, gazed out on two buttes that rose above Durango.

Silhouetted against a colorful evening sky, the rosy light poured through the window; lighting the fluffy comforter that covered a massive bed. Turning from the view, the bed beckoned and she went, sitting at beds the foot to kick off her boots. Surrendering to her exhaustion she lay back: but as she did she caught the gleam of a highly polished silver ice bucket on the antique dresser. With a sigh she stood and patted the silk comforter.

"Not *quite* yet." she whispered.

The dresser was one of the original items that had been shipped from the east back in 1870 when the hotel was first built; and stepping closer, she saw that the bucket sat on an equally old, thick tapestry runner that protected the polished wood from the beads of condensation that were running down the buckets sides. But more importantly, from that bucket a familiar green tapered neck poked out from the ice; a flowered bottle of Perrier Jouet with a a card tied to its neck. She smiled. *'Nice touch, Tell.'*

Untying the burgundy ribbon that held the envelope, she ran a fingernail under its flap and removed the card.

It was an old-time photo of a saddled horse standing beneath a spreading oak tree; a rope thrown over a high branch with one end tied to the pommel, and a knotted noose at the other.

Her forehead furrowing at the image, she opened it.

Welcome to Durango, Emma, it read. *Hang tight, Butch and Sundance will be arriving soon.*

Flopping back onto the bed, she gazed up at the high ceiling and placed the card over her heart. *'I wonder which one is Sundance?'* she chuckled, and glancing over at the slender glass neck protruding from the ice bucket decided she would drink the Champagne later.

What she needed now was a little nap.

~

Kelly opened one eye to a flashing red light on the phone.

'That's odd,' she thought. *'I must have slept through the ring.'* Blinking, she, stretched, and saw she had not moved one inch. The card was still in her hand, which rested on her breast; but sitting up, she saw a fully dark sky through the tall window. "Wow," she yawned. "I guess I really needed that." But still puzzled that she slept through the call she was waiting for, she looked over to see that the ringer volume had been turned off. Mystery solved, she called the front desk and a pleasant voice picked up on the first ring.

"Good evening, Miss Rowen. How may I help you?"

It took her a moment to realize that of *course* the front desk would know her name. She was on the guest register.

"Oh . . . hi. I just noticed that I got a call. Could you tell me if the caller left a message?"

"Of course. Just a moment." there was a short pause, then, "Yes Ma'am, but the caller didn't leave a return number, just a message. Would you like to come to the front desk, or shall I read it to you?"

Kelly was far too comfortable to leave the room.

"Read it to me please."

"Yes Ma'am." the voice said. "The message was: Meet Willie tonight at the 'Lost Dog.' Here the clerk paused.

"That's a bar just north of here, off of Main and Second Avenue, and between 12th and 11th Street. Do you know it?"

"No, but I'm sure I can find it. Thanks."

Smiling, she set the receiver back in its cradle. It had been quite a while since she had last seen Willie and was looking forward to an evening with him.

Rolling out of the bed, she removed the Champagne bottle from the bucket of melted ice, peeling the foil from its neck.

"The 'Lost Dog' huh?" she chuckled.

"How appropriate . . .."

Giving the cork a pull and a twist, it shot through her hand with a loud 'Pop,' ricocheting off of the ceiling only to be followed by a fountain of Champagne that foamed out, and over her hands. Not knowing what else to do, she brought the bottle to her mouth, bringing it all to a manageable level with some nose-tickling swallows. But glancing up, she saw her reflection in the mirror.

Standing in the Victorian elegance of a parlor room, still dressed and disheveled from sleep with her lips wrapped around the tapered neck of the bottle and Champagne dripping down her chin, she cut a comical sight. And as the absurd, and slightly sexy visual sunk in, she thought again of Teller, giggling as she pictured his approving expression.

Wiping her face, she went to the dresser, picked up one of the long-stemmed glasses next to the bucket, and filled it with what remained of the sparkling liquid.

Watching the tiny bubbles migrate up the sides of the glass she decided that the effervescence was a sign of her changing fortune; and with the recognition that opportunity waits for no woman, she began peeling off her clothes.

It was time for a shower.

= Chapter 37 =

Jane tossed a couple of packets of sugar next to the coffee cup in front of James and stepped back to light a cigarette.

"Milk?"

James tore the corners from the packets. "No thanks, blacks fine." But his spoon clinking against the sides of his cup as he stirred, he peeked up through his eyebrows.

Janey leaned casually against the counter, resting her cup on her belly and watching as he stirred. But then, blowing a smoke ring into the ceiling fan, she walked around the counter, hiked her white skirt and apron up her skinny legs, sat on the stool next to his, and pulling a glass ashtray full of butts across the counter, tapped her cigarette ash onto the pile and looked directly into his eyes.

"Alright slick, you've had your drink. Now, you care to tell me what brings you back to Cortez," her steel gaze dug deeper. "Without Jack?"

James tensed. He had hoped to assuage some of his guilt by sharing the blame. But now, sitting here under Janey's scrutiny, he was having his doubts. But, he realized. It was too late now to change his mind. So, while he sipped his coffee, he laid out a very general overview of the events that had taken place since his last visit. Avoiding any personal details that might assign blame while offering only the specific of Ben's deranged objective of killing Teller, and the possibility of Jack's being in danger as well, if, for no other reason than his probable, and unfortunate, proximity to Ben's target. Hoping he had covered all bases while still covering his ass, James finished his coffee and sat back, waiting for Jane's anticipated tirade. But to his surprise, instead of anger she simply nodded and ground out her smoke in the already butt-filled ashtray. "And just exactly *why* is your nephew wantin' to kill Teller . . .?"

James sighed, lifting his eyes from the melted ice cubes in his regrettably empty glass to meet Jane's accusatory glower. Earlier he had thought that this would probably be a mistake. Now he was *sure* of it.

"I'm not real clear on that, Jane." he sighed. It was becoming evident he would have to reveal more than he wished, and with that realization his gaze went to the bottle on the shelf: then, looking back at Jane, he said, "But from what I gather, Ben was attracted to Teller's girlfriend."

"From what *I* gather," Janey snorted, "*every* man is attracted to Teller's girlfriend."

James gritted his teeth, trying to keep his embarrassment hidden. "Yes," he growled, "I suppose that's true. But for some reason Teller beat the kid up pretty bad."

Janey sneered and lit another smoke.

"I've met Teller, mister. And he ain't the kind to beat up some kid just 'cause he's makin' eyes at his girl."

Dropping the match into the ashtray, she watched the wisp of dying smoke rise into the air between them.

"No sir," she said, eyeing James. "There's more to it than that."

James felt his anger rise, but wisely tamped it down.

She was right, and he knew it. But unwilling to tell her more than absolutely necessary, he decided to try a different tack. Regrettably, his voice took on the condescending tone he habitually used with people he considered his inferior.

"The *why* isn't the issue here, *Jane* . . . The *only* reason I came through this Podunk town was that I was on my way to try and find my crazy fucking nephew. And it was only on impulse that I stopped to let *you* know what was going on." James was so absorbed in his self-righteous speech that he ignored the slight smile that was forming on Janey's lips.

"I also thought that *maybe* you or your husband might have some idea as to what to do. After all, you *are* Jack's friends." His smug self-righteousness reaching its peak he paused and turned his gaze to the liquor bottles on the shelf.

"But," he sneered, "I see now that it was a waste of *my* time. So, if you don't *mind,* how about fixing me a drink and I'll be on my way." Turning from the liquor shelf he stared straight into Janey's eyes, expecting to see her humbled. But rather than fear, a sparkle of humor twinkled just as a deep voice from directly behind him rattled his cup.

"Got a problem here, honey?"

Jane's eyes glittered with amusement while James nearly soiled himself. "Naw," she grinned, "Slick here was just tellin' me some crazy story about Jack and his friend Teller." Taking a dainty sip of coffee, she reached for her crumpled pack of smokes. "And I *think* he might be askin' for some help, but he just don't know quite how to do it."

Her smile vanished. "Is that about right Slick, or am I missing something?"

James' hand involuntarily tightened, nearly shattering the cup he held. But slowly gathering his wits he exhaled the breath he had sucked in the moment he had heard Leroy's voice. And through a clamped jaw pleaded, "Please, could you not call me 'Slick?' My name is *James.*"

The weight of Leroy's hand fell on his shoulder, and a very large thumb pressed into the base of his skull.

"The man's right, Janey," Leroy's voice boomed. "You got no reason to insult him. Call him by his given name if'n that's what he wants." The big calloused hand slid slowly across his shoulder as Leroy moved around the counter to the coffee pot where the big man poured; and as he lifted the cup to his lips, James' heart gave an irregular thump.

The damn thing looks like a demitasse cup in that hand!

He gulped, his gaze going to the bottle on the shelf again, only this time dread overcame pride.

"I think I've had enough coffee Jane," he stammered, tipping his head in the direction of the shelf. "I'll have another Stoli . . . *if* you don't mind."

Janey ground her cigarette into the ashtray. "I don't mind at all, Sli . . . 'scuse me. James. First one was on me. Second one you'll have to pay for."

"No problem," he mumbled, and with a weak smile took out his wallet and laid a platinum AMX card on the counter with a shaking hand.

Leroy's massive palm slapped the card and shoved it back across the counter. "Don't pay her no never mind Jim. But there's no more after this one." He motioned at the wall clock with his chin. "It's still early, and it sounds like you got something to say. Now, I know you already told Janey here some of it, but if you don't mind, I'd like to hear the *whole* story."

James waited for Janey to pour; and the moment she placed it in front of him he lifted the glass and drank as if the contents would transport him far, far away.

Straddling the adjacent stool, Leroy glanced at his wife and nodded. "Okay Slick." He smiled, but his eyes were cold.

"Shoot."

James rattled the ice in his now empty glass, and nearly cried.

―― ― -- ---- -- ― ――
― ― ― ― ―
-- ---- --

= Chapter 38 =

Bristling at the laughing retreat of the Raven and blinded by warm blood, Ben grit his teeth against the pain, tearing the left sleeve from his shirt to wrap it around his head. But the blood pulsing from the three ragged gashes soaked through in seconds. Tearing away the soaking cloth, the white bone of his skull glistened from beneath the bloody flaps of flesh that were still attached.

Shaking in rage, Ben threw the rifle into the back of the Hummer; slamming the hatch and blindly stumbling along vehicles side, his wet, sticky hands leaving gory streaks along the once pristine paint. Reaching the door, he pried the door open, leaning on it to steady himself when he nearly collapsed; but crawling in he steadied himself on the steering wheel, pulling his right arm across his forehead to clear the blood. But the rough material snagged the hanging meat of the wounds: and as the flesh tore further Ben screamed in agony; salty tears mingling with blood.

Trying to jam the key in the ignition, the key slipped from his wet fingers and the demons in his head punished him with hot spikes. . . sobbing, he wiped his hands across the upholstery and picking up the key a second time, jabbed it into the slot so savagely it nearly broke off in the ignition. Incredibly, it bent only slightly and the motor roared to life.

A vicious snarl twisting his damaged features, he threw the transmission into reverse and stomped on the gas.

The vehicle jerked violently; straining to break free from the ancient tree trunk that anchored it: the steel bumper having hewed as deeply as if it had been an ax, leaving the weight of the tree leaning heavily against the crushed grill.

Screaming in rage, Ben pounded the dash with his fist, railing at the heavens while grinding the gearbox into four-wheel drive. The transmission engaged with a shuddering clunk, and Ben laid his full weight onto the gas pedal.

The powerful engine strained to free itself; the vehicle shuddering down to the rivets while the tree shook so hard against the mechanical onslaught that needles began to rain onto the hood.

Howling in madness, Ben's chest heaved in great, racking sobs but were drowned out by the shrieking of a motor that threatened to come apart.

But he would not let up. He pushed the pedal harder.

No vehicle was designed for this level of abuse. The rear end clattered as the frame twisted, bucking against the immovable object that held it tight . . . the engine screamed against a tree that groaned at the pull of steel. It was machine against nature, and something had to give.

Tires smoked as the torque increased.

Finally, some hidden flaw deep within the trees core succumbed to the incredible stress and it split with a thunderous crack; twisting and toppling sideways, crashing to the ground in a cloud of dust and splinters.

The sound of its demise echoed up the canyon, scattering the swallows that nested in the overhangs.

With a howl of triumph, Ben wiped the hot, salty blood from his eyes and stared through the shattered windshield. for he knew that if he followed the Raven, it would lead him to Teller.

— — ·· —·· — —
— — · — —
·· —·· —·

= Chapter 39 =

Tipping his glass, James sucked the last of the vodka from the melting cubes.

The drink had helped calm nerves that the strong coffee; coupled with Leroy's unexpected appearance had put on edge. But now, with courage born of pride, indignation, and Stolichnaya, he re-told the tale. Only this time, due Leroy's vigilant ear, he included many of the unflattering details he had left out in the story he had recounted to Jane.

But his liquor induced confidence quickly evaporated, and by the time he finished describing the affair with Teller at the lake he was so agitated he insisted on a third drink.

Leroy frowned but nodded to Jane, who leaned against the counter, a cigarette dangling from her lips.

A small amount of sympathy colored her skepticism as she listened to James' revamped story, but she had no intention of providing more liquor. But, with her husband's nod, she took James' empty glass, dropped in three cubes, and poured a healthy splash over the ice.

"Soda?"

James shook his head, picked up the glass, and downed the entire drink in one swallow.

Leroy watched James' adams apple bob up and down, waiting for him to continue, but he remained silent, staring forlornly at the empty glass. Leroy gave it another minute, then reached over and pried the glass from James' grip.

"You ain't going to find salvation in there, boy."

Janey ground out her cigarette and chuckled, "Honey, you ain't heard the part about his nephew wantin' to shoot Teller yet."

That got Leroy's attention.

Cocking his head, he frowned, "Is that right?"

James gave a weak nod.

Laying a massive forearm on the counter, Leroy leaned in, his grey eyes cold.

"Now why in the *world* would your nephew want to shoot *Teller?*"

Avoiding Leroy's probing stare by focusing on the teaspoon's worth of diluted liquor that mingled with the melting ice in the bottom of glass in Leroy's fist, James mumbled. "Because he's crazy."

"Hmmm." Leroy nodded. "Well, that's usually how it starts."

With a tired sigh, Leroy thumped the glass onto the counter and stood. "I'm going to go get the Caddy ready. Janey honey, why don't you go on and pack up some grub for the road. Slick, you come with me. We still got some talkin' to do."

Sliding reluctantly from his stool, James snatched up his glass, and drained the last of the liquid.

"Please," he whimpered. "My name is *James.*"

= Chapter 40 =

Little Raven continued to follow the Eagle as it sailed north above the highway, winding through a country of low mesas and long vistas to finally crest a rise where the little town of Mexican Hat came into view. Here the magnificent bird screamed its wild call and banked west; growing ever smaller until it was no more than a speck against the blue.

Now alone, Junior looked down at the fuel gauge. Empty.

Taking his foot from the gas pedal, the big car began to slow; the Buicks sheer weight putting a new spin on Newton's first law of motion.

Junior smiled. *'Apparently old Isaac wasn't driving nearly four tons of steel when he had that particular revelation'*

Fortunately, a gas station waited at the bottom of the long hill, and seeing the faded Shell sign, Junior gave a quick thanks to his personal gods as the old Buick coasted down the long grade, coming to rest under a dented steel canopy.

'This sleek hunk of steel is a hell of a ride,' he thought, *'but it was built for nineteen cent a gallon gasoline'.*

Swinging the heavy door open, he stepped out, pressed his fists into his lower back and groaned, *'and the concept of suspension was clearly in its infancy.'*

Thankful for the shade of the canopy, Junior leaned against the fender and pumped. And as the rapid 'dings" rung out, counting each gallon that poured down the gullet of the thirsty beast, he was thankful for his credit card as well.

But as he pumped, he felt a presence behind him, and turning saw three old Navajo men in battered straw cowboy hats admiring the car while remaining a respectful distance away.

The tallest of the three made a quick gesture at the Buick, commenting in tribal tongue to his companions. They all chucked, and Little Raven gave them a smile rivaling his uncles. "Yes, it *is* a nice horse." he replied in Navajo.

At this, the men's quiet laughs turned to surprised smiles and the dark man who had made the comment asked in English: "You are of the Diné?"

Proudly, and in the language of the People, William Gaagii Knowles nodded. "I am. But my horse is not."

He left the men laughing as he went inside to pay.

Selecting a bag of chips and a soda, he had a short, flirty conversation with the pretty young Navajo girl behind the cash register; and with a smile and a wave goodbye, walked out to the car.

The men were gone, and the street was now as empty as an old western movie set but for a candy wrapper that fluttered across the road in the light breeze.

~

Driving north, Junior reached the 261 turn off, wondering if this was the same direction the Eagle had taken. He felt that it was, and that thought gave credence to his sense that this was all some grand plan; and with the thought that he was no more than a small, but necessary player in the game, he gazed out at the expanse of big, empty country beyond his windshield. Emptiness of this magnitude provided more than sufficient room to lose one's self in one's thoughts.

As a lifeline, he turned the radio on, and pressing the 'seek' button watched the numbers scroll by. Eventually the radio locked onto a talk station; but after twenty minutes of listening to PBS rattle on about the globe's sorry state of affairs found himself sufficiently depressed and pushed the button again. The digital numbers scanned the airwaves until finally it locked onto some old Jethro Tull.

Junior smiled. Music was *much* preferable to reality.

The road climbed up the mountainside, and with Ian Andersons flute mixing with the fragrant scent of Pinion and

Cedar blowing through the open windows, William relaxed. He was very much looking forward to seeing his Grandfather again, as well as both Teller and Jack, and he was *most* curious about this 'bear' fellow that Teller had joked about.

Taking a left at the next junction he began his descent down southern shoulder of the Abajo Mountains and into the warmer air of Fry Canyon.

= Chapter 41 =

Teller leaned forward in his chair.

"When did you say Young Bill would be here?

Billy gave an indulgent chuckle. "I didn't say."

"Okay, Chief." Teller grinned. "Let me re-phrase. When do you *expect* him to arrive?"

Billy just pulled the brim of his battered hat down over his eyes and settled back into his rocker.

Teller had become accustomed to the old Indians retreats into silence. So, pushing up out of his chair, he hopped down the steps of the porch and headed towards the river. The bay was heating up and the cool water would do him good.

The smooth, rippled sandstone surface of this ancient seabed made for easy walking, and quickly reaching the sharp cut the river had made in the earth, he stood on its lip and looked down. The river was still muddy from the spring runoff but the visibility was acceptable for a dive. So, with the water promising to wash away both the heat *and* his apprehension, Teller pulled off his shirt, then sat on the ledge to pull off his boots. But when he stood to drop his pants the hot rock caused him to do a little tenderfoot dance.

'Damn,' he grumbled, reaching down to the buttons on his Levis. *'I need to get out of my boots more often.'*

Unzipping, he did a quick check to make sure there was no one around to offend. For while Teller wasn't particularly modest, he did have a modicum of respect other people's. However, he was alone; so, slipping off his Levi's, he drop kicked his boxers onto the rocks, stretched, and smiled.

The afternoon sun felt delightful on his naked skin.

Stepping gently to the stone lip, Teller stood, his arms at right angles and his toes hanging over the ledge, the warm breeze tickling the fine hairs on his body as he prepared to dive into the chilly water. Suddenly the hair on his neck rose, and he felt a powerful presence at his back.

Teller's first thought was that death was imminent: that Ben had found him and his demise was arriving by bullet, sent special delivery via lunatic. But a long second later, he found himself still standing: pain free, with no sound of a gunshot echoing across the sage and with no precious body fluids leaking from recently applied bullet holes.

Deeply relieved, he remained absolutely still, waiting.

But for what?

Closing his eyes, he sending out mental fingers; but they grasped only air . . . and as he stood, he realized that while the feeling remained, he sensed no malevolence. Only *power*. With that, he began to turn.

~

The bell on the screen door tinkled as Abbott pushed through and stood, gazing across the wild landscape.

Something was wrong . . .

He looked down at Billy. "Where's Teller?"

Billy opened one eye and tipped his head towards the lake. "He went that-a-way."

Abbott nodded. "Okay then, where's Jack?"

Opening his other eye, Billy noted Abbott's obvious anxiety. "I've no idea, Abbott. Perhaps he went with Teller."

Again, Abbott nodded. "Maybe. . ." Suddenly Abbott's expression was of a man who had made a difficult decision. "Billy" he said, leaning forward, "do you think this will all work out?" Billy raised his eyebrows and looked down at the cup at his feet. It was empty, and he wished it were otherwise. Ahhh, but that was a different problem altogether. He returned his attentions to Abbott.

"Which 'this' do you mean, Sir Bear? There are many."

Billy's response relieved Abbott's fretfulness, and a smile took its place; for in the days that had passed, he and Billy had reached a rare balance.

Having spent years in the field and countless hours interacting with the tribes of the Southwest; Abbott had developed a personal affinity for its people, and their culture. But in all of his searching, and of all of the men he had met, he had never *dreamed* he would find a man such as the one who sat across from him now: for Billy was a treasure trove of more than simply information. He was a living connection with the past. And, more fascinating still he was a man who seemed to be a conduit with the spiritual world. A world that, regardless of whether it had been lost, forgotten, or existed only in the minds of believers, was nevertheless exercising considerable influence on the lives of himself *and* his new friends.

As for Billy, Billy found great pleasure in not only Abbott's extensive knowledge, but of his instinctive understanding of spiritual matters beyond most Billagaana's grasp. But he particularly appreciated in Abbott a trait that he shared with his friend Teller. An inherent virtuousness, coupled with an incorruptibility of soul.

Billy was *quite* sure it had been this unique quality that had been instrumental in bringing the two of them together. And it was *that*, in combination with Teller's predilection for chaos which had most certainly attracted Coyotes attention.

At the mere thought of Coyote, Billy felt an internal harmonic vibrate within the universal fabric . . . But then, the hiss of a beer being opened calmed the vibration, returning Billy to the present. Abbott taking a drink and unaware of the cosmic interlude, continued.

"The 'this' I mean," he said, waving the can in an all-encompassing gesture, "is everything that has happened recently. Teller's surprise return, the Coyote, and of course, the discovery of the cave and its treasure. But for me, the event with Estebanico's spirit is of a special interest."

Billy, originally trying to simply placate Abbott, suddenly sat forward, his expression suddenly intensely curious.

"Estebanico's spirit? I don't believe you've mentioned this to me."

Abbott's forehead wrinkled. "Haven't I? Are you sure? Hmmm. Well, things *have* been a bit hectic lately . . . Well then. Perhaps *you* can help me understand it better. But before I tell you about that, please answer me this. You are familiar with the history as well as the origin of this gold. Do you think the discovery of these coins and stones will bring us misfortune?"

Billy's megawatt smile returned.

"My dear Abbott. *That* will depend on what you do with them." Leaning forward as if in confidence, a youthful gleam sparked in his dark eyes. "And *that* was an answer that should be quite obvious to a man of your intelligence."

With a quiet chuckle, Billy sat back in his chair, but his smile faded. "But, now, please tell me of Estebanico's spirit. For what occurred in that cave may have greater bearing on your fortune than you might realize."

~

With the comfort that no bleeding bullet wounds brought, Teller continued his turn towards the source of the unknown power: and as he rotated he was reasonably sure of what to expect. But, having no idea as to how it might manifest itself he made the turn with no small amount of trepidation.

Upon completion, the corners of his eyes crinkled.

There sat the golden-eyed Coyote, its head slightly tilted, with what could easily pass for a grin spread across his long muzzle, the look of smug intelligence unmistakable.

A smile of equal satisfaction crossed Teller's face, and he squatted on his heels to be at eye-level with this joker. Teller, however, had forgotten that he was naked, and his gonads made a pendulum swing across the rough sandstone. Bolting upright in surprise, he could almost hear Coyote laugh.

Glaring at the grinning canine he checked for damage.

"Screw you, Wiley," he grumbled. "Yours are all safely tucked away in a nice furry package."

Following a quick inspection and pleased that all was well he slipped on his Levis. "And a far superior design in *my* humble opinion." Now partially dressed, he sat cross-legged, making eye contact with the creature.

"So, you furry bastard, what brings *you* here today?"

The Coyotes grin vanished, and the creature's aura of amusement vanished as silent words of warning tattooed themselves across Teller's consciousness.

'Madness comes . . ..'

The sensation of Coyotes voice inside of his mind was uncomfortably invasive.

"Thanks," Teller smiled. "But I already know about Ben. Besides, I think *you're* responsible for this whole damn thing in the first place."

Coyote gave a shrug that was felt rather than seen. . . only this time the sensation manifested itself not in his intellect: but in his heart. Then, rising gracefully on all fours the Coyote tipped its ear to the sky as if listening. A moment passed, and turning its yellow eyes back to Teller, gave a shake of its magnificent coat. Suddenly the air was filled with an otherworldly dust that lifted and spread, scattering in every direction to glitter in the fading rays of the Sun.

At first, the cloud of dust simply expanded. But the motes began to drift and spin; forming patterns that quickly became small galaxies as they grew to rise and take their positions in the sky. Mesmerized by the cosmic display, Teller found himself suddenly weightless.

Now, he too began to rise; and as he lifted his very essence seemed to gradually dissolve into smaller particles; splitting into atoms that merged with the spinning dust-stars.

Suddenly, far away, a screeching caw split the silence and the spinning stopped.

He crashed back to earth.

Teller opened his eyes to a flurry of wings, and huge raven swept down, landed between he and the Coyote, and tilting its iridescent head, directed one shining black eye at him.

Feeling quite disadvantaged, Teller looked to Coyote; and saw that as it gazed at the bird, its quasi smile returned.

Immediately mistrustful, Teller saw that the Raven held what looked to be the bloody remains of a rodent in its claw: and turning its glittering black eyes to him, the bird took the gooey object in its beak and with three quick hops placed the item at his feet.

Curiosity winning over revulsion, Teller bent to pick it up.

It took only a moment to recognize what it was: a mass of human hair. . . it took a few seconds longer to realize that the hair was still attached to a chunk of bloody flesh. Teller reached down, picked it up, and holding bloody the piece of scalp between his fingertips looked at the Raven, who raised its beak, hopped up and down twice, and squawking happily, flew off.

Disgusted, Teller watched the bird go, then turned to Coyote.

Coyote watched Raven fly off as well. But once out of sight looked back at Teller and with the wink of a a golden eye trotted into the desert; blending into the sage just as he had done with Abbott on this very spot only a few days earlier.

Left staring into the sage where Coyote had dissolved, Teller dangled the Raven's prize between two fingers and called out, "Aren't you forgetting something?"

A spot of air shimmered above the sage but nothing more. Teller waited a moment longer.

Nothing.

He dropped the mangled clump of hair and flesh onto a rock.

"I'll just leave this here," he called out, "Just in case you want it later." Looking once more to the sage, he then raised his eyes to the sky where the bird had winged its way through the western sky.

With a shake of his head, he looked down at the flat stone where Ben's scalp lay to see that a trail of ants were already snaking up its side to enjoy their newfound feast.
Teller's lips pulled into a tight smile.

"I *seriously* doubt that *that* is going to make the little lunatic more prone to reasonable conversation . . ."

With a final glance to the sky, Teller returned to the ledge, dropped his pants for a second time, and dove, cutting deep into the water.

= Chapter 42 =

The click of heels on Oak treads echoed through the lobby and the desk clerks weren't the only pair of male eyes that turned to admire the woman trailing her hand down the staircase's highly polished rail. Dressed casually in worn jeans, boots, and a short jacket, she was still striking.

The eyes of the married men swiveled, assessed, then darted back to the faces of their wives: many a second too late while the desk clerk's smile widened with every step of her approach.

"Miss Rowen! *How* may I help you?"

The young man's eyes revealed hunger, his weasel grin reflecting the response he fantasized she might give. But Kelly simply smiled and placed a slip of paper on the counter in front of him. "I'm going out. If anyone calls they can reach me at this number." Eyeing the digits, his fantasy-fueled smirk followed her to the door. But as she laid a hand on the brass handle she spun on one heel. "You can erase those thoughts little boy," she said, the smile on her face as cold as it was sexy. "You are *completely* out of your league."

The young man's jaw dropped, guilty shame replacing his leer. "Yes Ma'am!" he gulped. "Of course."

Struggling to contain her laughter, Kelly turned, putting her hand to her mouth as she stepped through the glass doors and down the steps.

Following the 1800's replica streetlamps that lined Main Street, she headed north towards the "Dog," her steps light. It was gratifying to still be lusted after, and the kid was cute, but he was certainly no match for the man who held her heart.

~

Working his way through the noise and the crowd, Kip delivered Willie his first beer of the night.

"Here ya go Willie."

Looking up from the three-legged wooden stool, Willie nodded, took a slug, set the mug at his feet, and plucked the 'B' string.

"Hey Willie," Kip asked, "you heard from Jack?"

The tone of the string wowed down, then up again as Willie twisted the tuner.

"Nope."

Tugging on the bar rag that seemed to be permanently wrapped around his neck, Kip sighed, "that's too bad."

Willie glanced up. "Why's that?"

The smile that spread across Kip's face lit up like a kid on Christmas. "'Cause that guys the bomb! The girls still ask about him."

Willie smiled as he twisted a tuning knob. "Yeah, that *was* some fun." But then he frowned, "but the next morning was a bitch."

Kip snorted. "For *you* maybe. For me it was a slippery ride in the playground."

Willie squinted a red eye at the young man's smiling face and grumbled around the pick between his teeth. "Give it a few years son, give it a few years . . ." Turning his attention back to his guitar, he gave the tuning key another twist, and the string snapped. Biting down on the pick, he threw an accusatory glare at Kip, pulled a new pack of strings from the case, unwrapped a fresh 'A,' string, and wound it around the peg, mumbling as he did. "Did hear from Teller tho.'"

"No shit!?" Kip blurted, his excitement raising the pitch of his voice.

Willie bit down on the pick and twisted the tuner.

"No shit . . ."

The string tightened incrementally, and with a final pluck, he brought it into tune. Done, he looked up and smiled. "I'm supposed to take care of his girlfriend until he gets here."

He strummed a G chord, nodded, and bent to pick up his beer. "She should be in town any time now."

Kip started to speak, but suddenly a loud, drunken shout erupted from across the room.

Flashing Willie a quick smile, Kip tugged on the rag around his neck. "Gotta go man, let me know when you're ready for another beer." Willie thanked Kip's back and glanced up at the clock on the wall. He should probably give the hotel a call and see if Kelly had checked in yet, but he wanted somewhere with a little more privacy.

Laying the Gibson back in its case, he picked up his beer, stepped through the French doors and out onto the patio. Once there, he breathed a sigh of relief. It was quiet and warm . . . a *much* more peaceful environment. Smiling, he took a seat at an empty table beneath a grass umbrella and oriented himself according to the view. A view that consisted of the mesa above the fence, as well as a group of pretty young women who were drinking bottled beer two tables over, the tabletop littered with empty shot glasses.

One of the girls noticed him and turned her head to smile. Willie smiled back as he dialed the hotel.

It looked like it was gonna be a good night.

~

Tucking his pencil behind his ear, Kip bit his tongue. He could see that this table was going to be a problem. Assuring the loudest jerk of the group that yes, he *had* their order right, and he would be right back, he turned towards the bar and stopped dead in his tracks.

Whoa!

There, on the corner stool was a newly arrived patron. He had never seen the woman before, so she wasn't a local. But *damn* she was gorgeous. His priorities instantly shifting, he slipped into stud mode. *'Those idiots can wait.'* he grinned, moving her direction while straightening his shoulders; then, popping a breath mint, he covertly checked himself in the bar mirror. Satisfied, he pulled the rag from his neck, stepped up, and put on his most charming smile.

"'Evening, Miss. What can I get you?"

The corners of her eyes crinkling in a smile, she nodded at the wall behind him.

"Quite the selection of Tequila you have here."

"Yes Ma'am," Kip purred, resting his elbows on the bar and leaning close. "We carry sixty of the world's finest. May I offer any recommendations?"

Kip's suave act was smooth enough for the girls he generally dealt with, but the woman across the bar from him now was *nothing* like the schoolgirls that typically warmed these stools.

Pursing her lips, Kelly studied the young man.

Having been the subject of every possible form of machismo, she was used to the attention, and honestly, just a little tired of it. But, being a woman, and still amused from the little heartbreak back at the hotel desk, she played along.

"Your cute." she smiled seductively. "But I think I'll have a Milagro Anjeo in a glass. With ice, please."

Kip's ego swelled, with other areas quickly following suit.

"Right away, beautiful." He winked, sauntering towards the wall of bottles and smiling while a personal fantasy began brewing. *'Grrrr, Cougar . . .'*

Kelly hid her own smile behind her hand.

Returning with her drink, Kip wiped down the bar, dropped a napkin, and placed the tequila on it with a flourish.

"There you are pretty lady. And don't worry, this ones on me." Smiling, he looked into Kelly's eyes, fully expecting a response of gratitude. But instead of appreciation followed by coy interest, he saw something different, and somewhat unnerving. Her expression was not the fawning look he normally experienced at this point. This was something intrinsically more dangerous.

Lifting her drink, Kelly's eyes locked on his, and she took a sip. Then, lowering the glass to her breast as she ran her tongue slowly along her upper lip, she smiled, "So. What's *your* name?"

Kip's mind went utterly, and completely, blank. Every clever line in his arsenal, as well as every ounce of carefully cultivated sophistication vanished under the power of that smile. With his mouth working around unintelligible words, he stuttered like the town simpleton, trying desperately to untangle his tongue. Finally, following a seeming eternity of gulping and stuttering, he regained a modicum of savoir-faire.

"Kip," he muttered, holding out his hand, palm up. "Kip, that's my name. What's yours?"

Trying not to laugh, Kelly placed her hand in his palm and smiled seductively. "Kelly. Pleased to meet you Kip."

For Kip, the world went momentarily quiet.

But then a shout erupted from the back of the room and the spell was broken.

"Hey! Barkeep! How about those drinks?"

Kip blinked, and the world came rushing back.

"Hang on!" he shouted, "I'll be right there!"

With an apologetic frown he squeezed her hand. "Let me take care of these assholes and I'll be right back."

Kelly nodded while gently, but firmly, removing her hand from his. "Don't worry, Kip. I'm not leaving."

Kip's youthful exuberance overcame his polished facade.

"Cool!" he grinned, "I'll be right back!" Pulling on his towel he hustled down the bar.

Kelly watched him go

'*Men . . .*' she smiled and shook her head.

~

Willie hung up.

The desk clerk told him that Miss Rowen had indeed checked in, and that he was instructed to give the following number to whoever called. So, jotting the number down on a napkin, Willie pushed away from the table, patted the fat joint resting in his shirt pocket and glanced over to the girls across from him. They were getting boisterous, and he was happy to see a fresh round of drinks on the table.

He was right, he grinned. It *was* going to be a good night.

Punching in in the number the clerk had given him as he went back through the patio doors, he listened to it ring as he sidled up to the bar for a refill but Kip was nowhere to be seen. Scanning the crowd, he finally spotted him over in the corner with a table of boys that were already a little too rowdy for this early in the evening. It looked like they were giving him a hard time over something, but he seemed to be handling it.

'*Well . . .*' Willie grinned, reaching over the bar. '*Seeing how the boy is otherwise occupied . . .*' but just as the golden liquid began to flow into the mug beneath the tap, he saw a good-looking woman sitting at the end of the bar take a ringing phone from her purse and smile, "Hello?" and at the same time that same sultry, "Hello" came over *his* phone. Shutting off the tap, he picked it up.

"Kelly . . .?"

Hearing her name over her phone, *and* a few stools down, she looked to her right and saw a somewhat scruffy, but still handsome man in a battered cowboy hat. The fellow smiled and gave a hesitant wave.

"Hi Willie," the voice over his phone chuckled, and then, in a silky purr, said, "wipe that look off your face and come over here."

Willie blinked, thinking, '*What look?*' But his response was: "Yes, Ma'am!"

Hanging up, he topped off his mug and walked down the bar.

Kelly's smile was radiant as she slid from her stool to take his hand in hers. But Willie pulled her in for a full hug and released her, stepping back to grip her shoulders with outstretched hands while both sides of his handlebar moustache lifted over his grin. "It's been a long damn time Kelly! Teller said you were coming to town, but I sure as hell didn't recognize you sittin' there."

Picking up his mug as he took a stool, his smile lost a small degree of happiness. "Now, don't take offense, but Teller asked if I'd take care of you 'till he got here."

Kelly just patted his knee. "No offense taken, Willie. That's just Teller . . . he can be a bit . . . overprotective."

Willie nodded. "Yeah, but I can see his reasons. You're even prettier than the last time I saw you."

"And you're as handsome as ever." Kelly smiled, her heart warming at the blush her comment brought.

She loved Teller's friends. They were each and every one a rouge and a rascal: throwbacks from the days when men were defined differently, and she, for one, regretted the loss.

Bringing his mug to his lips to hide the blush, Willie gazed over the rim; catching a flash of anxiety in Kelly's eyes. His embarrassment vanished, and his voice grew serious.

"Okay, Kelly. What's Teller got himself into *this* time?"

"It's a long story Willie," Kelly sighed. "And tonight's not the night. I'm going to be here for a few days, so let's not worry about it now. Maybe we can talk about it over lunch tomorrow."

Willie nodded. He was old and wise enough to know when a woman wanted to keep a sorrow to herself.

"So there's nothing I can do?" he asked, putting his hand on hers. She shook her head and laid her free hand on the top of his. "No, Willie, not a thing." But her smile slowly returned and she looked into his eyes. "Except maybe play a few of his songs."

Willie grinned and raised his mug. "Hell, Kelly, that's easy enough. That's most of what I do anyway."

Her eyes brightened, and she raised her glass to his. "Well then, to our fool's safe return."

"To our fool, *and* his return." Willie repeated, and tipping back their respective glasses, they drank.

~

Kip, having successfully calmed down the six idiots at the back table without any trouble, turned back to the bar, anxious to get back to his quarry. But on seeing another man sitting next to his potential cougar, a genetic sense of proprietary possession surged, kindling his youthful testosterone. He was halfway across the room by the time he realized it was only Willie and immediately relaxed.

'Hell.' he chuckled, 'Willie's no competition.'

Slowing to maintain an image of cool nonchalance, he sauntered up and leaned across the bar.

"Everything's cool with those guys now." He winked, giving Willie a casual nod. "Hey Willie. What's up?"

Amusement flickered in Willies eyes as a smile played beneath his moustache. "Not much stud, what's with you?"

Kip paused, trying to gauge whether Willie's comment was sarcasm. But with his expression giving nothing away, he decided to respond by changing the subject.

"So, when you going to start playing?"

Willie turned and winked at Kelly, then turned back to give Kip a big smile.

"Just 'soon as you pour me and this beautiful woman here another drink." Kip's eyes flashed in jealous confusion, and Willie slapped the bar with his hat.

"Get to it son!" he barked.

Kip automatically jumped back a step, and wavering between anger and shock, reached for a mug, feeling more than just a little intimidated.

He looked to Kelly for direction, but she just smiled, and shrugged in silent diplomacy.

"What's the matter Kipper?" Willie shouted, "Ya deaf? Git this gal a drink and pour me a beer!"

Kelly, pitying poor Kip, slapped the brim of Willie's hat.

"Oh stop it, Willie."

Kip stopped in mid-pour, paralyzed. If anything, he was more baffled than before. The once seductive smile on this woman's face was now playful and familiar.

"Don't mind him, Kip. He and Teller have the same sense of humor."

Kip's mouth opened and closed silently like a carp. Until finally he looked at Willie and stammered, "what . . .?"

"Relax Kipper," Willie chuckled. I'm just rattling your cage. This here's Teller's girl, Kelly. I think you've heard about Teller."

Kelly gave a consoling smile. "Hello again Kip."

While Kip's ego was punctured, his curiosity quickly trumped his disappointment. He now looked at this woman with different eyes.

"You mean the same guy who Jack was talking about? That guy sounds *awesome!*"

Kelly's eyes widened, and her laughter rang like crystal.

"Good grief. You mean to tell me this poor kid's met Jack??"

Willie nodded. "Yep. Young Kipper here has gotten more than an earful about your boyfriend."

Kelly smiled and held out hand.

"Kip, you have my deepest sympathies, but I can still help. Give me a refill and I'll set you straight on some of the lies you've been told by these boys."

Willie handed his mug to Kip and looked up at the clock.

"This one too Kipper, it's almost time to go on."

Kip might have been confused, but he was happy. Putting Willie's mug under the tap, he reached up, pulled the bottle of Tequila down from the backbar, and smiled over his shoulder. "You gonna play, 'Sure felt right at the time?'

Willie reached over, shut off the tap as it spilled over the top of the glass, and picking it up, held it high. "Of course!"

Kelly shook her head and sighed, "of *course* you are . . ."

= Chapter 43 =

Teller was dry before he was even halfway back to the store. The desert air sucked the moisture from the air at an incredible rate even this late in the afternoon; but as he moved silently past the store's wooden steps he heard Abbott and Billy's voices. Pausing to peek around the corner, he saw them deep in conversation; and judging their expressions the subject was serious. But he saw no point in disturbing them. He was looking for Jack.

The situation had changed, leaving them in need of an exit strategy. And, while he had a few ideas, he still wanted to bounce them off his partner just to make sure he hadn't missed anything. But there seemed to be no sign of the man in or around the store, so he went to the chopper. But again, no Jack. That left nowhere but the trailer.

Rounding the shed where Billy's parked the Scout, Teller looked down into the darkening valley where the flickering yellow-orange glow of a small fire bounced off of the Airstreams silver skin. *'Success,'* he smiled, and with a waggle of his eyebrows, headed down the trail.

Jack was stretched out in a dilapidated folding chair staring into the flames; firelight reflecting in the liquid of the glass he held loosely in his right hand. Without bothering to look up he acknowledged Teller's arrival.

"Hey Tell."

"Hey yourself Jack." Teller smiled, pulling up a chair that was only slightly less abused then the one that held Jack. Pointing at the empty bottle that lay next to the fire, he asked, "Last of the stash?"

238

Jack shook his head, raised his glass, and took a halfhearted sip. "Naah, that one's dead, but I imagine Billy has a few more hidden away . . . he's funny like that."

Teller studied Jack. He looked tired, but more worrying was the concern in his friend's eyes. And Jack, noticing Teller's expression, lowered his glass and looked over at his longtime friend. "So then, what do you think we ought'a do buddy?'

Teller picked up the empty bottle, letting it dangle between his fingers as he gazed at the flames.

"'Bout what?"

A half smile touched Jack lips as several clever retorts came to mind, but his heart just wasn't in it. "Well," he sighed. "about the kid, mostly."

Teller gave a little snort. The memory of the Raven-delivered scalp was still fresh on his mind.

Holding the bottle so he could look at the fire through the glass, he smiled. "Oh, the kid is most *definitely* on his way."

Jack lifted one eyebrow suspiciously.

"And what makes you say *that?* "

Teller pulled the cork from the bottle, tipped it back, and let the small amount of liquor that remained trickle into his mouth. Then, with a tired smile, he put the bottles rim to his lower lip, took a deep breath, and blew one long hollow note, evoking the lonely image of a ships foghorn. The sound echoed across the dusky landscape: drifting away until the only sound remaining was the crackle of the fire.

"A little birdie just told me so." He sighed.

Setting the empty bottle between his feet, he leaned back into the rickety chair and put his hands behind his head.

"I don't, however, have any well-thought-out plans on what to do when he arrives . . . if that's what you're asking."

"Tell," Jack smiled, "you've never had *any* well-thought-out plans for *anything.* "

Teller looked up from the flames, eyebrows lifting as he wagged a finger firmly. "That's where you're wrong amigo. My seeming disorganization is only an illusion. The truth is that my life is an experiment in controlled chaos. It is simply that the subtle Zen of my existence goes unnoticed by the dulled masses." A star streaked through the sky just as he finished his comment. He watched it burn out and turned back. "You know my motto," he grinned. "Keep the enemy" But Jack interrupted with an appreciative chuckle.

"I know, I know. Keep the enemy confused. The problem, however, is that your friends are just as confused as your enemies."

Teller turned to Jack with an expression of hurt innocence.

"Jack." he frowned. "All my *friends* need do, is ask."

Jack gave a nod. "Alright then brother, I'm asking."

With his moment of brooding having passed, Teller smiled again. "Actually, Jack, that's one of the reasons I came looking for you. I have a question. Once this little problem with Ben had been concluded, what does *your* future hold?"

Jack reached down, picked up the empty bottle that Teller had dropped, and brought it to his eye, peering through the green glass at the flames.

"Well, old buddy, that kind of depends on the outcome now doesn't it?" Slowly lowering the bottle, he looked back at Teller. his expression grim.

"What happens if Ben is successful?"

Teller's expression was one of genuine disappointment.

"Jaaack," he drawled, pushing himself up out of the chair. "I got no intentions of *dyin'*."

Jack's worry slowly became a smile. He couldn't help but admire his friend's sense of self-destiny. He had never known Teller to be overly concerned with the capriciousness of fate. And on the occasions when misfortune *had* arisen, Teller's attitude was one of Que Sera Sera. He simply took things as they came and adjusted to life's disparities.

"Well," Jack smiled, raising his glass in salute. "That's real good to hear, partner, but what's your plan for *preventing* it?"

Teller chuckled. "I already told you Jack, I got no plan. But I doubt the kid's got one either, and *that* is to my advantage."

"Yeah," Jack nodded, "but he's crazy, which make him unpredictable."

Teller's smile turned wicked.

"You are absolutely right, Jacko, but he's hurt, he's angry, and he's lost the element of surprise. So again, advantage, me." Then with no preamble, he stood and began walking towards the trailer. "I'm going to go find a beer . . . you like houseboats?"

~

Billy leaned slowly back into his rocker, his face an expression of curious wonder. The fantastical tale spun by Abbott was almost beyond belief.

"So . . . the Great Spirit has taken the man who has financed the Peoples future."

Abbott considered for a moment and nodded.

"Yes, I suppose so. And ours as well. . . our financial futures I mean."

"Abbott my friend," Billy said, with a smile that chased away the shadow of his consternation. "I believe your future was determined when Coyote led you and Teller to that cave, and then the two of you, to me." His eyes twinkled, and he laughed aloud. "As your Christians like to say, the Lord moves in mysterious ways."

Abbotts brows rose and he smiled, "So now you're a believer?"

"Don't be ridiculous," Billy snorted. "But haven't you found that it's much easier to give a name to whatever deity you wish to either thank, or lay blame?"

Abbott thought for a moment.

"But that would make all gods the same."

An enigmatic smile touched Billy's lips, and he gave a nod. "Yes, and no. Let me ask you this. Are all men the same?"

A slow smile began beneath Abbott's beard.

"Yes, and no. But . . ."

"My dear Abbott," Billy said. "I do not wish to discuss the finer details of the workings of the cosmos. I remain sufficiently confused by the workings of man and his Gods as a whole, and more specifically, the particular God that is within our midst, *now*." Pushing himself from his rocker, he smiled down on Abbott's mystified expression.

"I am going to make some tea for our company. Would you like some?"

Without thinking, Abbott said yes. But with his next breath asked, "*What* company?"

"My Grandson." Billy answered. "He will be here soon."

But as he turned he paused, cocking his ear to the desert as if listening . . . suddenly, with yet another dazzling smile, he added, "As will others, it seems." With a pat to Abbott's knee, he turned and walked into the store; leaving Abbott alone and bewildered with the dry sound of a lone moth fluttering against the lantern.

——— — ‑‑ ‑‑‑ ‑‑ __ ———
——— ——— __ ——— ———
‑‑ ‑‑‑ ‑‑

= Chapter 44 =

Following James' confessional re-telling of the story, Leroy led him to the ATV parked behind the diner and motioning him in, headed towards a row of small Quonset huts huddled behind the larger aircraft hangars.

James, feeling angry and small, crossed his arms over his chest and stared across the tarmac in silence.

Leroy found this petty attitude annoying. But then again, he found *James* annoying. Ignoring him, he held his tongue until they pulled up to a pair of sliding steel doors, where he turned a disgusted eye to his mute passenger and motioned him out. At first, James hesitated, but the expression on the big mans face convinced him that it would be in his best interests to do as suggested. Grudgingly, he stepped out.

Leroy did the same, but paused, leaning on the ATV's canopy to study James across the roof. His grey eyes were steady and calm, but held no hint of friendliness.

Pulling a ring of keys from his overalls', he began spinning them around a large finger; and as they circled like the hands of a clock, time seemed to press down on James and he began to worry . . . suddenly the spinning stopped, and at the sound of the keys slapping against Leroy's calloused palm he jumped back a step. And Leroy, seeing this, made his decision. Selecting one of the keys, he inserted it into the heavy steel lock and gave a twist, pushing the big door open.

James shivered as he stared into the dark, cavernous interior; but when Leroy reached around the corner to flip a series of wall switches, banks of Fluorescent tubes buzzed and flickered; slowly illuminating the yawning abyss.

James' imagination had taken some dark turns while they rode, wondering what Leroy had in mind. And when he looked into that gaping black hole, he was downright frightened. But as he looked around now he felt his fears vanish along with his other paranoid suspicions.

He had expected a greasy workshop. But what lay before him was and area so clean one could perform surgery.

Polished stainless-steel tables lined the walls, gleaming beneath the bright lights, and above those tables perfectly organized shelves ran along the entire length of the building.

Engine parts by the hundreds lay spread across spotless surfaces like the exploded diagrams in manuals: each meticulously cleaned as evidenced by toothbrushes sticking from coffee cans reeking of toxic fluids.

At James' expression of astonishment, Leroy laid a beefy hand on his shoulder. "One little piece of grit in a piston at sixteen thousand feet could ruin your day Jim."

James gave a nod, acknowledging not only the truth of the statement, but noticing that he had gone from 'Slick,' to 'Jim.' A slight improvement at least . . .

"Yeah," he nodded, "Jack made that abundantly clear on our flight over."

It took a moment, but then Leroy remembered Jack's promise to introduce him to the fool that such a problem needed explanation; and as he put the two together he laughed his deep, rumbling laugh.

"Oh yeah, the oil pressure gauge . . . he said you were pissed about that."

James actually gave a slight smile. "Well, it wasn't so much the problem that bothered me, it was the *way* that he explained it." That produced another great, booming laugh, and Leroy motioned towards a large tarp-covered lump in the center of the room.

"Grab the other end of that, wouldja Jim?

James frowned, *'Well, it beats slick.'* then nodded, "Sure." And taking an end, on Leroy's signal, yanked.

The tarp floated up, and away; revealing a completely refurbished 1957 Cadillac Eldorado Brougham.

Lustrous under the lights, its stainless-steel roof matched the gleam of the surrounding tables.

"Wow!" James's exclaimed. "*Very* nice!" then, without thinking he blurted, "It looks like something Teller would have." A smile crossed Leroy's face as he pulled a rag from his pocket to rub at an imagined spot on the hood.

"Matter of fact, he wanted it." Leroy said, his grin growing larger. "They only made four hundred of these beauties, and Teller wanted to buy *this* one from me."

Picking up the tarp, he folded it into precise squares, set it on the counter, and taking a clean rag from the nearest bench began dusting the surface of the car.

James crossed his arms and leaned back on a table.

"Didn't want to sell?"

Leroy's deep laugh resounded through the building.

"Well, that, and the fact that he didn't have a dime to his name."

"Typical." James muttered under his breath.

Not hearing hear the comment, Leroy tossed the barely dusty rag into a barrel full of ones just like it and opened the driver's door. "Funny thing was," he said as he settled into the seat, "I got the feeling that for him it was only a temporary, and minor inconvenience."

Reaching through the steering wheel, he turned the key, and the engine fired: and as it began to purr his smile took on a noticeable element of warmth. "I knew I liked that boy at that very moment." But then, leaning out of the window, that smile took on a menacing element that chilled James' blood.

"Now Slick, get on in and tell me about this nephew of yours wantin' to kill my friend Teller."

___ __ -- --- -- __ ____
____ ___ ____ ___
-- --- --

= Chapter 45 =

Willie wrapped up his first set to a round of hoots and applause. But on looking down at the few crumpled bills that lay scattered among the loose change in his guitar case, he gave a sad shake of his head and scooped out the paltry pile, stuffing it into his pocket and joining Kelly at the bar. The place was packed but she had saved him a stool next to hers. Giving it a pat, she motioned him to sit.

"Great job Willie. You do Teller proud."

Willie dropped his hat onto the bartop. "Thanks Kell," he said with a half-hearted smile, "but it'd sure be nice if the rest of the crowd was as appreciative." Pushing the stool away, he leaned his elbows on the bar, rested his boot on the brass rail that ran its length, and gave Kip an expectant squint. Kip responded by sliding a fresh beer into his waiting hand. "There ya go!" he grinned as he moved down the bar to a group of pretty girls.

Willie nodded, drained half the glass, wiped the foam from his bushy moustache, and looked up at the clock.

"So, Kelly. What's *your* plan?'

She shrugged, "I guess I wait."

Willie gave a nod, looking down the bar where Kip was in animated conversation with the young ladies. Whistling to catch Kip's attention, he twirled his finger over both his and Kelly's glasses. "Another round, young Squire, and put it on my tab." Kip nodded, giving the girls a wink as he pulled the rag from his neck and strolled down the bar, wiping the surface as he walked. With a happy smile he pulled down a fresh mug for Willies beer, then mixed Kelly's with a flourish. "Yours are paid for as long as you're playin' Willie, and as for your gorgeous friend here, the drinks are on me."
Willie glanced at Kelly, then, turning back to Kip crooked his finger. "Hey Kipper, come here for a sec."

Kip's eyes narrowed in suspicion. But wrapping the rag around his neck he stepped close, and Willie leaned over the bar. "Buyin' drinks all well and good son," he whispered in Kips ear, "But don't be gettin' any crazy ideas . . ."

Tilting his head in Kelly's direction, he laid his hand on Kip's shoulder and gave a fatherly squeeze. "*That* one'll chew you up and spit you out." Raising his eyebrows knowingly, he sat back down.

Kip gave a nod, and he snuck a quick look her way.

She didn't seem to have overheard Willie's comment, but catching his covert glance, she smiled and at the flash of her perfect teeth he thought: *Yeah, maybe so, but I bet I'd love every minute of it.'*

Seeing Kip's expression, Willie shook his head in dismay. As a man, he could read exactly what was going through this young pup's head. Setting his boot back on the rail, he leaned over the bar a second time.

"Careful where you step, Kipper . . ."

Kip grinned wolfishly as he watched Willie turn to give Kelly a peck on the cheek.

"Time for my last set. Stick around and we can grab a late bite."

"Sure Willie." she smiled. "'I've nowhere to go."

Willie held out his mug, Kip refilled it, and throwing Kelly a wink, he headed towards the stage.

Kip watched as Willie took the steps up onto the stage and pick up his guitar. And as the next song was introduced he snuck another peek at Kelly's profile, wondering just *how* careful he needed to be.

= Chapter 46 =

Teller stuck his head out through the trailer door.

"No beer in there," he frowned. "Guess I gotta go to the store. Wanna come?" but not bothering to wait for a response he started up the trail; while Jack, still puzzling over his "houseboat" comment, struggled to get up out of the rickety lawn chair; and by the time he finally freed himself Teller was already halfway up the hill.

Jack was forced to step lively but catching up, stepped in, matching Teller stride for stride. "So, for the time being," he panted, "I'm gonna overlook the minor detail of Ben's being on his way here to kill you . . . What the fuck is this about a houseboat?"

A whimsical grin crossed Tellers face as he threw an arm over Jacks shoulder.

"Well, partner, I figgered we need a home base for a while, and I kinda like it down here." Teller waved his arm as if he were presenting the land spread out below to Jack as a gift. The last of the evening's light bathed the surface of the rock canyons in a soft orange glow, while shadows poured into the spaces between them like ink.

"Yeah, Tell," he nodded. "It *is* nice."

"Besides that," Teller said as they the crested the hill and the lights of the store came into sight. "I also happen to like my one, and only neighbor."

"Yeah," Jack chuckled. "You never *have* been one for crowds." Teller nodded in agreement, but then turned suddenly to lay his palm in the middle of Jack's chest; stopping him in his tracks and pointing towards the store with a grand smile.

There, in the lanterns soft light sat Billy and Abbott, each with a cup of tea, deep in conversation.

Teller spoke softly.

"That, my friend is undoubtedly the case. I *do,* however, appreciate good people. And yonder sit two of the finest examples I've yet to encounter . . . 'sides you of course, but that's a different thing altogether."

Jack laughed and followed Teller up the stairs and into the lantern-lit porch.

At the sound of boots on the worn floorboards, both Abbott and Billy turned to see them standing together, Teller grinning cheerfully. "Gentlemen!" he said, holding out his arms. "A *very* good evening to you both."

"Captain!" Abbott exclaimed. "Where have you *been?* I was becoming concerned."

"No need to worry old bear." Teller laughed. "Just out talkin' to God and man." He gestured a thumb over his shoulder at Jack, who stepped out from behind; smiling as he bent to retrieve the bottle of Scotch he had stashed behind the bench the day before.

"*That* being the man," Teller said, flashing Billy a conspiratorial smile, "while God remains in his furry form."

At that, Billy's smile gained wattage. But then Teller spied the teacup in Abbotts hand. Pointing a quivering finger at Abbott, he cried out in mock alarm. "And the end times must be nigh upon us! For that is surely a sign!"

At first, Abbott frowned, but then his smile flashed white beneath whiskers. "Fear not Captain, 'tis simply a change of routine."

Flopping into the nearest chair, Teller wiped his brow with exaggerated relief.

"Well then! Thank the stars that my worries are unfounded. For a moment I thought you may have drank all the Rocky Mountain swill in the Four Corners area, and the earth itself was about to burst open and swallow us whole."

Assuming a look of righteous indignation, Abbott growled,

"I *hope* you're not referring to my beloved Coors as 'swill'!" but then a sudden look of dread darkened his face and he turned to Billy.

"I've not drunk *all* the Coors . . . *have* I . . .?"

Chuckling, Billy blessed Abbott with a smile of benevolent compassion. "No, Abbott, you have not, although the in-stock supply has certainly dwindled since your arrival. But worry not, Sir Bear. I have made arrangements to have five pallets placed on board Teller's new houseboat, and both should be here tomorrow."

At this, both Abbott and Jack turned, staring at Billy, curiosity mixed with bewilderment. But then Jack turned to Teller. "You weren't shittin' were you?"

"About the boat? No Jack, I rarely shit about matters of such importance. But I *must* confess, the beer *is* a surprise."

Turning his smile to Billy, Teller said, "Tomorrow huh? Well then, it seems my credit is in good standing."

He turned back to Abbott.

"Well then old bear, while your supply of Rocky Mountain suds may be diminished, it seems is not yet decimated. So, in that light, may I get you one?"

Grinning mightily, Abbott nodded.

Teller turned to Jack. "And Jack, old friend. May I get you a glass and some ice?"

"Yes," Jack smiled, "you may, and thank you."

Teller nodded and turned to Billy. "And Billy, may I get you *anything*?"

Billy's smile was joyful, but his tone was oddly serious.

"Yes, Teller, as a matter of fact you can. There is a wooden box in my office, sitting on the top shelf of the gun cabinet. Would you be so kind as to bring it to me?"

Curious at the sudden change in Billy's demeanor Teller nodded. "Sure Billy. Top shelf?"

"Yes Teller. It is behind a box of shotgun shells. The key to the cabinet is in the top left desk drawer."

"Okay . . ." Teller nodded. "I'll be right back."

The tinkling of little bell on the screen door as Teller passed through sounded suddenly ominous; and Jack, who had noticed the change in Billy's demeanor as well, dropped his smile. "Anything I need to know about Bill?"

His dark eyes shining with affection, Billy weighed his options against his obligations, and smiled at the man who sat before him. A man he had known since birth.

~

Unbeknownst to Jack, Billy had met Jack's father at Camp Pendleton many year's prior; where, having been thrown together with hundreds of other young men from all over the country were whipped into shape for the impending war. But while Billy was put into a secret code-breaking program, Jack the first was relegated to lowly boot camp. However, once shipped off they found themselves in Iwo Jima, fighting alongside one another; and in the bloody horror of war they became friends. But wars end, and; and with goodbyes and good lucks the two men went their separate ways. But destiny often has plans other than those we make for ourselves, and many years later, in a two-bit rodeo in the tiny town of Snowflake, Arizona they were brought together once again.

Billy was riding bulls for prize money while Jack Senior was hustling cards for the local yokels' paychecks.

Jack was fast, and he was good. But when a group of cowboys realized that they had been relieved of their month's wages by an unnatural run of face cards they decided that this stranger was just a little *too* lucky, and in a demonstration of their displeasure, Jack the first's winning streak was cut short.

Billy, on the other hand, was doing well. With the competition nearly over and holding a strong first place he was on his way to winning the purse. But during a break, Billy went for a piss; and with the sounds of the rodeo clowns and the laughter of the crowd in the background he moved through the stink of the stables for a little privacy. But in the shadows, he stumbled across a man face down in the cow shit; both arms bent in unnatural angles.

Kneeling in the muck and laying a finger to the stranger's neck, Billy felt the faint pulse of life. So, picking up this beaten, slime-covered Billagaana, he carried him to his trailer, where he laid him carefully in the bathtub.

Gazing in pity at this poor soul, he turned on the shower and let the warm water wash away the ugly mix of cow shit and blood: and as the muck washed from the fellows bruised and swollen face, Billy had his second shock of the day. There, in the filthy water lay his old comrade in arms.

With it now personal, Billy gently loaded Jack Sr. into his pickup and raced to the Flagstaff hospital, leaving his prize money behind.

Fortunately for Jack Senior, his injuries were not life threatening, and with money hidden in a special belt wrapped around his waist the doctors were paid for their services. *Un*fortunately for Billy, however, the injuries required months of recuperation. So, with their shared past allowing him no alternative, Billy offered to share his small apartment near the Flagstaff campus as a place to mend.

During the course of his healing, Jack Sr. met a pretty young medical student on campus: and while he may have won her heart, the girl's father was less than thrilled with his daughter's choice in men. But, realizing there was little he could do, out of love for his "little girl" he accepted this nèer-do-well in the hopes that he might change. But he did not, and within months; to Jack's dismay and her father's outrage, she became pregnant. So, with the times being what they were, Jack Sr. reluctantly married the girl; passing his name to his newborn son while insisting that Billy become the child's Godfather. And Billy, being who *he* was, accepted.

Shackled, Jack Sr. remained in Flagstaff just long enough to complete his convalescence; spending his time playing poker with the young collage men and fleecing them out of their tuition. And once his bags were full, he disappeared, leaving his young wife alone and Billy as the child's unofficial guardian. And so, once again the wheel of fate was spun, and another ball dropped into place. . .

And so, the years had passed and that small boy had grown into a fine young man. A man Billy was as proud of as if he had been his own son. And *now* that man sat before him, holding a glass of Scotch, unaware of any of this history.

~

Jack waited patiently for an answer to his question, but Billy just shook his head.

"No, Jack. Nothing that concerns you specifically."

Jack had learned long ago that nothing was to be gained by pressing *any* issue with Billy. . . however he did find the lack of a smile on Billy's face unsettling.

"Okay . . . you think Teller will be alright?"

Billy's smile returned.

"*That* will depend on how he handles himself at a critical moment."

"I don't like the sound of that." Jack muttered just as the bell over the screen door announced Teller's return.

Stepping into the lanterns light, he held a glass of ice in one hand, a cigar box in the other, and cold six-pack tucked under his arm. "Still a few cases in back, Billy." Teller grinned. "It seems the Bear hasn't yet decimated the *entire* supply."

Setting the glass of ice on the table in front of Jack, he handed the box to Billy, plopped heavily onto the bench, and handed one of the beers to Abbott. Then leaning forward, looked into Billy's face.

"So Chief. What's in the box?"

——— — ‑‑ ‑‑‑ ‑‑ — ———
——— —— — —— ——
‑‑ ‑‑‑ ‑‑

= Chapter 47 =

Wilting under the critical eye of the big man behind the wheel, James slid into the Cadillac; reluctantly pulling the door closed behind him. Leroy gave a subtle nod, put the car in gear, and aimed it down the faded blacktop of the highway.

As the empty sage desert rolled by Leroy asked James to repeat the story he had told Jane earlier. But he was so obsessed with the imagined abuses he had suffered at Tellers hand that his tale was more a litany of complaints than a source of any real information. Leroy listened patiently for a few miles, then held up his hand, silencing James' whining.

"You can cut the bullshit right there, Jim. All I need is for you to do is tell me exactly what happened. Not how you think Teller ruined your goddamnd life."

James began a stuttering defense but Leroy's responding glare stopped him before he could whimper his first excuse. Clearing his throat, he began again more honestly this time; still striving to present himself in a more favorable light than the truth would allow.

As they drove along the old county road west, Leroy framed strategies while ignoring the obvious incongruities in James' story. He cared nothing for delicate egos. He needed to understand the enemy. So, as they wound between the rocky cliffs that hemmed in the cracked two-lane blacktop, he attempted to sift grains of truth from the mountain of exaggerations that was James' tale.

Soon enough, the tiny town of Aneth came into view; and having heard enough Leroy turned the Caddy around and headed back to Cortez. Only *this* time it was he who asked the questions; and rather than simply letting James steer the story he formulated a plan of sorts.

By the time they rolled up to the rear steps of the diner Leroy was confident he had a fair grasp of the problem. Putting the Cadillac into 'park,' he turned, and focused his grey eyes on James. "So then, Jim. Just exactly what happened the last time you saw the boy?"

At first, James was silent: but choosing his words carefully he described the makeshift hospital room he had set up in his home, followed with a selectively worded account of Ben's disappearance. Leroy raised an eyebrow, pressing him for details and when James reluctantly mentioned the photograph with the i.v. needle sticking through Teller's eye, Leroy leaned back into the brocade seat and stared at the upholstered roof.

Turning angry, unbelieving eyes on James he growled,

"Son of a *bitch,* boy! And you let the kid loose with a *rifle?*"

James' distress evaporated as all of his resentment and frustration came to a head. Arrogance smothering his guilt he lifted his fist and hammered the steel dash.

"God*damn* it!" he shouted, "I didn't *give* him the fucking thing! He *stole* it, *and-my-car!*" His anger now in full bloom he raised his fist to swing a second time but Leroy's hand shot out, enveloping James' entire fist in his ham-sized paw and halting it mid-swing.

The pain of Leroy's crushing grip caused James to yelp out in shock; and the astonishment of seeing his entire fist enclosed in Leroy's massive hand extinguished his rage.

Throwing James' throbbing fist back onto his lap Leroy scowled, "Careful with the car, son."

James sat, perfectly still, cradling his hand. Then, scooting across the seat he pressed himself up against the passenger door, massaging his crushed fingers while wondering what the hell *ever* made him think coming here was a good idea in the first place.

Seeing James cowering against the door, Leroy shook his head in disgust. . . Tilting the steering column up, he pulled on the chrome door handle. pushing the door open with his knee. Then he reached around to open the back door. The pillarless, suicide door design was one of the main reasons he had bought this model Caddy in the first place: for once both doors were swung wide it became much more accommodating for a man of his size. Unfolding gracefully from the cars confines he stood, stretched, walked around the car and politely opened the door.

"Step on out son."

As hesitant as James was to get out, he was even more reluctant to stay: but bearing in mind the fragile nature of his situation he wisely chose to accept Leroy's suggestion. As his foot touched the ground, Leroy closed the steel door with a solid "thunk," and laid a heavy arm over James's shoulders.

"Yer goin' home Jim." he said, guiding him towards his pickup.

James was unsure whether he was upset, or relieved. He liked to think he was no coward, but during that brief moment when Leroy's hand had been clamped over his fist he realized that he was no hero either.

Turning, he looked up into Leroy's eyes.

"What do you mean?"

It was a stupid question, and he knew it the moment it left his lips.

Leroy's response was non-threating but left no room for discussion. "I mean, Jim, that you should just go back home. Seems to me that you pretty much created this problem, and while I appreciate your drivin' all the way down here to tell me n' Janey about it, I don't think you'll be any more helpful than horseshit in fixin' it." Holding James by the elbow he opened the driver door of James' truck, eased him in, and leaned into the open window. "I'll give Jack a call to tell him we're comin,' and we'll be lookin' for your goddamnd nephew. *You* just scoot on back to Telluride and take care of whatever the hell it is you do up there." Pushing the truck door shut, he gave it a solid pat. "I appreciate you comin' down, Jim, I really do." But as he stepped away he saw the half-empty bottle of Scotch lying on the seat. Frowning, he reached through the window and gave James' shoulder an iron grip. "An' you might want'a keep that corked till you get home." Releasing his hold, Leroy turned, and walked back towards the diner.

James had sucked in his breath the moment Leroy's hand landed on his shoulder, and he was still holding it as he watched the big man walk away, terrified that he might change his mind and come back. But once his considerable bulk had passed through the diner's back door James exhaled a long breath of relief, started the truck, put it into gear and stepped on the gas, carful not to spin the tires.

As he made the first turn out of the airport the bottle of Scotch rolled across the seat and bounced against his leg. Looking down at it, Leroy's suggestion rang in his ears; but the minute he pulled onto the highway he glanced into his rearview mirror, grabbed the bottle, and pulled the cork with his teeth.

~

Janey stuffed a spare pack of smokes into her purse and smiled at the man who had shared her life since she was sixteen. "So, where's Slick?"

Leroy bent to give her cheek a kiss and picked up the cooler at her feet. "Honey, I sent that worthless sack home."

"Good." She nodded. "That prima donna would'a just been in the way."

Slinging her purse over her shoulder, she followed Leroy through the door, pulling the chain on the neon Coors sign as she passed. It flickered twice and died.

Once outside, Janey paused, and as the warm sage-scented air filled her nostrils, a private smile crossed her lips

'Bout time Leroy took me somewhere.'

Securing her purse over her shoulder, she locked the door and took the steps to where the Caddy idled smoothly: 50's rock and roll playing through the dash speaker.

Leroy leaned across the expansive seat and swung the passenger door open; and Janey, smiling at the gesture dropped her cigarette onto the asphalt and ground it out with her heel. Sliding across the seat she laid her head on his shoulder and rested her hand on his knee.

Leroy patted her hand and put the big car in gear.

After a few miles of listening to the radio overlapped with the hum of tires on the highway, Janey patted his knee and scooted away.

Pressing the chrome window switch she lit a fresh cigarette as the glass slid silently out of sight; and blowing a thin plume of smoke into the wind that whistled by, turned to her husband.

"What're you thinkin' Leroy?"

His bushy eyebrows furrowed, and he gave a crooked smile. "I'm thinkin' that our friend Teller sure has a habit of gettin' himself in a world of shit." but then the smile disappeared and he gritted his teeth. "And god*damnd* if he don't always drag Jack right into the middle of it with him!"

Chuckling, Janey stuck her cigarette in the ashtray and got on her knees to lean over the big bench seat.

"Ahh, now honey, that aint fair." she said, rustling through the cooler and coming back with a couple of soda cans. "You and I both know Jack always volunteers for whatever shit he ends up in. It ain't right to blame it *all* on Teller."

Leroy laughed. She was absolutely right. But his fatherly feeling for Jack were hard to shake. And the favors he was forced to call in to expedite that extraction from Arizona a few years back still rankled.

"Yeah. You're right, sweetheart, you're right. But dammed if Teller ain't always right in the thick of whatever it is." Taking a giant drink, he handed the empty can back to his wife.

"Do me a favor Janey, see if you can get Jack on the phone. I want to let him know we're comin,' and see if they've had any sign of this crazy kid."

= Chapter 48 =

Placing the box Teller had delivered reverently on his lap, Billy closed his eyes and began rocking gently. Abbott looked to Teller; who simply shrugged, wishing he had his guitar: while Jack sat back and sipped his Scotch.

The minutes passed with no one daring to disturb Billy with unnecessary conversation. Suddenly, a coyote's howl broke the silence. It echoed through the canyon, slowly fading until it blended into the many other chirps and rustles of the desert night.

Teller tipped his ear, taking note of how each creature's song was akin to an instrument in an orchestra: in, and of themselves, they were nothing more than a single, repetitive beat. But joined together they formed a grand symphony.

It was with this concept that he smiled, thinking how intricately interwoven the tapestry of the world seemed to be. Yet *his* life, and the events of the past few weeks were more like some mad, free form jazz than the glorious opus that guided the cosmos. And with *that* thought, he began composing a song that would encapsulate his life. The title, he decided, would have to be: *'You never see it coming.'*

Setting his boot heel to tapping out a rhythm on the worn wooden planks, he began out a rough melody line in his head when his ears picked up a faint, but distinct, rumbling in the distance . . . recognizing it immediately, he grinned. With strange events having become the norm as of late, his future being delivered in a 1950's steel package did not strike him as surprising. But with his muse now interrupted, he turned to Billy; only to find the old Navajo studying him. Eyebrows raised and dark eyes filled with humor.

"A unique sound, is it not?" Billy smiled, but before Teller could respond the coyote yipped again; adding cosmic approval to the unexpected arrival. Teller's gaze went from Billy's magnificent grin to twin yellow beams that scrolled across the sandstone walls in the distance as the vehicle wound down the switchback.

"Unique indeed . . ." Teller smiled, nodding in agreement while wondering what was next.

Billy studied Teller for a moment longer, then lifted the box from his lap and placed it on the bench at his side. Turning to Abbott, he smiled, "Sir Bear, would you be so kind as to bring the tea? It seems your future has arrived."

Abbott had been watching the lights as well, but with Billy's request followed by the odd comment, Abbott's forehead knotted in curiosity. "Of course," he nodded.

Billy smiled his thanks, pushed out of the rocker, and going to the stairs, laid his hands on the rail to wait. Jack went to join him, while Teller just sat, wondering what was in that box; but his curiosity was cut short as the twin beams of headlights swept across the porch, lighting Billy's smile in their twelve-volt glow as they passed over him; but then, quickly doused, left only a gleaming silhouette; reflecting starlight from its polished bulk: the cast iron engine ticking as it cooled in the sudden silence . . . but one by one, the chirps, rustles and squeaks of the desert night returned to fill the void created by the steel beast's arrival.

Expectancy hung in the air: then, finally, the driver's door swung open, allowing the weak illumination of the dome light outline a tall figure. But the heavy steel door thumped closed and the darkness was once again complete.

Suddenly, bright teeth flashed in the dark and Junior came bouncing up the steps. "Grandfather! it is good to see you again" and taking Billy by the shoulders he pulled him close, his smile one of both love and deep respect.

"I've missed you, Grandfather."

262

Releasing Billy with a final squeeze, he turned to Teller and held out hid hand "And it is *very* good to see *you* again, Brother Coyote."

Teller grinned. "And you, young Bill."

The bond of family blood pulsing deeply, Junior was delighted to be back in the company of this group, and while the two Knowles men's smiles lit the porch like beacons, Teller's was a close third.

Releasing Teller, Junior turned to Jack and seeing the ice-filled glass he held, asked, "You wouldn't happen to have another one of *those,* would you? It's been a long drive."

Jack rattled the ice. "As a matter of fact, I do. Hang on, I'll be right back." But just as he stepped towards the door, Abbott came barreling through, holding a tray of cups, saucers, and silverware. Unable to avoid one another they collided in a crash of grunts and rattling glass.

Jack, being no match for Abbott's bulk and momentum bounced sideways into Teller; ricocheting through the door and into the store like a pinball; while Abbott, spinning full circle juggled the tray, silverware clattering and cups threatening to spill; then, with a few deft ballet steps, spun yet again, dipped, and brought the tray to rest onto the low table, while calling over his shoulder to Jack.

"Grab me a beer while you're at it!"

For the first few seconds Junior stood his mouth agape. . . But then began laughing. "So *this* must be the beer drinking bear!" But looking into Abbotts quick brown eyes his laughter was reduced to a subdued chuckle.

"I'm very pleased to meet you, Sir." Junior smiled, holding out his hand. I have heard much, and I must say, the description fits you well."

Abbott accepted Junior's outstretched hand while casting a judgmental eye at Teller. "Is that so?"

"Now wait a minute," Teller laughed. "I didn't say-" but Junior cut him off, raising his hands and holding them palms out. "Please, Abbott, don't misinterpret. Everyone speaks *very* highly of you." but tilting his head back in order to look into Abbott's face, he smiled. "But there is no denying that you *are* a *big* man." Waving his hand as if to bring to attention Abbott's head of wild curls as well as the bushy beard framing his face, and the mass of curly hair poking from his unbuttoned shirt, he shrugged, "*and* rather furry." Then pointing a finger towards the tray that Abbott had somehow kept from spilling, finished, "and you do dance *quite* well." There was a moment of absolute silence. . . but then Abbott grinned, and the rest roared with laughter.

It was then that Jack came back through the door; but having missed the exchange saw only the two men clasping hands, Junior's head tilted back in order to look into Abbott's brown eyes, and Teller standing to the side, his laughter subsiding as he rubbed his shoulder.

With a smile, and a shake of his head, Jack stepped into the middle of the men, and passed the drinks around.

Thanking Jack profusely, Junior accepted his Scotch while Abbott, performing a surprisingly graceful pirouette, bowed, and took his beer.

"I stand guilty as charged good sir, and may I say it is a pleasure to meet you as well. Anyone who has survived a meeting with *this* man," he waved his beer can in Tellers direction, "has my respect. And any relation of Billy's is, without doubt, a friend of mine."

The sound of one set of hands clapping filled the porch, and Teller stepped forward, laying a hand on both Abbott's and William's shoulders. "Excellent!" he grinned. "All friends, as it should be." Turning to Junior, he motioned to the darkness beyond.

"So, young Bill. It seems that you've delivered my car, therefore saving me the tiresome task of returning to Tucson where I would once again be forced to reign in my lusty friends," He glanced pointedly over at Jack. "libido."

Jack just shrugged and smiled.

Teller grinned at Jack and continued. "And for that, I *truly* thank you. But, I also understand that you have in your possession some of the rewards of our investment. Is this so?" Little Raven glanced to his Grandfather, and receiving an imperceptible nod turned back to Teller.

"As to the first," he smiled, holding out the keys to the Buick. "You are most welcome. The trip was personally enlightening, and the car fit in in a most interesting manner. But, as for the second, I think you may want to avoid Tucson for awhile." Puzzlement showed on Teller's face as Junior dropped the ring of keys into his palm.

He didn't recall more than just the two keys on the ring: the original ignition key, and the trunk key. But now there were two more. One small brass key, and one old, tarnished skeleton key. Curious without doubt, he thought, but *that* was a question for later: the more immediate issue was Junior's warning. He slipped the keys into his pocket.

"Why should I avoid Tucson?"

Taking the chair next to his Grandfathers, Little Raven raised his eyebrows. "Do you remember Sheila's friend, Susan?"

Teller nodded, "Yeah . . ."

Jack snicker resulted in a withering glance from Teller.

"Well she's looking for you. It seems she's not used to not getting what she wants."

"And with her looks," Jack said, shaking the cubes in his glass, "I doubt that happens very damn often."

"You're just jealous Hawkins." Teller grinned. But his smile faded as he turned back to Junior.

"Look, I'm used to women being pissed off for something I've done, but for something I *haven't* done?"

"Not *yet* anyway." Jack chuckled into his glass.

Teller glared. "Shut up, Jack."

"I don't know, Teller." Junior shrugged. "All I *know* is that Sheila say's Susan's pissed because you never called her."

Teller pulled a beer from the plastic ring and sighed.

"As *I* recall, I *did* mention that I was otherwise involved."

"When did *that* ever make a difference?"

"Shut *up.* Jack."

"I meant to the *women,* Tell." Jack laughed.

Junior held up his hands in surrender. "Don't shoot the messenger my friend. Just a word of warning. She told Sheila that you've become a challenge."

He smiled, and Teller was again taken by the genetics of the Grandfather in the young mans face.

"Amen to that!" Jack laughed.

Teller turned. "Shut. Up. *Jack.*"

Amused by the banter, Junior was reminded why he had felt comfortable with these two from the very first.

"As I said. I am the messenger, nothing more. However, your problems with women aside, I *do* have something for the three of you." Reaching between his feet, he pulled his briefcase up into his lap and flipped the latches.

"Excellent change of discussion young Bill" Teller nodded. "Any imagined problem I may have with women five hundred miles away is a moot issue in the here and now. So, let us get to items of more immediate importance."

"Wise words." Junior nodded, and as the case opened all three men leaned forward in their chairs, anticipation hanging heavy in in the air.

Jack's phone rang.

"God*damn it!*" he growled, but on checking the number his expression of anger became one of curiosity.

"It's Leroy . . ."

Teller shrugged. "So answer it."

Junior looked at them both, leaned back in his chair, and clicked the briefcase shut.

Jack nodded, stood, and punched the answer button. "Hey, Leroy what's up? Oh, hi Janey." His voice faded as he walked down the steps and melted into the night.

Teller watched him go, then turned back to Junior. "you may continue."

"We don't need to wait?"

"Hell no!" Teller barked, rolling his hand impatiently. "There are no trust issues here. Proceed."

The latches clicking a second time, Junior opened the briefcase, removed three plain unmarked envelopes, and laying them on the table tapped the center one with his forefinger. "Each of you gets one of these.

"Rather undramatic." Abbott frowned.

Teller picked up one of the envelopes. "Some folks are just *never* satisfied." He smiled, and pulling out the enclosed letter, he read . . .

At first, he blinked in disbelief. But as a smile slowly spread he turned to Abbott. "Grizzly old chum, with what's in that envelope you will be able to purchase whatever drama you may deem necessary."

His brow furrowing, Abbott scrutinized Teller as he pried the envelopes flap, and pulling the correspondence from it confines, began reading as the sound of boots on the stairs brought Jack back into the light.

"That was Leroy. He said he's on his way down here . . ." But as he tucked the phone into his pocket his expression reflected his puzzlement. "He also wanted us to know that James came by to tell them about Ben."

The surprise on Teller's face was obvious.

"James drove to *Cortez?*"

Jack smiled, but it was without humor.

"I know. Leroy says that James feels guilty but he doesn't think he's to blame for Ben's wanting to kill you."

Teller nodded, picking up the remaining envelope and handing it to Jack.

"He's right."

"What do you mean he's *right?*" Jack choked.

"I mean it's not his fault." Teller shrugged. "Not really anyway. It's not like he gave the kid a gun and told him to go shoot me."

Jack's eyebrows lifted. "You sure about that?"

"No." Teller chuckled, "I'm not. But I like to think the best of people. Even when they're people like James."

Noting Jacks doubtful expression, he shrugged.

"Well anyway. I'm glad Leroy's coming down. I always liked that guy." But gesturing to the envelope in his hand, he smiled, "you gonna open that?"

Jack tapped it in his palm. "Am I going to like it?"

Teller looked over at Abbott, who sat staring at the contents. He was so enthralled he hadn't even noticed that he had knocked over his beer and the liquid was pooling at his feet. "What do you think, Griz?"

Abbott looked up and blinked. "Excuse me . . .?"

Teller turned back to Jack.

"I believe the Bears reaction should be all the answer you need. Open it, and then tell me what *you* think."

Jack looked again at Abbott, then glanced at Junior who simply smiled. Squinting at Teller's amused expression, Jack peeled back the flap on the envelope.

Folded into an accounts balance sheet were twelve cashiers' checks; each made out in the amount of eight thousand, three hundred and thirty-three dollars. In addition, written at the bottom of the balance sheet was the address of a bank in Flagstaff, as well as the code and account number of a bank in the Caribbean. Giving Teller a puzzled frown, he shook the envelope and a key dropped into his palm. It was a safety deposit box key: a key that was exactly the same as the one now hanging from Teller's keychain.

Teller grinned and nodded.

At the response, Jack went back to reading the deposits listed in the columns. His eyes moved left to right, back and forth until they reached the bottom of the page. It was here, where the total was listed that his eyes widened. The figure showed a combined total of four hundred thousand dollars.

Jack's eyes went from the sheet, to Junior.

"You shittin' me?"

Junior's face had framed a proud smile as he watched Jack read, but at his reaction his expression became one of surprised dismay.

"Jack. *That* is your share of what you and Teller left me in Tucson. But if you are able to provide me with the amounts you inferred to in the restaurant, well, *that* is another matter altogether." Jack nodded, and his eyes returned to the page.

Junior looked to Teller. "Is there a problem?"

"The only problem," Teller grinned, "is that Jack just got blindsided by a Coyote." And laughing, he started singing the first line to his new song:

"Well you never see it coming, it hits you then it's gone, if your thinkin' that you're ready, well I'm thinkin' that you're wrong . . ."

Chuckling, he stopped singing and dropped a hand on his partner's shoulder. "Well buddy, it look's like its time to look up Rumpled Joe, right? Jack? Jack . . .?"

When Teller had first started singing, Jack had closed his eyes and Teller had assumed he was listening to the lyrics. But now he just sat, tapping the envelope in his palm, eyes closed, lost in a fantasy of wet, bouncing girls in wet, bouncing rafts.

"Jaaack . . .?" Teller smiled, "Come back Jaaaack . . ."

Jack's eyes slowly opened, and he grinned. "Yes, Tell, I guess we do."

While all this had been going on, Abbott had been on his hands and knees, trying to retrieve the beer can he had kicked under the bench. And with it now in hand, he crawled from beneath the table and looked up at the three smiling men.

"Who's rumpled Joe?"

= Chapter 49 =

Janey ground the cigarette butt into the ashtray and looked over at her husband.

"Think we'll see the boy?"

Leroy frowned at the question.

"I doubt it, honey. The kid's got a pretty good head start and we only know where he's headed . . . we don't know which route he'll take ta get there."

Janey nodded and tapped a cigarette from the box.

"Hell, Leroy. There's only two ways to get there."

"Yep." he nodded, his eyes never leaving the road. "And we can only take one of 'em."

Jane leaned back into the seat and stared through the windshield at the headlights fanning across the blacktop, and with a sigh, closed her eyes in silent acquiescence.

~

"Janey . . . hey, honey . . .

Janey felt the nudge of a gentle hand.

"Honey, I'm gonna fill up, you need to use the head?"

Her eyes creaking open, she blinked at the fluttering insects bumping against the bright florescent lights that hung from the canopy above. Yawning, she saw the gas pumps and pushed the door open.

The answer was yes.

~

Outside of Blanding, Leroy spun the wheel west onto Highway 95, nearly spilling the large cup of bitter gas station coffee that rest between his legs. Cursing silently, he straightened the car he looked across the seat to his wife.

Jane's bouffant pressed against the headrest, she looked out at the stars; and blowing a long plume of smoke out the window, gave by a little cough.

"You need to give those damn things up, Janey." Leroy said, lifting the coffee to his lips and blowing across the scalding liquid in a futile attempt to cool it down enough to take a sip. "You know they killed that TV guy."
Janey gave no immediate response, and he expected none.

This had been an ongoing dialogue for the past twenty years, and he no more expected her to quit than she expected him to give up trying to convince her to do so.

Keeping her face to the window so he couldn't see her smile, she said, "I know it honey, but that Marlboro Man wernt near as tough as me."

Leroy gave a rumbling chuckle. "Weren't near as pretty neither." She laughed, and it was the laugh he remembered from their youth.

Smiling at the memory, he made a second attempt at the coffee; but his smile faded when he saw yet another crushed Jackrabbit in the glow of his headlights. It was the third rabbit he had seen in the past ten miles and this one a good ten feet off the road. Slowing, he steered so the headlights swept across the crumpled animal.

The tire tracks swerved away from the blacktop and through the dirt; where they crushed the poor creature and then bumped back to the highway.
Whoever had done this had done so out of sheer malice.

Squeezing the coffee cup between his legs, Leroy put the car in reverse, angling the car so that the bloody corpse was lit by the headlights. Muttering a silent curse, he parked and swung the door open.

"Wait here, hon."
He was still grumbling as he went to the trunk and pulled out a folding spade to cover the crushed rabbit with sand.

A few minutes later the dome light lit the interior and Leroy slid behind the wheel and put the Caddy into drive, and as they bumped back onto asphalt he looked over at Jane with a grim set to his jaw

"I think we found the route the boy took."

= Chapter 50 =

In answer to Abbott's question regarding, 'Rumpled Joe,'
Teller began recounting his trip to Tucson. Joyfully
embellishing each detail and colorfully weaving his way
through each and every event: working his way to the point
where he felt that the man who was 'Rumpled Joe,' could be
properly inserted to the story. But just as he was reaching the
crescendo, Jack slapped the table. "Jesus Christ, Tell!" he
cried, "cut to the fucking chase!"

His mouth snapping shut, Teller pinned Jack with a look of
amused disappointment, crossed his arms, and leaned back
into his chair.

"Fine then, Jack. *You* tell him."

Giving Teller a terse nod, Jack turned, looked at Abbott,
and condensed Teller's elaborate tale into one short sentence:

"Joe was a guy we met in a bar in Tucson who told Teller
here that he was some hot shot with the Bell Corp."

Abbott nodded and waited for Jack to continue, but Jack
had nothing more to add. As far as *he* was concerned his
explanation was more than sufficient. Abbott, however,
clearly felt otherwise. Frowning, he looked first to Teller,
then back to Jack, then back to Teller again: but with neither
man seeming inclined to inject further commentary, Abbott's
curly head swiveled back and forth until his gaze finally
came to rest on Jack. His brown eyes anxious with curiosity
he asked, "So then, *who* is Rumpled Joe. . .?"
Feeling fully redeemed, Teller broke into laughter.

"See Jack . . . this is *exactly* what I'm always telling you!
Facts alone are *boring*. Without the backstory Joe is just
another guy in a shitty bar with a shiny suit. Another loser

drowning himself in cheap booze and cheaper hookers. It's the *how* and the *why* that makes him, 'Rumpled Joe.'"

Jack grumbled, "yeah, but the suit was expensive."

"Yes, it was." Teller grinned. "Expensive but *rumpled.*"

Happily picking up where he had left off, Teller spun his tale, expounding on the details until finally reaching the point where Joe had claimed his position of hierarchy in the Bell helicopter sales division. Then, with a smile of supreme satisfaction Teller reached into his wallet and removed Joe's business card with a flourish.

"Here's his number," Teller grinned. "I want you to give him a call and tell him you want the newest stealth model . . . you know, something you can sneak up on unsuspecting rafts with." Jack grumbled with self-righteous indignation as he snatched the card from between Teller's fingertips

"Smart ass."

But between Tellers happy grin, and Abbott's failing struggle to choke back his laughter, Jack found it impossible to sustain the level of anger required to salvage his dignity. Seeing no other way out, he decided to agree.

"Look Tell. I'm going to have to think about it. A stealthy chopper's gonna eat up the better part of a Mill."

"Yeah," Teller shrugged. "that is likely the case. But don't expect *me* to help finance your perverse hobbies."

Seeing Jack began to puff up again, Teller turned to Abbott.

"And what of *you* my friend? *Your* needs are modest."

~

Billy sat quietly in the background, listening to the banter and suppressing a smile of his own.

He was truly impressed.

Following their teasing, the men shifted into a discussion regarding their sudden, and unexpected change in net worth. And as the conversation went on, not one of the three made any of the foolish declarations one normally hears with the onset of sudden wealth. But then again, he had expected nothing less from these men. They joked of course, but the heart of their debate was serious; including detailed, intelligent questions: seeking advice from his Grandson as to their wisest course of investment.

Comfortable that William could guide them properly, Billy wrapped his hands around his teacup and closed his ears to the conversation; thinking instead about the tale Abbott had related earlier.

The story of Estebanico's spirits release. . .

It seemed the legend was true: the man *had* escaped. But *how* did he come to die in the cave that Coyote had led Teller to?

Billy closed his eyes. The mysteries of the world were great, and some things could never be known.

But *one* thing was certain. In Teller, Coyote had found a recipient worthy of his attentions: and the undeniable moral fortitude of the friends whom Teller surrounded himself with was a revelation beyond Billy's most fervent hope. And as he considered the magnitude of these things, a howl cut through the night

'*Yes*. . .' Billy smiled. The mysteries were great.

= Chapter 51 =

The 'thump' beneath his front tire brought a malevolent grin to Ben's face; cracking the dried blood caked across a visage from hell

Rabbit number twelve . . .

But as the mile's passed his grin became a grimace of pain.

Glancing down at the speedometer, he saw the needle hovering at nearly ninety-five, the wind whistling through the holes in the windshield burning his wounds with cold fire.

But the pain only steeled his resolve.

Reaching down to stroke the Magnum that lay in his lap, he thought how fortunate it was that the Navajo Reservation was so lightly patrolled. It was *very* unlikely he would be able to control the madness a second time. As a matter of fact, just thinking about the patrolman who had pulled him over re-lit flames of rage that scorched his soul.

Burying the anger, his eyes jumped from the speedometer to the gas gauge where it bounced just above reserve; bringing memories of his uncle's warning to never let it get that low. He smiled through the pain. That was of little concern to him now. . . he had more than enough fuel to get him to his final destination.

Teller.

The joy that accompanied the thought of his nemesis' impending death brought a tremor that drove knives through his skull. He squeezed his eyes shut in a vain attempt to block the searing pain; but rather than relief, an image of Teller's face appeared, cruel and laughing. Ben squeezed his eyes tighter but Tellers smile only grew larger, mocking him further.

Opening his eyes as wide as he could, he screamed, but his cries were sucked away on the howling wind, and worse, the howl stretched his skin further, cracking the dried blood that caked his face; sending the dried flakes fluttering down his face, and with his tongue flicking out like a reptiles he licked them from his lips. They tasted of copper.

Rolling his tongue, he smiled at the foul taste, but a second series of fevered chills suddenly racked his body, the heat burning deep inside overriding all else.

Rolling down the window, he leaned his bloody face into the desert night. That was a mistake. Hurricane force winds tore at his scalp, the flaps of flesh peeling back to flap in the wind; the dead light of the moon reflected from the white bone of skull and bringing tears that streaked across his temples, mingling with the fresh blood that was now flowing freely from the freshly opened wounds.

Squinting into the wind, he leaned further out, but on seeing his grotesque reflection in the rearview mirror he let out a mad, choking cackle, screaming, "TELLER!"

His cry was lost to the shrieking wind; but through that wind the voices in his head returned, chanting:

Te-ller, Te-ller, Te-ller,'

Laughing, the demonic chorus repeated his name over and over until Ben could hear nothing else. . . but just as his insanity peaked, a Coyotes mournful howl punctured the night; the howl reaching Ben and bringing him back from the brink of absolute madness. . . but just barely.

Squinting a bloodshot eye down the side of the fender, he saw jackrabbit number thirteen freeze in the bright beams of his headlights.

Pulling his bloody head back into the cab, a malicious grin spread across Bens face and he took aim.

___ __ -- --- -- __ ___
___ ___ ___ ___
-- --- --

277

= Chapter 52 =

Billy looked to his Grandson. "Did you bring the box?"
Junior looked at this Grandfather hesitantly, then nodded.
"Would you bring it to me?" Billy asked.
"Of course."
Junior stood, handing Jack his empty glass. "Think I could
get a refill?"
Jack nodded.
The worn floorboards creaked beneath Italian loafers as
Junior went down the steps to where the old Buick sat, its
bulk a starlit shadow.
Teller watched Junior leave, then turned to Billy.
"Another box?"
In the excitement of Junior's arrival, the box that Teller
had retrieved earlier had been forgotten; but now Billy
picked it up. "Yes, Teller. One that is *this* one's sister."
As far as Teller was concerned there was nothing
particularly distinctive about the wooden container Billy
held. It looked to be no more than a plain, wooden; albeit
fairly large, box. Yet Billy held it as if it contained an
extraordinary treasure. But as he pondered the contents the
heavy 'thump' of Buicks trunk closing cut through the night,
followed by the creaking of stairs as Junior returned, stepping
into the lantern's light with the sister box tucked beneath his
arm. Billy nodded his thanks, took it, and motioned William
to take the seat next to his. Junior sat, smiling as he accepted
the glass Jack placed in his hand.
The men sat silent as Billy lifted the new box, holding it as
if judging its weight. Then, with an infinitesimal nod, he
passed it to Abbott. "*This* one is yours, Sir Bear."

"Why does Abbott get that one?" Teller frowned. "It came out of *my* trunk."

"My friend," Billy chided. "You have possessed Sebastian's car for only a short time, and it was Coyote that led you to it, just as he led the *two* of you to the cave of Estebanico."

He paused, and his smile warmed.

"You are a clever man Teller, and without doubt deserving of Coyote's attentions, but you are new to this."

Teller began to protest, but Billy held up his hand.

"In a moment, Teller, in a moment. Please, have patience."

Teller looked at Abbott, who, with a distracted, and slightly dazed, smile, nodded, and turned back to Billy, his mind reeling with the sequence of events.

First, an envelope that held a fortune, secondly, the curiosity of this conversation, and now, the sudden gifting of this strange box.

Billy smiled, and nodded as if he could read Abbott's mind.

"Sebastian and I have kept this to ourselves for all these many years, with Sebastian holding the key to my box, and I the key to his. In this way neither of us could open its sister. And while I still hold the key to Sebastian's box, *you* now hold the key to mine." Billy then held out his hand, opening it to reveal a small skeleton key.

Raising his eyebrows, he smiled at Teller.

"I believe *you* have its match."

Teller frowned, his gaze moving from Billy's smiling eyes, to the keys he held. Why would Billy think that *he* had the key? Then it came to him. It was the same type of key Junior had handed him earlier.

Reaching into his pocket, he took out his key ring.

The two worn keys that belonged to the Buick hung from the hoop, as well as the shiny new key that belonged to the deposit box. But between them was a small skeleton key . . . he had noticed it when Junior had handed the key ring to him earlier, but at the time, with more immediate issues on his mind, he had set those questions on the back burner.

'*Well,*' he smiled grimly, *it seems the heat has just been turned up . . .*' He held out the ring and jangled the keys.

"Well, Chief. What now?"

Billy smiled, and held out his hand, palm up.

"The key, Teller. Please."

Ben raced down the gravel road, searching for the gap in the canyon walls he had seen in his fevered dreams.

There! It split the wall, just as he had known it would.

Whipping the steering wheel hard to the right, the passenger's side of the battered Humvee skidded against the walls rock face, gouging a deep crease along the entire side of the vehicle and leaving a long streak of red paint on the sandstone's surface. Ben grit his teeth against the pain of the impact and continued his mad race down the rough road until finally emerging from the narrow canyon

Here, he slowed the vehicle to a crawl, staring at the lake before him. Its flat water seemed no more than a blacker hole in a black landscape: the twinkling of the lantern hanging from the building on the shore no more than a distant star on the edge of that darkness.

Knowing the lantern marked Teller's refuge, Ben shifted into low gear, steering the vehicle across the featureless landscape: his dilated pupils scanning for a trail that might lead him to a suitable spot for his task; and seeing two faint parallel tracks in the scrub he smiled crookedly. They ran along the ridge to a promontory that overlooked the pinpoint of light in the distance.

Perfect.

Extinguishing the headlights in favor of the less obtrusive fog lamps, he ground the Humvee's transmission into low four-wheel drive and took to the trail, crashing through the sage; the pungent odor filling the cab as gnarled branches were crushed beneath the weight of the vehicle.

The faint trail was soon lost, and Ben resorted to simply following the yellow beams of his fog lights towards a ridgeline that was no more than a black silhouette against a starry sky.

Crashing down through sand-washed gullies, then grinding back up over rocks and stumps, Ben pushed the vehicle far beyond the limits of its engineering, twisting the suspension while destroying the undercarriage; shearing driveline bolts and mounts until, with a clunk, the rear u-joint shattered and the drive shaft dropped to the ground, sparking and clanking, continuing to spin as the front wheels struggled to pull this once showroom-quality, rich man's toy up its final hill where it crested the rise: valves clattering like castanets as the motor sucked its last drop of fuel, jerked forward with a cough, and died, its final wheezing swallowed by the immense silence of the desert.

Ben sat perfectly still for a long moment: then, shattering the silence with a scream of frustration began to pound the steering wheel with his fists; but his anger spiked his blood pressure, and feeling as if his head were going to explode.

But Ben was beyond caring: about the blood *or* the pain. Using his fingers to clear his vision, he brought back his hands covered with viscous fluid that glittered black in the starlight; the blackness reflecting the emptiness of his soul; and with that emptiness threatening to swallow him whole, his fury snapped him back to his mission.

Kicking the door open, he stumbled to the rear of the vehicle, but his blood-slick fingers could not grip the hatch's handle. Howling in frustration he pulled his wet hands across his shirt, drying them enough to open the hatch and flip the latches on the rifle case.

A grim smile twisted his bloody visage as he lifted the lid.

There, deadly black against the green crushed velvet of the case lay the solution to all of his sorrows. The voices in his head cackled in demented joy as he lifted the weapon from its padding, slung it over his shoulder, and made his way to the edge of the overlook.

The location was ideal. The building that provided his enemy refuge was no more than a quarter mile away and the glow of the lanterns lit the small figures on the porch.

Ben smiled a dreadful smile.

Staggering to the cliffs lip, he lowered himself to the ground, cringing in pain as he settled himself into sniper position. Unscrewing the protective caps from the scopes lens, he brought the perfectly polished glass to his eye and the building jumped forward. *Now* he could see the individuals on the porch, but the light was still too dim to identify Teller. With a curse, he turned his eyes to the east where the first light of dawn colored the horizon.

The voices in Ben's head quieted. By Sunrise the source of his hatred would be dead, and he and Kelly would be together. . .

Steering around another crushed rabbit, Leroy glanced over to Janey, who snored lightly, her head resting against the window glass.

Feeling his bile rise, he was thankful she was sleeping.

Leroy found the sight of such callous disregard of any of Earth's creatures unpardonable, and knew that regardless of how tough as she acted, she would be as hurt as he was furious.

Checking his watch for the second time in thirty minutes, his lips tightened. They might just make the marina by daybreak.

= Chapter 53 =

Billy eyed the men around him. "It is getting late," he smiled, curling his fist around the keys that Teller had dropped into his palm. "Perhaps it would be better if we waited until morning."

Abbott's eyes lifted slowly from the box in his lap: a tangle of emotions plain on his face. "No, Billy. With all that has transpired I'm quite sure I could not sleep without knowing what lies within these boxes." His eyes darted to Teller for backup and as hoped, Teller nodded.

"Sorry Chief." He smiled, "but I agree with the Bear. My curiosity is mightily roused."

Swiveling to Jack, he asked, "What say you?"

"I'm not going to be able to sleep since Leroy called anyway," Jack shrugged. "Let's see what's in 'em."

Billy's gaze went to his Grandson.

Junior raised his Scotch to his lips. "In for a penny, in for a pound, Grandfather."

Billy turned to Abbott. "Very well." White teeth flashing against dark skin, he held out a small key.

"As you now possess the box, Sir Bear, I believe *this* is now yours as well."

Reaching out, Abbott took the key; holding it between his large fingers as if it were made of the most fragile of glass. But curiosity overcoming hesitation, he slipped the key into the lock and turned it slowly. A quiet 'click' followed an Abbott looked up, his expression impossible to read.

But then, with a slow intake of breath, he placed a hand on either side of the box. And as he pushed the lid up with his thumbs his eyes widened.

Laying on a perfect square of red fox fur was a necklace.

It was a necklace such as he had never seen, yet was still somehow familiar. His first thought was of pre-invasion Plains Indian breastplate, but it was of much simpler design, and the bones significantly thicker. Lifting one of the long, tapered pieces, he was startled by its weight. It was much heavier than bone.

Running a finger down the length of the yellowing patina, he wondered: Ivory? Yes, that's what they were. Ivory . . . and while they were similar to tusks, they were much too small. Teeth? Maybe; but too big . . . with a quick count, he added up thirty-two of the roughly twelve-inch objects: all tied together with a braided weave of what he presumed to be human hair: long, black, human hair, with each "Tusk" separated by a sequence of small round shells knotted between them. Lifting the necklace gently from its fur cradle, he draped between both hands and looked to Billy.

"What *is* this?"

Before Billy could speak, Teller answered,

"Whale's tooth."

All eyes turned to him.

"What?" he grinned.

"Whale's tooth?" Jack said, his eyes narrowing.

"Yeah. . . well, to be more precise, Whale's *teeth*."

Caressing one of the tapered pendants, Abbott nodded. "That *would* explain the Ivory."

Splashing Scotch into his glass, Jack set his bottle between his feet, looking at Teller with impressed annoyance. "Teller, how the *hell* would you know those were Whales' teeth?"

Again, Billy was delighted. The camaraderie between these three was superbly amusing.

"Come on, Jack." Teller said, "have a little faith. I've spent a lifetime travelling this big ole' round world, and I'm not near as dumb as some people wish I was." In the silence that followed, Teller looked first to Billy, and then to the object in Abbott's hands. "In Fiji that would be called, 'Wasekaseka'.

I saw one of these at the Bishop museum in Honolulu a few years back . . . and *those* particular teeth belonged to a Sperm Whale. Quite rare if it is pre-1800's Whaling industry, and more valuable still if so." He smiled, waiting for comment; but when no one responded he shrugged, and turned his full attention to Billy. "More to the point, Chief, is where did *you* get it? 'Aint many Whales in these parts."

Billy's eyebrows rose. "*That,* my friend," he said, "is where this mystery begins."

Shifting the box in his lap he slid the last key into its lock and lifted the lid, carefully removing the piece of rough fabric that lie folded within: and laying it on the table, spread it out and smoothed it with his palms. "These items were given to the ancestor of my grandfather by Estebanico at the gates of Hawikuh on the night before his capture."

Abbott returned the necklace to its case as Jack leaned in, rubbing his chin. "So then, what is *that?*"

What lay before them was an ancient Polynesian Tapa cloth: dots of various sized scattered sparsely across its surface, mixed with odd symbols that were connected by lines; which, in turn, led to other mysterious symbols.

Teller studied it for a moment, tipping his head this way and that. Suddenly, he looked to Abbott and smiled, "You thinking what I'm thinking?"

Abbott grunted as he ran a finger along one of the lines. "Some sort of map?"

"Exactly, Abbott old chum. But not a map. A chart. Or more precisely, a sailing chart. I recognize some of these symbols as celestial references. . ." he tapped the cloth with his finger. "You say that *Estebanico* gave this to your grandfather?" With the question going unanswered, Teller glanced up from the cloth to see that while the old shaman's eyes were focused on the colors that painted the horizon; his mind was elsewhere. What Teller could *not* know, however, was that Billy's spirit was in search of Coyote.

A long moment passed; and with a subtle nod, Billy's eyes refocused. "Yes. . ." he smiled. "But not my Grandfather. . . *his* grandfather's father's father . . . but, I am sorry to say, very little is known of what transpired. Only that it was given." But then Billy stood. "It is nearly Sunrise. Would anyone like Coffee?"

Teller smiled and shrugged. "It's too late for bed now. Sure, I'll take a cup."

Three nods from the others followed.

"Very well." Billy smiled. "I will be right back."

When Billy did return, he found the "Three Musketeers" gathered around the Tapa speaking in low tones as to not disturb Junior who had fallen asleep in his chair; but hearing Billy's boots, Teller glanced up; gesturing towards the sleeping man. "Long trip. . ."

Billy set the tray of steaming coffee on the table and nodded, his eyes warm with affection. "Little Raven never *was* much of a night person"

Sticking a finger through a cups handle, Teller raised a brow. "Maybe you should've named him 'Little Owl."

Billy's eyes twinkled. "Do you suppose that might have made a difference?"

"Naaa." Teller chuckled, rubbing his own tired eyes. "Probably not . . . but that aside," he sighed, pointing at the cloth. "As I'm up to my ass in riddles already, think you could enlighten me on *this*?"

Billy dropped into his rocker and motioned everyone to gather close. "Yes, Teller, I will try."

"As I mentioned earlier, there was very little known regarding the origin of these items. And while Sebastian had his own theories of course, this is what I *do* know. My ancestor spent considerable time with Estebanico, guiding he and his entourage through unfamiliar country. And although I can only guess, I think it fair to assume that the two men would have developed some type of bond, with Estebanico particularly, for one of my family has been a shaman and spiritual leader for the people from the time Coyote scattered the stars. And Estebanico's survival up to that point had been based on his image of shamanism, whether real, or simply pretense."

Teller sipped his coffee, filing this information into what he already knew.

"According to family legend," Billy continued, "there were *two* reasons Estebanico was searching for Hawikuh. Or, as the Spanish referred to it, 'Cibola'. The primary reason of course is that he had been commanded to do so by the Crown. But as a man whom had endured his many sufferings, and as an indentured slave, my guess is that his loyalties to the Crown were not voluntary; and this map one of the reasons he led Fray Marcos on such a merry chase."

Abbott too, had been listening intently while keeping his many questions to himself; but here he could no longer keep quiet. "So, you know the truth regarding their journey?"

Billy frowned.

"No, Abbott. I do not *know* the truth. I *know* only the story that has been passed down to me. and through that, I have developed a theory. But still, I am reasonably sure it is accurate."

"Well then." Abbott nodded, "*I* would certainly like to hear your theory."

"And you will, Griz," Teller chuckled, patting Abbott on the shoulder. "You will. But first things first."

Turning back to Billy, he tapped the Tapa cloth on the table with his fingertip. "As you may have gathered, Chief, Abbott here is very big on facts, while I am more intrigued with the greyer areas of life. . ." he paused, raising his eyebrows. "You mentioned *two* reasons for Estebanico's quest."

Billy's black eyes sparkled and he smiled.

"Ahh, yes. I am glad to see you were paying attention. So, while gold and power were the *King's* sole reason for exploration and conquest, other, less single-minded men often had less selfish, or at least more personal goals," and, he added with a wink, "Coyote often helped men such as these."

Teller grinned. "Duly noted. Please continue."

Billy looked to the East. With the sunrise, the cirrus clouds above the horizon were lit in varying shades of crimson; the first rays of morning fanning across the sky to push back the night once again.

"Beautiful, is it not?" Billy smiled.

Rising from his rocker went to the railing to gaze out at the colors in silence.

The other men joined him, each facing the sunrise: and while each contemplated their particular place in the coming day, none had any idea of the surprises that day would bring. Nothing was said as the long shadows grew shorter, but as one, the men turned their backs on the horizon and retuned to the table where the chart lay.

Once all were seated, Teller leaned forward, his elbows on his knees. "So. you left us at the second, and seemingly covert addition to the mission the King had assigned Estebanico."

"Viceroy." Abbott corrected.

Teller raised his eyebrows. "What?"

Abbott looked up from the chart. "It was the Viceroy Antonio de Mendoza that pressed Estebanico into service, not the King."

Teller exhaled slowly. "Does it really matter?"

"Of *course* it does!" Abbott barked. But then, smiling, shrugged, "no, I suppose not. In the end, the results were the same."

"Exactly!" Teller sighed, rubbing his forehead with his fingertips while giving Billy a tired smile. "See what I mean about his penchant for facts? Now, please, go on."

Billy chuckled. "Yes. Well, regardless of the *source* of the orders, orders were given and Estebanico set out, and during the course of his travels he encountered many tribes, and many strange people. But the one that concerns us, here, involves a man he met many miles north of present day Albuquerque."

Abbott gestured to the box that held the necklace. "The man he met carried these?"

Billy nodded, his gaze turning intense.

"Yes, Abbott, he did. But what is *more* curious is the story he told of where he, and they, had come *from.*" Billy's dark eyes went from face to face. Seeing that he had the full attention of all three men, leaned forward. "According to the story told by my forefathers, this man was unusual in many ways. First, he was dark. Not so black as Estebanico, but still a different shade than that of the People. Also, he was very large. Easily as tall as Estebanico, but much more muscular."

Teller and Abbott looked to one another; and while both held expressions of curiosity, Teller's was mixed heavily with skepticism. Looking back at Billy, he started to speak, but Abbott spoke first. "And this man was in New *Mexico*?"

"Yes," Billy nodded, "but technically it was not yet New Mexico."

"That small detail aside," Teller cut in, "what was this guy doing there?"

"An excellent question." Billy smiled. "And a *very* large puzzle to everyone travelling with Estebanico at the time."

"Wait," Teller said, scrutinizing Billy. "And it was *your* relative that was one of his companions?

"Yes, Teller. He was. They met in by chance during one of Estebanico's many separations from the Monk. As I mentioned earlier, my forbear was a shaman, and finding Estebanico both interesting *and* charismatic, he offered to be his guide. and serving as such, the two became friends. However, *that* is a story in itself, and one to be told at another time. For now, let us concentrate on the stranger."

Abbott nodded vigorously, while Teller, with a shrug rolled his finger. "Very well then," he smiled, "Go on . . ."

Returning the smile, Billy continued.

"This strange man traveled alone and spoke a dialect no one could fully understand. But he was also intelligent enough to have familiarized himself with the nuances of the languages of the tribes he had encountered during his journey. Enough so that he was able to communicate to some degree. And thus, following a long evening of discussion, this stranger took Estebanico to be the 'Chief' of the entourage as their colors and size were similar. But it was when he discovered *where* Estebanico was going that he took great pains to share his story."

"And the story was?"

"The story, my friends, was that he had come from a land far across the sea, and that he too, was searching for Hawikuh." With this bizarre revelation, Abbott voiced what Teller was still processing.

"You're telling us that a *Polynesian* man somehow made landfall on *this* continent, and was searching for the same Pueblo as Estebanico?"

Billy brought his teacup to his lips and gazed over the rim.

"So it seems."

"But that's impossible!"

Billy nodded, his eyes twinkling. "Yes, so one would think. But then, one would think that *your* recent experiences would be rather implausible as well."

Teller laughed. There was no arguing *that* point.

With a sigh and a grin, he stood. He needed a libation stronger than caffeine. But Billy smiled, "please, Teller, sit. The rest of the story is short, and our company will arrive very soon."

Teller nodded. He had no wish to argue, and had learned to accept Billy's ability to foretell future arrivals. Curious about both, the stories end, and the arrival of company, he took his seat. But as he did, a frustrated Abbott spoke.

"I'm sorry Billy, but how can this possibly be a *short* story?"

"Because," Billy said, "I *know* only a small piece." Wrapping both hands around his cup, he leaned forward. "And that piece being small it is short in the telling. So, here is what I *do* know, along with what Sebastian and I have surmised." Here Billy paused yet again, his eyes drifting to the east; and in doing so, his eyes passed over his sleeping Grandson. Smiling fondly, he leaned back, lacing his fingers beneath his chin as he divulged the tale.

"Needless to say, Estebanico's journey to this point had been arduous. They were days ahead of the Monk, their supplies were low and his men were in need of rest. So, making camp my grandfather's ancestor sent a few of his men to hunt while he stayed with Estebanico, wanting to hear more of this extraordinary man's incredible journey. You see, men of landlocked tribes, the story of vast oceans stretching beyond horizons was quite unbelievable. But for Estebanico had spent much of his life on oceans and ships. so, while this man's story might have been incredible, it was not beyond belief. And with the stranger's dark skin and powerful build, Estebanico was convinced that not only were they cut from the same cloth, but that this man was undoubtedly capable of such a journey. For *him*, the greater surprise was hearing of yet another vast sea on at the edge of this strange new world, and another land far beyond that."

Abbott had been carefully framing questions to ask at the end of the story but Teller had his ready *now*.

"Alright Chief, I'm willing to accept the possibility that a lone man drifted and or sailed across the South Pacific, and somehow land on the coast of North America . . . but *why* would he choose to hike a thousand miles inland?"

Billy presented his enigmatic smile. "Why do you assume he made the trip alone?"

Teller pursed his lips. "He *was* alone when he encountered Estebanico, wasn't he?"

"Yes Teller." Billy nodded, "He was, but only because his voyaging companions were not at all interested in further hardships. *They* were content to stay on the coast with the people who had found them on the beach and healed them. Surrounded with the comforts of the village, and a people who treated them as gods."

At this, Teller leaned back and laughed. "And they were, no doubt, *more* than willing to play that particular misconception to their advantage."

"Of course!" Billy laughed, his eyes sparkling. "When has it ever been different?"

But Abbott, who had been patiently waiting, leaned in. "Yes, but *why* did he travel so far inland?"

Billy pointed to the map. "As I mentioned, he was also searching for Hawikuh."

"But *why*. . .?"

"Ahhh," Billy smiled. "*This* is where the wisdom of the Creator of All Things enters, and, for we mere mortals, the seeming coincidences arise."

As he spoke these words, the Sun crested the jagged, butte-lined horizon, spilling light across the land, chasing away the shadows while illuminating the bottom of the porch's stairs where it slowly crawled up each step; creeping across the floorboards until its rosy fingers lit the worn tips of Billy's cowboy boots. Billy looked down, and smiling at this small thing, continued his tale.

"For the rest of the night our man recounted the tale of the arduous journey that had brought he and his companions to these distant shores. But this strange traveler said that he had been only one of many boats; boats that were meant to carry his people from their old home, to a new land. But after only a few days at sea a great storm had separated them, shredding their sails and sinking their companions' boats. Then, once lost and without sail, they could only drift with the currents, and as the weeks passed the men grew weak. Some died, but when hope would abandon them they would find courage in some small thing. But weeks passed, and as the situation grew ever more desperate a squall of rain finally came, filling the boat and the dying men's gourds with much needed water."

Here, Billy took a drink of his coffee and smiled.

"During this rain, a school of Malolo came skipping across the waters, landing into their canoe as they passed. The men rejoiced, for now they could eat. But, rather than devouring them all, our man counseled restraint, saving some to fix to a bone hook and cast it into the water in the hopes he might catch something larger."

For the first time since the beginning of the tale, Jack spoke up. "What's a Malolo?"

"Flying fish, Jacko." Teller said.

"Now just how the *hell* do you know that?" Jack snapped.

"I told you," Teller grinned. "I ain't near as dumb as people wish I was." Then turning to Billy, nodded, "please, go on."

Billy chuckled, and did so.

"Hours passed and nothing was caught, so the men began to argue, some wanting to eat the last of the fish. But as the discussion went back and forth, the line went taut and a fair-sized fish was hooked, and, while it was only one fish, it settled the argument. So, cutting it into small pieces, they ate frugally while our man took the head, placed it on the hook, and tossed it back into the sea.

The day passed, and it seemed that their hunger was worse than before they had eaten. But then again, the rope went tight. So much so that it nearly pulled itself from our mans weak grasp. But he held, scarcely believing his luck. This was a fish large enough to save them all! Lashing it to the bow of the canoe, he let the mighty fish pull, hoping it would soon wear itself out . . . but it did not. Night came and went, and by morning they discovered that it was not a fish at all, but a shark, and one as large as the boat itself! It pulled them for days, devouring fish as it passed, leaving the scraps floating behind for the men on the canoe to scoop up. And it was with these scraps the men survived. And as the great shark swam, it was always to the east. . . always towards the sunrise."

Teller refilled his cup. "Okay, Chief, that is a hell of a story, and we know that he made it to the coast. But we still don't know *how* he ran into Estebanico . . ."

"Because," Billy said quietly, "he was searching for his homeland."

Teller started to speak, but Abbott growled, "Shut up, Teller! Let the man finish!"

Silenced by Abbott's outburst, Teller smiled and shrugged, "My apologies. Please, go on."

Billy chuckled and continued.

"After weeks of continuing misery, one of the men spotted land in the distance. Rejoicing and taking the white shark's guidance and salvation as a sign from the gods, they made landfall, crawling from the boat to lay upon the sand, lost, and weak from lack of food and water, but alive! and while he did not remember how long he lay there, sometime later a group of brown-skinned people who spoke a language that was completely foreign to their ears found them, and after the shock of their discovery, brought both fresh water and meat.

Billy paused, his brow furrowing as he looked again to the east; then continued. "These people were smaller than his people, but as they were similar in appearance he thought they may have found the land of their migratory forbearers.

He and his crew were fed, and once rested were taken to the tribes Chief, where he was asked many questions. But of course, he understood only fragments of their meaning, not the words. But, once had at last answered everything that he could, he was allowed to inquire on the subject that was foremost on his mind, and *that* question was if this was his 'homeland.' The people of the coast understood none of what he said of course, except for one word: "Hawaiki"

"Hawaiki?"

"Yes Abbott. Hawaiki. That was the name for *his* people's land of origin. The 'homeland.' Hawaiki."

Jack nodded and said, "sounds a lot like Hawikuh."

Teller looked at each of them in turn, and then directed his gaze on Billy. "It also sounds a *hell* of a lot like Hawaii".

Billy nodded. "Yes, Teller, it does. But they had no way of knowing that. So, since that was the *only* word from this newly arrived "God" that the Chief of the coastal peoples understood, he gave directions to the only location he had ever heard of with a name that sounded similar. Hawikuh."

Abbott rubbed his beard. "What are the odds of that?"

"The odds are always in favor of the gods, Abbott." Billy laughed. "You should know that by now." At that, Teller laughed as well.

Abbott opened the box and held up the necklace.

"And he was carrying this?"

"Yes, Abbott, he was."

"I need a beer."

"I was wondering how long that would take." Teller grinned, calling out to Abbott as he walked through the screen door, "Bear, would you be so kind as to bring one for me?"

"Of course" came the muffled reply.

Teller sat in silence until Abbott returned with two cans. and opening both, handed one to him.

"Thanks pal."

"You're welcome." Abbott nodded, sitting, and looking at Billy. "So, what happened next?"

Pouring more coffee into his cup, Billy cradled it in both hands. "The man joined with Estebanico to discover if this 'Hawikuh' was truly the "homeland."

"But what happened to him after the battle in which Estebanico was captured?"

Billy shrugged. "There is no clear answer to that, Abbott. On the night of their arrival at the gates of the Pueblo, Estebanico gave the gold and stones to my ancestor and he and their small contingent waited outside the walls as Estebanico entered."

Here Billy looked to the east a third time. The high cirrus clouds were still tinged with color but were dispersing rapidly. With a sudden sense of urgency, he continued.

"And when the army of warriors came pouring from those gates everyone scattered, the Polynesian man at the side of my forefather. The next day they crept through the trees, and back to the walls of the city. And as they stood among the dead, this strange and formidable man gave these items to my ancestor and simply walked away."

Billy's small audience sat in silence as he took a drink, lowered his cup, and sighed. "My forefather hid for two days in the trees outside the walls, waiting. But the only thing he saw leave was a large raven. On the third day he rolled up his charge in a deerskin and began the long walk home."

"And that was that?' Teller asked, returning his attention to the chart.

"Yes, Teller. As far as I know, that was that."

Teller nodded, tracing his finger along one of the lines on the chart. Then, tapping one particular symbol with his finger, said, "I'd like to compare this with a more current map." Jack walked over to examine the placement of Teller's fingertip. "Why's that, Tell?"

"Because," Teller frowned, "This mark here is unlike any of the others."

= Chapter 54 =

The sun glinted from Cadillac's stainless-steel roof as it wheeled down the dirt road, a billowing cloud of dust in its wake: and although it was still miles away, Billy, sensed its approach. Smiling, he excused himself, going to the porch rail to gaze out at the mesa: leaving Teller, Abbott and Jack to study the charts.

Letting his eyes lose their focus, he allowed mind to drift: searching for Coyote. Suddenly an unexpected, but gentle touch to his shoulder pulled him from his contemplations.

Turning to Jack's smile, Billy looked the direction of his pointing finger. . . Billy saw nothing for a moment: but then a car's windshield flashed against the red cliffs as it wound down the final switchback to the flatlands. Recognizing it, Jack called to Teller, who, looking up and seeing the cloud of dust, nodded to Abbott, folded the chart and joined the other two men at the porch rail.

Four smiling faces awaited the Caddy as it came to a rumbling stop; but the cloud of dust in its wake continued on, obscuring everything until the fresh breeze from the Mesas rolled it across the sage, and away.

Waving the dust from his face with his cap, Jack went down the steps to the car and opened the door.

"Hi, Janey," he grinned, bending to kiss her cheek as he took her hand. Gratefully accepting, Jane laid her hand in his, stepping out to push her fists into the small of her back.

"Thanks, honey," she groaned. "I'm too damn old for sleeping in cars."

Jack laughed, and lifting her hand above her head, spun her in a gentle pirouette. "You'll never be old, Janey."

A girlish smile lit her face, and for a brief moment Jack's statement was true.

"Oh pashaw, ya big flirt." she said, standing on tiptoes to whisper in his ear, "You best be careful what you say, Jack. My husband's here ya know."

Jack grin grew larger. "Well then," he winked, "we'll just keep it our little secret."

Janey's giggle was overridden by the squeaking of suspension as the Cadillac tipped to one side and one of the biggest men Billy had ever seen slowly unfolded from its confines. Towering over the car, he laid two large hands on its shining roof, released a monstrous yawn, and seeing Jack, broke into an enormous smile.

"Jack!" he boomed. "Good to see ya again boy!"

Shading his eyes against the morning sun he turned toward the store. "And where's that goddamnd Teller? That sombitch better still be kickin,' 'cause I'd *sure* as hell hate to think we drove all the way down here too late to save his troublesome ass." For a moment, the only sound was the wind rustling through the sage. . . but then, from the shade of the porch a joyful laugh rang out; "Damn right I'm still here, Leroy! and it's gonna to take a lot more than some loony little shit like Ben to do *me* in. Hell, *I've* been workin' at it for years, and if *I* can't get it done that fucking punk kid doesn't have a chance. Besides," Teller cackled as he bounced down the stairs. "How would it look if I went and got myself all kilt before the Marines arrived?"

Tramping across the parking lot to Janey, he leaned down to give her a peck on the cheek. "It's *good* to see you again Jane." But as he stepped back. Leroy came charging around the Caddy like a loose rhino; grabbing him by the shoulders, lifting him off the ground, and squeezing him like an Accordion. "Airborne Rangers, asshole, *not Marines!*"

"Jesus Christ, Leroy!" Teller cried, slithering from Leroy's grasp. "You trying to save the kid the trouble of killin' me himself?"

"Quit complainin' Tell!" Jack hollered from the other side of the car. Leroy's just tryin' to make you a smaller target."

"Ha ha, ha," Teller glared as he shuffled around to the passenger side of the Caddy. "*Real* funny Jack."

With the car now acting as a buffer, Teller slapped the Sunroof and grinned,

"So, Leroy, you willing to sell me this piece of junk yet?"

Absolute silence fell across the parking lot, with Leroy's eyebrows lifting as he turned to Jack in disbelief. . . then turning back to Teller, a smile of grudging respect slowly turned the corners of his lips.

"Well Ghod-damn! Here I stand, after drivin' all night long just so's we could get here in time ta keep *you* from gettin' killed, and all you got to say is will I sell my *Caddy?* Boy, first of all, what makes you think I want to sell? but more to the point, what makes you think you'll be around to *drive* it?"

Teller walked back around the car, rubbing his rapidly bruising shoulder. "Well, for the first thing," he said, grinning through the pain. "I have money this time. As for question number two, I was kinda hoping you'd help me keep that demented little fuck from succeeding . . . but, in a worst-case scenario, you could always bury me in it."

Hearing this, Billy chuckled.

He had been standing in the shadows of the porch, quietly watching the scene play out, and after getting over the initial shock of Leroy's size, he once again found himself not only impressed by the quality of Tellers friends, but by Teller's resiliency. Wondering at the meaning of this turn of events, he heard a chuckle from behind and turned to Abbott, who, with an enormous smile splitting his beard gave Billy a wink and disappeared into the store.

It was time for more beer.

Back in the parking lot, Leroy gave a snort. "I aint going to sell my Caddy, Teller. Not to you, and not for any price. And I sure as *hell* aint gonna *bury* you in it!"

"Well then," Teller shrugged. "Guess you're gonna have to keep me alive so's I can borrow it now and then."

Still taking refuge behind the Cadillac, Teller took great pleasure in seeing Leroy's face turn red in frustration,

"Relax ya big 'ol bull." He laughed. "Why don't you and your lovely wife come on up to the porch. I have a couple of people I want you to meet." Raising his eyebrows, a crooked smile touched his lips as he looked at Leroy for a sign that he was forgiven. Leroy's head tipped ever so slightly and Teller took Janey's hand to lead her up the steps, and into the shade. Leroy watched them go; then, glancing over at Jack shook his head in amusement and set a big foot on the first stair. Jack grinned and followed.

All together now, Teller introduced them: first to Billy, and then to Junior, who, having woken during the commotion, was in the process of pouring himself the last of the coffee.

Giving the cup a wistful glace, Leroy asked, "any more of that?"

Little Raven poured the last few drops into his cup and shook the empty pot with a guilty smile. "Sorry . . ."

But just then Billy quickly between them, and removing the stainless-steel pot from Junior's hand, smiled, "Please, I'll make more. But in the meantime, may I get either of you anything else?"

Janey peeked around from behind her husband. "You kin tell me where the bathroom is."

Billy's megawatt smile lit the porch and he headed for the screen door "Follow me."

Janey did.

"Thanks Bill." Leroy called out, his eyes following his wife through the door: but the moment they were out of sight he turned to Jack. "Any sign of that murderous little prick?"

Teller's eyebrows shot up at Leroy's vehemence. "Whoa, Leroy." He said, stepping back and holding his hands up as if he were expecting Leroy to charge again.

"Is there somethin' we need to know about?"

Struggling to stifle his rage, Leroy hissed. "He's here, Teller. That little bastards *here* . . . the sonofabitch left a trail of dead Jackrabbits all the way back to Blanding."

Teller's eyes narrowed.

The news that Ben had arrived worried him more than he cared to admit and seeing Leroy this angry worried him even more. "He's a twisted little fuck," Teller nodded, "that's for sure," then, turning to gaze across the landscape, smiled, "but it's good to know he's here."

Jack had remained silent since Leroy's announcement. But hearing Tellers comment his expression became one of puzzlement. "And why in the hell would *that* be?"

"Cause now we aren't wondering *where* he is," Teller smiled. All we need to do *now*, is keep an eye on any high spots with a clear line of sight to this building."

"Christ, Tell." Jack exclaimed, waving his arm in a wide arc. "That covers about 360 degrees!"

Giving Jack a 'no shit' squint, Teller nodded. "I *know* that, Jack, so look for a spot that *you* would choose." Turning to Leroy, he smiled as he rubbed his bruised shoulder.

"Thanks for coming down Leroy. You didn't need to do it you know."

"Yeah, I did." Leroy said, giving Teller a look a father might give his wayward son. "And I knew it for sure once I talked to your chickenshit partner."

"Chickenshit *Ex*-partner." Teller admonished.

"Whatever." Leroy grumbled, "But when Slick showed up and told us about his nephew, I knew we had ta come on down." But then flashing an unexpected smile, he gave Teller a solid slap on the back, sending him nearly a foot forward.

"And hell, it gave me an excuse to get the Caddy out of the garage, and Janey out of the kitchen. 'Sides, I would'a never heard the end of it if we'd a stayed."

Teller regained his balance and glared, "Knock it off Leroy! And who in the hell's *'slick'*?"

"Slick is that polished piece of shit Jack here brought to Cortez." Leroy grumbled, jabbing his thumb in Jacks direction.

Jack slapped his leg and guffawed. Not only was he amused by Leroy's comment, he absolutely reveled in the good-natured abuse that was being bestowed upon Teller.

"Well, *I'm* glad you made it," he chuckled, but seeing Teller massage his new bruise, he added, "and we *both* appreciate the heads up on Ben. But take it easy on Teller, Leroy. Otherwise there won't be nothing left for Ben to shoot." Teller glared at Jack, muttering in caustic tones, "nice to have friends. . ."

Junior smiled from his chair, thoroughly entertained. The banter, along with everything else that had transpired since his arrival easily justified the long drive. Suddenly the slam of the screen door interrupted his amusement, and he turned to see his grandfather carrying a tray that held six cups and the coffee pot with Abbott trotting close behind, cradling a cold six-pack. Both Teller and Leroy turned to the arrival as well. Smiling, Leroy gave Teller a second, but far gentler pat on the shoulder, taking a cup from the tray and thanking Billy as he poured.

Teller glared at Leroy and stepped away, intercepting Abbott while deftly slipping a can from the ring and popping its top. "As I have said many times, Griz, great minds think alike." Lifting the can to his lips, a voice spoke from behind.

"At least thirsty ones do."

Teller turned just as Jack stepped up and pulled a second can from the ring. Raising it high, he grinned, "Salude!"
Teller returned the smile and touched his can to Jack's.

"Amen!'

Teller leaned into Abbott, gesturing towards the necklace and chart lying on the table. "Put those away Griz," he whispered, "that's a lot more explanation than I care to deal with right now. You and I can put *that* riddle together at a later date."

With a nod of understanding, Abbott covertly stuffed the necklace and the tapa cloth into their respective boxes, tucking both behind the bench just as the little bell on the screen door jingled and Janey's returned, smoothing her skirt and picking up the last remaining cup. "Thanks, Bill, I needed that." She smiled sweetly and poured, spooning sugar into the strong coffee.

"You fellas hungry?" she asked.

Leroy's face lit up. "Hell, honey, you know *I* can always eat." Turning to the others, he boomed, "How's about you boys?"

Abbott voiced an enthusiastic, "Aye!" and the rest followed.

Grinning, Janey pulled out her pack of smokes and shook one out. She was back in her element.

"Good! Where's the kitchen 'round here?"

At that, a laugh erupted from the chair where Junior sat. And as all eyes turned to him he simply tipped his cup in their direction. "It's good to be home again."

Billy laughed and his humor encompassed them all as he set his cup on the table and reached out to take Jane's elbow.

"Please Ma'am," he said, "Come with me. I'll take you to the kitchen in my trailer."

With a proud sniff, Janey shook her elbow free of Billy's grip. "Thanks all the same Bill," she snapped, speaking around the cigarette that dangled between her lips, "but I kin still walk on my own, and you kin cut the 'Ma'am crap too. I ain't no older than you."

Billy's smile grew. "Of course." he chuckled, releasing her elbow. "But on *that* particular, my dear Jane, you may be mistaken."

Teller smiled, pleased with the jovial feeling that had replaced the aura of doom previously encompassing the small area. But while he might be pleased he was still watchful.

Covertly scanning their surroundings, he saw no sign of Ben, or anything else that indicated a potential threat. But the very fact that nothing seemed out of the ordinary worried him, bringing the old cliché from some western movie to mind.

'It's quiet . . . too quiet . . .

The thought had barely passed when the desert silence was shattered by the bellow of a foghorn. The blast bounced across the water, echoing from the surrounding rock.

All conversation ceased as everyone began looking in different directions; searching for the source of the sound. But as the first echo faded away, a second blast reverberated across the water, louder than the first, announcing the arrival of sixty-five feet of sleek, black fiberglass, aluminum and tinted glass. Chugging into the bay it rounded the outcropping of stone that safety harbored the dock, the glass-wrapped wheelhouse reflecting brilliant rays of sunlight blinding everyone as it approached.

Shading his eyes, Teller's expression of stunned disbelief became one of stunned astonishment. This was *nothing* like the rental houseboats that the marinas offered. . . No, *this* was in another league altogether.

The boats massive bow carved a deep "v" in the lakes flat surface; gliding towards them while pushing white-capped waves against the cliff walls where they bounced back, splashing over the dock as the engines revved into reverse: the propellers sucking the green water into a bubbly vortex at the ships stern. Suddenly, large vinyl balls attached to heavily braided ropes dropped over the sides where they were squeezed to nearly bursting as they kept the steel hull from crushing the little wooden dock, the pressure rocking the structure all the way back to the store. And as the craft bumped, two men appeared on deck; one jumping out to wrap the bow-rope to a large cleat bolted to the docks floating platform while the other ran aft, pulling a second rope through the cat-holes; lashing it to another cleat at the opposite end of the dock. The ropes reached their limits, and with a showing of great skill, the pilot nuzzled up to the dock with no more than a soft 'bump'.

Teller stood speechless in the reflected light of this marvelous piece of floating architecture. Shaking his head in awe, he looked over at the baffled faces of his friends, wondering how Billy had managed to pull off *this*. But on the heels of *that* thought, the old saying: 'Be careful what you wish for.' came to mind. But just as he wondered what negative results could possibly come from this; his musings were interrupted by the sound of shoes on hardwood.

Turning to the second-story deck, he saw a man emerge from the shadows of the wheelhouse sporting a spotless white cap with braids on its bill and emblazoned with golden anchors.

Gazing down at the group gathered below, a smile shone white against a deeply tanned face: and basking in the glory of his arrival, he gave a salute, skipped down the solid oak stairs and crossed the deck, leaping lightly over the water.

Coming to halt in front of Teller he held out his hand.

"Congratulations!"

Teller, still in a state of semi-shock, smiled cautiously.

"Pardon?"

"Congratulations!" The man repeated, his hand still extended

"And what makes you think this is *mine?*"

Having grown tired of waiting for a reciprocal handshake, Neil reached down to lift Teller's hand and began pumping it enthusiastically. "Because *you,* Sir," he said, his smile growing toothier still; "Have the look of a man of taste and substance."

At first, Teller remained cool and aloof: lowering his eyes to his still bouncing hand. Raising his eyebrows, he brought his eyes from his hand to Neil's face; his expression disturbingly neutral. Clearing his throat, Neil called on all of his sales bravado, struggling to hold Teller's gaze while desperately wondering just how to release Tellers hand gracefully. But just as the sparkle was leaving Neil's smile, Teller felt a hand on his shoulder as a warm breath whispered in his ear, "Don't let this old hustler fool you."

Sighing in relief at his rescue, and emboldened by Billy's presence, his white teeth flashed. "I'm a salesman, son. . . I can see a sucker from a mile away, but the expression of a satisfied customer within a handshake's distance is infinitely more pleasing."

Gratefully releasing Teller's hand, he took Billy's instead.

"And how are *you*, Bill?"

Billy grinned, returning the handshake. "I'm doing well Neil." he laughed. "But save your sales pitch. Mr. Teller here is *not* your average client." Gesturing to the boat, he added, "But I do wish to thank you for delivery."

Neil's smile embraced them like a mother hen. "Delivered as promised." he said, as if nothing less could have been expected; then turning to Teller, held up his hands in submission. "First, may I beg forgiveness for my exuberance. As a purveyor of dreams, I often get overly enthusiastic; it comes with the territory and for that I apologize. . . *that* said, I assume you have a check?"

Teller grinned.

Upon their introduction, he had found Neil bombastic and overbearing. But now he saw what Billy saw: a P.T. Barnum character in a sailor's cap, but stepping back he laughed, "*Wait* a minute. . . you're askin' the wrong guy."

Blinking like a surprised owl, Neil looked inquiringly to Billy, who chuckled, and patted the string of gold braids that hung from the shoulder of Neil's jacket.

"Don't worry Neil. Little Raven will take care of you."

Teller's eyebrows lifted in happy surprise. "Well then," he smiled. "There you are . . ."

In that thin sliver of silence that followed, a cigarette-rough voice interjected, "Well gent's, that's all real nice and all, but what about breakfast!?"

Turning to the commanding tone, Neil expected someone much differed than the diminutive woman before him, made smaller still by the *very* large man who stood, his hand resting lovingly on her shoulder.

With the boat delivered and payment assured, Neil reflexively slipped back into his sales persona . . .doffing his cap, he spread his hands in an all-encompassing gesture.

"Madam. Upon this splendid craft is a fully stocked, completely gourmet kitchen, which! I've no doubt will supply you with whatever you might need." Then puffing out his chest, he smiled down on Janey and added a caveat.

"Of course, that *does* depend on just what it is you plan on preparing."

Janey rolled her eyes and he grinned. "Well, I suppose a celebratory meal *is* called for," adding, "that is, if you don't mind a floating kitchen."

Jane thought for a minute, then, tapping a cigarette from her pack put it to her lips, glaring at Teller as if daring him to refuse her request.

"Kin I smoke on this damn thing?"

Teller couldn't help but laugh at the ferocity of her expression.

"I think I can make an exception this one time, Jane."

"Good!" she grinned. Taking the cigarette from her lips stood on tiptoes and kissed his cheek, turned to Billy, and pointed her smoke at him.

"Come on Bill, let's see if there's any eggs on this tub."

_____ __ -- --- -- __ _____
_____ ____ __ ____ __
-- --- --

= Chapter 55 =

A hellish buzzing tickled the edge of Ben's consciousness, disturbing his twisted dreams. At first, it barely registered, but once aware, it became all he could hear.

Frightened, he struggled to claw his way out from the darkness; but it was so thick it clung to his soul; but finally sensing hope he sucked in a painful breath, and his eyes fluttered open.

His heart nearly stopped.

There, only inches from his nose, a lizard's expressionless black eyes studied him: its quick tongue gliding across its scaly snout. But then it was as if the reptile could read his thoughts; for as hatred filled him it scurried off, leaving him a view of the glittering lake in the distance. It was then that he remembered where he was, and what he must do.

Kill Teller.

With that thought, Ben attempted to rise, but the blood from his leaking wounds had dried during the night, fusing his cheek to his arm. Startled, scared, and only half awake, he tried to jerk free, but the bond was shockingly strong and all he succeeded in doing was to send a jolt of searing pain through his skull and scatter the hundreds of flies that had gathered on the blood leaking from his scalp.

Rising, they swarmed in a thick black cloud; circling as they repositioned to resume their feast.

That was the source of the hellish racket, Ben realized sickeningly. It was caused by flies! Those filthy little insects were responsible for the noise, and the horrid tickling; but with his cheek welded to his forearm he was powerless.

Gritting his teeth, he pulled, nearly passing out as skin separated. . . but hatred overcoming agony, he struggled to stand on wobbly legs; looking to a sun that was now just above the horizon. *'I'm late . . .* he moaned through cracked lips. Desperately thirsty, he limped back to the Hummer and pulled the door open. He needed something to drink!

Seeing nothing *on* the seats, he crouched and swept a hand beneath the driver's side. Hearing the crackle of plastic his heart jumped as he clutched madly, pulling a half-empty bottle of Gatorade from the dirt and trash.

Unscrewing the cap with trembling hands, Ben clumsily brought the crushed bottle to his lips and sucked greedily: but unable to control his swollen tongue most the piss-warm liquid simply dribbled down his chin and onto his chest. With a cry of frustration, Ben crushed the now empty container and threw it as hard as he could into the sage.

Wiping tears of self-pity on his sleeve, he stumbled back to his rifle, lowering himself gently into the dirt to bring the high-powered scope to his eye and dialing it in.

Ben's head jerked back in shock and he nearly shouted,

'What's a *boat* doing there?'

Putting a knuckle to his eye, he rubbed, and refocused the scope. He could no longer see the porch to get a clear shot!

Trembling with fury and fever, Ben lowered his rifle, and going to his knees began searching for higher ground.

There! about a quarter mile away was a prominent point where he would have a better line of sight.

Slinging the weapon over his shoulder he stood and staggered towards that high, flat mesa in the distance.

—— — -- --- -- — ——
—— —— —— ——
-- --- --

Chapter 56 =

Leroy's steely grey eyes scanned the shoreline while he and Jack discussed various strategies to keep Teller alive. But with the smell of sausage gravy and biscuits drifting through the French doors, he was finding it increasingly difficult to concentrate. His mornings *always* included a hearty breakfast. And while he had managed to ignore the delicious odors up till now, the smell of eggs and toast set his stomach to grumbling.

Dropping a meaty paw onto Jacks shoulder, he rumbled, "Come on, son. Its time to eat."

Jack lifted his nose to the delicious odors and followed Leroy into the boats salon.

Teller, Billy and Neil sat at the chart table ironing out the final details of the boats purchase; but on seeing Jack and Leroy enter, Teller slapped the tabletop with both hands and pushed his chair back. "Billy, *you* started this, and if Junior thinks it's a good idea and there's enough money to pay for it, then *do it*." He paused and looked at Junior. "There *is* money to pay for it, right?"

Little Raven nodded.

"Well then," Teller grinned. "Write the man a check!"

Flashing a salesman's smile, Neil laced his fingers behind his head and leaned back in his chair.

Teller looked at him and grinned, then turned to Jack.

"Gentlemen!" he said, holding out his arms as if to embrace them. "*There* you are, and just in time. Leroy, I do believe your lovely wife has breakfast nearly ready."

Picking up his empty coffee cup, he stuck his head through the galley door.

"And how may I be of service, sweet Jane?"

310

Looking up from the Wolf gas stove, Jane cracked the two eggs she held on the edge of the skillet and tossed the shells into the sink. "Hell yes, you kin help!" she hollered, mopping the sweat off her brow with her apron. "Clean off that table, find some plates, some silverware and some napkins, and don't fergit the salt and pepper." She paused, looked up, and smiled around her unlit cigarette. *"Please."*

"Yes, I will ma'am'" Teller grinned, "seeing as how you used the magic word and all." He ducked and pulled the door shut just as a third eggshell smacked the other side; and laughing, went in search of table settings.

~

The mood at the breakfast table was jolly; the sounds of everyone stuffing themselves filling the salon and leaving Ben and his heinous goal temporarily forgotten.

But finally, after sopping up the last bit of gravy on his plate with a last bite of biscuit, Neil threw his napkin onto a nearly spotless plate and leaned back in his chair.

Patting his belly with unadulterated satisfaction, he pulled a toothpick from his pocket, and prying a piece of sausage from his back molar, smiled, "Madam, *that* was delicious. I had forgotten what real home cooking tastes like."

Looking across the table at his crew, his smile took on a more authoritative quality. "Boys, I want you to show your appreciation by helping this young lady with the cleanup."

Grinning, his helpers jumped up, the younger of the two chirping, "No problem boss!" as he reached down to grab a plate: but as he did, Janey barked, "Dang it! You kids sit back down! I kin clean up this mess on my own."

The young man looked to Neil for guidance but it was Leroy who had the last word.

"Damn it now, honey, let these boys help. We got things to do, and it'll go a hell of a lot faster if you'll just quit bein' so damn stubborn!"

Jane glared at Leroy, her lips tightening around her cigarette in a repressed smile. "yer right honey," she muttered, then

311

looked at the men. "Okay then boys, grab them dishes and take 'em on into the kitchen."

Nodding his approval, Neil grinned and the men gathered up an armload of plates and headed towards the galley.

Seeing everyone scurrying about, Leroy bent down and gave his wife a kiss on the cheek, then, turning to Jack he growled,

"Come on Jack. Let's go have us a look around 'n figure out how we can keep Teller from gettin' killed."

Jack stood, but before he followed Leroy through the French doors he leaned down, tipped his head towards Neil, and whispered loudly into Juniors ear. "Watch this guy, William. He's the shady type."

Neil's expression of satisfaction vanished and his mouth went slack; dropping his toothpick into his lap.

Jack slapped him on the back and walked away laughing, while Junior opened his briefcase to remove the check he had prepared on Teller's behalf.

Smiling, he turned to Neil.

"I assume you have the documents of sale in order?"

~

Having piled a plate high while he helped Janey in the kitchen, Teller skipped the group meal and went in search of Abbott. He needed to speak with him in private regarding the necklace and the chart.

Finding him in the rear cabin, they had a short discussion agreeing that there was still much to know regarding the two objects, and that they would need to corner Billy in the hopes of prying this much needed information from him. However, Abbott pointed out that prying *anything* out of the taciturn Indian would be a near impossible task.

Teller, in full agreement, went to look for Billy.

While the boat was large, it could only provide so many paces to be, and rounding the wheelhouse, he came across Billy. He was leaning on the starboard rail; Junior and Neil on either side, with both listening to how Neil had come to have this particular boat in his possession; but just as he stepped into the end of the tale, Jane's voice came through the galley window thanking Neil's men for their help and telling them to scoot on out of *her* kitchen. Neil took this as his cue and reached out to clasp Billy's hand.

"Always a pleasure, Bill."

"Yes, Neil," Billy smiled, "it is. And I want to thank you again. I realize you could have made a much more handsome profit had you sold it to someone other than myself."

"Sure," Neil grinned, "but where's the fun in that?" then he held up his finger. "Excuse me for a moment." Turning, he crossed the deck, stuck his head through the galley window, and tipped his Captain's cap to Jane.

"It was a pleasure to meet you Miss Jane, and thank you for breakfast. It was de*licious*." Not bothering to wait for a response he turned to Teller and held out a hand that held a business card pinched between two fingers. "Mr. Teller," he smiled, "If you ever find yourself in need of my services in the future, please don't hesitate to call."

Teller's aversion to salesmen ran deep and he was hesitant to respond; but as Neil was a friend of Billy's, he accepted Neil's bonhomie along with the card. but as far as he was concerned, business was concluded. Neil, however, was so pleased with the day's business that he blissfully ignored Teller's attitude. Smiling, he threw one arm around Billy's shoulder, the other over Juniors, and said, "Follow me."

Chuckling, Teller followed the men down the steps to the lower deck.

Working their way to the rear of the boat, they found Neil's two-man crew waiting next to a small speedboat hanging from davits over the stern. Neil turned, grinned at Teller, then shouted a command. The boys lowered the boat into the water and Neil, jumping behind the wheel, gave a thumb's up and turned the key. The engine belched a throaty roar, causing exhaust to bubble up in a cloud of blue smoke. Laughing, Neil motioned his men in and with a wave of his cap, pushed the throttle forward.

The nose of the sleek craft rose like a rocket, and it was gone; leaving a twelve-foot rooster tail as it skipped across the surface of the lake: and the moment the boat cleared the projection of sandstone that protected the little dock, one of the guys threw out a slalom ski and was soon bouncing across the boats wake; his hoots of joy bouncing from the sandstone walls. . . suddenly Neil cranked the boats nose and the guy on the ski whipped through the rooster tail, flying straight up, then flipping and tumbling into the boats wake.

Laughing at the fitting ending, Teller turned from the stainless-steel rails and went back to the salon, dropping into a plush chair to stare through a bank of windows; scanning the jagged landscape, his focus intense.

Jack took a seat across from him; aware of what he was looking for but reluctant to bring up such depressing subject matter on this happy occasion.

"So, why did you buy this again?"

Teller was so intent on the convoluted country outside the windows, Jack's comment barely registered.

There were a *lot* of places for a lunatic to hide.

Holding up his glass, Jack rattled the ice. "I mean, Teller, this is one *nice* fucking boat."

Teller blinked, looked over at Jack, and rose from his chair, going to the east-facing window where he stood with his back to the room. Not wishing to show the depth of his concern to his companions, he smoothed the worry from his face, pulled the curtains closed, and went back to his seat.

"Yes, Jack," he smiled, "it is."

Deciding that Ben was a problem for later, Teller turned to Billy and grinned, "Chief. When I asked you to find me a houseboat, I wasn't referring to a floating *palace.*"

"I realize that," Billy shrugged. "But when Neil told me about this; well I felt it would be foolish not take advantage of the situation." Turning to his grandson, he smiled. "What do you think Little Raven? Was this a wise choice?"

Looking up from the paperwork that was still spread across the surface of the salon table, Junior nodded. "*I* think this is a remarkable investment Teller, and it will work quite well for what will soon be a much needed tax write-off." Then, following a brief pause, he grinned. "And I can always use a luxury getaway. The lake is a welcome escape from the Tucson summers and Grandfathers trailer is *much* too small."

Teller looked over to Billy, who simply smiled.

"Well, that's good enough for me." Raising his eyebrows, he turned to Jack. "Good enough for you?"

Jack shrugged. "It's not *my* money."

Teller's smile vanished. "No, it is *not*. But you might need a break from your little cabin in the woods during a cold Flagstaff winter." His smile returned and he winked,

"Particularly if you want to impress a certain gorgeous airport vixen."

Ignoring Jacks glare, Teller turned back to the group. "And that offer applies to everybody here. Each, and every *one* of you." A murmur of appreciation went through the room and Teller turned his smile on Abbott.

"So, Griz. What do *you* think of the Musketeers floating clubhouse?"

The corners of Abbott's brown eyes crinkled as he glanced about the luxurious salon. "She's a grand ship, Captain," he said, his grin slowly working its way through his beard.

"Mighty grand. And one deserving a fitting name. What shall you call her?"

At this, Teller paused. It was a good question; a very good question indeed . . . and one he hadn't yet considered.

Leaning back in his chair, he steepled his fingers, touched them to his chin and closed his eyes; and as he did the name slipped into his consciousness as cleanly as a trick card in a Magicians deck.

His eyes popped open, and the as slightest of smiles touched his lips, he uttered,

"Coyote's Dream."

As the words were spoken, Billy felt something prodigious occur. It was as if a new thread had been woven into the great web that holds all things together; with God himself plucking that cosmic string.

Smiling his brilliant smile, Billy bowed his head.

"An excellent choice, Teller. An *excellent* choice. And, as you will need to keep your dream somewhere, I would be honored to offer you my dock as safe harbor."

Teller nodded. He had felt the shift as well; and while not to the magnitude Billy had experienced, the note still reverberated within him. Shaking his head as if to clear it, he laughed. "Thanks Billy, but while your offer is generous, this dock will require substantial modification to accommodate *this* particular Dreamboat."

Jack smiled and lifted his glass. "Well, partner, as my dreams are peripherally attached to yours, I will be more than happy to lend my skills to the endeavor."

Abbott, not wishing to be left out, raised his bottle and volunteered his time and talent as well, with Junior following suite.

Teller, again appreciating the caliber of his friends, smiled as he looked around the room.

"Your offers are greatly appreciated and accepted. As the old saying goes, many hands make light work."

For a moment, murmurs of happy agreement filled the salon; but then the heavy thump of Leroy's fist rattled the table. All eyes turned to him as he shoved that fist into the ice bucket, pulling out a beer can tightly enough to put a kink in the aluminum. His expression grim, he studied the faces of the people before him. . . with a shake of his head he went to the double French doors to stare across the broken landscape with a battle-trained eye.

The room sat in silence as he slowly turned back to the room.

"This here is all well and good," he growled. "And Janey and me surely appreciate the use of your boat Teller. But let's not forget that right now there's a crazy kid out there with a rifle who wants to put an end to your fun." A buzz riffled through the group, and Jack added, "He's right, Tell. This is *real* nice. But we'd all like to see you around long enough to enjoy it."

Crushing the empty can he held, Teller sighed.

"Yes, Jack . . . I've not forgotten the lunatic child. And, as I told you before, I got no *intention* of dyin.' But as you two have pointed out, once again reality has reared its ugly head."

"And," Jack frowned, "this time it's got a gun pointed right at *you*."

"Always the voice of comfort, huh Jack?"

"I enjoy your company Tell." Jack shrugged. "I'd like to keep you around a little longer."

Abbott raised his can. "I second that, Captain."

Teller felt blessed that he was surrounded with friends such as these; but he also recognized that it was *he* who was responsible for their welfare and it was with this in mind that he made his decision.

"Very well then. Tomorrow morning we will raise anchor and head this ship south with everyone aboard. Everyone but *you,* Jack. *Your* gonna stay with me and we'll see if we can track that little fucker without gettin' killed." But before Teller could say another word, Leroy slammed his can on the table, crushing it while glaring through lowered brows.

"Sorry son, but that just won't do. I didn't come all the way down here just so's I could sit on my ass while *you* two dance around the goddamned desert doing recon on a homicidal lunatic!"

Teller stood to argue his point. But seeing Leroy with his wide shoulders blocking the light from the doorway and his close-cropped hair only inches from the ceiling, his resolve fizzled. The grey of his temples notwithstanding, Leroy still cut a formidable figure and his expression allowed no argument. Teller was about to make one final point when Janey stepped up and took her place beside her husband.

"*We* didn't come this far, Teller."

Abbott stood and joined them, his meaning clear.

Jack just lifted his glass.

With a smile of defeat, Teller raised his can.

"All for one?"

Bothe grinning, Jack and Abbott raised their vessels, and clinked them together.

"And one for all!

The rest of the group looked at one another, momentarily puzzled. But then, as one, they called out.

"And one for all!"

= Chapter 57 =

Ben struggled to pull himself over the waist-high ledge, crawling across the hard capstone to collapse into a fevered heap at the very edge of the cliff. It had taken him nearly three hours just to cross the ravine. And now, laying with his cheek pressed into the blessedly cool earth, he focused one grit-filled eye on the ruined Humvee in the distance.
Leaning on broken axels, it represented his last tenuous tether to reality.

His eye fluttered closed, and for one brief, exquisite moment, the pain subsided. But the respite was only a tease. The hellish buzzing of flies increased their volume, rising to compete with the screaming voices in his head.
The combination was unbearable.

Whimpering while pressing his hands to either side of his head, Ben reached for his rifle, intent blowing the voices from his skull: but as his finer touched the trigger, a calm, seductive voice cut through the screaming demons: a voice that quelled the rage.
The voice of reason . . .

'Kill Teller,' it spoke simply. *'And the girl is yours.'*
The smooth silkiness of the voice calmed him; and refocusing his attentions lowered the rifle and he smiled a cruel smile that stretched his skin, cracking the dried and dirty blood caking his face and making his visage more horrifying still; and now motivated by the thought of Kelly in his arms he dug his elbows into the dirt; pushing himself up and resting the barrel of his rifle on a flat rock while putting his good eye to the scope.

From his spot high on the cliffs edge, the entire port side of the mirrored glass vessel as well as the storefront and the parking area was visible. . . all he had to do now was wait.

But as he lay there his thirst-swollen tongue filled his mouth like vile cotton, and the voices returned; some babbling incoherently while others mocked his misery.

Fighting to keep the voices in his head from driving him further into madness, Ben pushed his face into the crook of his arm, trying to smother the cruel laughter, his eyes leaking tears of pain and fear. But lifting his cheek to blot away the tears, something moved just outside is peripheral vision.

It was only a speckled lizard attracted by his body heat.

The curious reptile crawled up the rifle barrel, pausing at the scope to study him with glittering black eyes. . .but its curiosity was cut short. Ben's hand shot out with surprising speed, snatching the little fellow up and stuffing it into his mouth with a mad cackle.

The tail wiggled between his lips; finally breaking free to drop to the dirt where it thrashed wildly.

Looking down, Ben's lips peeled back to reveal scale-covered teeth; his hideous smile growing as he imagined that tail being Teller writhing at his feet.

With that image burning in his brain he swallowed and brought the rifle back to his bloody cheek.

The voices were gone . . .

Making himself comfortable, he waited.

= Chapter 58 =

Following much discussion, Jack suggested that they do a perimeter search after midnight in the hopes that they might catch Ben sleeping. Thus lowering the odds of a shooting.

"Unless he's got a night scope," Jack said, "It's pretty hard to pull off an accurate shot in the dark."
Leroy nodded in agreement, but Teller was not as keen on the idea.

"True enough Jacko, but since we can't use a flashlight, it seems to me that we also have a pretty good chance of bustin' a leg while we're stumbling around in the dark."

Wrapping both hands around his glass, Jack sighed and leaning forward. "Well then Tell. What do *you* suggest we do? Just sit here and wait?"

Teller smiled and shook his head. "Nope. What *I* think we should do is get a little sleep and wait till dawn. Then, Jack, *I* think we should get in that chopper of yours and do some aerial recon. We might risk the chance of him taking a wild shot at the chopper, but at least we'll have a solid fix on his location. *Then* we know what we're dealing with." He raised his eyebrows, gauging their reaction.

"Damn it." Jack nodded. "You *are* smarter than you look." Allowing Teller a begrudging smile, he glanced over at Leroy. "What do *you* think?"

"Makes sense." Leroy nodded. "Makes real good sense. Lot less chance of the kid taking an easy shot at Teller here."

'Yeah," Jack grumbled, "but a lot *better* chance of him puttin' a bullet through at me or my helicopter."

Teller's laugh overrode the complaint.

"It's not gonna be *you,* Jack. Its gonna be *us.* And relax, you're gonna buy a new helicopter anyway."

Jack glared at Teller, but a small smile touched his lips. "Yeah, but let's not overlook the small detail of my needing to be *alive* to fly it . . ."

"Jack old chum," Teller laughed. "The chances that Ben could hit a moving target are so minimal that they're not even worth considering."

"And if you're wrong?"

Teller shrugged. "Then I'm wrong."

Jack shook his head, poured another finger of Scotch over melting ice cubes, and raising his glass, sighed, "All for one." But as he lifted the glass, Teller reached over and snatched it from his hand.

"Glad you still feel that way pal," he grinned, and lifting the glass in salute, tipped it back, drained it, and with a smack of his lips, handed Jack his empty glass.

"Now, your phone please."

——— — ‑‑ ‑‑‑ ‑‑ ‑ ———
——— ——— ——— ——— —
‑‑ ‑‑‑ ‑‑

= Chapter 59 =

Waving his hat to the boisterous crowd, Willie stepped out of the spotlight, leaving an empty three-legged stool in its wash. He had stretched out his second set and was worn out; but it had been worth it. The crowd was rowdy but generous and seeing his guitar case filled with crumpled bills he smiled and thanked the Lord for music, liquor, and Friday nights.

Taking off his cowboy hat he wiped his forehead with his sleeve; but as he knelt to scoop the money from the case a pretty girl pushed her way to the foot of the stage and tugged on his cuff. Willie pulled back, but she yanked him close enough to whisper in his ear while tucking a folded napkin into his hand.

Smiling noncommittally, he unfolded the note and read it.

His smile faltered, and he looked up from the napkin to the girl. Reading it a second time, the corners of his handlebar moustache lifted. "Really. . .?" he grinned.

"Really." She smiled back.

Shaking his head, he shoved the note into his pocket and scooped the money from the case, stuffing it into his pockets as he dropped the guitar into the empty case and snapped the latches closed. Looking up, he winked,

"I'll call you later and we'll just give that a try."

A triumphant smile lit the young woman's face and she returned to her table of giggling friends; who, with varying levels of envy, turned to judge him with their eyes.

Raising his eyebrows, Willie put two fingers to the brim of his hat, picked up his old Gibson and left the stage.

Feeling invincible he weaved through the crowd, fantasies of the notes contents filling his head. But when he saw Kip on the stool next to Kelly's the visions scattered.

Kip was leaning dangerously close, and that was bad enough; but when one of his hands disappeared beneath the polished bar top Willie hurried his pace. *'Dumb kid'* he muttered, and as he shouldered his way through the crowd the loud chatter of bar noise inexplicably subsided; and in that rare second of near silence Willie heard a brittle: 'snap' followed by Kips cry of pain just as the noise ramped back up.

Maneuvering around a big guy holding a pitcher in both hands, Willie found Kip hunched over on his stool clutching his hand; his face a mask of agony. Willie looked at Kip, and with a grunt of disappointment slid his battered guitar case under a stool and turned to Kelly. He hadn't seen what happened, but her expression held no remorse.

"You okay?"

She gave him a tight smile. "Oh, *I'm* fine, but young Kip here may need to see a Doctor."

Looking into her eyes, Willie's questions were answered.

With a nod, he took off his cowboy hat and dropped it on the bar. "Do I even *need* to ask what happened, Kipper?"

"I'd rather you didn't." Kip hissed through clenched teeth. Willie smiled as he shook his head and picking up a clean mug, pushed it under the tap.

As it filled he turned to Kelly. "*You* want to tell me?"

"Don't be too hard on him Willie," she smiled. "It was just a little over-exuberance on his part. I think he can understand my reaction."

Willie nodded and took his mug from beneath the tap.

"You need to see a doc?"

Kip, with the expression of a puppy that had just been kicked held out his trembling hand. "I don't know man." he whimpered. "What do you think?" His hand was shaking so badly that Willie had to hold it in both of his in order to gage the damage; and turning it gently this way and that, he shook his head. "There's only one thing we can do son."

Locking Kip's wrist, he took the dislocated finger and with no fanfare jammed it back in place.

Kip's face drained of all color. Then, squealing in surprise as much as pain, he yanked his hand back, looking at Willie like he had just been kicked again, only harder.

"Jesus, Willie!" he cried. "That *hurt!*"

Willie shrugged, took a big drink and wiped away the foam on his moustache.

"Well son, maybe that'll teach you to keep your hands to yourself, *and* to take good advice when it's given."

Kip's mouth tightened as his face went red with humiliation.

Willie looked to Kelly, and giving her a wink that Kip couldn't see, admonished, "I warned you 'bout that son."

He waited expectantly for a moment, then nudged Kip with his elbow. Kip looked up and glared as Willie tipped his head in Kelly's direction: but finally getting the hint, turned to Kelly; humbled, yet youthfully defiant. With downcast eyes he muttered, "Sorry Ma'am."

Bringing a manicured nail to Kip's chin, Kelly lifted his face; and looking into his eyes, smiled, "Sometimes Cougars bite . . ." His finger forgotten, Kip's mouth would have fallen open if Kelly's finger had not been supporting it.

"I, uh, but I, uh, didn't, uh,"

Willie held for a moment, then broke into laughter. "You'll learn son," he guffawed, "you'll learn."

At that moment Kelly's cell phone rang.

Seeing the incoming number, she let Kips chin drop, then, slapping his cheek playfully, winked at Willie and turned from the bar. "Tell!" she laughed, "Where *are* you?"

Hearing Tellers name, Willie tuned his ears to Kelly's voice, while Kip, no longer the center of attention slunk away to find some ice for his hand. Willie watched him go, sipped on his beer while listening to the one-sided conversation but Kelly gave nothing away.

Finally hanging up, she turned a dazzling smile his way.

"Jack's going to be here tomorrow, Willie. Want to go to the lake?"

~

Saying goodbye to Kelly, Teller tossed Jack his phone.

"Okay partner, just as soon as we've flushed our homicidal little quail I want you to take that chopper east over to Durango and pick up Kelly. She's expecting you."

Jack tucked the phone into his flight jacket, stood, and looked at Teller expectantly.

"So, what am I supposed to do for money?"

Teller paused, stared at Jack for a second, then cried, "Jumpin' Jesus, Jack! You've got a hundred grands worth of cashier's checks in your pocket. What the fuck do you mean, *"what am I gonna do for money?"*

Jack grinned. He did things like this simply because he loved to rattle Tellers cage. Giving an innocent smile, he shrugged, "but those are cashier's *checks*, Tell. I've got no *cash.*"

Looking over at Young Bill, Teller gave a sad smile

"And *there* sits the idiot Musketeer."

William's dark face broke into a smile as Teller turned his attention back to Jack.

"Well, Jack. I realize that this may seem terribly complicated, but they *do* have banks in the town of Durango. Therefore, I suppose you *could* take a cab into town and after *cashing* one of those checks could then pick up Kelly as planned." Jack was trying to find the hole in Teller's logic when Abbott, who had been sitting quietly to the side, spoke up. "That *would* make sense, Jack."

"Or," Junior interjected, "I could give you a company credit card. I could use the write offs, and we could just subtract the figure from what I'll owe you on our next transaction."

Jack smiled and looked at Teller, who gave an exasperated sigh. "I don't give a shit, Jack. If that's what you'd rather do, then do it. But you still need to go to a bank and get some damn money! I *don't* want to have this conversation again." Jack's smile expanded, and he turned to Junior.

"I'll take you up on that offer my friend. As far as *I'm* concerned, the less cash I show, the better."

"True," Junior said, "but you fellows *do* need to get some type of Company set up for write-offs, as well as the many other perks that a Corporation enjoys."

Now it was Teller's turn to smile. "We've been discussing that option Young Bill." he said, tossing a meaningful glace at Jack. "But as we're new to the game, what say you help us out with the details?"

"Of course!" Junior smiled, "but right now I'm tired."

Laying back on the couch, he closed his eyes. "So, what I would like to do is catch a few winks. We can talk of Corporations come morning. Is that alright with you?"

"Absolutely." Teller smiled. "Make yourself comfy and pick a bathroom and a bed. I've no idea whether we're stocked with soap and towels, but you're welcome to whatever you can find . . . I'm gonna be up for awhile."

Little Raven's feet came off the couch and he stood. Then, with a bow first to Teller, then to Jack, and finally to Abbott, he smiled. "Well then gentlemen, I shall bid you goodnight." With that he strolled down the hallway.

Watching him go, Teller muttered, "Good man."

"Agreed," Jack nodded. "And that good man's example is worth following." Setting his empty glass on the table, Jack walked away.

Abbott watched him go, and then turned to Teller.

"How many bedrooms are on this boat anyway?"

"I have no idea, Griz." Teller shrugged. "I haven't left this room. But as far as I'm concerned, this here couch looks pretty damn comfy."

"Then Captain," Abbott said, lifting his bulk from the chair, "I shall leave you for the night. But before I go, may I be so bold as to ask what *you* think of the chart and the necklace? because they have certainly roused *my* curiosity."

Teller nodded. "And mine, Griz, and mine." He sighed and leaned back in his chair. "But I'm afraid that is a mystery that will have to wait, for at the moment we are balls deep in *this* one." Abbott nodded, "Yes, of course. I'm sorry Captain, you're right. Well then, I suppose I will see you in the morning."

"With any luck," Teller smiled. "You shall."

Chuckling, Abbott picked up a heavy tapestry blanket that was folded across the back of the couch and wrapping it loosely around his shoulders wished Teller "Goodnight" along with the pointless platitude: "and try to get some sleep."

Teller promised he would, and Abbott, knowing full well that he would do nothing of the sort, smiled, went through the French doors, and took the stairs to the upper deck.

～

Abbott emerged onto a deck that was blissfully silent.

The silence, combined with the gentle breeze, was a pleasant respite from the day's frenzied activities, and stepping to the center of the deck, Abbott stood, listening to the soft lapping of water against the hull. It was a lovely, peaceful sound, and with its steady rhythm in the background, Abbott began circumnavigating the deck; taking the cushions from the chaise lounges that were scattered across the deck and laying them in the middle to create one large mattress.

His task completed, he pulled up one of the now cushionless chairs, plopped down, and unlacing his boots, kicked them aside to wiggle his newly liberated toes in the cool night air.

Abbott's weary bulk seemed to grow lighter as he turned his face to the vast night sky; and allowing gravity to pull him from the lounge chair he slid down onto his improvised bed, lacing his fingers behind his head and gazing up at the dense road of stars that was the Milky Way; and while he could not help but feel insignificant in the presence of such grandeur; even the magnitude of that infinite canopy could not diminish the scope of the events that had brought him to this moment, this place, this night. And now, contemplating the cosmos and his place within them, he found it impossible to absorb all that had happened in the span of this past month; and the more he thought about it, the more overwhelming it became: the enormity of events proving to vast to comprehend. And so, with his thoughts spinning with the stars, his eyes fluttered closed. . . and for the first time in weeks no coyote howled from the canyons, nor did one disturb his dreams.

= Chapter 60 =

Ben's eyes creaked open. . .

Curled in a fetal position and wet with the heavy dew of the high desert, his teeth chattered while his body burned with a fever that left his skin damp with a cold and clammy sweat. With a groan he rolled his head roll to the east where his bloodshot eyes took in the first faint light of dawn.

Dawn!!

Panicked, he rolled to his knees. He had missed his opportunity to kill Teller!

Pushing himself up, he wobbled, weaving as he struggled with a dizziness that made the ground feet spin in and out of focus. Suddenly a vicious cramp twisted his guts; and doubling over he violently regurgitated the partially digested remains of the second, larger lizard that he had tried to eat during the night in his mad hunger.

The dimwitted creature had been attracted by Ben's body heat hoping to find a meal. But instead of being rewarded by primitive instinct the lumbering reptile had ended up on the wrong end of the food chain.

It had been killed it easily enough, with Ben using one of the many available rocks to bash in its head. But with no knife to gut and skin it, and no fire to cook the meat, he had torn into its scaly skin with his teeth like a wild thing, eating it raw. His demons had driven him to such savagery, and he was now suffering the consequences.

Following a series of gut-wrenching purges, the last of the poisonous meat was eliminated, leaving him sprawled out in the wet, stinking dirt, gasping in misery. But as he wiped the last of the shiny scales from his broken mouth he found himself oddly revitalized. Rolling over, he stared into the blue sky. The shaking had subsided and while he was soaked in sweat, his breathing had returned to normal.

With a low groan, he picked up the rifle and brought the scope to his eye. . .

With the morning light chasing away the shadows the boat's details were gradually becoming more distinct, and as he panned the deck he saw the silhouette of someone behind the curtains of a widow that was lit from within.

A hideous smile stretched his swollen lips and he spit out the last of the reptilian residue, arranging himself in sniper position and dialing the scope on the silhouette.

Suddenly the Sun crested the horizon; lighting the land and bringing with it the first hungry fly of the day.

Attracted by the stink of puke and blood, it landed on his tender wound; its tiny feet dancing across the bloody gash and tickling the exposed nerve endings.

But Ben's eye remained glued to the scope.

He would not be distracted.

= Chapter 61 =

Abbott jerked awake to an unseen, yet vivid presence that permeated the morning's breeze: and holding his breath, he glanced around. . . The sensation held no malice but the portent of something crucial in the wings was unmistakable.

Apprehensively rolling from the dew-damp cushions, he padded down the stairs to find Janey, comfortable in a pair of faded sweats in a lounge chair with a crossword puzzle balanced on her knees.

"Coffee'll be ready in a few," she mumbled around the cigarette dangling from her lips.

Abbott thanked her and peeked through the French doors to see if Teller was up. He was. . . still at the table, forehead in hands, intent on the old chart that was unrolled and being held down at the corners by four empty beer bottles on paper napkins.

Abbott called out, "Morning." And stepped into the salon.

Teller looked up, grunted, and tilted his head towards the coffee maker.

With a shrug, Abbott went to the kitchen and began opening cabinets. Locating the one that held cups, he placed two on the counter and waited for the coffee maker to complete its last phase of percolation.

Leaning against the counter, he looked at Teller.

"I thought *that* was a mystery for another time." he said, pointing to the chart.

Teller grunted. "It was. . ."

Abbott nodded, waiting for Teller to elaborate, but the coffee maker beeped and the tiny red light turned green.

Abbott waited a moment longer; but as it seemed Teller

had nothing more to say, he removed the pot, filled his cup and began searching for sugar. There was a row of opaque glass canisters on the counter, and by opening them one by one he happily found the third filled with small packets; and stirring one into to each cup, carefully placed one to Teller's left and took the chair on the other side of the table

"So, what changed?"

Teller smiled without looking up.

"Didn't we talk about going to Hawaii awhile back?"

"Yes," Abbott nodded. "It *was* mentioned."

"Well this," Teller said, tapping the chart with his finger. "Is our itinerary."

Abbott's expression becoming one of puzzled interest, he stood, and walked around the table to look at the chart.

"What *are* you talking about?"

Teller's eyes twinkling, he folded the chart and tucked it away in the table's wide, shallow drawer.

"What I'm talking about, Griz old chum, is our future! but I'm afraid the details must wait." Sliding from his seat, he went to the couch and picked up the green bottle that lay on its cushions. "I found *this* in the wine cooler!" he exclaimed proudly. It was a bottle of Crystal Champagne.

Abbott frowned, "But what about the-"

"I know!" Teller interrupted, beaming. "This boat has a *wine* cooler!"

"No, no," Abbott said shaking his head emphatically. "I was not referring to the *wine cooler*. I was talking about the chart, and-"

Teller waved him off, gulping the last of his coffee. "I already told you grizzly. All questions must *wait*."

Swinging the bottle, he headed towards the French doors.

"Come on amigo, it's time to christen this baby."

Seeing there was no point in arguing, Abbott fell into the spirit of Teller's enthusiasm. But as they reached the doors he placed a hand on Teller's shoulder.

"But what of the others?"

Teller stopped in mid-stride, his eyes narrowing at the hand on his shoulder. "Abbott. It was *we* who were led to that cave, and it was *we* who made the trek out."

"Yes Teller." Abbott agreed. "But it was Jack that flew us there the second time, and it was *he* who helped *you* save *me*." Teller's brows lifted and he gave a nod. "Quite true, Abbott. Quite true. And you make a good point." Turning around, he set the bottle on the chart table and disappeared down the hall. A moment later Abbott heard muffled voices; the volume quickly escalating with Teller's laughter drowning out Jack's complaints. A few minutes later Jack came grumbling down the hallway; Teller a few steps behind, Jack's boots in his hand.

"Goddamn it, Tell!" Jack cried, "at least let me get some fucking coffee."

Grinning, Teller graciously offered Abbott's services.

"Sir Abbott, *if* you would be so kind as to pour our grumpy friend here a cup of joe, perhaps we could get on with the christening." Balking at Tellers orders, Abbott nearly refused; but the expression on Jack's face convinced him that for the moment, perhaps diplomacy was the wisest course of action. Within minutes Jack held steaming cup of black coffee in one hand while running his fingers through his hair with the other. "Thank you, Sir Bear," Jack mumbled gratefully, pulling on his boots while giving Teller serious stink eye

Teller ignored them both, slapping the bottle in his palm.

"Good!" he grinned. "The Three Musketeers are again united. . . let us proceed!" Leading them from the cabin they walked into the pink light of the early morning. The rosy light bounced from every surface, reflecting from the mirrored windows while illuminating the deck in a magical wash. Immersed in that soft, pink glow, Teller led his friends to the starboard side of the boat where he stood on the bow, the breeze riffling his hair. Suddenly Abbott felt the wind shift, and the powerful presence he had felt earlier returned.

— — -- --- -- — —
— — -- --- -- — —

Ben lay, stone still, watching the boat through the rifles scope; and while the Sun's warmth helped to drive away the chill it also increased the flies' activity. They now swarmed around his bloody scalp, their endless buzzing competing with the cacophony of voices inside his head, while their tiny feet danced across putrefying flesh; tickling exposed nerves.
But Ben allowed none of this to affect his concentration. His eye remained glued to the scope.
But as the Sun rose, so did the temperature.

Soon the heat from the rock had created a shimmering, hypnotic veil between Ben and his target, and as he twisted the knurled knob to focus the scope through its diaphanous curtain, paranoid thoughts began to worm their way into his fevered mind. . . *'Kelly is there crying, waiting for me!'*
But at this, the demons only laughed.
Rubbing the sweat from his eye, he frowned, *'It's been too long . . . something's wrong.'*

Suddenly, he saw movement. Someone was walking between the store and the dock. Excited, he swung the rifle barrel; disengaging the safety while dialing the scope. But it was only an old woman with a bag in one hand and a cigarette in the other. *"Shit!"* he cursed, swinging the barrel back to the boat while pressing his eye to the scope.
His disappointment vanished and his wicked smile returned.

Three men were now standing on the deck, with Teller on the bow practically glowing in the desert light; then he kneeled and lifted something over his head.
Smiling, Ben focused the crosshairs just above Teller's ear, and put the lightest of pressure on the trigger.

— — -- --- -- — —
— — -- --- -- — —

Teller knelt to place his palm on the deck, smiling in wonder. The soft pink light bounced from every surface and the very air seemed filled with magic; and as he turned to look over his shoulder at his friends he saw his joy reflected in their faces. Feeling blessed in beauty and love, he lifted the bottle slowly over his head; speaking quietly, but with great reverence.

"For the Gods, for the Musketeers, and for Estebanico."

The bottle reached its zenith on the last word; and as he prepared to bring it down upon the bow his voice gained volume.

"I hereby christen this boat, Coyote's Dream."

As he spoke, the bottle shattered.

—— —— —— ——— —— —— ——
—— —— ——— —— ——
—— ——— ——

Ben's stomach was on fire!

Throwing down the rifle, he rolled onto his side, his eyes wide in horror. Thousands of red ants had appeared from nowhere and were now biting him mercilessly; each bite a burning needle stuck beneath his skin. Brushing handfuls of the little monsters away he jumped up, glancing back at the boat and grimacing in pain as the ants continued their vicious attack: but this was no time for distraction.

Snatching the rifle back up, he brought it to his shoulder and put the scope to a tear-filled eye, sweeping it across the water. The boat jumped forward as he spun the dial.

There! *There* was the head of his antagonist, still holding the bottle by its broken neck, bloody foam running down his arm.

Demonic laughter filled Ben's head as Teller's face came into sharp focus. With his goal now within reach he took another step towards the cliffs ledge, and began to slowly squeeze the trigger . . .

The laughter was suddenly silenced by a screeching "Caw!" as two powerful forces struck simultaneously; razor sharp talons ripping across the side of Ben's tortured head while a massive weight plowed him from behind.

The shot went wild as he stumbled forward, trying desperately to maintain his balance while swinging the rifle in an instinctive attempt to connect with the unseen assailants. But with the force of the dual strikes crippling his already tenuous bodily control, the additional momentum of his angry swing spun him around. And like a puppet whose strings had been cut, he toppled over the cliff's edge, flinging the rifle over his head as he tumbled backwards.

For the briefest of moments, Ben felt as if he were floating: and in those final few seconds of consciousness his field of vision was filled by a huge raven, its wings silhouetted against a blue sky: while the head of an extraordinarily large Coyote peered over the ledge.

What Ben did *not* see as he crumpled against the rocks was the Coyote's smile, and the wink of a golden eye.

The guns report came milliseconds after the bottle above Teller's head shattered, its echo rolling across the water while everyone hit the deck to scramble for cover.

Jack skittered behind the anchor winch; but seeing that Teller had taken refuge behind a large deck box only a few feet away, elbow-walked across the deck to tuck himself close. "You hit?" he asked, peeking over the box.

"No . . . I don't think so." But then saw the blood dripping from his hand; and in the same instant noticed that he was still gripping the neck of the broken bottle.

"Damn it!" he growled, throwing it into a coil of rope.

Grabbing Tellers hand, Jack examined it quickly; a smile of relief flashing across a face that had turned pale.

"You got lucky . . . just looks like a cut from the glass."

Teller flexed his hand. *"That's* good news amigo," he smiled grimly. "but where the hell did that shot come from?

"I don't know, Tell." Jack said peeking around the edge of the box, "but there were two of 'em."

"Yeah, and he missed both times."

"Like I said," Jack nodded. "you're lucky."

"Yeah," Teller grumbled, "Lucky me. . ."

Hunkering further down behind the box, the two men eyed each other. With no further shots, Teller motioned he was going to take a peek; and slowly maneuvering an eye above the lid, scanned the area. Wiggling his eyebrows, he slowly stood, crooking a finger at Jack.

"I think we're clear . . ."

Jack stood, and they moved cautiously across the deck. But on reaching the site of the christening, Teller looked down at the blood on the deck

"Where's Griz?"

"Don't know," Jack frowned, going to the starboard side of the boat while praying he wouldn't see Abbott's body floating in a pool of blood.

Suddenly Abbott's shout rang out and Teller, smiling in relief, set off running across the deck, leaving a trail of bright red blood as he came to a skidding halt, leaned over the rail, and shouted, "Abbott!"

Abbott's muffled voice called from beneath the dock.

"Captain! Are you alright?"

"Christ on a crutch," Teller muttered, shaking his head. "I'm fine! Now get yer ass out from under that dock, ya big coward!"

Poking his head from the shadows of the dock, Abbott paddled to the ladder, pulling himself up onto the platform where he rolled onto his back; spitting out water and gasping for air. And Teller, from his place high the boats deck, looked down at his pathetic friend and shook his head.

"You look like a big furry fuckin' carp!" he laughed.

Abbott glared, and lifting one dripping arm, raised the middle finger of his left hand.

Teller was laughing all the harder as Leroy came around the cabin at a trot, holding a Desert Eagle 50 caliber magnum low in both hands arms extended; and when he saw the blood smeared across the deck he pulled Jack aside.

"What the *hell* is going on here Jack?"

"I'm not real sure, I can answer that Leroy," he said. "We were getting ready to christen the boat when two shots came outta nowhere. Then, nothing."

Seeing the perfectly round bullet hole in one of the big mirrored windows, his eyes dropped to the trail of blood that led to Teller.

"He hit?"

"No, but the bottle he was holding was."

"What bottle?"

Jack stood quietly looking at the pool of blood behind the anchor where he and Teller had crouched.

"That's not important Leroy." He snarled as his anger overrode his shock. "Let's go find that fucking kid."

Leroy looked down the blood-streaked deck, tucked his weapon into his waistband, and ran after Jack, reaching the boats aft, where they jumped, clearing the six-foot span in one long leap, hitting the dock and sprinting towards the chopper,

Halfway there they ran into Janey.

On hearing the shots, she had dropped her bag of groceries and ran towards the boat. But on seeing Jack running towards her with her husband on his heels, had stopped, bending over with her hands on her knees to catch her breath. Relief that he was unharmed coursing through her heart. Grabbing him by the arm, she steadied herself as she looked up.

He was furious.

"What the hell's goin on Leroy?"

Smiling grimly, he took her gently by the shoulders, and with a kiss told her what had happened.

Her eyes going wide, she asked if Teller was alright, to which Leroy just smiled.

"Ahh, the boy's fine honey, you know how lucky that sonofabitch is. Now git on back to the store and grab some supplies for cuts and such." Janey nodded, gave her husband a kiss, and ran back the way she had come.

~

Within minutes Jack had the bird in the air and two sets of eyes were scanning the desert scrub. Five minutes out and just under two hundred feet of elevation, Leroy spotted the wreck of the Humvee.

"Over there." he pointed.

Following Leroy's finger, Jack tipped north. Minutes later they were hovering over the vehicle.

The sound of the rotors drowned out any attempts at conversation, but there was little need for talk. Both had been in similar situations many times before: and, as neither man could see any signs of life much less danger, Jack didn't hesitate to bring the chopper within a few feet of the ground. Leroy looked at Jack, nodding as he drew his weapon and jumped, zigzagging through the scrub towards the battered vehicle. Jack gave him a few moments to clear, then set the rails on the ground, flipping switches and toggles with one hand while unbuckling his harness with the other. Pushing the door open with his foot, he reached behind his seat, pulled his weapon from its holster, and jumped out, racing through the sage; but as he drew close he slowed. . . Leroy was walking around the once showroom perfect toy, running his finger along its side as he went. But as Jack stepped up, he paused, laying his hand on the crumpled fender as he slowly turned, astonishment plain on his face.

"What in the hell is *wrong* with this kid?"

The vehicle looked like it had been in a demolition derby.

The passenger's headlight was not only shattered, it was filled with what looked to be thick, sticky amber, while dried blood was spattered across a front bumper that was twisted under the right front fender, nearly poking into the right front tire, chunks of furry flesh stuck between the bars of the crushed grill. . . the passenger side quarter panel was caved in, the paint scraped away on both sides while the driveshaft was bent backwards beneath a flat rear tire.

Jack stepped up and shook his head.

"Well, whatever's wrong with him, he sure wasn't planning on driving out of here."

"No," Leroy murmured, his eyes narrowing. "He sure as hell wasn't. Which brings us to the next big question. Where is he *now?*"

Jack's eyebrows lifted, and he pointed to the scuffed trail Ben had left in the dusty soil. It wound down into the gully and up the opposite bank, weaving towards an outcropping in the distance where a large raven circled in wide, lazy loops, riding the thermals that rose from beneath its prominent point. Bringing his field glasses to his eyes, Jack trained them on the bird, admiring its glistening blue-black feathers as it circled, thinking, beautiful yes . . . but *what* was it circling?

Lowering the lenses to the earth beneath the bird, he saw that scuffmarks had displaced an inordinate amount of soil around a man-made stack of rocks. Squinting, he tried to identify the odd form that lay near the stones. . . it appeared stationary yet shimmered with movement.

Frowning, he handed Leroy the binoculars. "Something strange over there."

Leroy took the glasses, scanned the area, and handed them back. "You're right. Let's go see what it is."

~

Twenty minutes of clambering down through the ravine and back up the loose grade on the other side brought the two men against the same ledge that Ben had hauled himself over the night before. Leroy's steely grey eyes narrowed as he took his Desert Eagle from its holster, motioning Jack to do the same. Then, with a tip of his head he rolled over the little wall, instantly coming to his knees to swing his weapon in a wide arc. Jack came right behind; and standing back to back, they circled, weapons held out and ready.

But there was no sign of Ben.

Leroy's forehead creased in puzzlement and looking over his shoulder at Jack, slowly lowered his weapon.

Jack nodded, but kept his weapon raised, cautiously following the faint trail of scraped earth before him. Leroy hesitated, scanning the empty country around them once more before following. Soon they stood over the blood-soaked soil where Ben had lain in wait.

Leroy, seeing the stack of rocks on which Ben had rested his rifle, knelt to pick up one of the spent shell casings while Jack bent to examine the remains of a large lizard.

The shimmering he had mistaken for movement was no more than a cloud of flies that swarmed over the savaged, bloated carcass; and seeing where Ben had ripped the lizard apart with his teeth, disgust twisted Jacks features and he turned away to see Leroy holding up the spent shell.

Happy to have something else to consider, Jack reached out, but his eyes were drawn to a cluster of footprints that weaved like dance steps up to the cliffs ledge.

Cocking his head, he looked up at the Raven that still floated in slow, lazy circles against the cloudless blue sky and holstering his pistol, he walked to the cliff's sharp edge.

There, far below, Bens body lay crumpled among the boulders: sunlight glinting off the chrome barrel of the black rifle broken in two.

— — -- --- -- — — —
— — — —
-- --- --

= Chapter 62 =

Slouching in a deck chair while Janey bandaged his hand, Teller fidgeted while staring at the tiny chopper in the distance.

"Goldang it!" she muttered around her cigarette. "Hold still!" Teller chuckled, and she glanced up from her work.

"See anything?"

"No." He smiled as he tried to pull away, but Jane grabbed his wrist and brought it back to her knees.

"Hold still dang it! I'm nearly done . . ."

Teller sighed, then hollered, "Hey Abbott, grab a couple beers and bring me the binoculars would ya please?"

"In a minute." The French doors muffled Abbott's response, but in truth Abbott had no intention of doing anything for Teller because he was avoiding him.

After the shooting Abbott had come back aboard, endeavoring to explain that he had tripped and fallen overboard while scrambling from the gunshot. *Not* jumped out of cowardice as Teller had accused. But knowing that Teller was unlikely to let it rest Abbott had decided to avoid him until he tired of the game.

Janey cinched the final wrap on Teller's hand.

"There ya go honey. All patched up."

Teller looked down at swaddling. "Thanks, Janey." He smiled, "You and Leroy going to stick around for a while?"

Janey pursed her lips and blew a long plume of smoke into the air. "I don't know hon. that'll depend on what Leroy wants to do." She patted his bandaged hand and smiled down on him. "I sure wouldn't mind takin' a little vacation tho.' Not if you wouldn't mind us stayin.' "

343

Teller looked around for Abbott, who was yet to bring him a beer *or* his binoculars.

"Damn that cowardly bear." he grumbled, swinging his feet from the lounge chair onto the deck.

"Hell no, Jane. You two can stay as long as you like."

Janey pinched her cigarette between two fingers and started to speak, but Teller leaned in and kissed her cheek.

"I'm serious Jane. Stay as long as you want." Holding up his bandaged hand he smiled. "Give me a second Janey. I'll be right back."

Taking the steep stairs two at a time, he popped through the glass doors to find Abbott at the table with Billy and Little Raven.

Junior glanced up and gave him an apologetic smile.

"Sorry Teller, I slept through the whole thing."

Teller shrugged, "It was for the best Young Bill. You would have only made another target." But turning to Abbott, his smile turned caustic. "You forget about me Pal?"

"No." Abbott sniffed, "something more interesting came up."

Teller's eyebrows rose. "More interesting huh? Tsk, tsk, adding insult to injury. Just what I'd expect from the likes of you." Pushing past them to the fridge, he removed two beers with his good hand, closed the door, and made his way back through the salon. But as he passed a second time, Abbott held out his hand, fully expecting Teller to give him one of the cold bottles. But Teller kept walking, brushing away Abbott's paw. "Sorry," he shrugged, "I don't believe in contributing to the delinquency of ungrateful bears. Besides, I've important surveillance work to take care of up on deck and I may get thirsty." Then pointedly turning his back to Abbott, he looked into Billy's bright eyes.

"Hi, Billy." He grinned.

"Hello Teller." Billy smiled back. "I'm happy to see you unharmed."

"Well," Teller frowned holding up his bandaged hand. "Not *completely* unharmed. . . *Relatively* unharmed."

"Yes, yes," Billy nodded, "relatively . . . a key detail that applies to nearly everything . . . oh, and by the way, the name you gave your boat did not go unnoticed."

"Unnoticed by whom?"

The old Shaman reached into his pocket, removed a small box he had recently carved from mesquite, and holding it in the palm of one hand, lifted the lid with the fingers of the other. There, in a nest of fresh sage leaves lay the coyote carving that Teller had first found lying atop the gold in the chest in the cave. The little coyote remained curled as if asleep; its tail wrapped around its nose . . . but *now* one eye was most certainly open, glittering yellow, and looking undeniably amused. Looking up from the carving, Teller saw that Billy's dark eyes held a quiet humor equal to that of the little coyotes.

Questions began to reel through his mind, fracturing like the images in a kaleidoscope: each overlapping the last; with every potential answer creating a dozen new questions. Finally, with a low chuckle, Teller gently pushed the lid closed with his fingertip.

"Well then, what is *your* opinion, Chief?"

Billy's smile was enigmatic. "My *opinion* means very little, Teller. I do believe, however, that you have started something that-" Suddenly the chop of the helicopter's rotors rattled down the canyons; breaking the spell.

Billy shrugged, handed Teller the little box, and turned to the rest of the group. "Come," he said, "let us go hear what our friends have found." But as the last of them filed through the French doors he turned to Teller, his black eyes sparkling.

"Take care of coyote," he smiled with a wink.

Teller watched him go, but said nothing, for there was nothing to say.

Stepping from the salon, he went to the rails and stood, watching his friends gather to wait for Jack.

Smiling, he returned to the boats cabin feeling as if he were emerging from a dream. And with a soft laugh put the little box into his pocket; wondering just what the old Shaman might have meant.

= Chapter 63 =

It was nearly noon by the time Jack lifted off, tipping the chopper east towards Durango; and Kelly.

Everyone had gathered on the porch, listening intently as he and Leroy told of their gruesome discovery; each reacting with their own level of shock and sorrow. Even Teller, being the target of Ben's madness, felt a small degree of pity.

Not for the boy's actions, for he found the selfishness of those actions unforgivable. But for the boy's slip from sanity.

~

Much later things had calmed. Leroy and Jane had gone back to the boat, while Abbott, Junior, and Billy sat in the shade of the porch discussing what the future held, rather than what the past had delivered.

But Teller sat alone, wrapped in silence.

Having commandeered Billy's rocking chair, he had positioned it at the top of the stairs facing west: west, towards the grand backdrop of the sacred peaks and to where a large black Raven still floated in an azure sky.

~

Time marched its endless circle; the discussion circling as well, with more questions raised than there were answered; yet no asked Teller's opinion, nor bothered him; for it was clear he preferred his solitude.

But still, Billy kept a watchful eye, gauging his mood.

Morning stretched into afternoon for there was much to discuss and the mysteries were great. But for Teller, their words were no more than meaningless noise.

~

Suddenly, and without a word, Teller pushed himself up and out of the chair, leaving it rocking silently as he walked down the steps towards the cliff where Benny had been found. The three men watched him cross the parking lot, growing smaller with every step, slowly vanishing into the rippling lake of heat that lay across the land.

= Chapter 64 =

Teller circled the ruined vehicle, pausing every so often to examine a specific dent or scrape. He was astonished at the amount of damage Ben had inflicted, fascinated that he had gotten it this far.

'An impressive force, crazy.' He thought.

Looking down at the three sets of footprints that led away from the vehicle, he followed them down the draw; scrambling back up the loose rock on the other side to jump over the short wall. Pausing to gaze down at the blood-stained dirt, he shuddered at the lizards remains, then walking to the edge of the cliff, stood, the wind ruffling his hair.

The view was remarkable. Ben couldn't have chosen a better location for his failed deed. The shining mirrored glass of the houseboat threw squares of reflected light across the scrub landscape: illuminating the rock face below his feet: and with the front of Billy's store so plainly visible he could make out the small figures that sat in the shade of the porch, he thought again of the insanity that had driven Ben, and of his good luck. 'Yes,' he thought with the slightest of smiles. *'There is a fine line between success and failure.'*

Turning to the profoundly blue expanse of southwestern sky, Teller saw that the Raven was no longer a shadow against its depth: and with the bird's absence, an odd pang of loss tickled the edges of his soul: for it seemed that here, on the edge of the world, something important was both ending, and beginning. . .

Easing himself down, he dangled his legs over the ledge to gaze at the sad, broken figure below.

When Jack and Leroy had first told him of Ben's death, he had insisted that no authorities be called in. There was absolutely *nothing* to be gained by doing so. . . the situation would be impossible to explain, and to have them all pulled into the investigation that would inevitably follow seemed pointless. Besides, who would *believe* the story?

And, he had pointed out, any outside scrutiny into their newly acquired finances, *or* their future undertakings would only create problems for all concerned.

Looking down once more, Teller reached into his pocket and took out Jack's borrowed phone. He would call James to tell him of Ben's death, and at that point James could handle things as he saw fit. This was his problem now, and in honor of their past friendship he felt he owed him that much.

~

Teller put the phone back in his pocket.

The conversation had gone much easier than he had expected. There had been no screams of denial, nor shouts of blame. James had simply accepted Ben's death as if he had expected nothing less; and, surprisingly civil, said goodbye.

With the events of the past month having left him exhausted, Teller lay back, putting his arm over his eyes, calming with the sounds of the wind.

But woven within the breeze came soft words. . .

'Small decisions lead to great changes.'

The oddly familiar voice seemed to float within his head, yet he sensed a physical presence as well.

Lifting his arm, he looked up at Coyote silhouetted against the sky, golden eyes shining with humor.

Raising an eyebrow, Teller smiled.

'Yes. . . but why me?'

The simple answer that rang through his mind was laced with amused respect. *'Why not you?'*

Teller smiled, closed his eyes, and laid his arm over them once again.

~

Much later, Teller awoke.

Coyote was gone and he was alone. For a moment he simply lay where he was, feeling the steady beat of his heart as he gazed up at the darkening sky. . . then, swing his legs up onto the ledge, he stood, dusting his hands on his pants as he lifted his nose to the breeze.

It held the smell of sage and hope.

    Tipping his ear to the timeless music of the wind threading the canyons, Teller closed his eyes; for that within that endless song he imagined he could hear not only the blades of the helicopter, but the sound of laughter.

    With a nod, he stepped to the cliffs very edge and touched his fingers to the brim of his worn hat.

    "Goodbye, Ben. Sorry about your luck."

    Suddenly a soft gust of wind rustled by; Coyote's last words woven into its whisper.

On hearing them, Teller laughed,

    'Indeed. Why not?'

The End . . ..

: AFTERWORD :

This book was written during a long and brutal period of illness: one that very nearly killed me. But, as Teller discovered, Yin follows Yang, and the scales always seem to balance. Thus, during my recovery I was blessed with one of the most remarkable creative episodes of my life.

Now I have always been a storyteller and a songwriter, and, on more than one occasion, have been accused of being a bit of a bullshitter as well: and while that, dear friends, may, or may not, be true. I have, however, long held the belief that a little imagination can always make the truth more interesting. But the point is this. For years I have been told that I should write a book. Not only due to my ability to spin a yarn, but because there is a select group of people out there who have heard my many unbelievable tales enough times, and over the span of enough years, to accept the possibility that at least portions of them, are in fact, truth. Which, I suppose, makes this a work of fictional fact. Or, if you prefer, factual fiction. Regardless, nearly all of the locations in this story *do* exist and are taken from my personal experiences in and around the Four Corners area. . . As for the historical storyline of Estebanico, the "Arab from Azzamoor," this is a verifiable fact. He was a very real, and very interesting footnote in the expansion of the Spanish Crown's early, cruel, and frequently inept attempts in "discovering" the Northern Continent of the New World.

Everything I have written concerning Estebanico (Or Estevanico depending on the records) is based on either written or oral historical records. Most were taken from the journals kept by those whom he traveled with, while others were pulled from various sources that are easily available for any of you who may wish to delve deeper than this story provides. So, while I have embellished many facets of his existence and personality, I believe the picture I paint is quite close. The main point where I diverged from the records was the differing opinions of his demise, and in doing so, I have indulged in what is commonly referred to as: "Artistic License." And this is because the story of his death at the hands of the Zuni has long been the subject of contention in historical circles. Some say that the records indicate that he was killed by the Zuni Chiefs for telling the lie of there being a great army a day a two behind him. And, while one would *assume* that this lie was created in order to save himself, it seems to me that such a lie would be far more likely to get one killed than to provide sanction.

Still others argue that he was killed along with most of his entourage for religious retribution; for the priests and shaman of the villages were in fear of losing their status by this strange and imposing figure. Still others claim he was killed merely for his pomposity, or perhaps for his hounds and green plates. But, there are still others who think he may have escaped. And I, like these few, prefer to believe that someone of his skills, intelligence and adaptability would have found a way to avoid being killed by a people as civilized and advanced as the Zuni: regardless of the unfortunate circumstances of their meeting.

~

Now, as for the Dreamworld that Teller and Abbott experience, *that* is a very personal place, and is the heart of many myths and beliefs of tribes across the globe. And while we are all invited into this "outside reality" from time to time, it is filled primarily with creatures of our own making. However, that is not the case here. The deity of Coyote is both an interesting, and important element of Navajo culture and history. And while Raven is also included in my story, and *does* receive mention in the lore of many of the Southwestern Tribes, he plays a far more influential role in the ancient world of the Northwestern Tribes, than that of the Navajo. I simply felt that combining the two helped the storyline. Another case of Poetic license, if you will.

Regarding the other Characters in this novel: let me put it this way. Teller and I were, and are still, quite close. As for the rest of the cast, each and every one is to some degree, real. But with them, as in the rest of this story, I have allowed myself considerable latitude in imagination, and in a slight twist to an old phrase, the names have been changed to protect the guilty. And by the way, all of the songs that Willie preformed at the "Lost Dog" are also real and will soon be available for your listening pleasure.

As for the guitar straps described. They too, are quite real.

A very talented friend whom I referred to as the "Moon Queen" in the novel crafted them, and due to her frequent forays south of the border, we have expanded her title to "Queen of the Spanish Moon." However, in the real world she is known as Kimberlie Gilbertson, creative genius of Ruliens Lost Muse, and can be reached at . . . wait . . . here's the free plug! www.ruliens.com (You're welcome Queenie!)

Now, back to the songs. All the tunes mentioned throughout the novel will soon be available on my upcoming CD or streamed through one of the many media outlets.

P.S.

Stay tuned! There is a second Novel in the works involving the crew and the Tapa Chart, and there are already new tunes bouncing 'round in Teller's head.

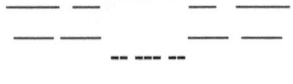

I truly hope you have enjoyed the reading of this tale as much as I have enjoyed the telling.
If so, my goal has been accomplished.

*

All three books in this trilogy are now available and may be purchased through Amazon, Barns and Noble or through my personal website:

DenverCDavis.com

Cheers!

www.ingramcontent.com/pod-product-compliance
Lightning Source LLC
Chambersburg PA
CBHW051325250626
47155CB00007B/2454